By Blood Sworn

The Dagger Chronicles
Book 2

Janice Jones

Amberjack Publishing
New York, New York

Amberjack Publishing
228 Park Avenue S #89611
New York, NY 10003-1502
http://amberjackpublishing.com

This book is a work of fiction. Any references to real places are used fictitiously. Names, characters, fictitious places, and events are the products of the author's imagination, and any resemblance to actual persons, living or dead, places, or events is purely coincidental.

Publisher's Cataloging-in-Publication data
Names: Jones, Janet, 1965-, author.
Title: By blood sworn / Janet Jones.
Series: The Dagger Chronicles.
Description: New York, NY: Amberjack Publishing, 2017.
Identifiers: ISBN 978-1-944995-22-5 (pbk.) | 978-1-944995-38-6 (ebook) | LCCN 2017930879
Subjects: LCSH Bodyguards--Fiction. | African American women--Fiction. | Vampires--Fiction. | Werewolves--Fiction. | Supernatural--Fiction. | Fantasy fiction. | Action and adventure--Fiction. | Paranormal romance stories. | BISAC FICTION / Occult & Supernatural
Classification: LCC PS3610.O62563 B93 2017 | DDC 813.6--dc23

Cover Design: Dane Low

Mama

Our story ended much too soon. With a heavy heart, I begin another without you. Ever my hero; forever in my heart.

Prologue

From his position behind the glass, he waited. What else could he do? In this century, he was at a disadvantage. Witchcraft continued to elude him, as it always had. And Brice Campbell couldn't tell a spell from a fast food menu, so Tristan was forced to watch and wait.

Giselle worked day and night—page by page. The "clean room" was off limits to Tristan. Something about how the magicks she used to transfer his consciousness could be interrupted if he stood in that room for even a few minutes. He felt like he was back to his old self, but she insisted he wasn't.

"You need more time for the blood to take hold permanently," she warned him over breakfast.

Tristan sighed. More time. He was tired of that phrase, quite honestly. Over the centuries, waiting was something he had come to know intimately. But if he had to wait any longer, he'd surely go mad. He reached up to press the little white button that operated the two-way speakers.

"How much longer?"

Giselle peered over the top of her glasses at him, her gloved hands poised over the delicate pages of the book of dark magic she'd been painstakingly scanning for the last three hours. With her hair pinned up in a bun and covered in a matching bonnet, she looked like a surgeon.

"This may take a while." The mask over her mouth moved as she spoke. "You should go on with your day, Tristan. You'll just be bored watching me."

Tristan pressed his right palm to the glass and tapped it

lightly with the ring around his finger as he held the button down. Giselle continued to pass the slim lighted wand over the page. He watched the tedious process in painful boredom. "Sorry, I'm just anxious."

"So am I, but scanning two thousand pages will take time, Tristan. My program will decipher the text but not instantly. Most likely this language is dead, so we may have to wait even longer for the translation."

Tristan stepped closer to the glass. "Don't you have a spell that can turn that into something we can read?"

Giselle shook her head, and he could tell she had a smile on her face. "My magic isn't strong enough for this. But I do recognize some of the words here." She leaned closer to the book, and Tristan saw her eyes narrow as the mask over her mouth moved. "It says something about a *dzhadazhiya*—that's Bulgarian."

"For what?"

She looked up at him with something akin to fear and disbelief. As she scrambled over to the messy desk in the corner, Tristan sighed.

He released the button while he waited. All this babble about dead languages and ancient glyphs had given him a massive headache. "Giselle," he growled under his breath, then pressed the button again. "What does it mean?"

A leather-bound journal lay open on the desk. She flipped the stiff pages quickly, stopped, appeared to read the words scribbled on them, then looked up at him.

"Dhampir," she announced with a grin in her eyes. "That's what my people called them, anyway."

Tristan suddenly felt lightheaded. He let his weight fall against the glass as he smiled at her. "Are you sure? Please tell me you're sure."

"The doctor made references to a hybrid program, but there were problems," she said, almost under her breath as she shut the journal. "I have to go over this, without interruption," she said then hurried back to the workstation. "I'll let you know when I'm done."

He left the observation room in a good mood. Down the long, dim corridor, Tristan practically danced toward the freight elevator. In the bowels of this museum, among the cement walls and dank smells, he felt safe. This place reminded him of home, his underground fortress in the desert. The home and family that hunters invaded and destroyed.

He reached the freight elevator just as his phone buzzed. He was surprised that it even worked down here. The thick cement walls and spider-web of electrical wires should have blocked the signal. He looked at the screen with a small grin. Some good news, finally. The shifter had surfaced.

According to his source, Kit Blaze had arranged to meet with Alex Stone in a few hours. Tristan wondered how long it would take before she cracked. Shifters were not known for their strength of character. For the right price, they'd give away all to the highest bidder. This woman had proved to be no different. Apparently, she felt Alex Stone would protect her.

"Oh how wrong you are, my dear," Tristan whispered to the empty freight elevator when the door slid open. He stepped inside. "She can't protect you—not from me."

Chapter 1

Her stomach knotted at the sight: the position of the bodies and the chaos of the room. But, worst of all—the thing that would give her nightmares—was the look on the children's faces, smeared with blood, as they grinned at their dead parents.

"Damn shame, huh?" someone said behind her. "I thought this was supposed to be against their rules—turning little kids."

"It is," Alex muttered as she pushed her way through the agents while they documented the scene. But when she reached the couch, a strange sense of déjà vu came over her. It was all too familiar.

His bulky body was blanched and perched awkwardly on the faux leather couch; its light-colored pillows stained dark with his blood. Of the two victims, he had definitely gotten the worst of it. While one had fed from his neck, the other had ripped through both wrists like a chainsaw. And he was beyond bled dry. Alex could see the outline of his skeleton against his shrink-wrapped skin.

From the looks of it, the mother had come through the front door and dropped her groceries outright when she saw the carnage. Her shoes were covered in smashed fruit and spilled milk—drag marks paved the way to where she was now.

Alex pulled on a sterile glove as she made her way closer to the body. She couldn't help but notice the sick similarities to scenes from the past, years before, in times she had hoped were long gone.

It was Tristan's twisted idea of fun. Turn the children and send them after their own parents. His signature catch-me-if-you-can move. The sick bastard.

Was he here? Was he close? she wondered as she watched the dark blood congeal on the couch; its smell coated her nostrils then planted itself in her brain.

"Why do you think they trashed him so badly but left her almost pristine?" one of the agents asked as she snapped pictures of the scene.

Alex glanced at her. It was a good question. She turned her attention to the dead woman, the mother, sitting so very still in her rocking chair in the far corner of the room.

The woman's hands, stained with blood that traveled down from her wounds, lay in her lap, almost peacefully, as if resting. Alex could tell from the pattern of bloodstains and the way it was smeared after congealing that one of them had brushed her hair and reapplied her makeup after her death. Maybe in a childish attempt to make her look alive. Some last, tragic moment of humanity that flickered in their almost dead hearts.

"They loved her," Alex said softly, but loud enough to be heard by the agent.

"Love?" The agent hummed. "You buy your mother flowers when you love her, not bleed her to death."

Alex turned to the agent and motioned toward the father. "Him? No love lost there," she sighed with a shake of her head.

Another gruesome memory popped to the surface. Something about the father and the savageness of his death brought to her mind a small town in Utah. The father there had been torn up just like this one. But not a biological father—a step-father.

The mother had been fed on as one of them sat in her lap. That was clear. It would have been the smaller one, the younger one, the boy, held in her lap. The marks were a deep purple color against her blanched skin. The boy had tapped the vein in the bend of her elbow—a hellish mockery of a nursing child.

In her mind's eye, the chair rocked back and forth as the boy guzzled his first meal as a vampire. What did he care that his mother's life spilled from his small mouth to the beige carpet? The mundane trappings of modern life meant nothing to a fledging vampire as he sated the first pangs of a thirst that would last the rest of his unnaturally extended life.

"So they hated their father," another agent said. "What else is new?"

"I don't think he's their father," Alex said as she looked around, absorbing more and more information from the scene. Her eyes trailed down from the body perched in the rocker to the pool of mostly dried blood at her feet. She stopped when she saw another clue: footprints—two sets.

"She's wearing a wedding band," the agent replied. "And it matches his."

The agent's words drew her attention away from the prints. "So? That's doesn't mean he was their father," Alex replied with a quick glance toward the young vampires.

All along the walls were pictures of the woman and the two children, but without the man. In contrast, on the mantle was a wedding picture of the two adults without the children.

The wedding looked simple, even with the exotic Hawaiian locale. Lush and green beyond description, the mountains behind the bride and groom filled the background. No fancy dress or giant cake.

He was probably her second marriage, Alex surmised. *Maybe it had been a second marriage for both of them.*

"See those pictures?" she asked with a nod toward the wall. "They're still hung, perfectly straight and clean."

"So?"

"So, look around you. Those pictures are of the mother and the kids."

"And . . .?"

Alex pointed to floor around the couch. "See those

pictures, the ones with the man in them?"

"Yeah."

"They ripped those to shreds."

"That doesn't mean he's not their father," the agent replied. "Maybe he was beating them, or worse." The agent frowned as she picked up a crumpled piece of a picture, still covered in blood.

"He's not their father," Alex stated firmly. "How did you catch this case anyway?"

They stepped closer to the man's body, and Alex examined the neck wounds—one on either side. They didn't match. On the laminate floor around the couch were bloody prints of the nine-year-old boy's bare feet, the thirteen-year-old girl's flip flops, and another set—slightly smaller than the father's, but not quite as small as the mother's.

"The mother works for Strategic," she answered. "Dr. Carlisle made her the Executive Assistant to the Head of Field Ops here just last month."

Alex stared at the wedding pictures again. That would explain their Hawaiian wedding. If she was in field assignments, then she was making big bucks. It would explain why Tristan chose her too.

"Those footprints there," Alex turned back to her discovery in front of the rocking chair. "They match those by the couch."

The agent turned to one set then the other but didn't seem to grasp the significance of what Alex was telling her. Then a glint of recognition blinked in her eyes.

"They had help," she grinned and nodded.

They looked to where the giggly children sat—hands cuffed behind their backs—against the opposite wall. One of them would lead her to the third one.

"Where's the other one?" Alex asked coldly as she walked over to them.

"Other what?" the girl giggled as she bumped her little brother.

“The other kid,” Alex said between clenched teeth.

They looked at each other, shrugged, and then burst out into high-pitched, childish laughter. Alex looked at the children for a moment, watching them laugh. Remorseless. Twisted.

They aren’t really children any longer, she told herself as she pushed down the revulsion and pity turning in her gut.

A thought occurred to her. She picked up the evidence bag, lying nearby, and pulled out old airline tickets and the man’s wallet. She thumbed through the cards until she found what she was looking for. Sandwiched between his AmEx and an old arcade card was a picture of a kid. His red hair was messy but clean, and the braces on his teeth looked brand new.

“Who is this?” Alex demanded as she held up the picture to the monstrous siblings.

“Ronnie,” the boy squealed just before his sister bumped him, hard. “Ow! He’s Chuck’s kid,” he finished softly, frowning at his sister.

“Was he looking after you while they were in Hawaii?” Alex asked as the knot in her stomach tightened. Tristan got to Ronnie, somehow, and then *he* turned them.

“Yeah, so?” the girl sneered.

She looked around again. All the drapes were drawn, pinned together, and taped on each side. Along the top, more duct tape sealed the fabric to the wall. There was no sunlight in this room, at all. There was even a pocket door that separated this room from the kitchen, with its big bay window that would fill that room with warm sunlight in the mornings.

“What happened when you tried to leave this room?”

They looked at each other then back at Alex.

“The sun burned us,” the boy whined.

The agents parted as Alex moved quickly toward the pocket door. She slid it open, but the light only reached so far into the room. As long as the children didn’t venture too close to the threshold, they wouldn’t be burned by the light.

Alex tossed the wallet at the woman. "Check all the rooms—be careful. He could still be here somewhere."

The agent flipped the picture over. "Why would he still be here?"

"Because they can't go out into the light—not yet. They're newly turned and haven't had the fake stuff. He'll be close."

The agent grinned at the picture, "He shouldn't be hard to find if he's hiding from the sun."

"Then find him," Alex barked.

The woman turned and left without another word. Two other agents followed behind her. After a few seconds, Alex could hear them as they searched through the rooms, as things fell to the floor and glass broke. Strategic would foot the bill for anything that needed to be replaced, if anyone actually showed to bury these two.

"Who did this?" Alex asked the children again. This time, her voice was laced with steel, but they just laughed again. "Answer me!"

"We did," the girl answered, a smile on her young lips. "Are you *slow* or something, lady?" More laughter from the two newly born vampires. She didn't have time for this shit.

Alex knelt down in front of the little monsters and looked up at the guard. He nodded. Without a word, he pulled out his gun and pointed it at the girl's head.

"Not to them," Alex replied. "Who did this to Ronnie?"

The gun had an effect. It always did. "Our new father," the girl said hastily.

Her brother nodded in agreement. "Yeah. Chuck the Schmuck deserved it anyway."

"Why?" Alex asked over their nervous laughter.

"Because he was a schmuck," the boy rolled his eyes at Alex. "You *are* slow."

"And what about your mother? Was she a schmuck too?" Alex asked.

The children's giggles stopped cold, and they glared at Alex. She could hear the growl in the back of their throats like animals. It was nothing at all like a childish imitation of a growl. This was the real thing.

"Don't talk about our mom like that, *bitch*," the girl spat as her top lip curled to reveal a nice set of new fangs. "She was the best mom ever!"

"She couldn't have been that good," Alex said innocently. She wanted to fan the flames—get one of them to tell her something useful. "After all, you killed her."

They lunged at the same time, quick as snakes. But Alex was faster. She grabbed them both by their necks and slammed them back into the wall. Each of them struggled, writhing under her grip for a long moment, even with their hands handcuffed behind them. They both showed surprise at her strength before calming from exhaustion. When they were calm again, Alex handed the boy to the guard but kept the girl pressed against the wall for a moment longer.

"What did Ronnie tell you about your new father?" Alex asked. Her voice was calm, but her heart raced in her chest.

"Just that he was rich and powerful," the girl replied. "And he would take better care of us than Chuck ever could. And we'd be young and powerful forever, just like him."

"What's his name?"

She shrugged, shook her head. Streaked in electric blue wash-out hair dye, her stringy blonde hair was caked in blood and oil. It hadn't been washed in a few days, judging from the smell.

"When is he coming for you?" Alex continued to keep the timbre of her voice calm.

The girl kept quiet, her lips one thin line as she pressed them together. Alex grabbed her by the ankle and dragged her across the sticky wooden floor toward the big front windows. She pulled the heavy drape to one side. The tape that held it closed ripped loose, taking paint flakes with it. When Alex held the girl's foot in the sharp rays of mid-afternoon sunlight, she screamed as her flesh began to sizzle and blister.

"When?" Alex repeated as she held the drapes closed again.

As her brother yelled and struggled with two agents across the room, the girl roared and cried while her injured foot smoked. Before the last blister sealed itself again, Alex stuck her foot back in the light.

"I don't know! I swear," the girl screamed and wiggled to get loose.

"Stop it! Stop it!" the boy yelled from across the room.

Alex let the girl drag herself into the cool shadow again, but she followed. When she stopped, the girl curled into the fetal position then blew on her charred foot.

"You know something. And you will tell me, or I'm going to throw both of you into the sun."

They glared at Alex, and their animal growls filled the room. The sound vibrated off the walls then down Alex's spine. The boy rolled his eyes up then back at Alex.

She slipped off her jacket, dropped it to the floor, then stepped back into the center of the room. Just then, she felt his presence above her. Absent of any kind of remorse for what he'd done, she felt his anger and hunger settle around her like a curtain.

He crashed through the ceiling like he'd been shot from a cannon. Sheetrock exploded everywhere as the people in the room scattered in all directions. The ceiling fan just missed Alex as she rolled out of the way. The children yelled as they were pulled away by the agents. When he landed, crouched low and growling, Alex rolled to her feet with a death grip on the silver blade she had pulled from the sheath on her thigh.

"Let me guess," she smirked at the boy. "You must be Ronnie."

His long new fangs dropped slowly as he smiled. His red hair was still messy, but now it was dirty, and, like his clothes, covered in dust from the attic and blood from the scene. The dank smell of old boxes and sweat grabbed at her lungs and she almost lost her breakfast. When he shook his head like a wet dog, the muck flew out toward her.

"And you must be my next meal," he laughed.

He was about her height, but the portly build he had when he was human had been transformed slightly. Now he could break through solid sheetrock, wood framing, and possibly a brick wall if he wanted. Ronnie scanned the room as if doing a body count for later.

"Don't get too excited," Alex replied. "We just need some information from you, and then these nice people will take you and your brother and sister somewhere to get you some help."

"We don't need help," he glared at her. "You do!"

His razor-sharp nails cut through the air in front of her nose as Alex jumped back. The momentum put his back to her long enough for her to get him into a chokehold. But Ronnie had other plans. Two powerful elbows to her solar plexus and he was out of her grip and up the far wall like a spider monkey on caffeine.

The children cheered him on as he clung to the wall above them.

Alex clenched her teeth against the pain. "Get them out of here!"

The agents did as they were told. The children were pushed into a small bathroom as they yelled and cheered. With the sound of squealing children muted, just enough to take the edge off, Alex could concentrate on Ronnie. She stepped closer as he stayed glued to the corner of the ceiling.

"Come on, Ron," Alex tried to grin. "Don't make this hard on yourself."

He laughed, and sheetrock dust trickled down on her head. As he slid down to the floor again, his laughter stopped, and the creature inside him surfaced. She could see the weak muscles in his arms and shoulders expand and bulk. His beautiful green eyes turned black as his fangs extended to their full fighting length.

"This ain't gonna be hard on me," he growled as he rolled his head around like a boxer ready for a prize fight. "You, on the other hand . . . beat down time! Can't you see how strong I am? I'm a superhero!"

Alex could remember that feeling: the thrilling rush of it, how all of your muscles pulsed with it all at once, the taste of pure vampire blood. Not even she was immune to it, as she'd found out the hard way.

"You're not a superhero. You're just a kid that has been violated in the worst possible way, and, for that, I'm sorry. When you come down, it's not going to feel so good, trust me," she said.

"Come down? I'm never coming down," Ronnie laughed. "He said I never have to come down!"

Alex stepped closer, and he moved back. Could he feel her power too? Did he know she was different? "He lied. Tell me who he is and I can finish this, finish him."

Ronnie's roundhouse kick sent Alex into the bookcase behind her. As the cheap romance novels and self-help books tumbled down around her, she slammed a hardcover into his face as he charged. His prominent nose broke as he fell back onto the coffee table with a loud bang.

She tried to avoid using the blade. It was pure silver and would hurt like a son-of-a-bitch. The only time she used it was to kill, and she really didn't want to kill this kid if she didn't have to. This wasn't his fault. Not really.

"He didn't lie," he cried as he snapped the bone back into place. When he spat out his own blood, the clot landed in the dad's hair. "He loves me, and I'm going to be at his side forever!"

Alex shook her head and he growled as he charged again. He swung wildly at her, but she could tell he was losing his energy. He needed to feed again soon.

"Who is he, Ronnie?"

He laughed as he wiggled his hips and smiled at her. "My stepsister calls him 'Magic Mike'."

Creed must be completely insane to do this on her turf.

She tried not to punch this kid in his grimy face as she stepped closer.

"Tell me where he is."

"Close," Ronnie smiled. "I can feel him." He licked his bloody lips. "If I bring you to him, I'll be rewarded! Maybe he'll let me keep you for a while."

It was Alex's turn to laugh. Creed did not like to share, and she was not ever going to be some turned child's toy. If anything, Creed would try to keep her for his own personal amusement. She knew that for sure.

"You are not up to this, kid," she smiled at him.

"Let's see," he smiled back and picked up the leg from the broken coffee table. Swinging it like a bat, lamps and vases shattered in his wake. He moved her backward.

"I don't really want to hurt you," she sighed as she felt the heat of the setting sun at her back. The kitchen would be filled with natural light in just a few minutes, then night would fall again. "But I will if you make me."

Ronnie threw the table leg like a spear. It sailed past her head and buried in the wall. They traded punches and kicks, then she cut the back of his hand with the silver blade.

"Damn! That hurt," he barked as the cut sizzled, scorched from the silver.

"It's supposed to hurt."

He studied his hand, licked the wound, then spat. "That is gross!" A little puff of smoke came out.

He lunged at her, fangs fully extended as his hands reached for her throat. She dropped to her butt then her back. When she extended her legs, Ronnie was pushed into the sunlight of the kitchen. She jumped to her feet as he screamed. Once he landed on the kitchen table, his clothes burst into flames as did the rest of him. In a few seconds, he was ash then a giant black stain on the wooden table.

"Damn," Alex groaned as she picked up her jacket.

"Now what?" one of the agents asked.

"Clean this up," she answered as she opened the front door.

The sky was a brilliant orange canvas of light that would give birth to a clear, starry night. On the way back home, she'd pick up two bottles of tequila; she was going to need both to drown the bad dreams.

As she made her way back home through light traffic, Alex cursed Ramsey for the 911 text to come to this scene. Ever since she had taken over the Tracker team, the brief time between work and sleep was occupied by his attempt to exert control over her like never before.

Access to classified files was the trade-off. Now that she was completely back inside, she could request information previously deemed "need-to-know" before. As a temporary agent with a specific project, Alex didn't need to know what the Trackers had been up to over last few years. Her assignment was clearly defined and restricted to bringing in the test subjects for evaluation. She'd almost finished that job when all of this came up.

Her phone buzzed in the hands-free holder attached to a speaker. She tapped the answer button on the steering wheel.

"How'd it go?" Ramsey's familiar polished tone boomed. "Anything interesting to report?"

"One of the company's Executive Assistants and her new husband were murdered," Alex replied as she came to a stop at the traffic light. "Your team is bringing in their two children."

"Why?" Ramsey harped. "We're not a daycare center."

As traffic moved again, she rolled her eyes. "The children killed them."

"Oh," he sighed. "I still don't understand why we can't let the kids go to the local authorities."

"They were turned and killed their parents," Alex huffed. "That's why."

She thought she heard a low snicker come from the line, but why would he laugh at that? The whole situation was messed up, and she wished she could get to the truth some other way.

"How old are the kids?" he finally asked. In the background, she heard a rapid typing sound.

"I have no idea," Alex replied. "Maybe eight and twelve or so, I guess. The oldest one was around sixteen."

"What? Wait, I thought you said there were two of them," Ramsey snipped.

"There are now," Alex stated. "I had to dust the oldest."

Now she was sure he was laughing. His snicker reached her ears; she wanted to reach through the phone and rip out his throat.

"Of course you did. What would an investigation be without you killing someone?"

"Look," Alex hissed as she snatched the phone free. "He turned his brother and sister and watched as they killed their parents. He was not coming with us without a fight."

"We'll get a story on the local news by morning," Ramsey replied. "Nothing too dramatic. House fire should do the trick." More typing. "Looks like they just moved in, so no nosy neighbors to wonder about the activity around the house."

Alex remembered a cable television van and a moving truck out front. All the people around the house were pretty much ignored. She wasn't too keen on them setting a fire, but anything else would raise too many flags. Couldn't have the neighbors thinking a serial killer was on the loose or anything.

"What will you do with the kids?" she asked.

"See if they can identify the idiot vampire who turned them," Ramsey answered. "After that, the Council will send a courier to retrieve them. They've been notified."

She almost dropped Creed's name, but she decided against it once he mentioned the Council. That information would be useful to her later. If she told Ramsey, he'd have a kill order placed on Creed. She needed him alive, for now. Apparently, no one got Ronnie's reference or Ramsey would have made some smartass remark about it.

"How'd you find out about this, anyway?" Alex picked

up the conversation again.

"The Missus was due back today. When she didn't show or answer her phone, a co-worker got suspicious."

As flimsy as that excuse was, Alex let it go. Right now, she had bigger things to worry about—much bigger. The fate of strangers wasn't even in the top 100. Neither was what would happen to the newly-turned vampires being transported to God knows where for interrogation.

As a general rule, children were off limits. Human children were much too impulsive to be turned before a certain age. Children, especially as young as the ones she had just met, couldn't be trusted to make rational decisions. Everything was structured and filtered for them by the adults in their lives. They took instructions and did the exact opposite every time. Plus, these children had fed on human blood.

Usually the newly turned were eased into drinking fresh blood straight from the source. They'd be taught to endure the thirst, to control it in case they had to go without to stay safe. But once you get a taste for killing, you always want more. Then no one is safe.

To allow creatures like these to feed without restraint meant mistakes would be made. If the body count suddenly began to rise, the Council would notice. And, if they did, so would the human government. Blame would be placed solely on the Council, and they wouldn't like that.

If the children couldn't learn to feed without killing, they would be punished. Alex hoped they could be rehabilitated. This wasn't their fault. It was Creed's. And, for his misconduct, he might be executed. That thought filled Alex with a strange sort of pity—not that she hadn't wished Creed harm, but that was a long time ago. Now, to think that she held the power to bring about his demise, Alex felt a little scared of the possibility.

"Well," Alex said as she turned into the private drive of her house, "if there's nothing else, I've got work to do with my team."

"No, we'll take it from here," Ramsey's perpetual snide

tone scratched at her nerves. “Try not to kill any of them until after the conference.”

Before she could throw as many curse words as she knew at him, he was gone. The smartphone in her hand held her entire work life, so crushing it in her grip would not be a good idea. As she pulled up to the front door, all she wanted was a good workout, a stiff drink, and a long night’s sleep. Maybe she’d skip the workout.

Chapter 2

They'd been here for almost two weeks. In that whole time, this was the first opportunity she'd had to get him alone. An aching need gnawed at her insides. She welcomed this release and craved his bite as well.

Sebastian fed greedily from her as the sex reached a fever pitch. Erin held on tight. Much to her own surprise, she kept up with him. Each thrust fill her with a euphoria she could not explain. As she begged him to go deeper, harder, she welcomed the approach of her own release. Everything, heightened by the drugs and the addictive chemicals of his bite, slammed her senses, and she screamed.

Not that Sebastian was an aggressive lover, but he was a young vampire whose powers continued to grow every day. Erin knew he held back; he thought he had to because he still thought she was just human. Without the supplements Coop gave to her in secret, she wouldn't be nearly strong enough.

His assault on her neck eased as he climaxed and rolled from on top of her. Wrapped in the sleeping bag they found in the corner of an old caretaker's cabin, Erin listened to Sebastian's purr of satisfaction, then he blew out a hard exhale.

"You okay?" he panted at her.

She drew in a big breath, rolled over on her side. "Of course."

Sweat rolled down her face and dropped on his broad shoulder only to evaporate on his hot skin. As the enzymes from his saliva and the drugs in her system mixed, Erin felt her body react to the combination. She welcomed the high that would stay with her through the remainder of the night.

They dressed quickly and left the cabin together. The others were under the impression they were on a run, or so the rest of the team wanted them to believe. Erin knew better. She was aware of everyone's suspicions, but she didn't care. Sebastian was a distraction—a little excitement to break the monotony of training for the next assignment.

As they began to run back to the main house, they didn't say a word. Then Sebastian stopped and cursed under his breath.

"Maybe we should take a quick swim," he said as he eyed the water a few feet away.

Erin looked at him, then the lake, then back at him with a frown. "Are you crazy? It's freaking cold! What for?"

"Alex is gonna know we . . ." he replied as his left eyebrow went up.

"So what?" Erin laughed. "If we run back, the sweat will mask it anyway. She's not a freaking werewolf, is she?"

They both began to run again.

"No, but close," Sebastian huffed. "Shit."

Erin pulled him to a stop. "What did you say?"

The look on his face told Erin he'd made a big mistake. A slip of his tongue that was now ammunition for later.

"She's . . ." Sebastian stumbled over the thoughts as they formed in his head. "Those pills—she's still taking them and, well, they've changed her."

"Are you fucking kidding? You have to be kidding," Erin squealed. "How do you know that?"

He turned to walk away, but she stopped him. "She told us," he answered. When Erin pulled him around to face her, he looked into her eyes. "She showed us stuff in Vegas."

"What kind of stuff?"

When he took a deep breath, he could smell her excitement in the air. If he didn't keep going, she would just go ask Alex herself. He knew Erin well.

"She can move objects with her mind. Her sight and hearing are better than most vampires. And she says that she heals way faster than before."

Erin's mouth moved into a weird grin as she shook her head at him. "Bullshit," she laughed. "You're lying."

"I swear. I saw it—felt it."

"Felt what?"

"The energy," he almost whispered as if anyone could hear them. "When she moves stuff there's this vibration around her. It's pretty impressive."

"All of this because she's still taking those pills," Erin frowned. "Why wouldn't Dr. Carlisle tell us? Why wouldn't she let him figure out why it worked with her and no one else?"

Sebastian sensed some anger from Erin. Her eyes seemed glassy, and there was an edge to her tone. Why would she be so upset by this? Was it that Alex had left her and Amy out again?

"I don't know. Maybe he didn't think it mattered anymore."

Erin turned away. "It matters. Why should she be the only one?"

"The only one?"

"Never mind," she muttered as she turned.

He grabbed her arm and spun her back around to face him.

"Don't tell anyone about this. We promised her."

Erin just grinned at him as she tried to pull free of his grip. When he tightened his hold, her face contorted from the pain. "Erin," Sebastian demanded, "nobody, not even Amy. If Alex finds out I said something, she'll most likely kill all of us, so keep your mouth shut."

Sebastian could see the wheels turn in Erin's head. If he could, he would have made her forget, but he didn't have that ability; not that he knew of anyway. He couldn't think of a lie good enough to at least throw some doubt in her mind. He was busted.

"Alright, geez; I swear!"

With a small push, they continued their run back to the main house. Then he stopped again with a sharp curse.

"What now?" she said as she stopped too.

"I forgot to reconnect the ultraviolet lights," he groaned and turned to go back.

Erin grabbed his arm and spun him back around. "Too late now. The sun's almost down anyway. We'll do it tomorrow. It's fine."

He looked at her for a few seconds, and she turned on the innocent, little-girl stare of hers, the one all men were weak to. He shrugged and they jogged on. At the main house, sweaty enough for everyone to notice they'd done more than run, they entered to find their teammates going over blueprints and strategies in the kitchen.

The only person who didn't look up was Amy. Erin knew she had a massive crush on both her and Sebastian but was too timid to do anything about it. Too bad for her. Erin had no sympathy for her weakness or her wounded pride. If she wanted him, she could have him, but she'd have to make the move. Until then, Erin would enjoy the ride, and to hell with Amy's self-esteem. Besides, she'd smooth it over later, and everything would be just as before.

"How was the run?" Kai snickered. David tossed a bottle of water at Sebastian.

"Fine," he replied as he cracked the cap.

Xavier brushed his fingers over the corner of his own mouth when Sebastian looked at him. "Got a little something on your mouth, dude."

Embarrassment flashed red on Sebastian's face as Erin and the others watched him wipe at his mouth then grin like a guilty schoolboy. Erin took a cold energy drink from the refrigerator then sat next to Amy at the table. As she stared blankly at her tablet, Erin nudged her.

"What?" she said without even a brief glance in Erin's direction.

"What are you so into?" Erin replied as she leaned into Amy.

Amy nudged her away. "My assignment. Alex wants us to have this stuff memorized before we leave for Vegas." She continued to tap the screen and read.

"Relax," Erin giggled. "There's not gonna be a test, Amy. I'll cover you if there's something you can't understand."

Angry, Amy stood, gathered her things and left the kitchen without a word.

"Really, Erin?" Sebastian frowned at her.

"I was just joking," Erin sighed as she waved him off.

"No, you weren't," Xavier stated. "You were being a bitch."

"Yeah," Kai joined in. "More than usual too."

"Shut up," Erin growled at them. "She's gotta learn to take a joke and to be a little tougher, especially now. If she wants to stay on this assignment, she's gonna need to get that weepy thing under control."

"She's doing fine," David answered.

"You think Alex is gonna accept 'fine'?" Erin shook her head. "You heard her. If Amy can't control her emotions, she can't control her power. If she can't control her power, she is of no use to us."

Sebastian dropped the empty water bottle in the trash and turned to Erin. She could see he was angry at her, but it was hard for her to understand why. They all knew what she said was true. Amy was the weakest link in the chain. Did they really need Amy? Her magic was unreliable. Which made her unreliable, didn't it?

"She's fine," Sebastian stated as he passed Erin. "Leave her alone."

He left the room, followed by Xavier and Kai. David stayed seated across from her.

"You guys should cool it before Alex finds out," he said as he tapped on his laptop.

"So what if she does?" Erin snapped at him. "What's it to her?"

David grinned as he closed the machine and tucked it under his arm. On his way around the table, he took a shiny green apple from the bowl on the counter. He stopped next to Erin as he took a big bite.

"Some friendly advice," he said as he crunched on the apple. "She ain't Coop. He didn't care, but she will. Cool it."

When she was alone, she wanted to scream at the top of her lungs. No one told her what to do or who to screw, no one. As long as it didn't get in the way of the assignment, she wasn't going to let Alex Stone or Amy get in the way of the bite high she'd grown fond of. *So what if Alex finds out? It's just sex anyway.*

"I swear, Sire. That's all I know," the girl whimpered, barely able to lift her head. "I'm so hungry." There was no need to keep her bound—she was too weak to try an escape. Even if she did, the tracking device embedded behind her right ear would keep her within their reach. "Please," she begged from her knees on the dusty floor of the cell.

Over the last two weeks, they'd gotten nothing of use to them. Adam was beginning to think he'd lost his touch. Maybe he'd grown soft over the last hundred years of living in this modern world.

Whoever controlled her had a very strong hold. Her master must be smart and possibly as old as he and Conner in order to accomplish that feat. But there's always a trace, a thread to pull to release the information. As a Master, you left that thread to keep your progeny under your thumb—safekeeping precious information or blackmail material from others. This skill was extremely handy in a pinch.

He needed more time to get to that thread, but Adam feared his time with her had come to an end with little to show for it.

"Let's go over it one more time," Adam replied as he stood over her. She reached out with a shaky hand. "Why

Alex Stone and the Trackers?" Her fingers just missed the cuff of his tailored slacks as he stepped back.

In her weakened state, she fell, face first, to the floor. He could smell salt in the air from her tears. Her head rose slightly. "We were told to find someone called Dagger. I guess he thought the woman and her friends might know where to find him." Then she was face down in the dirt again, but this time she laughed.

Adam reached down and pulled her head up by her dirty hair. He pitched her back against the small cot she slept on and still she laughed. Her stained fangs barely pushed through her gums and she screamed when they fully extended. The rodent blood they'd given her kept her alive, but their strength came from real blood—healthy, strong human blood. She was like a newborn, weak and vulnerable. Kneeling down, Adam's stare stopped her laughter.

"In your current state, the sun will fry you to a nice pile of pretty ash," he grinned as he stood up again. "Who should we send them to?"

Dirty tears slid down her even dirtier cheeks. He wasn't sure if they were from fear or the laughter. He thought fear of a painful death might flip some switch in her brain—bring back a memory or two.

"You can't kill me," she coughed as she tried to pull herself up from the floor.

"Why not?" Adam smirked down at her.

"You need me," she smiled as she scrambled forward on her hands and knees toward him. He kicked her backward again and she landed flat on her back with thud. "I can lead you to him."

Adam kneeled again and took her chin in his hand. "Him, who?"

She shook her head. "Not until we have a deal."

Adam moved a greasy piece of dirty hair held across her face by sweat. "Convince me of your worth, and I'll consider it," he hissed and dropped her head back to the floor. Her clammy skin left a residue on his hand. When he reached into his jacket pocket, a crisp white handkerchief appeared. After he wiped his hands, he let the soiled cloth drop to her chest.

"Tristan," she whispered as she wiped away her tears. "He calls himself Tristan."

Adam turned with a growl, "Liar! He's dead."

The young girl's laugh, though weak, stung him deeply. "Aren't we all, technically?"

His hand flew out before she could blink. The smell of her tainted blood filled the room as soon as her lip split open. "If you betray us, the way you're doing him, staking you in the sun will be the kindest thing I could do to you," he said as he towered over her—his shadow turned the blood on her lip a dull, muddy shade. "And I have never been known for being kind."

"I'll need more than rats to feed on," she replied. "And a finder's fee."

Adam took a step back to pound on the steel door of her cell. Two females stepped inside. One stood beside him and told him he was needed back in Vegas. The other helped the girl to the cot then waited. "Get her cleaned up and properly fed," he ordered. "When she's ready, send me a message, and I'll meet you at the safe house," he added as he left the cell.

Adam pulled as much as he could from her brain. Instructions imbedded in her subconscious told her to capture the witch—bring her to an abandoned warehouse and wait for further instructions. Adam had sent a team there a few days ago. But the cobwebs indicated it had been empty for years. The social media site she received her messages through was a bust too. The information was automatically deleted after a very short amount of time. Their hackers assured him the information was deleted from the servers as well.

"We should have killed him when we had the chance," he mumbled as he exited the building. Inside his Escalade, he turned up the jazz music he loved so that it filled every square inch of the vehicle. The soft leather seat welcomed his weight easily. On the hour-long drive back into Vegas, he wouldn't think about Jason or Alex or even the conference.

Miles of sand lay ahead, but he was fine with that. Velvety smooth, Chet Baker's rendition of "My Funny Valentine" took Adam back to that smoky jazz club in Harlem around 1950 or so. Jason was still pretty young at that time, for a vampire anyway, and had grown very fond of a very young Elvis. Adam convinced him to join him for a night of "real" music, and he agreed.

On the bill that night: Miles Davis. A god as far as Adam was concerned—then and now. Back then, all musicians were gods. Real music was live and performed in places off the beaten path. Today, live music is bastardized for stadium performances and car commercials. Sound morphed through devices that kill the soul of the music and those who perform it.

He made sure to invite a then-human Nicole Hansen that night too. When Adam first laid eyes on the eighteen-year-old, she was working for a business associate of his as his personal secretary. Three years later, she'd become the man's mistress. It had been ages since he'd even thought of the man. Adam grinned as the memories came back.

Robert Caine, investment banker and trophy husband to a spoiled New York heiress, had invited Adam to lunch at his country club one bright Sunday afternoon. At that time, Robert was in his late thirties—old for the mid-twentieth century. With two awful and bratty sons, Robert hired Nikki as a favor to an old college friend. Over afternoon scotch with Adam, he proclaimed his undying love for the young woman with the killer figure and enchanting blue eyes.

"I know it's a bad idea," Robert sighed, "but I can't help myself."

Adam agreed that it was a bad idea, but he understood.

"It will be the death of you, Rob, if Gladys finds out. Why risk it?"

"She makes me feel needed. I don't want to be without her," he replied with a slight blush to his cheeks. "Can you blame me?"

"No, but I don't have a rich wife holding the purse strings, old man," Adam chuckled with a sip of thirty-year-old scotch. Back then, you could drink your lunch and go back to work. Back then, smoking was a mark of distinction and taste. No one cared about lung cancer or secondhand smoke.

Robert nodded, "Lucky you."

Robert had come to Adam for help. He wanted to purchase an apartment for his young lover, discreetly—a place where he could go and satisfy his ego, a place where an older man with a young and beautiful girlfriend could pretend. He asked Adam to purchase the domicile in his name, and he agreed. But Nikki soon tired of Robert's broken promises to leave his wife for her. And, as all things do, Robert's tryst with Nikki ended.

At the time, the little three-bedroom flat cost him thirty thousand dollars. Adam let Nikki keep the apartment for another twenty years or so because he owned the entire building. He found that he liked her company most of all. One evening she came to Adam with an interesting proposition.

"I could be very useful to you," she smiled over dinner and drinks that evening. "I know things and people that could help you."

Adam smiled back as he waved for another bottle of wine. "Help me with what exactly?"

She dropped her pointed chin and looked at him through long dark lashes. "You'd be surprised at what a man will tell you under the proper conditions," she winked.

"No, I wouldn't," he winked back.

Her red lips pressed together as she moved closer to him. When she placed her hand on his as it rested on the table, he could feel the warmth and the blood coursing through her veins. It was intoxicating to be close to someone so young and alive.

"Take you, for instance," she whispered. "I know what you are, Adam Craig."

"And what do you think you know?" Adam replied as he moved closer. Part of him knew she didn't know the truth, she couldn't. But part of him was afraid he'd have to kill her before the end of the night to keep his secret.

"Robert says you have secrets," she answered with a sparkle in her blue eyes. "He says you're a dangerous man with dangerous friends."

He laughed then gave her hand a pat. "Well, he's half right," he replied as he picked up his drink again. "What else did he tell you?"

"He told me lots of things," she said. "Mostly about who's stealing from whom and where they keep their mistresses. He says knowing where the bodies are buried is more lucrative than his real job. Is that true?"

"It can be," Adam replied as the waiter placed the bottle on the table.

"Then maybe we can do business," she said as she poured. "I know you own my apartment. I'd like to stay there, so maybe we could come to an agreement of sorts."

That night she became his little fly on the wall and his lover. She was very good at gathering information. She was very good at a lot of things.

Chapter 3

She clung to him, moaned his name with each thrust. When all ten nails sank in under his shoulder blades, Jason's fangs slid into the vein at Nikki's neck, and her sweet blood flowed. Down his throat, it tickled as it filled his empty stomach. As he climaxed, she screamed and laughed through her orgasm. After a minute, he eased from between her warm thighs, rolled over, then put his back to her.

Nikki had a voracious appetite, especially during sex. Just as he was about to leave the bed, she wrapped her powerful thigh around him from behind and sank her fangs into his neck and began to feed. The pain shot through him like a lightning strike. Then she began to rub herself slowly against him. She moaned as she pleasured herself and fed. He gripped her thigh and rode it out.

When he felt her body shudder and the pull of her mouth begin to weaken, Jason knew she was finally done. A small kiss at the back of his neck signaled her complete satisfaction even though he had nothing to do with the last part. With her naked body pressed against him, Jason pretended she was someone else. After a few minutes, she sighed.

"You seem a million miles away," Nikki purred, warm breath on his back. "Worried about the conference?"

Jason didn't answer. Truth be told, he wasn't worried about the conference—he could handle that. His thoughts were elsewhere. Anger had burned through him the moment Nikki showed him the newspaper item a few hours ago. She had wanted to punish Jason, and the sight of Alex wrapped around a sport's team owner on the front page of a gossip rag felt like punishment to him. She'd made it a point to drop the paper where he could see it and commented on how happy Alex looked on another man's arm.

"Don't they look sweet together?" Nikki hummed over drinks in the casino bar. Adam had barely glanced at the picture, but Jason fought the urge to set it on fire and shove the flaming mess down Nikki's throat. "I wonder if he'll be her plus one for the wedding."

Jason shot Nikki a dirty look, to which she laughed. Later, upstairs, she came on like nothing had happened. She crawled all over him like a starving beast, and his desire got the better of him. Instead of denying Nikki, he took her to bed in hopes of stopping the green-eyed monster in its tracks. It didn't work.

When she nibbled at his ear, he squeezed his eyes shut and wondered where Alex was. He'd intentionally ignored her call earlier, but now he wanted to hear her voice. She and the team were scheduled to arrive in Vegas in a couple of days though.

"Just going over everything in my head," he answered when Nikki tugged playfully at his ear with her teeth. "You know how I am."

"Yes," she giggled in that same ear, "I do. I know you better than anyone else in the world. There is no one better suited to be your wife than me. We are perfect."

Over the last sixty or so years, she was the constant in this ever-changing world. Always there—no matter what. She and Adam were his only family now. Countless lovers, friends, and enemies had come and gone, but they, the three of them, were forever.

He could still remember when he first laid eyes on Nikki. The beautiful and vivacious human with the gorgeous figure, silky blond hair, and piercing blue eyes. She was stunning, and she knew very well how to make that work for her. In the smoky jazz joint on a hot summer night in Harlem, Jason, like every other man in the place, fell head over heels for her. Jason was determined to make her his—body and soul—until the end of time.

I should have been more careful what I wished for, he mused to himself as the feel of her tongue on the back of his neck brought him back to the present. After a few minutes, she was asleep—her arm slung lazily over him. With agility, he moved it so as not to wake her, then slid from the rumpled bed. Once he was back in his robe, he left her bedroom as quietly as he could.

At the other end of the hall, the master bedroom, his domain, was quiet and clean. The darkness would have been total if not for the thin sliver of moonlight that seeped through the narrow opening of the heavy drapes. He reached for the lamp on the nightstand as he sat down on the soft bed, but he decided to leave the darkness all around him. Comfortable in his luxurious cave, Jason let his eyes adjust fully to the lack of light, then picked up his mobile.

Her name, as it blazed across the screen, caused his heart to tap hard in his chest. His excitement embarrassed him, but he redialed anyway.

"Well," her voice calmed his excited heart, "way to make a girl wait."

"Sorry," Jason hummed then leaned back against the pillows. "I was tied up."

Alex's laugh made him wish she was next door, not three states away from his reach. "I'm sure you mean that literally."

"I'm guessing you received Adam's package?"

When Adam told him he had sent an actual uniform for the Tracker team to wear while on duty during this trip, he knew Alex wouldn't allow it.

"Yes, we did, and no," she sighed.

Jason laughed at the girlish response. "I figured as much. Is that the only reason you called—to tell Adam to go to hell?"

"No," she replied. "I could have called his private line for that. I called to congratulate you."

"On what?" he asked.

"Your engagement," she replied. "Don't you read your own press releases?"

"What are you talking about?" he replied as he tried to keep his voice calm.

"Umm, there's an announcement on the dark web," Alex said. "Jasper's column."

Jason turned on the light and shut his eyes as it hit them. He snatched up the tablet and reached the website quickly. There it was.

"So," she cleared her throat, "when's the big day?"

He chuckled because he didn't know what else to do. "I, we haven't set one yet. Look, Alex—"

"Hey," she replied, "you don't owe me any explanation. I mean, it was just sex, right?"

Jason felt a twinge of anger suddenly. Did he make any promises to her that he shouldn't? Did she to him? He could have been slightly more forthcoming with her about his relationship with Nikki, but he never had to be before. But if he were being perfectly honest, his feelings for Alex were dangerous.

"Is that what you think?" he asked.

"What would you call it?" she giggled nervously. "You're engaged. You should have told me before we got involved."

"We weren't engaged then," he replied. "Not officially anyway."

"Not officially? Is that supposed to make me feel better?"

He suddenly realized who put that item on the dark web—Adam.

"Nikki and I have an open relationship." He'd hoped that would stave off the fight they were about to have, but it didn't.

"Open to what?" Alex sniffed back. "Interpretation?"

Jason couldn't help the slight chuckle at her retort. Alex

did have a way with cutting through the bullshit, didn't she?

"I care for her," Jason continued. "I won't lie about that—not to you. Nikki and Adam are my family. My feelings for her won't change, but I have feelings for you too."

The silence on the other end was deafening—painful. He could hear her breathing. When nothing came from her, he continued. "For the last hundred years I have worked my ass off to get to the top of this world, Alex. Nikki and Adam have been the driving force behind me, and I love them both, deeply. Our world, the mixing of races, it doesn't bode well for anyone in my position to . . . Well, the Council expects certain things in return for its support. I agreed to their terms before I met you."

"You don't want to lose favor because of a human," Alex replied. "I get it."

"Do you?"

"This was a mistake," she whispered, and Jason felt his heart drop.

"I know," he whispered back, and it left a sour taste in his mouth. "I wish . . ."

"Don't," she interrupted. "Just makes this harder to do."

"What? Wait!"

That was all he got out before she was gone. He showered and dressed, then headed for Adam's office. With every step, Jason tried to clamp down the anger, but he knew by the time he reached the office it would be at a boiling point. It didn't help that he kept going over the article in his head either.

Jasper Jake's gossip blog was extremely popular with the supernatural set nowadays. He was the supernatural world's equivalent of Perez Hilton. And, somehow, everything he wrote about came true. Jason rapped hard on Adam's door then entered before he heard a reply.

"Have you seen this?" he asked as he dropped the device on the desk in Adam's line of sight.

"Yes," he replied as he pushed it back toward Jason. "I put it there."

Jason swallowed enough bitter anger to choke a horse. As his sire, even now, Jason was obligated to show Adam respect. Even if it wasn't always returned.

"Why?"

Without even a glance at Jason, Adam continued to stare at his giant monitor as if he wasn't even there.

"Because it's time. To everyone's surprise, you have your seat in the Lower Chamber. Conner just notified us."

Under different circumstances, Jason would have been overcome with delight at the news. But it didn't matter because Adam had intentionally delivered the one-two punch so Jason wouldn't start an argument.

One reason after another stood in the way of an official announcement of his engagement to Nikki. Over the past few months, he'd been inundated with email, and visits about this meeting. Once Alex entered his life, he wanted to delay it even longer. In the back of his mind he knew Adam would force his hand though.

"What has that got to do with making this public without my permission?"

As soon as the words escaped his lips, Jason begged them to come back. As Adam rose from the leather chair, his eyes burned through Jason.

"You really want me to answer that," Adam said in a low tone of voice. "Or should I give you a chance to define 'permission' before I rip out your throat?"

He wasn't going to apologize—Adam would lose his shit for sure if he did. Over the years, Jason had learned the hard way that Adam did not accept apologies. You made a mistake, you faced the consequence—period.

"The announcement should have come from Nikki and me. It may seem innocent to you, but this makes me look as if I can't make any decisions without you, Adam. Not even when I marry. I worked my ass off to get that seat," his voice rose. "No one handed that or anything else to me, ever!"

Adam's right hand twitched with the sound of Jason's

shout. When he stepped away from the desk, Jason knew not to move a muscle. Adam pushed his hands into his pockets as he faced Jason fully.

"We had an agreement," he stated calmly. "Once your appointment came through, you and Nikki would announce your engagement."

"Had I known about one," Jason replied, "I would have done the other."

"Had you not been preoccupied with texting that . . . woman like a love-struck teenager, you might have noticed Conner's email," Adam proclaimed through gritted teeth.

Jason couldn't stop the grin that emerged on his face. Now he knew what this was really about—Alex.

"Since when do you care who I take to my bed?" he continued to grin.

"Since it started to interfere with everything else," Adam answered with a scowl.

"Like what?" Jason asked. "I've done everything you've asked me to do. The meeting is set. I'm even meeting with Adelaide, as instructed." He snapped his hand to his temple, clicked his heels together, and gave Adam a salute.

Again, he stopped himself from steppimg back when Adam moved forward. Now he could feel the immense power that always radiated off the Pure. It hummed against his skin now.

"Don't say that like you're doing me a favor," Adam snapped at him. "Her vote helps us move forward. Helps you succeed! Don't forget that!"

"I haven't," Jason snapped back. "But don't you forget I'm not a child! I decide what happens in my private life—not you!"

"Careful," Adam growled low.

"Or what? You'll send me to my room without supper? You'll rip my throat out? Do it! Better dust than a puppet on strings!"

"I am your sire, your maker! I gave you life eternal. You begged me to make you a vampire! You pledged to do as

I instructed for a place in the Council, and you have it—because of me!" Adam barked.

"I agreed to follow the rules of business—and I did," Jason hummed. "I sacrificed and fought hard for what I have. I played the game and won. I didn't agree to have you control every aspect of my life."

"I taught you that game," Adam replied. "And I helped you in a fight or two, remember?"

"Yes, and I will be forever grateful, but I can handle this," Jason stated.

"End it."

"Why?"

Adam looked him in the eyes and Jason felt that power again. "Because I'm asking you to."

"Do you think I'm the only member of the Council with a human lover?" Jason grinned. "I'm not naïve, Adam. Even the high and mighty Conner Gale has had a human or two."

"That's different," Adam growled.

Jason began to let his confidence get the best of him. He leaned back against the desk, crossed his legs casually and smiled at his angry sire.

"Because I'm not of pure blood," he sighed. "I wasn't born a vampire."

"Yes," Adam answered as he crossed his arms over his chest. "You were not born but made! I said end this ridiculous tryst with that woman. You have too much to lose if you continue."

"You mean you have too much to lose," Jason said as he stood up straight again. "You have your precious reputation, of course. And there's Conner's favor to consider."

"I don't need Conner's favor," Adam snapped, "you do! End it!"

"No!" Jason barked with no thought as to the consequence. Before he blinked, Adam had Jason's head between his solid hands. Out of instinct, he grabbed his wrists. The pressure on his ears lessened just a bit because of it.

"You can't have her," Adam growled in Jason's face.

"I already have!"

His back slammed into the door before he could brace himself for the impact. Any harder and Adam would have put him through the heavy wooden door. It had been years since Adam had put his hands on Jason out of rage. Hard fought sparring matches were one thing. An all-out display of power was quite another—for Jason anyway.

Jason put everything he had into his punch. It landed squarely and snapped Adam's head to the right. The loud crash of the crystal tumbler set as he slammed into it gave Jason a boost of confidence. His fist hurt like hell, but it was worth the healing of broken bone later. Before he could throw a jab, Adam's paw of a left hand clamped around his neck. Jason dropped his fist in the bend of Adam's arm, but that didn't loosen Adam's grip at all. In fact, it tightened.

"This is the Jason I know and love," Adam hissed close to his face. "I'm done watching the other make a fool of himself over a human!"

Jason's feet left the floor. Then his back slammed against the wall. This time what little air he had in his lungs jumped out and he slid to his knees. The taste of his own blood shot electricity through every limb. Back on his feet, two quick jabs sent Adam backward. He heard glass crunch under his feet as he got his balance again.

"Stop telling me what to do!" Jason barked as he delivered a swift and powerful roundhouse that caught Adam's perfect chin. "Are you going to tell me what position to start with on my wedding night too?"

Adam smiled as he rubbed his chin, then licked at his bloody lip. "Do you want me to, or was that rhetorical?"

Jason had to laugh as he sat down on the edge of the desk and pulled in oxygen to fill his lungs. Adam tossed a bar towel at him. He grabbed a handful of ice and placed it in a towel for himself.

"Are we really fighting over her?" Adam moaned as he pressed the towel to his bruised chin.

Jason shook his head, but he was pretty sure they just had. His left hand throbbed and twitched as it began to heal. Blood, fresh and direct from the source, would speed it up.

"I need to take care of this," Jason said as he stood up and held his hand to his chest. "Can we talk about this later?"

Adam followed him all the way to the winding staircase. Jason was wrapped in Adam's arms before he could take another step.

"You are all I have, Jason," he said in his ear, "you and Nikki. We can have everything we've ever desired if you would just trust me."

"I do," Jason answered, unable to pull free of Adam's bear hug. Suddenly, Adam's cold bloodied lips pressed to his cheek. Jason could smell Adam's blood on his skin when he was pushed away.

Adam held Jason at arm's length to look him in the eyes once more. Over the years, he'd accepted that Jason was the closest thing he had to a son. It only made sense for him to marry Nikki. They made more sense together than he and Alex.

Adam knew from the moment Jason laid eyes on Alex that there would be problems. Jason could never resist a woman who could take him or leave him. All of the women in Jason's circle seemed to not be able to live without him. Alex seemed to not need anyone at all.

Jason was drawn to her arrogance and attitude. Nikki's "definitive femininity" caught Jason's eye, but Alex's bold independence is what piqued his interest. Everything combined made Alexa Stone hard to compare to anyone else in his life.

Adam couldn't deny Alex's talent. He wouldn't deny her differences, either. Something about her just wasn't right. Both he and Conner agreed she had secrets, and vampires love secrets.

"Then end this relationship with Alex," he sighed. "For your own good."

He could see the question in Jason's mind before it came from his lips.

"Her being human can't be the only reason," Jason sneered. "It never bothered you before."

Adam released Jason and stepped back. He didn't have the words to explain their suspicions. Conner noticed something when they met a few weeks ago. Something he couldn't prove—not right now. So had Adam, but he had just thought it was his imagination. He and Conner couldn't have imagined the same thing, could they?

When Jason spoke to Adam, his eyes were cast down. "Your plan worked—the announcement on the dark web. Alex already called to tell me we're done. You win."

"We all win," Adam declared as he tried to take Jason in his embrace again. But Jason avoided Adam's arms as he stepped back, bowed, and turned toward the staircase without another word.

Jason climbed the stairs in silence as Adam watched him disappear from view.

After he cleaned up the mess in his office, Adam showered, dressed, and left the house alone. The drive to Ashblood didn't take long. His standing appointment was long overdue.

CHAPTER 4

Looking over the map of the new location for the meeting, Alex tried not to feel excited. It felt sort of stupid, but she was amped about going on this mission now. After reviewing the original plan, it was decided that the castle wasn't exactly a safe place for the meeting. There were too many caverns underneath to insure proper protection of the attendees and, logistically, it just sucked. And then the electrical fire kind of squashed that idea altogether, so they needed a new plan.

The Palace of the Parliament in Bucharest became the new venue after a couple days of discussion with the Council. As the seat of the country's government, it was easier to move around, spacious enough to accommodate all the attendees, and beautiful to boot. With long marble hallways and exquisitely decorated meeting rooms and offices, everything was already in place to host something of this magnitude. Best of all, it was close to all the hotels.

The team had to know every inch of the facilities and grounds by the time they landed.

When Ivy came out of the house with a drink in one hand and a bottled water in the other, Alex slipped the tablet back in the pack at her feet and pretended to study the pictures on Ivy's laptop instead.

"You know," Ivy hummed as she placed the water in front of Alex and sat down again, "you should maybe get a checkup before you leave, huh?"

"I'm good," Alex shook her head as she looked over the wardrobe the team would wear during this assignment.

Their uniforms would be made from next generation fabrics that would adapt to almost any temperature. When their body temperatures rose above a certain level, the fabric would cool them. If it dropped, the fabric would warm them. Sebastian's, of course, would have some design changes specific to the way his body worked, but everything was ready and working perfectly.

Body armor never looked so good. Cool leather jackets hid next generation Kevlar that would stop standard and modified ammo. Unless the odds were against them and someone hired a sniper, they were ready. They would be the best equipped bodyguards in the world.

"Are you nervous at all?" Ivy's voice broke into her thoughts.

"A little, I guess," Alex answered then turned the laptop in Ivy's direction. "It's been a long time."

"Well, let one of them take a bullet for him," Ivy replied as she nodded toward the house. "I'd like my partner back here in one piece." She pulled the laptop close with a nod of approval. "The design turned out pretty cool. Do you like them?"

"I really do," Alex smiled. "I'm sure the team's gonna love them. Maybe Strategic will buy the designs when we're done with this assignment."

"Maybe," Ivy sighed. She sipped her wine as she stared at the screen. "Why are you really going to Romania with them?"

Alex looked up at her. "I told you."

"Yeah, now I want you to tell me the truth."

After she pushed the half empty glass away, Ivy sat back and waited.

"Coop just needs some help," Alex lied—had been lying about Coop and what happened since she'd been home. Until they found proof, he was still alive as far as anyone not on this assignment was concerned, and that included Ivy. "He's a little out of his league on this one." She smiled, but Ivy didn't smile back.

"You got out."

"I'm still out."

Her uneasiness drifted toward Alex in waves. It stung her brain. Usually, when Ivy was nervous about something, Alex knew what to expect. But, this time, her senses were taken by surprise. She'd never felt this before from Ivy.

"Doesn't look that way from where I'm standing," she hummed. "What do you know about mergers and acquisitions anyway? You hate that stuff."

"I don't have to know anything about mergers and acquisitions," Alex answered. "I know people. That's what they need—someone who knows people."

"I thought this was just a meeting about some kinda land deal or whatever," Ivy grinned before she finished her wine. "Why would Jason Stavros need an entire team of bodyguards to meet with some CEOs in Transylvania?" She giggled as she tapped the empty glass nervously. "Seems like overkill to me."

"I've seen people get killed over less," Alex responded then immediately wished she hadn't.

"See," Ivy shook a long finger in her direction as she stood, crossed the bar of the outdoor kitchen, and pulled a bottle of Patron from the shelf. With two shot glasses between her fingers she came back to the table. "I knew you were holding out on me. What's really going on?"

Alex took a deep breath then stood with the bottle of Patron and led Ivy, shot glasses in hand, deeper into the park-like backyard, past the lap pool with its colored lights that changed in a preprogrammed pattern. The surface of the cold water rippled as the breeze skipped across it.

They climbed the wooden steps of the deck, and Alex lit the fire pit as Ivy sat down on the comfortable sofa, curled her legs underneath her, and waited. Red and yellow flames jumped, and the wood popped as Alex sat down and poured two shots.

"Remember when I told you about vampires?" Alex asked as she stared at the fire. "How they were real, I mean."

Ivy nodded slowly. Her deep brown eyes turned amber by the firelight.

"Yeah," she replied. "You showed up at the campus Halloween party in hunting gear. Everyone thought it was the coolest costume ever. Who knew you had tracked a nest to the Frat House down the street?"

Alex laughed at the memory. "That hundred bucks for first prize came in quite handy as I remember."

Ivy smiled as she stoked the fire. "So, Bucharest?"

"This meeting," she began, "it's about the Supernatural Community and a credible threat to all of us."

"What kind of threat exactly?" Ivy inquired, suddenly more interested in what Alex had to say. "What does it have to do with you and these bodyguards?"

Alex ran her fingers through her hair as the breeze picked it up. "Sometimes we'd do things for them in return for certain favors: technologies, medicines that we couldn't get, or hadn't discovered yet."

"How does Jason Stavros factor into this?"

"He's just been appointed as the representative of the entire vampire population of North America."

Ivy took the warm tequila shot in her hand and sat the bottle down on the ground. "The body in Vegas," she said, "did that have something to do with this meeting?"

"We're not sure yet. That's one of the reasons I'm joining the team on this assignment."

"And the other reason?"

Alex took another deep breath. She'd just bragged to Jason about how she kept Ivy safe, away from this kind of stuff. If Ivy told anyone, she wouldn't be safe anymore.

"A friend of mine was killed while I was in Vegas. I think that does have something to do with this meeting, so I'm in again."

Ivy gave her a knowing nod as she stared into the flames. "Why did you leave?"

"I was hurt on my last mission," she whispered, trying to hold back the memory. "The vampire we were after . . .

he almost killed me."

"How were you able to fight that vampire?" Ivy replied, turning toward Alex again. "Or any vampire for that matter?"

"The program was formed around a supplement my father created that gave us certain abilities: strength, stamina, healing; we could do what almost any vampire could do as long as we stayed on the pills."

"And if you didn't?"

"We'd go back to being normal," Alex lied again.

"Did you stop taking them?" Ivy asked. "I mean, after that assignment? Is that why you were in the hospital?"

"Sort of," Alex answered. "That's a long story. Maybe when I get back, okay?"

"Sure," Ivy smiled and gave her hand a pat. "So, Jason Stavros is a vampire."

Alex laughed and relaxed some. In true Ivy style, she'd give Alex her space, for now. Besides, Jason was a much more interesting subject.

"Yeah, intel's a little sketchy on just how old he is," she grinned, "but I'm pretty sure he's close to a hundred."

"Damn! He looks good for an old man."

"He's good at a lot of things," Alex laughed and blushed slightly. "For an old man."

"You slept with him, didn't you?" Ivy laughed too. "I knew it! He can come to the launch."

"Yeah, I'm sure his fiancé will love the new line," Alex sighed.

"Fiancé? Since when?" Ivy hummed.

"I just saw the announcement," Alex replied. "So I wouldn't count on him accepting that invitation."

"Please," Ivy frowned. "He's still crazy about you, fiancé or not. Besides, he's not married yet."

"Close enough," Alex replied just as a gust of wind sailed across the backyard and excited the fire in front of them. She stood, scanned the darkness to the west of them, then took a deep breath. Ivy began to rattle off the names of the men Alex could invite instead of Jason like she was reading her grocery list. "Shhh . . ."

"What?" Ivy picked up the almost empty tequila bottle and looked in the dark sky like Alex. "What is it?"

Alex took the bottle from Ivy's hand and dropped it on the padded couch cushion. Once she had Ivy by the wrist, she pulled her back then pushed her toward the house.

"Go inside," she said. "Get the others. Go!"

Ivy held her long hair as it danced in the wind around them. "What's wrong?"

Alex shook her head and looked up into the clear, starry sky. "Go, Ivy! Go now."

Another shove sent Ivy onto the concrete patio with a stumble. Once inside, Alex heard Ivy curse. Then she turned her attention to the scent that led her into the darkness.

Sebastian felt the presence of vampires before he heard Ivy scream for them from below. He was halfway down the stairs, Xavier and Erin bringing up the rear, before Ivy reached the bottom step.

"What's going on?" he asked as he took her by the arms.

"I don't know," she said as she shook like a leaf. "She took off after something. She told me to come and get you."

He ran through the main living area after he told Erin to watch after Ivy. Through the kitchen and out the back entrance, Sebastian pulled in a breath and the sour sting excited him.

He and Xavier reached the gatehouse just as the twins and Amy exited. Sending Amy to the main house, the rest of the team ran in the direction of Alex's scent. They followed Sebastian in silence, but they smelled of excitement. Looks like they would get a chance to use their training tonight.

The flare lit up the sky at the far end of Alex's ten-acre

estate. The property was serving as a training facility for her team until they left for Vegas. With them close to her, she could be sure no one would interfere with what she wanted to teach them. After the attempt on her and Jason's lives in Vegas a couple of weeks ago, it made sense for them to all be in one place. What was hard for Alex was sharing space with six twenty-something, superpowered, special agents for the government. Quiet time was nonexistent now that they were here.

The light died over the caretaker's cabin, which sat unattended next to the man-made lake. Alex's legs fell into a rhythm. Her muscles warmed up, and she picked up speed. From behind her, she heard the others rush in her direction. They'd better hurry, or they'd miss the fun.

Another flare went off overhead. This time, right over the three-room cabin by the lake. Given time, she would have remodeled it for guests—if she ever had them, which she didn't. But she wasn't given time, was she? She was given an ultimatum: join this mission or stay bound to the company forever. Some choice.

Her legs kept up the pace easily. A familiar rhythm guided her feet. At the halfway mark, a thought formed in her mind. *Why hadn't the flood lights covered the entire lakeside in irritating ultraviolet beams?* They had promised even the slightest intrusion would trip them.

"Fuck," she huffed to the dark. "How'd they get past that? Did they fall from the freaking . . ."

The realization struck her hard. The first flare was to get her attention; the second may have taken out the power source for the security lights. She slid to an abrupt stop. All around her were the sounds of the night—creatures that preferred to go about life in the dark. From a few miles north came the smell of a fireplace. From behind her, her team came in fast.

As she tightened her focus on the shadows, she saw four figures. The clouds shaded the moon as it tried to help her see. Two figures stepped between the shadows, clothed in black. In the blink of an eye, the other two had circled behind her.

"A little far from home, aren't you?" Alex said.

"The Mistress sent me," they replied in unison.

This breed of vampire, Clan Cantu, had a collective mind. One sire with several children all linked psychically, like a puppet master that could pull strings from hundreds of miles away. They spoke as one, in first person.

The shrill timbre of their voices was like nails on a chalkboard. It tingled over Alex's scalp.

They took one step forward and grinned. "I have something for you—a gift from the Mistress. If you accept, her debt is paid in full."

Alex clenched her fists then stretched her fingers out again. "I understand."

They giggled. "I know you do."

Once Sebastian's yell reached them, the two figures behind her turned and disappeared in that direction. She hoped they were ready; the Cantu loved to play.

"Are you ready?" the other two chorused with one more step forward.

Whisper soft, the evening breeze swept across the clearing they stood in. Alex pulled the hoodie over her head and dropped it to the ground. Her white tank top would make her easy to see, but this breed could see in pitch black so that didn't matter now.

Clan Cantu were the only vampires that had not adapted to daylight. They lived in darkness, caves mostly. Tucked deeply in the Canadian Rockies, one might happen upon a group, if they were unlucky. She'd been unlucky once and lived to tell the tale.

The Cantu vowed, hundreds of years ago, not to side with humans. To them, humans were prey and the enemy. They separated themselves from the rest of the vampire population so there was only one reason they were here now.

For payment, they will offer their unique abilities

to the Pure. Only for the vampire elite will they deliver special messages. And they will only accept human blood as payment.

"It's been awhile," Alex sighed as the creatures removed their hoods.

"It's like riding a bike," they replied. "You should never forget."

Smooth, pale skin and slanted, black eyes, the Cantu's deep red lips spread into wicked smiles. Their teeth, fighting for space in their mouths, were gleaming white. Incisors, razor-sharp and big, extended past their bottom lips. With jet black, pin straight hair pulled back into tight ponytails at the base of their long necks, Alex did the same with her hair. The only exception was they had shiny black razor blades threaded through the ends of theirs—she didn't.

When the beaten-up fighting sticks landed at her feet, she rolled one to the top of her foot then flipped it up into her hand. She quickly flipped up the other.

"I see you haven't completely forgotten all I taught you," they smiled at her.

In the distance, her team had their hands full with the other two Cantu. She could hear Cantu laughter and the swarm of curse words the guys let loose on the breeze. Even a simple sparring match with a Cantu could frustrate the calmest of warriors.

"Well," she sighed, "let's get to it then."

"Let's," they laughed.

"To your right," Sebastian yelled from the ground. His shoulder was dislocated.

Before Xavier could react, the small creature had swept his legs from under him. When his back hit the cold ground, a little giggle filled the air as it backflipped away with a wink.

"I hate these things," he groaned, rolling to his knees and running after it.

Sebastian snapped his shoulder back in place and followed. He didn't think it was possible, but he was tired and he could tell the others were too. The two creatures led the four of them closer to Alex and two more identical figures.

As she traded strikes with both, Sebastian and Xavier found themselves trading Tai Kwon Do moves with the one between them. As Sebastian kicked at one side and was blocked, it kicked Xavier into the air with very little effort.

On Xavier's right, the twins didn't fare much better. Kai cursed with every jab he threw. David, struggling more than he should have been, dodged a ponytail as it swung out. They'd learned early on about the razor blades tied to them. Somehow, Sebastian felt like that was cheating.

It hardly seemed possible, but the creature disappeared like magic as David and Kai both threw punches at it. They stopped short of knocking each other out when they realized their opponent was gone.

"Hey," Kai yelled as he looked around wildly, "come back here!"

Hearing the snap of a twig, David ducked and stayed low as he forced an open palm into the shadow he hoped was the creature. He felt his hand slam into a body of wiry flesh and muscles. The creature stumbled back with a surprised look on its ghostly face.

"Not bad for a human, huh," David boasted with what was left of the air in his aching lungs. At least they'd slowed the creatures' pace a little.

All of its ragged teeth appeared as both creatures stopped their assault. They came together in front of the team with Alex and the other two close behind them.

"I've fought better," they said together. Then, as Alex battled a few yards away, they brought their hands up as if to pray and bowed at the group.

The guys looked at each other then back at the Cantu. They bowed, careful to keep their eyes on the creatures. The Cantu straightened, turned and ran toward Alex.

Xavier was the first to step forward. "What just happened?"

Kai rubbed his bruised chin. "I think we won."

Just then the sound of Alex grunting put them all in motion.

"Shit," Sebastian hissed. "Alex!"

Her lungs worked overtime as she blocked and defended herself against two Cantu. She'd forgotten how fast they could be. But she surprised herself with how much she remembered from her time with them. Being able to match them move for move meant she was probably ready for anything.

Cockiness can get you hurt, which she soon found out when one creature spun around and whipped a ponytail her way. It sliced effortlessly through her bare arm, and she yelped. They laughed, of course, at the drawing of her blood. She acted quickly. Her advance caught one off guard. As it turned to repeat the maneuver, she stepped back and jerked at the strands of hair on the lethal ponytail. The razor blade and the hair it was attached to fell silently to the ground.

Both Cantu faced her and she twirled the sticks up into a defensive cross pose in front of her face.

"She's slow," they said to each other. "Much slower than before."

Their heads shook as they turned to her and laughed.

"You're out of practice," they shrugged their boney shoulders. Then they stepped back and smiled big. "And you've put on weight too."

Alex had just enough air in her tired lungs to say, "Bite me." She reached down to retrieve the razor blade.

They laughed a witchy cackle as they looked at each other.

"Invitation?" they asked each other, then turned their eyes back to Alex. "If I had more time and had not been warned by the Mistress not to be greedy, I would."

Alex smiled, tossing the fighting sticks to the ground at their long feet.

The one to her right tossed a black wooden box at her feet as the other tossed a red leather book into her hands.

"The Mistress offers this warning," they stated. When their companions joined them and her team fell in line next to her, she examined the book. "Be sure you are ready. Be sure you have exhausted all other avenues before you choose."

"What do I do with this?" Alex asked as Kai picked up the box. "Where's the weapon?"

"There's nothing in this thing but a weird looking bracelet," Kai said showing them the box. Purple silk covered the inside. Nestled within was a metal bracelet with a glass tube embedded in it. She thought she recognized it, but she didn't have time to figure it out.

"I don't understand," Alex said to the creatures. "What was all this for, if not to tell me what the hell to do with it?"

"I was just testing you," they giggled. "I wanted to see if you still remember what I taught you. You need more practice."

Alex glanced at the book as David held it up in the dim light of the moon. The language was unrecognizable to her—or any of them, for that matter.

"I don't understand," she huffed.

"You will," they replied with a deep bow to them all.

Another flare went off above them. When the light died, the Cantu were gone.

"Now what?" Xavier sighed as they walked back toward the main house again.

David flipped through the book, shaking his head. "I don't even think this is a real language. Looks like bullshit to me. I think this is skin, not paper," he frowned and closed the book.

When they reached the pool, Alex took the book from him.

Well, at least she didn't have to come up with their

payment. It was the Mistress who chose them to deliver the gift, so she would handle that. Alex was sure Ashblood Manor had a good supply of fresh human blood on hand. Leave it to the Mistress to send her something so powerful she couldn't even figure out how to use it. Maybe Alex should have asked before she let the Mistress cash in her debt.

"Too late now," she mumbled.

Chapter 5

He was glad for the silence. His tormentors had been called away, suddenly, which meant he wouldn't be on the menu tonight—hadn't been for almost ten days now. That Sasha chick had gone missing, and it was all hands on deck to find her. Ben secretly hoped the bitch was dead, but they hadn't found any proof one way or another.

The change in him was coming slowly, but it was coming—he knew that. What he would eventually become was a mystery. The doctor told him, early on, that he was among a rare few who couldn't be turned. At a cellular level, the virus would mutate into something but not vampire. He wasn't sure if he still had enough of the supplement in his system to fight the assault, but he prayed that he did—harder than he ever had in his life.

On a positive note, if the search for Sasha took longer, maybe his body would have enough time to heal itself—reverse the damage. When he had taken the last of the pills he managed to squirrel away before being abducted all those weeks ago at the cabin, Ben hoped it would be of some help in that process. If not, he wanted Alex to be the one to end his life.

His hands, fingers elongated and almost skeletal, reminded him of a dead body. He didn't have the balls to look at his own reflection anymore. The last time he looked, he smashed the mirror anyway. Their constant feedings drained him and left him looking barely human. His dark wavy hair was dull and brittle. Once strong and white, his teeth felt loose, soft, and coated in something grainy and sour tasting. His lips were cracked and it hurt when he licked them. The dried blood caked in the corners of his mouth was hard now. His skin was leathery and pale green, unless his vision was failing him too.

Ben was still too human to take his own life, no matter how much he wanted to die. He still clung to his mother's Catholic faith. "Suicide is a sin," she had said. "You won't get into heaven if you do that." That was the last piece of advice she'd given a sixteen-year-old Benjamin Palmer. The next week, she was gone—accidental overdose is what the official report said. Ben knew better. She'd struggled with addiction all of her life, or his life, to be more precise.

His father had left her because of it. His grandparents had taken him in and treated him very well. But he missed his mother more than he thought possible.

One bad memory was replaced by another—the loss of another woman he loved, but it was his fault that time.

Ben's memory of her as she sat by the barred window of the visitors' lounge was still very vivid. She flipped cards on a small wooden table. The two Marine guards looked bored at the sight. Everyone else sat on one side of the massive waiting room probably wondering the same thing Ben was wondering—*what the hell?*

When the guards had spotted him, one approached Ben, stopped, and offered a perfect salute. Winnan, his name tag reflected, was a Lance Corporal according to the bars on his left shoulder. Since he had saluted a civilian-clothed Ben, he must have already been briefed.

"Sir," Lance Corporal Winnan announced as he snapped his hand down again. "I have to make sure you're not armed. Sorry, sir."

"No problem, Marine," Ben replied as he raised his arms and allowed LCpl. Winnan to pat him down.

It was a little embarrassing—being patted down in front of everyone in the lounge, but Ben played along. Once he was done, he asked Ben to remain where he was until the room was cleared.

Everyone was politely ushered from the room in an orderly fashion. They were being taken to a smaller waiting area. Ben watched in confusion. Then he turned back to Alex. The other guard, a Private First Class Hayes, stood just behind her at attention. She shook her head and shrugged at Ben.

"Clear," he heard Winnan bark. "Go ahead, Colonel."

She stood slowly as the guards stepped back to a safe distance. At least that's what it looked like to Ben. Alex looked small and fragile in faded blue scrubs, white Keds, and a grin. He could tell that she'd lost weight. Her dark hair hung down to her shoulders, limp and dull. Hair tucked behind her ears, she looked like the little girl he'd met all those years ago.

Ben began to walk toward her; his arms went up as he got closer. But Pfc. Hayes stepped up quickly, pushing his arm out to stop Ben. "Sorry, sir," Hayes sniffed.

Ben saw her roll her eyes again as he stepped into Hayes's personal space with a smile.

"Really? What do you think I'm gonna do Private? Stuff her in my pocket and run?"

Winnan stifled a chuckle as he gave his partner a quick nod. "It's fine, Hayes. I'm sure it'll be okay, right, Colonel?"

"Of course," Ben replied with a grin at Pfc. Hayes as he pushed past him.

When Alex was in his arms, he felt a quick prick of electricity. She squeezed him back then stepped out of his arms politely. Waving him to the empty chair opposite hers, they sat down together. The game of solitaire was gathered up by LCpl. Winnan. He tapped the table twice, then left the deck stacked neatly in the center.

"We'll be over there, sir," he said to Ben, "just in case."

Ben winked at him and they walked away. At the exit, they stood at parade rest. Ben could see them in the mirror on the far wall as they watched them. Winnan shot Alex a nasty look.

"Damn," he grinned, "what the hell'd you do to him?"

She grinned back, "Beat him at poker." She rubbed her neck as she cut a glance at them. "Lost a month's pay to me last night."

Ben laughed, "Sucker."

She laughed too, but it seemed different. Hollow and weak, her eyes didn't reflect her humor. They didn't dance the way that Ben remembered. He didn't like what he saw in her eyes at all.

"So," he sighed, "when you gettin' out of here?"

"Not sure," she rubbed her neck.

"You look fine to me," he lied.

"I feel fine," she answered. He figured she was lying too.

Ben leaned in slightly. She stayed where she was. He could see the Marines tense a bit through the mirror.

"Your . . ." he paused when she frowned at his near mistake. Alex and her father didn't have what could be referred to as a "father/daughter" relationship. "Dr. Carlisle would have been here, but something came up in Washington," he lied again.

"The program always comes first, right?" she sighed.

"I'm sure if he thought you really needed him, he'd be here," Ben replied and felt the pang of disgust at his insensitive words. She clearly thought her father would be here instead of him. He thought the same until Dr. Carlisle told him something came up at the last minute.

"Guess he thinks I'm alright then, huh?"

"You're not?"

She took another quick glance at the Marines. When her eyes met Ben's again, he felt another jolt of electricity. She shook her head as her eyes filled with tears.

Ben's temper ticked up. The muscles in his legs tightened as he prepared to stand and yell at the guards. If one of them had touched her, he was going to kill them both and take her from here. Her cold hand landed on his arm. With a vice-like grip, he stayed seated.

"Alex," he whispered, "if someone tried to hurt you, tell me. We can get you out of here now."

One tear slid down her cheek. Then he felt it again—that shock, but this time it actually hurt a little. The table wobbled too.

"No one can hurt me, can they?" she whispered. "Not really, right?"

"Hell no," he replied as her hand trembled in his. "What's wrong?"

Her grip tightened on his hand. "I'm perfect," she continued to whisper. "I'm perfectly human. Tell me I'm perfectly human, Ben."

Ben's knuckles rolled as her grip locked on them. Any more pressure and he was sure she would break his fingers.

"Alex," he said in the calmest way possible. "I'll tell you anything you want to know, as long as I get to keep my fingers."

Without taking her eyes from his, she released his hand. He stretched his fingers out, wiggled them around to get the blood flowing again. She placed her hands in her lap.

He noticed the Marines had gotten closer. Maybe under the circumstances, that was best.

"What do you want to know?" he said to her.

Ben could remember the look on her face, even now. The smoldering anger in those brown eyes. Back then he thought he imagined them turning a light amber color, but now he knew he didn't.

"Am I human?" she whispered.

"Yes," Ben replied.

"Completely?"

The feeling of his lungs tightening in his chest came on suddenly, just like it did back then. He could still feel his heart race and his palms sweat as his mind refused to formulate a lie good enough to fool her. His mouth went dry in an instant.

"Not—" he started, but the end was cut off when her hand clamped around his neck.

The memory felt as real now as it did when it happened

all those years ago—his body as it rose from the chair, then being pulled over the small table like a paper doll. He even remembered the cards as they spilled to the floor in slow motion. All the while, her expression never changed. Calm, cool, and collected, Alex's grip on his throat trapped air in his lungs that wanted to get out.

"How long?" she hissed in his face. "How long have you known?!"

Ben scratched and pulled at the iron claw as it closed off his windpipe, but it didn't move. As one Marine tried to help remove her hand, the other put her in a choke hold.

"Let him go," Pfc. Hayes barked, but to an almost unconscious Ben, it sounded watery and distant. And, just like that, she let go.

But Hayes found that challenging someone like her wasn't covered in Marine boot camp on Parris Island. She forced her elbow into his solar plexus twice, then donkey-kicked all two hundred solid pounds into the far wall. He shattered the mirror on impact.

Winnan dropped Ben, who was still gasping for air, behind him then drew his side arm on her. Alex stopped, raised her hands, and grinned at them.

Before Ben could form a single word, Hayes hit her from behind, taking them both to the floor. He forced her arms behind her and cuffed her quickly. What surprised Ben most was that she wasn't resisting. She could have killed both of them in record time and been out the door and off the property before anyone knew what had happened.

"Don't fucking move," he barked down at her as his knee kept her pinned to the floor. Blood streaked down his neck, staining his starched collar. When he saw it on his hands, Hayes cursed and dropped his knee in her back again. A small grunt of air came out, but she still grinned.

"You alright, sir?" Winnan puffed.

Ben just nodded. A commotion broke out behind him as two orderlies rushed in, followed by a nurse. Hayes held her down as the nurse gave her some sort of injection. When she was jerked up from the floor she winked at Hayes and he cursed at her.

"Sir," Winnan said as he looked him over. "We can drop her crazy ass back in solitary, if you want."

"Back?" Ben cleared his throat. "What do you mean back?"

"She goes there a lot," Hayes grumbled as he smirked at Ben and Winnan. "I think she likes it."

"No," Ben croaked. "It's fine." They let him step closer to her, but Winnan warned him to stay at a safe distance. "You need to talk to your father."

Her grin faded. "Run," she said in a clear voice, "fast. When I catch up to you, I'm gonna put you both in the same box."

As they led her away, she didn't struggle.

All of his calls and requests for another visit were denied after that. He never stopped trying though.

Coming back to the depressing present, Ben felt a weird sting on his face. His fingers came back wet from tears, real ones.

"Well," he sighed, "at least I can still feel."

That gave him hope. If human feelings were still possible, then maybe he wasn't as far gone as he thought. Rolling into the fetal position, Benjamin Palmer thought hard about Alex Stone. So hard, his head began to pound.

It took years for her to speak to him again; a couple more for her to trust him. Maybe not fully, but still. After they started working together to fulfill her contract, he knew he would give his life for her. Right now, he hoped that feeling was mutual.

"She'll find me," he said to the dark, stale air around him. "She'll save me—I know she will."

Adam watched as the volunteer stumbled from the room, barely able to stand without help. The guards he had assigned to their prisoner nodded at him as they passed. When he entered the room, he could still smell fresh blood in the air. If there were a window, he would have opened it to release that stale stench into the night.

A young woman sat up in bed, then licked her lips with a grin. “Thanks for the snack,” she said in a breathy sigh. “I’ll take a ginger next.”

Adam didn’t respond. He just stared at her with disgust in the pit of his stomach. Her drunken stumble toward the small bathroom filled him with anger. She washed her face and hands, then returned to the bed as he waited.

Some of her wounds were almost healed. But the worst of them would need more time and blood. Unfortunately for her, they were out of time and Adam would not give her any more human blood. She had to look as if she were tortured when she returned to her master.

“How do you feel?” he asked when she was settled again.

She stretched out on the bed and tried to strike a seductive pose. Adam thought it was just some ridiculous notion she conjured in the moment. He’d rather be burned alive than touch her for any reason but to cause her pain.

“Silly child,” he said as she stroked the rumpled bed sheets.

“I could use something with a little more kick,” she giggled.

Giving the mattress a pat, she grinned. Adam checked the urge to strike her. He had no desire to indulge her juvenile attempt at seduction. He crossed through the room and sat down in the chair instead.

“Maybe your sire will accommodate that request when you return,” he said.

“So we have a deal?”

“Yes.”

Her eyes danced when she smiled and sat up straight and tall. “You won’t be disappointed—I swear! I’ll be the best spy ever!”

"I'm sure, my dear," Adam replied.

"But," her smile faded, "what will I tell him? He's smart. He's gonna wonder where I've been all this time."

Adam shook his head as he held his hand out to her. She rose from the bed then knelt in front of him with a smell of fear. Her hand trembled in his.

"You're not going to tell him anything, really," he replied. "You won't have much to tell."

He took her face in his hands as he smiled at her. Now she was confused and afraid. She had every reason to fear what was coming next.

"Tell me what to do," she whispered, "what to say so that I can please you."

Her dull brown eyes closed. When she tightened her grip on his thighs, he entered her mind. A tangled mess of memories greeted him. He made his way through the chaos easily. She was so young and weak that it hardly took any effort. At the memories he wanted to erase, Adam felt the slight tremble of her body become a full on shake.

"It hurts," she moaned and tried to force him from her mind.

She couldn't, of course, but the effort amused him. Just as he was about to erase everything from the last two weeks, which would include the fight, he stopped. In that moment, he decided to leave it there. Maybe it would prompt Tristan to come out and play. He liked the thought of using Alex as bait.

When she groaned and squirmed in his grip, more pressure on his thighs brought him back to the task at hand. Her eyes were shut tight against the pain. Her fangs dropped to fine points out of instinct. The pain caused her body to react to protect itself.

As he pulled her closer, Adam tightened his grip on her head.

"It's the only way, I'm afraid," he grinned as she struggled against his mental assault. "I could lessen the pain, but . . ."

As he began to scrub at the memories, she screamed. Thin streams of blood trickled from her nose, over her chapped, dry lips, then stained her once clean shirt.

Adam wanted her master to see Alex Stone in action. Adam wanted this girl's failure to anger Tristan as much as Alex winning angered him now. Revenge coaxed Adam to put more force behind his intrusion on this girl. For the first time since Alex Stone entered his life, Adam realized she may be out of it, for good, before the end of the conference. Her death might hit Jason hard, but he would get over it. The end of that relationship meant Jason had proven his loyalty to him and Nikki. Adam knew Jason wouldn't let a human get between him and what he wanted most: power and a place at the table.

Later, back at the compound, Jason paced the narrow space between the door and Adam's desk. In an effort to defend his decision to let the girl go, Adam had fielded call after call from minor Council members all day. He looked about done being polite.

"We have her location," Adam snarled before emptying the short glass of Scotch. "I have a team tracking her as we speak."

Jason wasn't sure who was on the other end of the call, but he was sure it wasn't Conner. Conner expected him to call later—without Adam. The video clip of Alex and the Cantu was one of those things Conner needed to know about right away.

"I don't have to explain myself to you, Valen," Adam hissed. "Who cares if she dies? If we get what we want, I don't care if they stake her in the sun until she's dust!"

He dropped the mobile device on the desk and scratched through his wavy salt and pepper locks. Jason could see the frustration wrapped tightly around him. Adam was not used to being questioned or doubted, not by anyone. The lower voting members of the Council offering up their two cents on this matter did nothing but make him want to kill.

He felt the vibration in the air before he heard Adam growl out loud. Silently, Jason watched as Adam pulled back every bit of anger he had, then he looked up at Jason with a calm expression.

"Why are you standing there like a guilty child?" Adam sighed. "Sit, please."

Jason did as he was told. "You really shouldn't let them get to you like that. You really don't have to explain anything to them."

Adam gave him a slow nod, but he wasn't focused on Jason—he could tell. His brain was elsewhere. With a look of defeat, Adam sat back in the chair then covered his face with his massive hands. They dropped suddenly and he grinned.

"You're right," he replied. "I'm so used to playing politics, I've forgotten my place. Second chair at the table means I don't have listen to them blather on about tradition. I know what I'm doing, and if they don't like it, so what?"

It was strange to see Adam so rattled by the nonsense of the lower chamber members. Sometimes it was hard to imagine Adam ever being one of them. His rise to the high chamber was bloody and hard fought. Jason remembered all too well what that cost Adam—and him.

Chapter 6

Her business card was moist and wrinkled. Kit held it tight as she weaved her way through the mid-afternoon crowd at DFW International Airport. She couldn't shake the feeling of being followed. Since boarding the flight in Miami, Kit had the creepiest feeling of being watched, and she didn't like it one bit. As a feline shifter, her senses were heightened, especially to threats—seen and unseen. Right now, she couldn't see trouble, but she could feel it through every pore.

When she deplaned in Dallas, that vibe grew stronger. After she passed through the sliding glass exit doors, she grabbed the door handle of the Uber she'd called on her way down the concourse.

"Shit," she hissed as something on the underside of the handle pricked her ring finger on her left hand. She immediately put the tiny wound to her mouth.

"You alright?" the young driver asked as she opened the back door.

"Yeah, thanks."

Kit tossed her overnight bag next to her on the backseat. Kit Blaze, Vegas call girl, told the driver where to go as she looked back nervously.

"First time in Dallas?" he drawled at her through the rearview.

"Yes," Kit replied as she examined her finger.

"Well, welcome to Texas," he chuckled, put the car in motion, and began to tell her about all the tourist stuff she should see while she was here.

Kit Blaze was not a sightseer. Kit Blaze was a mover—a shaker. Movers and shakers didn't sightsee, they were seen. As she took one last look behind them, a wave of relief washed over her. That feeling—creepy and heavy—just disappeared like magic. She didn't care why. All the tension she'd felt for the last four hours just melted away. With her head against the seat, she closed her eyes and relaxed.

"You okay, ma'am?" her driver asked her through the rearview.

"Yes, fine," she grinned. "Thank you."

The white Toyota Prius with the weird little symbol on the front windshield glided down the highway headed for a nice boutique hotel a few blocks away from Alex Stone's headquarters. The driver noted the light traffic and perfect spring-like weather for a November afternoon. She just tuned him out. Alex would meet her in the hotel bar. Kit sighed. A good, stiff drink was just what she needed right now.

"Where are you going in such a hurry?" Ivy hummed as she followed Alex out the front door and to the elevators. "Hot date?"

"Lunch meeting," she replied over her shoulder. "New model. Might put Vic's angels to shame next Valentine's Day."

"Anyone I know?" Ivy grinned as Alex pressed the button a couple of times. She needed to get to the hotel before Kit to make sure she wasn't followed.

"I doubt it," Alex grinned back.

When the doors opened they both stepped inside the steel box. Ivy pressed the lobby button then leaned back against the wall. "Maybe you should at least tell me where you're meeting, just in case, I mean."

"In case what?" Alex answered as the numbers ticked down from thirty-five.

"You get hung up," Ivy shrugged, "or worse, God

forbid." She raised an expertly arched brow. On the bottom floor, they stepped out together. Ivy kept pace with Alex all the way to the revolving glass doors then Alex turned to face her.

"It's just lunch," she said with a shake of her head. "Go back upstairs, please."

"Swear," Ivy stayed rooted to the spot. "Swear to God this has nothing to do with Jason Stavros."

Alex rolled her eyes, place her right hand over her heart and raised her left. Ivy just stared into her eyes for about five seconds then walked away. "This is business," she heard Alex say to her back.

It seemed odd that she thought she felt Alex's stare burn a hole through the back of her head as she waited for the elevator. When she stepped inside again, Alex was gone. All the way back up, Ivy pushed the urge to follow her down. That fight she had with her own conscience had begun. Ivy wasn't an operative—not that kind anyway. Her degree was in Psychology. At Quantico, she was the best profiler in her class.

The doctor looked so proud at Ivy's graduation. She wondered what Alex could have done had she been allowed to have a regular life. Instead, Alex was battle trained. There was no way Ivy could trail her and not get caught.

As Ivy passed her assistant, she told her to hold her calls. Inside her office, at her desk, she tried to work. From her mobile, she dialed his number. One ring. Two rings. Then he picked up.

"Ms. Rose," he sounded happy. He was never happy. "How nice to hear from you."

"Dr. Carlisle," she replied. "I just wanted to get you caught up. This seemed like as good a time as any, but I can call back if you're busy."

"On the contrary," he chuckled. "I'm never too busy for you. How are things going?"

Ivy suddenly felt sick to her stomach. His sweet demeanor was so out of character that she thought she would vomit. But her guilt gnawed at her insides too. Dr. Carlisle did seem to care for Alex like a father should—sometimes anyway.

"Fine," she answered. "Alex just left to meet with the hooker, so we have some time."

She could hear a slight electrical hum in the background. Then it disappeared with the sound of a door as it slammed shut. Then a weird silence.

"Do you have any idea what she might be doing?" he asked. "With a hooker, I mean?"

"I believe she has information for Alex regarding the attempt on Jason Stavros a couple of weeks ago."

"Thank you for the update," he stated with another chuckle, "but, you could have emailed that report."

"Right," Ivy sighed. "Well, if there's nothing else . . ."

"I'd like to ask about my daughter and the vampire," he stated. "Are they lovers or not?"

Ivy felt her cheeks burn with embarrassment. Not once in the entire time she had been on this assignment had he ever asked about any of Alex's companions. It just felt weird to even be discussing this with her father.

"I'm pretty sure she's slept with him," Ivy answered.

He was silent for what seemed like a long time, but it was only a few seconds.

"And has he fed from her?"

"I have no idea."

"I thought she told you everything."

"She wouldn't tell me that," Ivy replied. "And if I asked, she'd get suspicious."

"Maybe. But I'd like you to ask anyway."

Her stomach was doing backflips now. Ask a superpowered ex-assassin if she let a vampire drink her blood? Right. How would she make that sound like a casual question?

"Why would you care what she does with Jason Stavros?"

"Because I need to know," he replied with just a hint of anger in his voice. "And you take your orders from me, so . . ."

"How am I supposed to bring that up exactly?"

He laughed at her. "The same way you bring up everything else. Open that pretty, little mouth and ask. Ask her if he's fed from her and how."

"What do you mean, how?" Ivy said.

"A bite," he replied in an annoyed tone. "Was she stupid enough to let that happen?"

Ivy's head began to pound. "Fine. Anything else?"

"Yes," he answered. "Are you still seeing that escort, what's his name—Mason Creed?"

"Not the way you mean," she replied.

Again, the odd silence. Then she heard him cough. "I think you should make one more appointment with Mr. Creed."

Ivy looked at the phone then put it back to her ear. "Why?"

Dr. Carlisle had never seemed to care, one way or the other, about her relationship with Creed. Although Ivy never offered up any real reason for continuing the arrangement, she let him and Leland Ramsey believe he was a wealth of information regarding Alex and what she did for the five or so years she went off radar. Truth was, Ivy had known about Mason Creed for at least two years before they discovered he had some connection to Alex. Once the doctor got wind of his relationship with Alex, he went ballistic at first.

"You're not serious," she remembered him practically barking at her over the morning debrief. "My daughter! What proof do you have?"

Back then, she thought Dr. Jonathan Carlisle's bark was much worse than his bite. Over the years, Ivy found that his bite could be deadly, in more ways than she had ever imagined.

Sweat had rolled down her spine as she sat in that

cramped little office of his at Area 51. It was practically a freezer every day, but with him barking in her face, it felt like the desert.

"He told me," she almost whispered. "I mean, he bragged about having this tough, little black chick on his payroll for a while. He described her perfectly. I'm sorry, Dr. Carlisle."

When he crushed the stainless steel coffee mug like it was made of Styrofoam, Ivy knew he didn't just create supplements for the new crop of supersoldiers that would be known as The Trackers, he took them as well.

"What else did he say?" he grunted, which brought her attention back to him. "Does he know where she is now?"

"I don't think so," she replied. "He said she just took off."

His brow furrowed as his usual expression turned hard and mean. That poor coffee carafe slowly turned into an expensive paperweight. After he pressed it into a funky shape, he took in a deep breath then pushed it out.

"Keep close to him for now," he stated in his usual authoritative tone.

"Of course, Doctor," she replied.

He really didn't have to tell her to stay close to Creed. Back then, she would have done just about anything to stay close to him. Well, if she were being honest with herself, she was doing anything he asked to stay next to him.

Now, as Dr. Carlisle laid out her new assignment, she regretted doing it. Regret was a strange beast. No matter how much she tried to turn it into a memory, her time with Mason Creed morphed into a deep regret. She'd allowed herself to be used by both Strategic and him.

"I think he knows more than he's telling you, Agent Rose," she heard Dr. Carlisle say. "I think he may be using you for something. Let's see if you can find out before it's too late."

She was snapped back to the present by the same words she was thinking. Strange? *Not really,* she reminded herself.

Everybody uses everybody else, don't they?

"He's using me to get to Alex," she sniffed. "He wants a blood sample."

Dr. Carlisle chuckled for some reason. "Why?"

"I don't know," she stated. "I'm just supposed to get it for him. If I don't, he's threatened to tell Alex about our relationship."

"How much time do you have to produce it?"

Ivy drew in a breath. "Not much."

"Then let's not disappoint the man," he said. "I'll have a sample sent to you immediately."

Ivy couldn't believe what she was hearing. This man had no concern for his own daughter's safety. "What?"

"You'll have a sample first thing in the morning," he repeated.

"If it doesn't show traces of the supplement, he'll suspect," she answered as she shot the finger at the phone.

"You let me worry about what needs to show up in her blood," he answered. "You just let him know you have the sample, but you want to meet with his boss personally to deliver it."

"And if he says no?"

"I guess you'll have to convince him to agree."

"How?"

"The same way you got to him in the first place," he said with that irritating chuckle of his. "On your back."

The hotel she booked for Kit wasn't far. For a November afternoon, the air was fresh, and a big yellow sun kept the chill away as she strolled toward her destination.

She had to give Kit props for contacting her through the company. Discretion was a priority. Kit understood that better than anyone. Whatever she knew, Kit was ready to tell. But was Alex ready to hear it?

If Jason was lying, what would she do? If someone else was in play, it was too late to hope for an elimination of the threat before Romania. Her luck was never that good. The problem would follow them. It would follow them all the way to a city steeped in the past, a city where an Irish writer first saw a Romanian Count feed on human blood and live forever.

Chapter 7

"I consider her my friend," Mistress Bianca said. "I don't understand why you can't just tell her the truth."

Michael tossed a couple of shirts in the soft leather weekend bag as he cradled the phone between his shoulder and ear. "We're trying to protect them, Mistress—all of them."

"And your father agrees with this plan?" she sighed. Then she giggled. "Of course he does." She fell silent and Michael felt his heart sting at asking someone he respected and loved, in an odd sort of way, to lie to someone she considered a friend.

That thought seemed strange though. A powerful pure-blood vampire with an allegiance to a human—who would have thought? When she sighed again, Michael knew she had just agreed to back the story he would tell Alex. Michael Gale, A.K.A Michael Dean, private counsel for Ashblood Manor and, as such, for Mistress Bianca as well.

"Thank you, Mistress," he offered, but he knew she was not happy. "I owe you one, again."

"Yes, you do Michael *Dean*," emphasis on his false name. "And I will collect, one day." The line disconnected before he could say goodbye.

Being indebted to her was not a good thing, or so he'd been told. Michael was a man of his word though, and whatever she asked of him in return, he would do.

Checking his voicemail one last time, he listened to a message Alex had left asking him to call her when he got a chance. She was set to return to Vegas tomorrow night, so he was catching his own flight back in three hours. The company jet was being used by his brothers, so he was stuck with a commercial flight from JFK. He didn't care. The only thing that mattered was to get to Vegas before Alex Stone.

His phone buzzed in his hand. Another text. The car service would be there in twenty minutes. He dropped his bag at the private elevator then did one last check. His briefcase contained his tablet, a couple of magazines, and pens—pretty standard fare for a last minute flight.

Bianca offered one of her private apartments, in case Alex checked, and the use of a pretty sweet ride while he was there. The 918 Spyder looked like a car a douche lawyer in Vegas might drive. As Porsches went, it was pretty awesome though. He deleted the picture Bianca sent, picked up his briefcase, and placed it next to the bag by the elevator. His phone buzzed once more.

He glanced at the screen and shook his head, "Hello Con." As he tapped the speaker function on screen, he poured warm synthetic blood into a glass.

"Everything ready?" Conner asked.

"Yes," Michael replied. "I should get there by early afternoon. What's wrong?"

"Why do you think there's something wrong?"

Michael took him off speaker. "Because this is the third call today."

Conner laughed. Michael shook his head again. "Sorry. I'm just nervous I guess."

"I'm the one that should be nervous. She has sort of a short fuse, by all accounts."

"Well, I trust you've covered you tracks, Michael. If not, you deserve to get burned," Conner chuckled. "So to speak."

"Bianca has agreed to play along," he assured his father. "If she checks my story, everything will go as planned. Stop worrying so much."

"You're right," Conner stated. "I'm making a big deal out of nothing. Just don't underestimate her, Michael."

Michael emptied his glass and smiled. "Did you just say

I was right?" He laughed deeply and he could hear Conner do the same. "Well, that only took about a hundred years for you to say to me."

"Yes, well, it was very painful, so don't make me repeat myself for another hundred."

"Con, please relax. Just let me handle this. It's just drinks anyway. I don't think she's going to reveal anything earthshattering over wine and cheese."

Michael could feel a slight change in his father's demeanor over the phone. But how sure was he about Alex? Could he be convincing enough? Would she pick up on anything that would connect him to his family? Michael shook those thoughts out of his mind. He'd done this too many times to doubt himself over a human.

"Well, call when you arrive," he heard Conner announce. "How long will you be there?"

"Just until they leave for Romania, then I'll be back home."

"Good. I may have something for you when you return. Since Jason's detail includes some of our best, you may need to follow up on the girl for Adam. Pick whomever you wish to back you."

"Sure," he replied. "But don't forget that meeting on The Hill next week. I sent you the figures last night."

Gale Enterprises was a legitimate bioengineering firm with contracts all over the world. Its current project was to provide state-of-the-art prosthetics for returning military personnel from overseas.

They were also in negotiations to overhaul the security systems for a multibillion-dollar complex, still in the planning stages, tasked with cyber-crime. This complex would be fully contained. There was also a small drug company that wouldn't be small much longer. Their stem cell research was leaps and bounds ahead of everyone else. He hadn't had a chance to go over all the details and specs, but it looked next-level futuristic, and he wanted Gale Enterprises in on the deal.

"Yes, I planned to have that lull me to sleep later," Conner chuckled.

"Funny," Michael replied as a tiny beep sprang from the receiver. "My car's here. I'll call you later tonight."

"Have a safe trip," Conner said.

Michael pressed the elevator down button, and the doors slid open. With his briefcase swung over one shoulder, he slid the leather duffle into the elevator with his foot. As he descended, he assured his overprotective father once more, "I'll be fine, old man."

"I know," he replied, and was gone.

On the ride down, Michael wondered what kind of parent he would have made had his child survived. Conner worried about every move they made, constantly. They were grown men, but he always seemed to worry. Every mission, no matter how simple, Conner reminded them to be careful. As if they didn't already know that. Maybe he shouldn't be so hard on his father though. After their mother was assassinated, Conner had turned into the most overprotective vampire father in history.

He shrugged. "He could be worse," he said to no one.

The big steel doors opened on the modern lobby of his building on Manhattan's Upper East Side. Generally speaking, business types passed without noticing him. Some gave a quick nod, others gave no acknowledgement of his presence at all. For a vampire to go unnoticed in a lobby filled with humans was a testament to how well he was able to appear as human as the next guy. They fit into this new modern society, just as they'd planned.

Michael breezed through the automatic doors and was hit in the face by a biting north wind. Heavy and real, his leather jacket kept the stinging blast from his body quite well. Not that this weather really bothered them much, but the amount of blood he took earlier might not be enough to keep him looking human if he stayed outside for much longer. The colder he became, the paler his skin would get. If it got too pale, people would notice.

Snow tumbled down the sidewalk at his feet as the chauffer, bundled up like a sled driver, took his bag after he opened the back door of the town car for him.

"We should make the airport in plenty of time, sir," the driver's voice muffled as he climbed in behind the wheel. "Should I turn up the heat?"

"No," Michael replied as he shook off his jacket. He was getting hot. "It's fine unless you need it."

He heard a slight chuckle as his driver pulled his checkered scarf loose and laid it on the seat next to him. "No, sir," he laughed as he spoke to Michael through the rearview when they stopped at the red light. "My wife's got me pretty well bundled!"

Michael laughed too. *Must be nice to have someone waiting at home for you to return,* he mused. *A woman who cared about you when you were away and welcomed you home when you returned to her.* His bed partners didn't care much past what trendy night spot he'd be taking them to for the evening. Or if he owned the penthouse.

There were a few that were actually down to earth, but with his coming and going, they didn't last long. They asked too many questions that he couldn't answer. Jealousy was usually the culprit in the end. His reputation as a man who couldn't be tied down was a challenge to most human women. Vampire women too, come to think of it.

Vampires knew the score though. As a member of a powerful family, Michael was expected to put that first. Business was paramount, not romance. They all knew what it meant to be with Michael or one of his brothers. It meant no questions and no commitments.

Social events, the ones he had to attend anyway, were the prime showcase for the vampire elite. His father threw the best and most popular Dark Ball every year. No one wanted to be left out but some would be. So if a woman happened to be dating a Gale man around that time, it was because she wanted to be his plus one.

A thought struck him. *What if Jason invited Alex this*

year? Wouldn't that be crazy funny! "No way," he whispered under his breath.

"Sir?" the driver interrupted his vocalizing.

"Nothing," Michael replied. "Just talking to myself, sorry."

"No problem."

Michael threw that idea out immediately. Jason didn't have the guts to invite her to the ball. Especially now that his engagement had been announced. It was already the talk of vampire society. Now that Jason had a seat in the Lower Chamber, the Council would monitor his every move. Michael suddenly felt sorry for Jason. His life was about to change, and sometimes that was not a good thing.

His phone buzzed on the seat. He placed it to his ear without thinking to check the ID. When he heard that voice, he wished he had.

"Busy?" she asked with a bit of humor in her voice.

"If I were," he replied with a dry sigh, "would it matter?"

"Not really," she replied in the same manner then giggled. "I hear you're off to Vegas again. Should I be worried?"

Michael checked the urge to hang up. Evangeline Margot, daughter of the leader of the largest vampire house in France, was once his girlfriend. She, on the other hand, pretended she didn't know the definition of *ex-girlfriend*.

"I'm working, Evie," he always called her Evie. "What do you want?"

"You're always working, Mike," she never called him Mike because he hated it coming from her. "That's the reason we broke up."

It was Michael's turn to laugh. "The reason *I* broke up with *you* was because you had a very loose interpretation of our relationship. You took my absence to mean you could fill the void with any warm body that would have you."

Michael had a long list of other reasons he broke it off, but that was at the top. The last time he returned from a mission, she had taken up with a Saudi Prince. He wasn't sure which family, but it didn't really matter. All of his friends had warned him about her, like good friends should, but he didn't want to believe it. Evangeline was convincing. When she said that she loved you, she really did—at that moment. But she lived from moment to moment, so she said that a lot.

"I was just having fun," she whined. "And you were no fun anymore. What happened?"

He rolled his eyes as he felt his temperature begin to rise again and it wasn't from the manufactured heat of the car. "I got bored with competing for your attention. Or maybe I'm just growing up."

Her shriek of laughter irritated him. "Hardly! I heard about that little wager between you and Varga in Rome. You totaled his racecar for a few grand and that diplomat's silly little daughter. That's real mature."

He had to laugh. That bet was stupid. Cost him a million and a half of his own money, but he had impressed the daughter, and she was lots of fun, as he recalled.

"Why are you calling me?" he sighed.

"Well," he heard her take a big breath as she was prone to do when she was excited about some harebrained idea. He was bracing himself for a gem. "A bunch of us are going down to Mexico this weekend . . ."

He cut her off with a quick, "No."

"You haven't even heard what I want yet," she whined. He could see her stamp her feet like the spoiled brat she was.

"I don't care. The answer is still the same."

"God! Don't be such a prick," she huffed then realized her mistake. "I mean, please Michael. I'll make it up to you when you join us."

The last time Evangeline and her cronies used the house on Playa Zicatela, they almost burned it to the ground in a drunken haze. It took over a year to remodel and he had missed the best surfing there in years as punishment from Conner.

"Well, that does sound awful tempting," Michael dropped the timbre of his voice and Evangeline giggled, "but, no."

The line clicked and he laughed so hard the muscles in his stomach ached by the time he reached the airport.

Sunlight. How beautiful it was here. Clear blue skies were complemented by a nice, sweetly-chilly breeze. *Texas is alright so far,* Kit thought as the car weaved in and out of traffic, and she relaxed against the seat.

She'd heard the joke millions of times—"if you don't like Texas weather, just wait a minute; it'll change." But the driver kept saying how great the weather had been over the last few weeks. November was shaping up to be one of the better months, he had said.

"Although it's only the first week," he chuckled. "So that could change in an hour." He howled with laughter and slapped the wheel as he continued to make good time to downtown Fort Worth.

As the car slowed, Kit opened her eyes. They'd hit some traffic. She sat up straight as he eased into the lane that led to her hotel. "We're just a couple blocks away," he said as he craned his neck to get a better view up ahead. Kit never understood that. Unless he had some kind of superpower, he wasn't going to see anything more than a couple cars ahead of him in all that mess.

The digitized numbers on her smartphone indicated she had plenty of time, but she felt uneasy again. She mapped the walk from their current location and decided she had the extra ten minutes to walk it.

"I'll walk the rest of the way," she said then tapped the driver and handed him a pretty good tip. The car slowed to a stop at the corner and he told her it was straight ahead—just four blocks. Outside the car, she swung her overnight bag over a slim shoulder and began to walk with confidence down the busy sidewalk.

Some of the shops she passed already had Christmas decorations up in their windows. Jaunty tunes floated around the sidewalk as people window-shopped on their trek to work. All of a sudden, a warm, sweet smell reached her nose. The combination of pastry and coffee wrapped around her and pulled her close. The dainty little shop one block from her hotel was inviting and so quaint, she couldn't pass it up.

"Maybe just a little 'pick-me-up' for the walk," she giggled to herself as she passed through the threshold and took a deep breath.

Sugary goodness was crammed in every corner. All the shelves were draped in festive colors. When she reached the counter, the round, little elven woman smiled and called her "honey." Kit pointed to the golden-brown bun under the glass as her stomach rumbled in approval.

The elven woman slid the treat, cellophane and all, into the pink bag with a small bottle of water and thanked her for coming in. Back on the sidewalk, Kit found she had a bounce in her step. Probably from the million grams of sugar in the bun she was devouring, but who cared?

When she felt the tingle in the back of her throat, she stuffed the pretty pink sack into the open pocket of the overnight bag slung over her shoulder. The cap of the water bottle let out a puff of air as she opened it and took a quick sip. The tingle became a warm sting as she took a bigger gulp of water. It lessened just a bit as she spotted Alex a few feet ahead of her on the sidewalk and picked up her pace. Kit cleared her throat, coughed to stop the feeling of her windpipe closing off and she tried to swallow a little bit of water. Then she stopped, dropping the bag from her shoulder as she struggled for air. The man walking next to her grabbed her arm as she began to fall.

When the man next to Kit laid her gently on the concrete, Alex pushed her way through the crowd. On her knees, Alex made mental notes of what she saw: sweat on Kit's brow and upper lip, her lips turning blue as the air became trapped in her lungs by the closing of her windpipe. The man leaned over Kit, checked her mouth, and was about to give her mouth to mouth.

"Don't," Alex barked as she pulled him back and began to pump on Kit's chest. "She's not choking. It's poison." Counting off the compressions, she just wanted to keep her heart pumping until real help came.

"How do you know?" he said frantically as he dialed 911.

Alex nodded at her lips as she continued to try and save Kit. She was gone—her one and only lead. Alex heard the last few beats of her heart as she stopped compressions and placed her ear to her chest to be sure. That's when she saw the card in Kit's partially closed fist. She pulled it loose in the commotion of EMTs pushing through the crowd. She would have gone for the phone, but the uniform had already picked it up and trapped it inside his latex glove.

"Ma'am," he said to her. "Do you know this lady?"

"Not really, no," Alex replied as she and the bystander stood at the same time. "I . . . we were meeting for lunch."

"Why?" he said.

"Business meeting," Alex replied as she balled the card up and slipped it inside her pocket. "She's a model."

"Well, we'll need you to come down to the station," he replied as he waved to a portly guy in a bad suit, "give your statement."

When bad-suit stepped up, he had a paper cup in his hand. Alex assumed it was coffee. But, by the looks of him, it could have been bourbon or something equally as inappropriate for a plainclothes homicide cop to drink at lunch.

"Whatcha got, Crane?" he growled.

"Ms.?" Crane turned back to Alex with a raised eyebrow.

"Stone," she replied extending her hand to the detective.

"Ms. Stone was meeting the vic for lunch," he said as

they shook hands.

His grip was warm from holding the coffee. At about five foot nine, ten maybe, the detective looked like he was counting the days until retirement and driving his wife nuts full time.

He carried about ten to fifteen pounds of extra weight around his middle, and there were hints of gray at his brow. His brown eyes probably had a shine at some point. His handsome brown skin showed signs of dryness around his eyes and the beginnings of creases around his full lips.

"Detective Hart," he smiled. Then he released her hand and squinted. "Do I know you?"

"I doubt it," Alex replied.

"You just look familiar," he rubbed the stubble on his chin, emptied the cup and tossed it in the tall metal trash can next to them. "You're famous? Actress, right?" His crooked grin and chain-smoker's chuckle flushed his round face a reddish color.

"No."

Hart let his eyes travel down her body then back up like he was looking at a road map. He shook his head then grinned. "You sure we haven't met before? I never forget a face."

"I'm sure," Alex grinned back.

The sound of the gurney being rolled down the rough sidewalk turned his attention to the scene again. As the EMTs zipped the body bag, a gust of wind pushed through the crowd. Alex felt the shiver roll down her spine as the metal bed on wheels was lowered with a loud bang then back up again. It disappeared down the sidewalk as Hart gently nudged her forward in the same direction.

"We need to go down to the station," he said close to her ear. "It's not far. We can walk it, if you want."

"Sure," was all she said. There was no way to talk her way out of this one. They had the phone. She had already admitted she knew her. They would have every number Kit had called in a few hours. The only thing to do was to play along.

Hart kept them at an easy pace. He assured Alex this wouldn't take long and she didn't need a lawyer. Not to answer a few questions, right?

"I'll try not to take up too much of your time," Hart said as he held the door to the station house open for her. The desk sergeant nodded as he pressed the button under the desk to let them through the electronic door.

"My desk is right down at the end there." He nodded at the square space in the center of the large room.

The "Bull Pen" held at least ten identical desks. Hart led the way to the messy one at the back. He pushed some papers into a drawer he opened with his foot and nodded toward a chair for her to sit in.

Detective Hart eased his stocky body down on the brand new desk chair. Ergonomic and practical, it didn't even squeak under his extra poundage.

This station had only opened a few months ago. Alex could remember watching the ribbon cutting on her way for coffee one summer morning. Now, as she sat on a nicely cushioned chair in a police station across from a detective, she realized he probably wanted to pin the whole mess on her.

Two questions formed in the frontal lobe of Hart's brain: *How do I know this woman?* and *Why do I think she knows more about that vic than she's gonna tell me?*

She tried to release his thoughts gently, but the second she disconnected, he pulled the top drawer open, popped two pain relievers, and downed them with a swig from the bottle of warm water sitting next to the phone. With no clue as to why a sudden spike of pain came and went, Detective Hart turned his tired eyes on Alex.

"So let's start with the easy stuff first; what's your full name?"

His fat fingers poised over the flat black keyboard as he waited for her to answer. She gave him all the pertinent information and waited for his hunt-and-peck typing to catch up to her words. He cocked his head to the side with his eyes on the screen. He wasn't squinting, which meant he had good eyesight for a guy who stared at a computer screen all day. His index fingers dropped stiffly on the keys a couple of more times before he stopped and looked at Alex again.

"I've seen you somewhere before," he stated. "News Anchor?"

She shook her head, crossed her legs toward him. "I own a clothing company—underwear, actually—Bite, Inc. Maybe you've bought something from my men's line?" Alex almost laughed out loud at the thought. If this guy owned anything that didn't come ten to a pack for five bucks, she'd be very surprised.

"Naw," he frowned, "that ain't it."

She couldn't help the giggle that escaped. From inside her other pocket, she slid a pristine white card over to him. He looked scared to touch it at first, then he tapped it on the fake wood desk with a grin.

"I'll be damned! Still, I can't help but think I've seen you somewhere before today."

Before Alex could move him to a new topic, a voice cut through the office noise around them. A young woman, about Alex's height and weight, strolled confidently down the narrow aisle toward them. She wore a standard issue Glock 9mm on her right hip and a badge clipped on the front of her belt on her left side.

"That's because you have seen her before, we all have," she smiled as Alex stood and shook her hand. "Detective Fallon Andrade," she said with a tight grip on Alex's hand. When she released it, Alex knew what she was before they were seated again.

This vampire lady cop with the raven hair and perfect green eyes wanted to intimidate Alex Stone. What she didn't know was she wasn't dealing with a witness; she was dealing with a hunter who knew a predator on sight.

"She was mixed up with that casino guy whose car blew

up a couple weeks ago, remember?" she said angling a stray chair next to Hart. "And she's got a pretty hot company right now too!"

"That was actually a little over a month ago," Alex added with a smile.

Detective Andrade's loosely bound ponytail looked silky under the harsh office lighting. Green eyes provided the pop of color her gray V-neck sweater needed to enhance her overall appearance. A pair of gold earrings adorned her ears, each bearing a symbol that Alex didn't recognize. With black slacks to complete the outfit, she crossed her legs and smiled.

"Yeah," Hart yelped, "that's it! You're right, Andrade." He shook his head as he pecked on the keyboard again. "Hey, you're dating that guy, right?"

"Geez, Hart," Andrade scolded. "Rude much?"

Alex grinned at them. "It's alright, detective, really."

"Sorry," Hart mumbled as he shot his partner a dirty look. "Pretty bad shit out there, huh? I mean, his car exploding and stuff."

"He was lucky he wasn't seriously hurt," Alex replied.

"Yeah," Andrade hummed as she watched Alex closely. "Too bad about the driver though."

Alex just nodded politely. The lady detective gave Alex the impression she knew more than she should have about what happened in Vegas. Maybe she wasn't as innocent as she tried to appear.

"So," Hart moved on, "you were having lunch with the victim?"

"Yes."

Detective Andrade leaned over and placed an elbow on her thigh. Her green eyes blinked twice, then Alex felt the attempt to intrude on her thoughts. Alex decided not to block her attempt and instead pushed a thought her way—just so she'd have something to report to whomever she worked for. She let Detective Andrade have the last contact she'd had with Kit—Alex's phone conversation with her a couple days ago.

It was fairly innocent. Just a quick exchange of where they would meet and what time. Satisfied with that, Fallon backed out slowly, leaving a dull and short-lived pain in her head. Fallon was not very good at this trick. Her sire wasn't either, which would explain why she was never able to do it without giving herself a headache.

"And where were you meeting?" Hart continued his questioning.

"Brimstone Bar and Grill," Alex replied.

His confused expression as he typed made Fallon and Alex both grin. Fallon rolled her eyes and shook her head. "If there aren't any golden arches out front," she smirked and bumped him playfully, "it's lost on him."

"It's inside the Hotel Asylum," Alex replied with a nod.

At least he looked like he knew of the Hotel Asylum, Fallon mused as he pecked the keys again and she took over questioning Alex Stone.

"Brimstone's a pretty nice place," Fallon said. "Special occasion?"

"Business," Alex replied, eyes locked on Fallon's. It made Fallon uneasy but she figured she hid it pretty well, like any good cop would. "We were going to talk about building our Valentine's Day campaign around her."

"She's a model," Hart hummed, tapped awkwardly on the keyboard, then tapped the monitor. "Some place called Desert Beauty, outta Las Vegas."

Fallon reached across his round belly, angled the keyboard in her direction and clicked on Kit Blaze's head-shot.

Her eyes bounced from photo to photo of Kit in various outfits and some with not much more than a smile on the screen.

"Wow," Hart whispered next to her. "She doing anything else here besides modeling?" Hart directed the question to Alex after he cleared his throat.

"Not for me," she replied.

Fallon stayed glued to the screen while their voices droned on in the background. Then she felt Hart nudge her, and a thought popped from his mind into Fallon's: *"God, fantasize on your own time, Andrade!"*

Fallon felt the blush begin as she tucked a loose strand of her wavy hair behind her ear.

"Do you know if she was seeing anyone else after her meeting with you?" Hart asked.

"No," Alex shook her head.

Fallon smirked, "No, you don't know, or no, she wasn't seeing anyone after you?"

Alex grinned back. "No, I don't know what she had planned after our meeting."

An icy chill filled the space around them. She tried to enter Alex's mind again, but this time she must have done something wrong because a sharp pain spiked behind her right eye. It watered and blurred her vision as she sat back in the chair and groaned.

"You alright, Andrade?"

"Stupid allergies," she hissed and wiped a tear away.

"The uniform says you think she was poisoned," Hart continued as Fallon checked her face on her phone screen.

"Just a guess from the condition of the body," Alex replied nonchalantly.

Fallon and Hart looked at each other then back at her.

"Her lips were blue and she was sweating. There was a slight sweet smell on her breath when I leaned down to check her airway. There was nothing we could do for her. It acted fast."

They were silent, and Hart looked stunned. Fallon just leaned back in her chair and cocked her head to the side.

"How do you know so much about poison?" Hart leaned over the desk and whispered.

"My father's a scientist."

"Really," Fallon frowned. "What kind of science?"

"Infectious diseases, viruses," she replied. "Genetics."

"Poisons," Fallon added with a blink of her green eyes again.

"Poisons."

Hart and Fallon looked at each other again, then Hart pecked that note on the screen. He tapped the mouse then his small printer came to life. The pages popped out, one after another. As Fallon looked them over, Hart filled the silence.

"Does your father work here somewhere?"

"Washington," Alex replied. "DC."

Hart let out a low whistle as he nodded at her. "Big time, huh? What's he do for them exactly?"

Alex grinned when Fallon handed her the paper to review. She scanned it quickly then signed the last page. Handing it back, she looked at Hart who was still waiting for an answer to his question. "It's complicated. He heads a research group."

"What are they researching?" Fallon jumped in.

"Why?" Alex said.

"Just wondering since it sounds so ominous," she replied.

"It's not. Pretty boring stuff, really."

"Military?" Fallon asked.

"Classified," Alex replied, "and unless you have a line direct to the Oval Office, I can't really tell you more than that."

"Well, Ms. Stone," Hart said as he stood and extended his hand to her. Shaking it rather weakly, she smiled at him. Fallon found it easy to compel Hart to dismiss Alex and any thought of her having anything to do with Kit's death. "Thank you for your cooperation. If we need anything else, we'll contact you."

"No problem," Alex replied. "I just wish I'd been more help."

"We appreciate what you have done," Fallon stated, shaking her hand too. "Thank you, it's been very interesting."

Hart frowned and shook his head as he sat back down to finish the report. She would make sure he officially stated Alex Stone was no longer a person of interest. She had given her full cooperation and no further investigation of her would be necessary. Fallon escorted her to the exit. In fact, she walked Alex all the way outside before she said anything.

"I owe you an apology."

"For what?"

"Hart," Fallon shrugged. "He's not very tactful, sorry."

"You mean about Jason Stavros? Don't worry about it. The media puts a slant on everything."

"Yeah," Fallon continued to smile. "Like I read somewhere that the Tracker team's still in town—staying with you. Why is that?"

Alex turned to her, moving to the side so as not to block the entrance before she answered Fallon's question. "They're the focal point for the new Spring line. We're looking for a wider demographic."

Fallon didn't really care about demographics. She wanted something interesting to report to her boss. "But how come they're staying with you?"

Alex kept her expression and body language easy and loose. Whatever this woman was after, she wouldn't get much from this conversation. Once she was back at the office, Alex was going to make it a point to have Erin crawl all over her life and find out what the symbol on her earrings meant.

"They hate hotels," Alex giggled. "I have a house in the 'burbs. It's far enough out that we don't have to deal with noisy neighbors, you know?"

"I guess since they're pretty hot right now, that was a good move," Detective Andrade smiled. "I mean, with their connection to 'Mr. Popularity' and all."

"Just a weird coincidence," Alex replied. "Bite is looking for a fresh face, and Stavros is looking for a solid investment. Having the Trackers on as muscle for the trip," she sighed, "is what we like to call a bonus."

"Yeah, lucky you," Detective Andrade stated.

"Lucky me," Alex grinned.

The lady detective nodded and extended her hand to Alex. "*Obrigado pelo seu tempo* (Thank you for your time)."

Alex took her cool hand and matched the firmness of the detective's grip.

"*O prazer e meu* (My pleasure)."

Detective Andrade went back inside, and Alex descended the stone steps to the sidewalk and walked back to her office. She sent a text to Ivy that she was on her way back. She asked about the meeting, but Alex didn't answer.

Taking in a big breath, Alex pushed it out and focused on the vibration behind her. Andrade was tailing her. She smiled as she slowed to an easy pace so the detective could keep up. Obviously, she was planted in the PD to spy on the department or her. Alex didn't know which yet. But she would find out who the pretty lady cop worked for, and then she'd use that information the way a good assassin would—against them.

Chapter 8

Detective Fallon Andrade fell back a few paces when she realized she might be too close to her target. During her training on mixing in with the human population, she had learned how to read people and situations so as not to be discovered. Fallon took shit for being a turned human with a thick skin. But she worked hard and pushed through the ranks of a program for potential protectors of the vampire elite. Then she made one dumb mistake and landed here.

There was nothing wrong with being a police officer in a metropolitan city, but for Fallon Andrade, it seemed like punishment. Her crime? Losing herself to love—or, rather, really mind-blowing lust.

Fallon had done well right up to the point where she was ordered to take this crap job. Fast cars. Lots of money, access to the most beautiful women in the world—all of that came to a crashing halt one night five years ago. All she had to do was keep her charge safe. But that wasn't the reason she was exiled to the Lone Star State punitively. She kept the lovey and quite talented Romani princess safe during her first visit to an American and mostly human city. What she failed to do was focus on the job, instead of her charge's tight bod and beautiful smile.

In retrospect, she should have checked her libido at the door, but where was the fun in that? As great as that whole experience was, Fallon vowed to never again let a beautiful woman interfere with her duty to her clan. So here she was in Texas, trailing another pretty woman, but she wouldn't let her new sire down on this one. If she messed this up, Michael would have her head—literally. Pull this off and Fallon was on his security team at Gale Enterprises. And she wanted that spot more than anything she had ever wanted before—next to the Romani princess.

It was clear that the shifter's death was intentional. Someone must have tied up a big loose end with her demise.

According to everything she knew about Alex Stone, the word quit was not in her vocabulary. When she picked up Alex's scent again, Fallon was confident in her ability to keep this situation contained and Alex Stone out of the line of fire.

Fallon stopped at a safe distance when she saw Alex enter a sandwich shop. Just then, her stomach growled, and she realized she hadn't eaten since breakfast. As her mind pondered lunch, Alex came out with a big bag and a bounce in her step. Down two more blocks, she entered the glass and steel monument to her own success and Fallon grinned as she dialed Michael Gale.

"Fallon," Michael hummed as he enjoyed a pre-lunch pick me up. He mixed a bit of fresh blood in with his black coffee. As soon as the smell crawled up his nose, he grinned and started their conversation the way he always did: "What's wrong?"

Her sigh amused him as it always did. This was their little game. Even if she was reporting something mundane, he'd always ask what was wrong. Mostly because she always chased the good with the bad.

"Why is that always the first thing out of your mouth?" she sighed again. "I mean, that hurts, Michael." When she laughed, he sat back and took another sip of coffee with a grin on his lips.

"Sorry," he replied. "How are you Fallon? Having a nice day so far?"

"I'm good, Michael," she giggled. "Thanks for asking."

"My pleasure. Now that we've established the repair of your feelings, what's wrong?"

The whole minute of silence between them took away Michael's grin. When she whispered, he was sure no human would be able to hear it, but she came in loud and clear to his ears.

"The shifter is dead."

As he placed the hot coffee down, he waved the waitress over for the check. "How?"

"Alex Stone says poison," she answered. "ME confirmed."

"What kind?"

"The kind that kills," she answered with a slight hint of humor in her whisper.

"Fallon."

"I don't know yet. He'll have something by the end of the week."

Michael cleared his throat. "That's too long," he said then emptied the mug. "Speed that up."

"Sure," Fallon laughed. "Would you like me to wave my magic wand or flash my boobs at him?"

Michael moved briskly across the parking lot to his loaner and jumped inside. After the phone paired with the speaker device, he pulled out into Vegas Strip traffic. "I don't care how you do it, just get me the name of the poison."

"It's not gonna be that easy," he heard Fallon state, but this time she had an edge to her voice. She was irritated.

"It shouldn't be easy," he replied. "You won't learn anything if it's easy. Get that information, Fallon—two days, understand?"

"Yes, Sire," she growled. "Two days."

She hung up with a curse she probably thought he didn't hear. Michael laughed as he jumped on the freeway and headed toward Ashblood Manor. The Mistress needed his advice on something and he was in no position to refuse.

As the red Porsche roared past everyone else on the road, Michael thought about Fallon Andrade, that dark-haired, green-eyed beauty from Southern Ireland who everyone told him was a waste of his time—as far as making a decent bodyguard out of her. She was too unpredictable they all said. But Michael found he liked that about her.

Fallon was not the most popular candidate for the open spot at Gale Enterprises, but she wanted the spot more than anyone else. Every shit job that came down the pipe, she took. You had to admire that, at least.

As he drove up the long private drive to the valet, he told himself he had made the right decision. She'd get the job done and keep Alex safe. Michael tossed the keys to the attendant and took the briefcase from his grip.

Ashblood looked regal and quiet at this hour. As he entered the foyer, he reminded himself that this little favor wouldn't release him from his deal regarding Alex Stone. He was sure he'd have to kill a president to repay that debt.

Chapter 9

"Well," Erin said with an adjustment to the round glasses on her nose. "You were right. Detective Fallon Andrade, age 34, born in Dublin in 1982 to a Brazilian Diplomat and his Irish wife. Pretty boring stuff on her life there. The trail here doesn't pick up 'til about six months ago."

Alex paced in front of the glass wall of her office as Erin sat on the small loveseat to give her report on Andrade. Going over that afternoon's events in her mind, Alex knew something was missing. As she sipped from the less than cold bottle of water in her hand, Erin nibbled on the sandwich and waited for Alex to start up the conversation.

"So there's no transfer records—no police academy records," Alex practically whispered. "Nothing that connects her to this place at this time."

"Nope," Erin sighed with another small bite of the veggie sandwich. "Sorry, boss." Her fingers sailed over the keys again then stopped. "Hold up. I've got a death certificate from six years ago. Looks like your lady cop died in a car accident in London in 2010."

Alex spun around and leaned over the back of the couch for a better look. Andrade's hair, a brassy blonde color then, was pulled back into a schoolgirl ponytail. The wicked smirk and dazzling green eyes reminded Alex of someone with bad things on their mind. The senior cycle picture looked standard for a teenager in the private school system. She was maybe seventeen at the time the picture was taken. But Fallon Andrade of Dublin, Ireland wouldn't live to see her thirtieth birthday.

Her office door swung open and Sebastian and Amy walked in laughing. Sebastian went to the small bar on the other side of the room and brought back two bottles of water for Amy and Erin. He took the chair while Amy sat next to Erin and stared at the screen.

"Is that her?" Amy asked. "She's pretty."

"She's a fake," Alex replied as she took the chair opposite Sebastian. "She was DOA in a car accident six years ago."

"Where'd she come from?" Sebastian asked staring at Alex because she was staring at him. "The Council?"

"Maybe," Alex shrugged. She turned her eyes to Erin and Amy. "Did you find anything on the symbol?"

"Yeah," Erin smiled then tapped her smartphone screen. Amy handed it to Alex. "It's a designation for a kind of free agent. She broke a rule, probably recently. She's trying to get back into someone's good graces."

Alex tossed the phone to Sebastian. "Can you find out who she's working for?"

He studied the design with a frown. "Maybe, but not before we leave tonight." He tapped the screen then his phone buzzed. Handing the phone back to Erin, he pulled his own from his pocket. "I've never heard of a free agent program, but then again, I've never broken any rules," he smiled. "At least not any that would get me placed on vampire probation."

"Lucky you," Alex hummed as she stood and stretched. "I guess we should get back to the house and get packed. Vegas, here we come."

They followed her out the door after she packed her backpack and told her assistant goodbye. Ivy would be in charge until she returned sometime before Thanksgiving. Her assistant handed her a large manila envelope and wished everyone a safe trip.

His ass was numb. Perched on a flat rock since a little

before sundown, Cory shifted his weight to soothe the pain. He checked his phone—his friends had better be on their way or they'd never make it in time.

As a breeze blew across the sand toward Groom Lake, Cory zipped his track jacket up to his chin then blew his warm breath on his cold hands. The chill of the coming night wrapped around his hooded curly 'fro as he prepared himself for what came next. Once his buddies-in-crime, Wes and Tommie, arrived, they'd be inside in no time. He knew that for sure for some reason.

Just as he was about to text Wes, the sound of an engine echoed in the distance. At first he thought it was his friends, but Wes's piece of shit Ford pickup needed a tune-up. This sound was of a well-maintained and practically new vehicle. Cory could tell. He could tell a lot of things lately. Since getting out of the "looney bin," as his stepfather put it, he could hear things and feel things that he was sure no one else could: sounds from way in the distance, smells from the next block. It had all happened suddenly and had really freaked him out. The doctor had warned him that there may be some side effects to the medication, but still.

Cory eased his sore butt from the rock then stretched his body out on the sand when he heard the Jeep coming from the opposite direction. Behind the low stack of old rusted water pipes a few inches in front of him, he watched the base patrol bounce along the fence line for one last check before shift change. With the light dimming slowly in the western skies, they wouldn't notice him. He hitched his way up here so there wouldn't be a car to find, if they even checked that back road—which they wouldn't. When his friends got here, they'd see what they needed to see, snap a couple pics for proof, and be long gone before morning or the night shift rounds.

Right now, he was behind that imaginary line that separated trespassing on public land from trespassing on Government property, so he felt safe. But once they crossed that line, entered the fence and the lone building out here, all bets were off. To get pinched then would mean Federal time or worse. Much worse, he feared.

"Stop," he whispered to himself. "Nobody's getting caught."

As he peered through the dry brush, he was careful not to break any of the brittle branches. The brand new army Jeep stopped along the fence, exactly as he knew it would. The guards talked and laughed as the headlights lit up the chain link. This whole scenario was just like his dream: two young military guards charged with the simple task of checking a fence line out in the middle of nowhere. In another minute, they'd bounce along the sand to the next checkpoint and his friends would come over that sand dune behind him. Then they would find the loose section of fence, crawl under it and along the dark ground until they reached the lone building with a number stenciled on all four sides. In and out before the next pass by the guards and home before sunrise. Easy. Maybe.

In the dark of his mind, Cory knew this place like the back of his hand. He should. He'd been dreaming of it for the last two weeks. While the patrol sat and did whatever they did on the outskirts of what was commonly referred to as Area 51, he checked his phone again. If they had left at the arranged time, Wes and Tommie should be arriving any minute now. So this patrol had to get rolling or they'd all get busted.

Like they'd read his mind, the patrol rolled away. A small sandstorm trailed behind the Jeep. Cory heaved a sigh when he heard Wes's old Ford clanking in his direction. He could even hear the doors slam and their trotting feet across the sand. They talked about going to a bar after this to pick up chicks.

Tommie's laugh echoed around the canyon. A sharp pain at the base of Cory's skull cut off the sound suddenly. He found that when he concentrated, he could stop the noise, but it was always followed by that sharp pain and a slight dizziness. *The price you pay for silence,* he thought as he turned his head and saw his friends rise up like magic.

At the top of the dune, Wes looked almost seven feet tall. Tommie came up on the low side of the dune and they descended together. Cory stood up and Wes waved then lost his footing. As he tumbled down the sand, Tommie chased after him, laughing at the top his lungs. Wes's wiry arms and legs looked like a tangled mess as he rolled down the dune. Tommie picked him up by his collar and brushed sand from his jeans as he continued to laugh. Cory waited and tried to keep his temper in check. When they were close enough for him not to yell, he shushed them.

"Hey," Tommie said with an apologetic shrug of his bulky shoulders. Standing about six feet tall, he'd decided to take up Mixed Martial Arts. Wes was his unofficial trainer. "We made it."

"Just," Cory hissed as he turned back to the fence. "The guards barely left."

Wes pulled a flask from his back pocket and took a sip. "We got lost. Sorry, Cory." He handed the metal container to Tommie.

"You mean you got drunk," Cory replied as he took the flask from Tommie and took a long draw himself. It tasted like battery acid, but it steadied his nerves.

"So," Wes said then clapped his hands together. "We gonna do this or what?"

The loose length of fence was easy to find even in the dark desert. Cory followed his memory to the exact spot, dropped down on his knees, and took a deep breath. He reached out and slipped his fingers through the metal gaps then stopped.

"What's wrong?" Tommie whispered as he and Wes took a knee behind him. He felt Tommie's elbow. "Cory?"

"Nothing," he answered. "Just gimme a second."

"It's the right place, right Cory?" Wes asked. "That's the building you saw in your dreams. It's even got the same number: 370-8."

Cory stared at those white numbers against the dark

background. He nodded while he pulled at the metal fence. It gave a low yawn as it rose from the sand.

"Cool," both his friends whispered.

The cold sweat rolled down Cory's spine as the breeze swept past them. He crawled under the fence, held it up for his friends, then they followed him toward the building.

Covered in shadow, they crawled all the way to the back wall then stood up. Backs against the stiff metal, Cory's head began to spin.

"Gimme that flask," he whispered as he slipped his hand inside his front jean pocket.

Wes slapped it in one cold hand as Cory popped the white pills in his mouth with the other. Taking a long draw that emptied the flask, he felt the pills slide down his dry throat and hit his empty stomach. In a few seconds, the sweat and fear were gone.

Given what Cory knew about pharmacology—which was practically nothing—he was fairly sure most medication didn't act as quickly as this stuff. As the dizziness dissipated and his internal heater switched back to normal, he didn't really care. As long as the voices stayed quiet and the sweats didn't come back, it didn't matter, did it?

Being in this drug trial saved his parents a ton of money. And Dr. Gilcrest wouldn't steer him wrong anyway. He was a solid dude. His mother had been seeing him for a few months now—since her return from the Middle East. Her nightmares seemed almost as bad as Cory's, but then she had seen a lot in that combat zone. As a nurse assigned to the medical unit in Fallujah, Mrs. Norma Lucas had patched and stitched up all kinds of soldiers—men and women who had given limb and life in a war very few people agreed with. When she got home, she still carried what she'd seen with her. Dr. Gilcrest helped lots of vets. And now he was helping Cory too.

His mother's benefits paid for his treatment but not the experimental drugs. That's where the drug trial came in. When Dr. Gilcrest suggested it, they'd jumped at the opportunity. So far, it kept the voices and nightmares at bay. Cory couldn't say there were any side effects yet, like his hair falling out or something worse. He figured that would come later. For now, all he wanted was to get through tonight and take what he found to Dr. Gilcrest—if he found anything. He trusted Dr. Gilcrest.

His friends followed him down the dark path beside the old building, still pressed to the wall in the safety of the shadows. When Cory heard another engine growl, he stopped short and they bumped into him. Wes and Tommie chuckled.

"Shut up," Cory hissed over his shoulder. They stifled another chuckle as Cory kept them still until the Jeep rolled away.

When they reached the front, Cory stopped again and peered around the corner. He saw a guard house in the distance. His sight sharpened on the small building, and he could see one guard sitting at a desk just like in the dream.

"What the hell?" he muttered under his breath.

"Now what?" Tommie asked.

"This is insane," Cory replied. "I can't believe this shit. Can you?"

"Ever since you got out of that hospital, you've been able to do some pretty awesome stuff," Wes said. "Maybe they did some experiments on you, you know, secret shit just to see what would happen."

He saw Tommie nod his head in agreement, then they laughed again.

"Assholes," Cory grinned then checked the guard station one more time. "I'm gonna check this building. You guys stay here."

"Are you sure you wanna do this?" Tommie sighed. "Maybe we should just go back. What if we get caught?"

"We didn't get caught in the dream," Cory reminded him.

"You don't know that for sure," Wes added. "You always wake up screaming when we open the door, remember?"

Cory had to admit he was right. He never got any further than the door when he woke up in a cold sweat, his heart racing as if he'd run a marathon. That's why he decided to do this. He had to know what was behind that door. He had to know what he was so afraid of.

His friends had volunteered to come along, especially after they found out the coordinates Cory kept dreaming about were at Area 51.

"You don't have come with me," Cory stated as he prepared to step out of the darkness. He blew on his cold hands because he knew they had to be warm to open the door. Its electronic lock wouldn't open unless his hand was warm.

"Are you kidding?" Tommie squeaked. "I'm in, buddy!"

Wes stared at Cory then nodded. "If we get busted, you're gonna have to explain to my Dad why he has to fly to Cuba to bail me out."

"Just stay close and quiet," Cory whispered.

They stepped out one at a time. Still keeping to the shadow of the building, Cory led the way with Tommie in the middle and Wes checking the rear. At the door, the lock looked just as it had for the last two weeks. Cory rubbed his hands together as he blew his warm breath on them then pressed his right hand on the glass pad.

Chapter 10

"You shouldn't have done that," Alex stated as they sat in the lobby of Jason's hotel. Adam had just briefed her on the girl from the airport fight. He'd wiped her memory and set her free with a tracking device embedded behind her right ear. "Playing around with her memories will just cause more problems. Tristan is as old as you, if not older. He'll figure it out. Then he'll do something like he did back home—something that will draw attention we don't want."

"All the more reason to pick her up now," Adam replied. "We know Tristan's out. We should settle this before we leave."

Alex sat back in the comfortable chair and shook her head at him. "We know where she is. We know Creed's involved. You said you couldn't get a clear picture of Tristan, so it could be bullshit—her dropping his name."

He was silent. Because he was pure, Alex couldn't read his thoughts and she wanted to more than anything right now. She had never been able to read pure-bloods. Her father said it was most likely because they were born vampires, their genetic makeup was vastly different from the turned. Alex figured it was because she was mostly human and, therefore, too weak to read their thoughts. To her, that was a weakness she wished she could overcome.

"And if he follows us to Romania?" Adam asked as he leaned toward her. "I will not risk Jason's life on a hunch."

"You don't have to," Alex replied. "He won't follow us. Too risky."

Adam nodded and Alex turned to see Jason coming toward them. "And if you're wrong?"

"I signed on to protect him with my life," she answered as they both stood and faced him. "I'm good at what I do, Adam. I've never lost a client."

"You better not or he'll be the last client you lay eyes on."

Jason's gaze bounced from Alex to Adam and back. He shook Adam's hand and kissed her cheek. "Do I want to know what you two were talking about?"

"Just going over some last minute details," Adam replied. "Right?"

"Right," Alex answered. "I think we're on the same page now. If you two would excuse me, I have other business to attend to."

She bowed to Adam and he bowed back. Jason asked Adam to wait as he followed her.

"Where are you off to in such a hurry?" he asked as he took her elbow gently and pulled her to a stop. "We need to talk."

"We talked, remember?" she said. "Anything else will have to wait until later."

Jason pulled her closer, placed his warm lips to her ear. "The plane takes off at midnight. Don't be late."

When he kissed her ear, it sent tingles through her body.

"I won't," she answered as she backed away.

The snow that fell outside the limo window made New York seem tame. It was anything but. Conner watched as his son approached the car after saying goodbye to his friends. His friends climbed into a cab as he climbed into the backseat of the warm limo and nodded in Conner's direction.

Rockefeller Center disappeared as the car pulled away from the curb and into early evening traffic. Snowflakes, the ones that hitched a ride on the young man's coat, melted quickly into the carpet at his feet. His navy blazer was slightly wrinkled as he shrugged his peacoat off his slim shoulders.

He placed the coat on the seat across from them; a black cord stretched from his smartphone to his ears. The bass vibrated around the close quarters they shared. Conner continued to take inventory.

His yellow, maroon, and white striped tie hung loosely around his neck. The white dress shirt was new and starched, but his khaki pants were frayed at the cuffs and his loafers needed to be replaced soon, along with the brown leather belt around his waist. Conner tapped his arm, and the young man pulled the earphones out with a slight eye roll.

"You'll ruin your hearing," Conner commented.

"Sorry," he mumbled as he tapped the screen of his phone.

"How was your day?"

The young man shrugged. "Fine. Yours?"

Conner pulled at a loose thread on the teen's lapel. "We should replace this before it falls apart."

"It's fine, Con," he huffed then brushed Conner's hand away.

"How was the trip to DC?" Conner continued trying to coax a conversation out of his moody teenaged son, Andrew Gale—Drew for short.

"Boring," he answered. His foot tapped absently. Conner had learned over time that this meant he was angry. "I've been in the White House lots of times. It never changes." He gave Conner a quick smirk then turned his head back to his window.

"What's wrong?" Conner asked.

Drew turned to his father. His brown eyes burned with anger. They'd argued before he left for the trip this morning. And the argument, apparently, was not over yet—at least not for Drew.

"You know what," he sighed. "Are you ready to be reasonable about this?"

Conner cocked his head to one side, turned his body slightly to look Drew in the eyes. "I am being reasonable; you just don't agree with my decision."

"I don't agree that it's your decision to make," Drew replied as he matched Conner's posture and tone.

Conner swallowed the shout he wanted to let out at his son. At least he wasn't afraid to speak his mind. "And whose decision is it?"

"Mine," Drew replied. "I don't understand why I have to wait until my twenty-first birthday. I'll be eighteen next month."

"Go on," Conner replied.

"I'll be old enough to vote and go to war. Why won't I be old enough for that?"

"We're not talking about electing a President or you joining the military. We're talking about changing everything that you are, Drew. I just want you to enjoy being human for a little while longer."

"Why?" he mumbled. "It was hell until I came here."

"You have friends and soccer; I know you enjoy those things," Conner replied as he ignored his last statement. "Don't give that up so easily."

"I won't give it up after I'm turned, Con, I swear."

"You would have to, Drew," Conner answered. "We couldn't take the chance of discovery."

"I could hold back," Drew assured his father.

Conner shook his head as he faced forward again. "It's not that easy. Besides, you like to win too much."

"Who doesn't?"

"You would have an unfair advantage."

"That's not the reason and you know it," Drew huffed as he faced forward as well.

He forced the earplugs back in and turned up the music. Before Conner could pull them out, he jerked around, snatching them out again.

"You turned Zu when he was nineteen," he sniffed.

"That was different."

"Why?"

"Because he almost died. I was not going to let my son die if I could save him."

"Sometimes I wish I was dying," Drew growled then turned away. "Then maybe . . ."

Conner grabbed the phone, cord and all, before Drew could shut him out again then pulled him around to face him by his lapels. "Don't you ever say anything like that to me again," he growled. His fangs descended and Drew began to shake with fear. "I am your father and I say when you become vampire—if you ever do!"

Of his six sons, Drew was the youngest. Of his four adopted sons, Drew was the only one still human. Conner knew it bothered Drew, but he would not turn him until his twenty-first birthday, if ever.

"I'm sorry, Con," he heard Drew whisper after he'd released him and put some distance between them. Conner just nodded but didn't look at his son. "I mean it. I shouldn't have said that."

Conner gave his leg a pat. "It's fine, son, really."

Drew slid closer and placed his head on Conner's shoulder. Conner kissed his forehead as they rode through the dark streets of New York in silence.

Back at the penthouse, Drew went straight to his room. Conner listened as he climbed the stairs and closed his bedroom door. He took off his jacket and tie, rolled up his sleeves, and began to prepare a sandwich for his youngest son.

With the turkey and wheat bread sandwich, a glass of almond milk, and a banana on the tray, he climbed the stairs slowly. Conner tapped the door with his foot and waited. He never entered their rooms without being asked first. He could respect their privacy as long as he was never given a reason not to. Inside the room, a lone bedside lamp blazed. Drew sat on the bed with a book in his lap.

Conner could smell bath soap and toothpaste in the air. He saw the towel Drew had abandoned on the floor after his shower. Once the tray was on the bed, Drew put it in his lap.

"Thanks."

"My pleasure."

He watched as Conner reached down and picked up the stray towel. As he folded it, Drew began eating his late dinner. "I was gonna pick that up."

"Of course you were," Conner grinned at him as he walked across the room to his private bath and laid the towel over the rack. Back at his bed, he watched him eat.

"I'm not a kid anymore, Con."

"I know you're not."

Drew took one more bite, then pushed away what was left on the tray. After he emptied the glass, he ate the banana in three bites.

"I think I understand."

Conner sat down at the foot of the bed. "Do you?"

"Forever's a long time," Drew replied.

"Ours can be," Conner answered with a nod. "Sooner than you'd like, you will have to let go of your human friends. They would eventually notice you're not aging at the same rate as they are. That would be really hard to explain at your forty-year reunion—you looking twenty and some of them balding and gray."

"I guess so," he nodded with a grin.

"Don't worry," Conner said. His worry radiated all over the room. "We will discuss this more when the time comes."

Conner stood, picked up the tray, then leaned over and kissed the top of his son's head. At the door, Drew called to him.

"What would we discuss, exactly?"

Conner leaned on the door frame and gave Drew a thoughtful gaze. He could remember the twelve-year-old pickpocket who joined his family five years ago. A tough little bastard who had survived on the streets of New York

City since he was seven years old. Now, at seventeen, he was one of the heirs to the Gale Family billions and in three more years, he'd be immortal.

"What you want to do when you grow up. Where you fit in the company. How you want to die."

He didn't expect the fear in Drew's eyes at that last statement, but he was glad it had that effect on him. The terror hit Conner's heart though. It wouldn't be easy to turn his human son. That's why he wanted to wait. They had to die in order to turn. Dying was never fun, and Conner was not looking forward to taking Drew's mortal life. He secretly hoped Drew would change his mind—wait even longer after he found out what the process was, but he knew he wouldn't, and Conner would have to kill him to keep Drew forever.

Chapter 11

"Really?" Alex smiled as they pulled into a well-lit parking lot on the outskirts of town. "Batting cages?"

Michael laughed. "Why not? It's not like this is a date, right?"

They climbed from the convertible at the same time.

"Right," she answered.

He tossed a helmet at her as they walked toward the last cage, traveling down the gravel path lined with portable heaters. It was pretty empty, but Alex figured it was best to be as far away from the few humans out here as possible under the circumstances.

As a kid, these kinds of places were her training ground—environments where humans let their guard down and vampires hunted without fear. Amusement parks were the worst, only because it was hard to follow people onto a rollercoaster.

Vampires hunted in places like these because it was like shooting fish in a freaking barrel. The blood of children filled with all those tasty chemicals was hard to resist. Adrenaline could be awfully intoxicating to a vampire, especially a hungry one. They could smell excited teenagers from a mile away. Is that why he picked this place?

Alex gripped the aluminum bat and waited for the pitch. The hollow clunk of bat and ball as they connected echoed through the air. They watched as the white ball sailed out to the homerun sign.

"Not bad," she heard Michael say over the sound of the

machine as it prepared to send another ball her way.

"I don't really know what I'm doing," she lied, then sent the next two pitches out in the sticks as well. Then Michael whistled as the machine stopped and waited for more coins.

"You seem to be doing pretty well for someone who doesn't know the game."

Michael took her place in the cage. He swung the bat around to loosen up his shoulder muscles then took a pretty professional looking stance at the plate.

"Let me guess," Alex said as she pumped coins into the machine. After she was outside the cage, she leaned on the chain link fence. "You used to play baseball?"

He shook his head then swung at the first pitch. When the ball took flight in the opposite direction, Michael smiled. "One of my college buddies is a pitching coach for a farm team. He lets me practice with the team sometimes."

"When you're not working at the manor," she replied as he hit two more balls out into the darkness. He missed the last pitch then turned in her direction.

"I lied to you, sorta."

"About what?"

He walked up to the fence that separated them and slipped his fingers through the holes above hers. As he looked down on her, Alex suddenly had the urge to run so she didn't hear what he had to say. She was tired of secrets.

"I don't work at the manor," he answered. "I mean, not like you think. I'm legal counsel for the manor—for the Mistress."

"Oh," Alex sighed. "I thought . . . nevermind. Why didn't you just say that the night we met?"

"I guess I didn't think you'd talk to me if you knew," Michael grinned down at her. "People hate lawyers, you know?"

That innocent "forgive me" look in his blue-gray eyes had an effect on her for some reason. She did forgive him, but now she'd be more careful what she said to him. He was no different than any other vampire.

"Is she in some kind of trouble?" Alex asked as Michael exited the cage and she followed him back to the equipment booth. They took a table on the patio and he ordered two beers.

"The Mistress is never in trouble," Michael answered with a wink. "You should know that."

"Yeah," Alex replied. "That was a dumb question. You were there for pleasure then?"

"Does that bother you?"

"Why would it?"

They stared at each other as the waitress sat the beers down and smiled at Michael. She left with a glance at him over her shoulder and a sideways smirk at Alex.

"Answer my question," Michael broke the silence.

"I did," Alex replied as she tapped his glass with hers.

"No, you didn't."

She tried not to, but she smirked at him. "No, it doesn't bother me. It does surprise me though."

"Why?" he asked before drinking half the beer in one swallow.

"I don't know," she shrugged. "You don't seem the type. You live a pretty comfortable life, especially if you work for the Mistress."

"So?"

"So, you're handsome, easygoing. Why pay for what you can get freely?"

Alex could see the slight blush on his cheeks. Then he emptied the glass and waved for another.

"Nothing is ever free," he hummed. "Especially the affections of a woman."

Alex adjusted herself in the uncomfortable plastic chair. "You're not paying for affection."

"True," Michael agreed, "but you have to admit I'm right."

"Maybe."

He thanked the waitress for the new beer. "What about you? Why were you there?"

"Business."

"What kind of business?" he asked, his attention focused on her.

"Personal," she answered.

Michael sat back and nodded with a serious look on his face. "Are you in trouble?"

Alex grinned but didn't answer.

He wasn't sure how to take her sexy grin and cryptic silence. If she had been any other human, he have would just compelled her to tell him what he wanted to know.

He'd studied every piece of information he could get on the entire team. He knew what they were capable of and how to avoid an all-out confrontation with any Tracker. What he didn't know was how she really fit in the scheme of things.

As he sat across the small table from her, he could feel her power—the deep vibrations bouncing between them that set his senses on edge. Now he understood why Stavros wanted to keep her close. Her scent was so intoxicating and warm. Michael wanted more than anything to move closer, but he wouldn't. He shook loose from the thought of tasting her blood as she tapped his foot with hers.

"You okay?" she questioned with a bit of concern in her voice.

"Yeah," he chuckled nervously. "I'm just trying to figure you out, that's all."

"What's to figure out?" she shrugged.

"The Mistress thinks highly of you," Michael changed the subject.

"I feel the same about her," she smiled.

"How'd you meet?"

"Dark Ball."

Michael almost choked on the beer. "Sorry?"

"We met at this important party, Dark Ball. You've never heard of it?"

"I have," he replied. "I'm just surprised you've been to one."

"Why?" she said before she emptied her glass. "Because I'm human?"

"Well, yeah."

She laughed and he was pretty sure she meant it to sound condescending—and it did.

"Don't be such a snob," she said finally. "Pure-bloods are so arrogant about that stuff." She shook her head at him with a playful look in her eyes. "I know how to act in *proper* society," she stated with comedic emphasis on the word "proper."

"I'm not a snob," Michael answered. He waved for the check. "And I'm sure you could fit in anywhere you wanted." The waitress dropped the white paper on the table and thanked Michael for coming. She never even looked at Alex again. "How'd you know that I'm pure blood anyway?"

"Easy," she answered as they walked through the gate toward the parking lot. "That look on your face when I mentioned the Ball."

"What did you think of it?" Michael replied. "The Ball, I mean."

"Just a big, fancy room filled with hot air and old money," she answered with a little laugh.

"I guess you have been to one then," he said with a chuckle. "Anybody I might know?"

"Huh?"

He laughed, "Your date."

"Oh," she nodded. "Probably not."

"Vampire?"

"Nope."

Michael drew the keys from his pocket and they gave off a jingling sound. "Important human? Figures."

Alex bumped him lightly. "Meaning?"

"I'm not the only snob here," he grinned as he returned the bump.

"I'm not a snob," she mocked him as best she could.

As they approached his car, two big guys dressed in cargos, long sleeve t-shirts, and hard expressions stepped away from a pristine, white Chevy SUV parked on the right side of the almost empty lot. As one man raised his phone to his face, the other gave them a nod and a small salute. The pair passed them, and Michael felt her tension bump into his.

Alex took Michael's arm out of instinct, mostly. She wanted to let him know they might be in trouble and make the guys that had just turned back think they hadn't noticed. A few feet from the car, one of them yelled.

"Hey!"

They stopped, looked at each other then turned around to face the men.

"Yeah?" Michael answered.

"Nice car," the one said with a nod. "Must suck on gas though, huh?"

"Not that bad," Michael said. "Why?"

The two men stopped a couple feet away. Alex could smell the bad cologne as it was carried by a breeze. She couldn't see any weapons, but that didn't mean anything these days. Those heavy boots weren't for stomping grapes.

"I guess the ladies love fast cars," the other chuckled as he looked Alex over. "What do you say *draguta* (sweetheart)?" he grinned at her. "You into fast cars?"

"Look, we don't want any trouble," Michael said as he stepped ahead of Alex.

"I was talking to the lady," he said with a rough Romanian accent. The grin disappeared. "V*ampir murdar* (dirty vampire)!"

Michael took a step because he could speak Romanian too. They both laughed when Alex pulled him back and took his place in the guy's personal space.

"*Care a fost draga nepoliticos* (that was rude, sweetheart)," she replied.

The men grinned at each other. Then the second man moved up to his partner as he pushed his hands in his pockets. His light brown hair was spiked on top and cut close on the sides.

One side of his mouth curled as he looked down on her. "*Fata dura* (tough girl)," he growled in perfect Romanian.

Alex replied, "*Mai dure decat crezi* (tougher than you think)."

His movement was fluid and fast. His knee came up and his foot whipped out. The hiking boot swept past Alex's face as she stepped to one side then pushed his leg away.

He seemed surprised at how fast she was. Then he seemed even more surprised when she came up behind him and punched him in the left kidney. As his knees buckled from the blow, his friend approached Michael just as quickly.

"Are you as tough?" the man said to Michael.

"Why don't you take a swing and found out?" he smiled.

This man was about Michael's height but much heavier. The bulkiness of his body was matched only by the boulders that were his fists. Per Michael's invitation, he took a swing and missed. Not to be outdone, Michael held back, just a bit, on his jab. It snapped his head back, but he shook it like a dazed dog and came back for more.

His right hook took Michael by surprise. It was solid and twisted his head to the right. As Michael thought, the man's hands were like rocks and the impact of the punch rattled Michael's teeth. When he picked Michael up by the front of his t-shirt, his jaw was set tight and his eyes flared with hate. He grunted as he tossed Michael into the air.

When he landed on the windshield of their SUV, Michael felt his own natural defenses kick into high gear. The feeling of his fangs as they cut through his gums hurt like hell, but that's what happens when a vampire gets angry. When his vision sharpened on his attacker, the taste of his own blood granted him permission to kill.

Then the sound of glass as it shattered into a million pieces drew Michael's attention to Alex. Her opponent was knee deep in someone's passenger side window. She pulled the door open wider so that he was stuck between the car and the tangled metal of the now useless door.

Michael was up and off the SUV before the man could get to him. His razor-sharp nails swiped smoothly across his opponent's face as he tried to carve his name in the man's cheek. While the man grabbed his bloody face, Michael pulled a metal pole from the cement and swung it like a bat. The man's head snapped to the right as Michael forced the sharp end of the pole into his gut. A wounded cry escaped into the night as he went down on both knees trying to pull the pole loose.

"Is that tough enough for ya?" Michael hissed as he walked around the man, took hold of the bloody metal pole and with a quick jerk, pulled it through him. Face down in the dusty parking lot, the ground turned red as the rest of his blood pooled under his body. Michael licked the blood from his palm then spit it on the dying mess.

Alex and her attacker traded hooks and body punches as Michael looked for something else to use as a weapon. Before he could reach them, Alex landed at his feet. She wiped away the blood from a gash on her cheek as she stood up. She wobbled and Michael caught her before she fell.

"Need some help?" Michael asked as she shrugged out of his hold, rolled her sleeves up and wiped her bloody hand on her jeans.

"No thanks," she replied in a huff. "I got it."

With that, she ran at the other man at full speed. He had a wide catcher's stance as he blocked the roundhouse then the right hook. His powerful thighs pushed the seams at the sides of his pants as he kicked her into the light pole with a laugh. The ring on his right hand sent sparks over her head as it scratched the metal and missed her face.

Her tuck-and-roll was perfect. She was on her feet then on his back before he knew what was happening. They whirled in increasingly desperate circles as Alex wrapped her arm around his neck and applied so much pressure that he was forced to his knees, which gave her time to readjust her hold on him. With her feet on the ground again, she grabbed the back of his head and slammed him, face first, into the light pole. Michael heard his nasal cavity crunch on impact. Then he heard the familiar pop as Alex broke his neck in one smooth motion.

She dropped to her knees, fishing her phone from her back pocket as he approached.

"Two bodies," she coughed as she held her side. "I need this cleaned up now." She slipped the device back in her pocket then looked up at Michael. "You okay?"

His hand hovered over her. "Yeah," he sighed, pulling her to her feet again. "You?"

She just nodded as she leaned over, placing her hands on her knees and pushing out a hard breath. "You should get out of here before someone sees you. I can take it from here."

"I'll wait."

"I don't think I'm gonna need a lawyer," she tried to smile, but the cut on her cheek turned it into a grimace. "Not this time, anyway."

He wanted to protest, but she was right. He had to leave or risk someone showing up that could blow his cover story. "Call me later. I just wanna be sure you're alright."

"Michael," she sighed as she stood up straight again. "Best non-date ever."

In her personal space, Michael took in the smell of her blood when he inhaled. The combination of blood, sweat, and anger mixed as it hit his brain then his stomach. An overwhelming urge to feed from her came on like a blow to his head.

"This is the most fun I've had in a long time," he grinned at her. Without really knowing why, he reached out to touch her face where the blood was. She caught his hand with a shake of her head.

"Glad you had a good time," she replied as she forced his hand back down.

"How are you going to explain this to the cops?" he said. "I mean, I could help."

"No, you can't. And the cops won't be involved, so no worries there."

"You got a little dizzy there for a second, what happened?"

He watched her roll that question around in her head.

"Not the first time I've been clocked like that," she answered. "He was stronger than he looked."

Michael's ears began to ring as the sound of big vehicles rose from the distance. They were maybe ten miles out but coming in fast. He would have to go in the opposite direction to avoid them.

"Go," she said, then spun him around and nudged him forward. "Now."

Safe inside his car, he sped away with one last look in his rearview. There she was, crouched over the body, going through his pockets like a thief. He shook his head with a smile.

"Couldn't be helped, huh?" he asked as he tapped the device in his gloved hand without even a glance at her. Alex watched the cleanup team work quickly. Some questioned the staff. Others, dressed as police, took statements they'd toss later, after insurance claims were paid and people were happy again. "Mr. Ramsey would like to speak with you when you get a chance. We'll get you to your plane when you're ready."

"Where are the bodies going now?" Alex asked as they were place into heavy plastic bags on gurneys, zipped in, and wheeled away.

"Dr. Carlisle's lab," he answered. When he closed the cover on the small table, he held it behind him and stared at her. "Do you need medical attention, ma'am?"

"I'll take care of it on the plane," she answered.

He just nodded with a bored expression on his face. From the looks of it, he'd been pulled from bed. A faint bath soap smell hung in the air and he needed a shave.

His flight jacket was navy blue with gold and white stripes around the wrist, hem, and collar. With S.A.M. stitched over his heart, he looked more like an exterminator than anything.

"It's not a problem," he replied. She shook her head, and he nodded again, then excused himself politely.

A happy-go-lucky recruit trotted in her direction. She tossed an identical flight jacket at Alex with a smile. "When you're ready, I'll escort you to the plane. Your team and Mr. Stavros have been briefed. Mr. Craig will meet us at the gate."

"Great. Let's go," Alex replied as she slipped the jacket on and followed her escort to a black SUV, unmarked and running.

Chapter 12

"Jesus," Cory heard Tommie whisper right next to him. "What the hell is this place?"

He wasn't sure how to answer that question as his flashlight jumped from strange device to even stranger device while they crept through the warehouse. Some of the equipment looked decades old, some centuries old. Big, human-sized cages sat in the far corner covered in dust and rust from what he could see. Wes bumped into a steel table and the sound echoed everywhere.

"Be careful," he rasped as Wes rubbed his hip bone and nodded.

"What do you think this is for?" they both heard Tommie ask.

As Cory turned in his direction, his flashlight lit up the old-fashioned device. It was made of colored glass and looked like a giant genie's bottle—like from that old television show. There was clear plastic tubing attached to the lid and metal spouts all around the bottom with small white teacups positioned beneath them. Cory stood next to Tommie and reached out to touch one of the spouts. It was cold. When he pulled his finger back, it was covered in a dusty, rose-colored residue. He sniffed it then wiped it on his jeans.

"What does it smell like?" Tommie whispered.

"Dust," Cory answered and stifled a sneeze. "It's just dust."

Tommie directed his light on the glass container as he stepped closer. "Then what's that?" He put his face close to the glass and frowned.

Cory did the same. Inside was something thick and dark. When Tommie pushed the bottle, it sloshed heavy and sticky on the sides. Cory knew in that moment what it was. He knew what all the strange devices were.

"Let's go," he said as he pulled Tommie away and toward the door.

"What's wrong?" Wes asked as he opened a small container and sniffed. "This shit is freaking awesome! Let's take something as proof."

"No," Cory growled as he pulled Tommie toward the door. "Leave it, Wes. We're outta here!"

The dizzy feeling came on all of a sudden. He lost his grip on Tommie's sleeve as his knees gave out. Inches of dust puffed up around him as Cory landed on the floor. Voices came at him from all directions, and he pressed his hands to his ears to block them. But they weren't coming from outside; they were inside his head. When he squeezed his eyes shut, he saw a woman in a parking lot somewhere. She was fighting like some crazy ninja. The man on the attack scratched her cheek with a silver blade of some sort and Cory felt it: that burn of skin separating and then the feel of blood as it slid down her cheek.

"Help her," he moaned as his friends pulled him from the floor.

"Help who?" Tommie said. "Cory! Who do we need to help?"

And just as quickly as it started, it stopped. Cory's eyes opened wide and adjusted to the flashlight in his face. He pushed Wes's light away then Tommie's.

"What happened?" Cory whispered as he looked around confused and afraid.

"You saw someone who needed help," Tommie answered. "Who did you see Cory? Can you describe her?"

Cory stared at the darkness in the distance and tried to bring the memory back, but it was gone. As they helped him to an old desk chair, Wes kneeled in front of him.

"Cory," he said calmly. "Can you describe the woman you just saw?"

"No."

"Try," Tommie hissed down on them.

"It's gone," Cory whined and shook his head.

Wes mumbled something Cory couldn't understand, then he stood up. Tommie moved behind Cory and before he could react, Tommie jerked his arms behind his back as Wes pulled a syringe from his jacket pocket. When the entire space filled with light, Cory knew he was in trouble.

"What the fuck?" Cory barked and struggled, but Tommie had an iron grip on him.

"I'm sorry, buddy," Wes replied then held the syringe high. A small bit of whatever was in it shot up in the air. "You should have tried harder to remember."

"Remember what?"

"Was it her?" Tommie grunted in his ear. "We need something to go on."

Cory struggled, but he was tired, too tired to get loose. Then the prick of the needle in his neck got his attention. The mixture burned as it spread through his neck and down his body until everything below his chin was numb. He barely felt the army guys enter the room, pick him up from the floor, and load him onto the gurney they brought with them.

All the action around him seemed watery and slow. The voices were distorted by the drug spreading through his system like wildfire. After he was strapped to a table, he was covered in a thin, white blanket. He counted the light fixtures in the ceiling as he was rolled out the door. Ten. He counted ten old, gray flood lights. Was that important? If he was going to die, then no.

"Get him back to the lab," he saw Wes's lips move, but his voice was so mangled he wasn't even sure it was Wes anymore. The man he gave the order to saluted him and he returned the gesture.

He felt the bump of the gurney being loaded into the

back of the ambulance. The doors being slammed shut sent a pain through his head. The last thing he saw was Tommie's wavy image over him as they bounced down the road.

"Sorry," he heard Tommie say. "I'm really sorry about this, Cory. Maybe the autopsy will tell us more."

Cory's brain registered that because he tried to get loose. When the blackness came Cory thought he heard someone call him a test subject. Then they called him a failure, just like the rest. Cory wanted to hold on to consciousness, but it slipped away from him. His last thought was he hoped the autopsy wouldn't tell them a damn thing.

After Michael assured Mistress Bianca that Alex was fine—better than fine, she was freaking fantastic—her personal driver rushed him to the private plane gate at McCarran. The rushed shower and change of clothes refreshed him, but his pulse still raced from the fight. It raced from the memory of her in action too. She had hesitated for half a moment, and that's why the Romanian was able to almost slice the side of her face off. Michael wondered what could have caused her to pause like that. She wasn't afraid. In fact, she looked like she enjoyed the fight more than she should have. Well, he didn't have time to figure it out now. His father expected a report.

As he crossed the tarmac to the Gulf Stream, his phone buzzed in his hand.

"Alex," he sighed as he climbed the stairs and joined his brothers inside. "Are you okay?"

Her voice battled over the background noise on her side. "I'm fine," she yelled. "I just wanted to make sure you got home in one piece. No one followed, right?"

"No," he answered as he shushed his brothers and buckled up. When the engines roared to life, he hoped she didn't notice. "What's all the noise?"

"Clean up," she said. "Thanks for the help."

"My pleasure," he replied.

In the air, the landing gear went up, and Michael took the bottled blood his brother Sean handed him.

"Look," he heard her say with less noise in the background, "I have to ask you for a huge favor, Michael."

He emptied the bottle and nodded for another. That fight took more out of him than he thought. "Anything."

"You can't tell anyone what you saw me do out there," she said.

"Your secret's safe with me," Michael replied lightly, despite the feeling of a stone settling in the pit of his stomach. He was about to report everything he saw to his family. "But I'm still not really sure what happened. Who were those guys anyway?"

"When I find out, you'll be the first to know," she replied with a bit of humor.

"Thanks," he said. "When can I see you again?"

"Well, I'm leaving the country for about a week," she said. "I'll call you when I get back. I owe you one."

"No, you don't," Michael said. "But I like that you think you do, so I'm gonna let you pay me back."

He heard someone yell her name and she told them to give her a minute.

"I gotta go. Thanks again for the save."

She was gone before he could say goodbye.

"So," Sean hummed with a small grin on his face, "how was Vegas?"

"Boring," Michael grinned back as he flashed his bruised chin at his brother. "How'd you guys get here so fast?"

Raphael, the brother with a genius IQ, came down the narrow aisle from the cockpit. Their pilot always let him land and take off. It was sort of a running ritual now. "We were done in LA, and Con said you got your ass kicked, so we came to pick up the pieces."

They laughed as Michael emptied the second bottle.

His head stopped hurting and his spine snapped back into place. He could feel his cracked ribs mending too.

"I didn't get my ass kicked, but thanks for the lift."

"Where's the woman?" Sean asked in that polished, English professor accent of his. "Did she clean up the mess?"

"Yes, she did," Michael replied as he tried to stretch his arms over his head, but the roof of the plane was too low for that. He'd have to wait until they were off the plane. "She's pretty good. You should have seen her."

"Well, Con's anxious to hear what happened," Raph replied. "Do you know who sent them?"

"No. Maybe it was payback for Kit Blaze."

Raph and Sean shook their heads at him as they took the leather seats across the narrow aisle.

"The Mother says no," Sean replied. "She never uses humans anyway."

The Mother he referred to would be the leader of the Shifter Kin. Her name was Cordelia, and she was mother to the four oldest alphas in the breeding class. She was furious over the loss of Kit, but stated, in no uncertain terms, that Alex Stone was not to blame for her death.

"Did they say anything?" Raph asked. "I mean, before the beat down?"

"Not really," Michael chuckled. "We pretty much went from 'hey' to bloodshed."

Sean reached into a backpack on the seat next to him and pulled out a laptop. After he set up the connection to Conner, he turned it toward Michael. When his face appeared, he looked pissed.

"Are you alright?" Conner said.

"Yes," Michael answered.

"Jason says she needs stitches—what happened?"

"We were headed back to the Strip and were attacked. Two humans with short fuses, Romanian accents, and no brains. I think they were dosed."

"Romanian," Conner stated with a raise of an eyebrow.

"That's not at all strange."

They all chuckled, then Conner sighed.

"Pawns?"

"Most likely," Michael nodded. He could tell his father's mind was filled with all kinds of questions, just not ones for him.

"Which one of you were they after?" he asked.

"Well, it wasn't me. Not this time. I do believe this is about Alex Stone," Michael answered with the sudden realization that she was in a lot of trouble. He wanted to ask to be sent to Romania now.

"That's what we were afraid of," Conner sighed. He shook his head absently and looked back at the screen. "Once you're all home, we'll discuss this further. See you when you get here."

"Goodnight, Con," Michael waved at the screen. Sean closed the laptop.

Chapter 13

Alex grunted through gritted teeth. "Jesus! I can feel that, you know."

Surgical gloves covered his hands as Adam stitched the cut down the right side of her back with near perfect precision. The local he had given her had started to wear off. He probably hadn't given her enough on purpose.

"One more stitch," he said.

The sharp sting of the swaged needle as he pulled it gently through her skin forced Alex to concentrate on Jason's hard expression as he watched from the door of the medical bay aboard the plane. They had taken off just an hour ago.

"Done," Adam said as he secured the big bandage over his work. He removed the gloves and dumped them and the bloody gauze in a red bio-hazard bag along with her tattered shirt. She heard the thud of the needle as it landed in the bottom of the empty sharps container. "I'm sure by morning that will look like a scratch, but for now, it's a serious injury and you should get some rest."

That was code for no sex with Jason tonight, so kick back and fire up Netflix.

"Thanks," Alex groaned in pain as she sat up and Adam handed her a clean hoodie to cover herself with. She sat there in a white bra covered in blood. "I'll clean up the rest, if you don't mind."

Adam sat the red bag next to her on the table with a nod. "Jason, when you're ready, we have some things to go over."

After he was gone, Jason entered. He watched her gingerly slide one arm into the hoodie then the other. When it was zipped, he sat down on the stool across from her with an angry expression on his face.

"How do you feel?" he spoke low. Alex could feel the tension bounce off her already aching body. He leaned forward, placed his elbows on his thighs, and laced his fingers together. "Can I get you anything?"

Alex shook her head. "I'm fine."

Jason opened his mouth but closed it without a word being spoken. His long legs stretched out and he rolled toward her. They were almost eye-to-eye—her on the table and him looking as though he was about to examine her.

"Who were they?"

"I don't know."

"Did Strategic find anything?"

"Not yet."

His eyes dropped down to the bag next to her. When his nostrils flared, she placed it behind her in a lame attempt to keep the scent away from him. That was impossible under the circumstances, but she did it anyway. The feel of his hand as it pressed the bandage shot pain all over her body.

"That hurts," she said as he pulled away.

"I meant for it to hurt. What you did was dumb and dangerous."

"Yeah," she giggled, "that's what I was going for."

Jason stood up straight and she had to drop her head back to look him in the face.

"This isn't funny," he growled, but it was weak and filled with more pain than anger. "What were you doing there?"

Alex pushed him back—the pain of looking straight up was unbearable right now.

"I was meeting with someone about business."

"This business?"

"No."

"Then you shouldn't have been there," he replied. He

walked away then turned back to her from the door. "Get some rest. We'll talk more later."

Sebastian and Xavier appeared in the doorway as he disappeared.

"Take this," she said as she handed Xavier the bag. She took the sharps container, and turned it over so the needle dropped into her open hand. After she attached it to her shredded shirt inside the bag, Xavier closed it with a knot. "Wrap it up in a towel or something and don't let me forget you have it. When we get to Paris, I'll dispose of it."

He took the bag and left.

"You gonna be okay?" Sebastian asked.

Alex popped two painkillers and nodded. "Where's my room?"

Sebastian led the way from the medical bay and past a common area that divided the plane in half, where the rest of team watched a movie.

On this flying hotel, their bedrooms were on one side of the plane, along with a conference room slash office combo and a small kitchen. Jason's quarters were on the other side of the common area. Adam's private space was the closest to the cockpit upstairs. Adam's personal body-guards and Nikki had taken an earlier flight to prepare the hotel and meeting space.

They stopped at the last door in the hall. Sebastian pushed the cabin door open and allowed her entrance. Her bags were on the bed along with fresh clothes and a tray of food—a sandwich, fruit, and a bottle of water.

"Anything stronger than water on this crate?" she grinned at him.

He returned the smile as he backed away. "Be right back."

Alex moved slowly to the small bathroom. The shower was just big enough for her and she wondered how the guys fit if theirs were as small. She turned on the shower with a sigh. She hoped Adam's bandages were waterproof because she needed this shower. Bad.

Stripped from the dirty jeans and hoody, she stepped inside the stall and exhaled as the warm water hit her body. The bodywash smelled like cucumber and mint. She poured some on her head then into her hands. As the grime and blood disappeared down the tiny drain, so did her pain.

With her hair blow-dried and her body wrapped in the towel, she pushed the door open to find a bottle of tequila on the bed and seven shot glasses waiting to be filled. When she was dressed in a tank and track pants, she sat down and ate the sandwich and fruit. She'd share the tequila after she had time to think about what had happened back in Vegas.

The softness of the bed surprised her. For an airplane, it was pretty decked out, but then again, it should have been. As with everything she knew about the relationship between humans and vampires, when at all possible, they could share like good little neighbors. This massive beast was once an Air Force One. Impossible as it sounded to her, she had checked it out a couple of weeks ago and confirmed it.

Her eyelids became heavy as the mattress contoured itself to her body. She hardly felt any pain now. *That could be the painkillers,* she reminded herself. Going over everything in her mind from earlier, Alex's brain stopped the instant-replay of her and the bad guy when another movie took over.

The images came out of nowhere: the antique flood lights as they rolled past her line of sight, the busted up equipment she could see as clearly as she could see the man in front of her, the smell of dried blood as if it were right under her nose. But it wasn't her nose. And it wasn't her eyes seeing those things.

Someone else's eyes scanned the giant storage area. When they panned left to right, she recognized the two frats boys assigned to Cory Sims a few months ago. They were supposed to keep him safe while he acclimated back into "normal society." The doctor had high hopes for him.

He'd survived his first transition.

The dormant powers had begun to wake and he struggled at first. That's why he'd been placed in the hospital—to help with that transition. When he was released, two handlers were assigned to him. He believed them to be his best friends since fifth grade. In reality, Thomas Hall and Wesley Bradley were military police cadets on their very first assignment. And Cory Sims was a test tube hybrid released into the wild—the doctor's feeble attempt to create, in lab, what Alex was born as.

All of a sudden, she felt a needle at her neck, then the images were gone and she was sitting up in bed.

"What the hell?" she whispered to the empty room. Her eyes opened when she heard a knock on her door. "Come in."

Her new team filed in, one young face at a time. With very little space to accommodate them, Alex watched them settle around the room, and Sebastian took a seat next to her on the bed. Once the shot glasses were distributed and filled, she and Sebastian settled back against the head board.

"So," Xavier started the conversation. "What the hell happened out there?"

"We may have a third player," she replied, then they all emptied their glasses. "Someone doesn't like me very much."

"I don't suppose they introduced themselves first," Amy wheezed as Kai took the shot glasses and placed them on the small table by the door. "I mean, before they tried to kill you?"

"No, sorry," Alex smiled. "They wanted me to believe they were Romanian, but they weren't."

"How do you know for sure?" Erin jumped in.

"The speech was too proper," Alex replied, "too polished. We'll know more by the time we land in Paris for the night."

By now, the wound Adam had stitched felt tender, and the sharp pain was replaced by a dull throb when she moved. It was a good sign that she'd be her old self by morning. If anything kicked off during the stop in Paris, she'd be ready.

David cleared his throat and everyone focused on him. "Dr. Carlisle would like a vid-con once we're settled into the hotel. I called ahead and reserved a conference room."

Alex leaned forward at the waist to stretch a little. When she flexed her feet, she felt her back muscles try to resist. "Why does he want a face-to-face?"

David shook his head. "Just said to make sure we're all there."

"Then I guess we should get some sleep. It's gonna be a long day tomorrow," Sebastian yawned and stretched as he slid off the bed. The others filed out the door with a round of waves at her.

"Hey," she said before Sebastian closed the door. "I need you to do something for me."

"Sure," he agreed, but apprehension sat in his blue eyes as he waited.

She stood, turning her back to him. "Take that bandage off."

His fingers were cold as they peeled the extra sticky tape and bandage from her skin. A low whistle came from him then the feel of his cold fingers touching the stitches attached to her back.

"Damn," he muttered.

"How's it look though?"

"Not that bad considering," he replied. "Bleeding's stopped, and the skin looks like it's almost intact again. Maybe a couple more hours and you can lose the stitches."

He tried to replace the bandage, but she stopped him. "Leave it. I think that's slowing the process."

Sebastian eased the door closed and put his back to it as they stared at each other. Ever since she'd told the team her secret, he'd made a mental list of things he wanted to know. From the looks of the wound, her healing was almost equal to a pure blood vampire. And as he remembered from the fight in the bar, so was her strength.

"What's on your mind?" she asked.

"Why did you take this job?"

"The great pay." She grinned as she bounced the small bottled water between her hands.

"You don't need money," he replied then interrupted the next lie she was going to tell. "And don't say because of Matt, Ben, or even Coop, because you have enough resources to hunt for answers on the low."

"Why use my own money when Strategic can foot the bill?" she answered.

"Bullshit," he replied.

He watched her continue to bounce the water between her hands. She put the bottle down on the nightstand, finally, as she sat down on the bed. Sebastian slid to the floor and got comfortable.

"Someone let Tristan out," she stated. "Someone took Ben, killed Matt, and maybe Coop too. I should have been able to get something from Matt's blood, but I couldn't. The more I think about it, someone may have tampered with it. Why?"

"Keep us from finding the killers?" Sebastian replied. "Give Tristan more time to do whatever he's trying to do?"

"To bring us to Romania," Alex shook her head at him, "where almost every supernatural group in existence will be . . . in one place for the first time, ever."

"Why though?" he mused as he scratched at his leg. "They have to know this will be the most heavily guarded meeting on the planet."

"Maybe they don't care," she sighed. "Maybe it's not about anyone at the meeting."

A thought rolled around in her head—he could tell by the way she chewed on her bottom lip and stared into space.

"It has to be," Sebastian stated. "They tried to blow Jason up, remember?"

Alex shook her head again. She cracked open the water bottle and almost emptied it.

"No, his car blew up. He wasn't inside, and he didn't get hurt. Oren did."

"So they suck at explosives," he grinned. "David and Kai said the device was crude, amateurish." He cocked one knee up and laid his arm on it. "Or maybe that was meant for you."

"Nope," she answered. "No one could have known I'd be in that car with him. He was going to that meeting alone."

"Then Oren was the target," Sebastian felt a surge of excitement at the realization. "It was meant for Oren."

Alex grinned and nodded. "Oren was the target. So was Kit."

"And they're both dead now. So what's the link?" he asked.

"I'd say Jason, but he didn't have a link to Coop, so . . ." Alex replied before she emptied the bottle.

Sebastian stepped closer to Alex, dropped his voice to a whisper. "He kinda did."

"What?"

"This job," Sebastian offered. "This job's been our number one priority for months. So, in a sense, we're all connected to Jason."

"All except me," she answered. "How'd Jason even get my name?"

"From Coop," Sebastian replied.

Alex sat back down, stared at Sebastian for a few seconds. He wasn't sure what was about to happen, but she looked agitated.

"This thing between you and Erin," she said, "it stops now."

A quick flutter in his chest and his breath caught in his lungs. He thought they'd been so careful. Erin even bragged the other night about how maybe she wasn't as bright as everyone said she was.

"I . . ." he began then stopped when she gave him a don't-lie-to-me look. "It won't get in the way."

She leaned back into the pillows. "It stops now. This job

is our priority."

"I know that," he replied.

"Do you?" she sighed then sat up straight again. "These types of relationships between team members—it's not a good idea."

"Does that mean you, too?" Erin's voice came from the other side of the door. She opened the door without knocking. Alex and Sebastian turned their heads in her direction. She stood there with a look on her face that gave Sebastian the impression she was going to go head-to-head with Alex.

"Of course," Alex answered. "I don't lay down rules I don't follow myself."

Erin gave them a slight grin as she turned away, then turned back. "And what if we disagree?"

Alex stood slowly and Sebastian stepped back. When she was in Erin's personal space, fear spiked the air in the small cabin. "Then when we land, one or both of you get on a plane back to the States. And, honestly, I don't care which one of you goes."

"Yes, ma'am," she hummed.

"Good," Alex grinned at her. "I'm gonna go raid the pantry. When you're done, let me know what you've decided."

"We're in," Sebastian said as she pushed past Erin. "No problem, right Erin?"

"Right," Erin agreed, but Sebastian could see anger bruise her mocha skin with redness as she answered.

Alex took the bandage Sebastian still had in his hand, and they left her cabin together. She went in the opposite direction as Sebastian trailed behind Erin to the sleeping quarters.

"She's the boss, Erin," he said softly.

"Yeah," she replied as they continued to walk toward the rooms. "She's the boss. She calls the shots and we follow like good little soldiers."

He pulled her to a stop. "I'm staying on this assignment."

Erin stepped closer to Sebastian with a weird look in her eyes. When she brushed her hand across his crotch, a small giggle escaped from her mouth. He let her lick at his bottom lip until she bit it, hard.

"Shit," he hissed as he pushed her back. "What was that for?"

The taste of his own blood filled his mouth as he licked it away. Erin just stared at him with no real emotion. He'd grown used to her being distant and cold after intimacy, but he chalked it up to her past: strict parents who had her entire life planned out. They never showed her affection, according to her, anyway.

"One last bite," she giggled again, "for the road."

Erin didn't say anything else as they continued through the quiet plane. When he reached his cabin, he looked back to see her disappear through the door of the room she shared with Amy.

Xavier, head covered with a small pillow, was already asleep. On his own small bed, Sebastian fluffed the pillow under his head and decided Alex was right. He and Erin weren't really serious anyway. What was serious was their real mission—to find Coop, if he was still alive.

Their investigation of Jesse Cooper had started months ago. His alleged crimes? Treason, followed by espionage, money laundering, and a host of other things. Sebastian could hardly believe it. No one could. He had almost told Alex, but maybe now wasn't the best time. Maybe tomorrow. Maybe never.

From the laptop in her pack, a muffled ping reached her ears. Cross-legged in the center of the bed, she pulled the device onto her knees and opened it. A video call was queued in a secured program used by one person. Alex took several deep breaths, then tapped the icon she'd labeled "contracts" just in case. His face appeared illuminated by the computer screen. Everything behind him was in deep, deep shadow.

"How are you?" Leland smiled then put a crystal glass to his lips. When he moved the glass to spin the liquid around, its single ice cube plowed through the ripples before settling.

"Fine. Any news?"

"Bad news, I'm afraid. Another test subject has disappeared. Cory missed his appointment with Dr. Carlisle a couple of days ago. His parents reported him missing a few hours ago."

"So? Maybe he's out with the frat boys," Alex replied.

"The frat boys were the ones who told his parents he didn't show last night," Leland smirked.

Alex smirked back. "The frat boys are lying. And I'm halfway to Paris," she huffed. "On assignment. For you. I can't help you look for the body from here."

Leland scratched lightly at the side of his face as his eyes bore straight through her. A slim, mocha-colored hand placed a fresh drink in his line of sight and he gave the owner a nod.

"Why do you think they're lying?" he asked with an amused look on his face. "We've found no evidence of any foul play yet. Scorch just got to his apartment."

Scorch, one of the company's *cleaners*, could completely sanitize any situation in a matter of hours. If the target was already dead, he would make sure there was no DNA to be found, no fingerprints, not the slightest indication anyone ever existed. That included birth certificates, bank records, and employment files—even Social Security records. Everything, gone.

"Pick up the frat boys, and let the Professor have them," Alex grinned. "He'll get the truth."

Leland squirmed slightly in his comfortable looking chair. The Professor was the best interrogator Strategic had on the payroll. His methods may have been rather unorthodox, but he got the job done every time. After he took a long sip of the golden liquid in his glass, Leland looked at the camera again. "They're off the reservation. We have a team looking for them now."

"Where are you looking?" she asked.

"On campus, his apartment," Leland answered. "The boys said they waited all night at an off-campus bar for him, but he never showed. Where should we look now?"

"Try the old hanger at Groom Lake," Alex replied. She saw him pick up a small notepad. "Building number 370-8."

"That's awfully specific," Leland stated in the most bored way possible. "Almost like you were involved."

Alex just laughed and she could tell it irritated him.

"Dr. Carlisle has come up short identifying your attackers," Leland continued when he didn't get a reaction from her. "Lucky for you, the Mother says she didn't order a hit on you, so we're stumped."

She shook her head, more at the situation than his statement. How did they ever get anything done after she left?

"Well, color me surprised," she said with a fake yawn and stretch. "We're done, right?"

"Yes," he groaned. "Our futures may be going down the drain, but don't you worry your pretty little head one more minute!"

"I won't," Alex smiled as she straightened her numb legs. "When we get back, you can tell me how disappointed you are in me. And pretend I care what you think."

He disconnected, and Alex laughed so hard she felt a stitch pop loose. When she stood up, the thin silk thread lay on the bed. She picked it up, wrapped it in a tissue and placed it inside her pack. That would be burned as well, when they got to Paris.

Chapter 14

After the obligatory warning from Adam to keep his mind on business, Jason finished off two bottles of wine before he realized it wasn't helping. He still wanted to know what Alex was doing out there and who she was doing it with.

His shower didn't help much either. Stretched out on the bed, Jason absently went through his notes for tomorrow. In Paris, he was scheduled to meet with Adelaide and her daughter at their estate in the French countryside.

As the current leader of the clans in France, Adelaide wanted to add her two cents to the briefcase full of two cents from all over the world. Jason was in no mood, but he had no choice.

Adam briefed him fully on how to handle Adelaide. He told Jason to be patient, listen and nod. Basically, just smile pretty, let her have her say, and move on. Adelaide insisted on lunch at her estate. Her daughter was home and she wanted Jason to meet her.

Evangeline was pretty enough, Jason supposed as he tapped the screen to flip through the many images and articles on her notoriously shameless daughter. Her exploits were well documented all over Europe. One famous actor, singer, and politician after another.

Jason stopped when he finally recognized someone. Someone he'd met a few times but didn't really care for—Michael Gale, Conner's second son and Head of Security for Gale Enterprises. It didn't really surprise Jason that he and Evangeline had dated. They just looked odd together. And, with her draped over Michael like a cheap suit, they looked even more mismatched. Jason shook his head and closed the page on the device.

"I guess there's no accounting for taste," he said as he finished off the last bit of wine in his glass. The small knock would have gone unnoticed if not for that scent—strong and exciting—catching hold of his senses. Of all the things he would miss about Alex, her scent was the thing he'd miss the most. Had he known their last sexual encounter would be the end, he would have kept her in his bed longer.

"Am I interrupting anything?" Alex asked as she stepped inside and closed the door.

"Not at all," Jason replied. "Are you feeling better?"

He didn't rise from the bed and she didn't move from the door. A battle of wills had begun. Or so he hoped. Was she fighting an urge to climb into bed with him? What he fought was anger toward her about tonight. What better way to extinguish it than angry sex! But, with everything else that had happened tonight, she wouldn't offer herself to him ever again.

"Yeah," she nodded. "I'll be back to normal by the time we land."

"Good," he answered, before he went back to the tablet in his hand.

Every synapse in his brain was on high alert. The smell of her blood, the look on her face—all of it set his insides on fire. Not to mention her attire. Underneath the black cotton tank, he could see her breasts—nipples pressed against the fabric. As his eyes traveled down her bruised body, he noted that those long brown legs were covered by track pants, to his disappointment.

As casually as he could, he placed the tablet to the side. "Was there something else?"

When she cocked her head to the side, Jason grinned.

"I guess not," she replied. "I'll let you get back to work."

Jason nodded, "It's going to be a long day and I've got a

lot on my plate."

"Sure."

"You understand, right?"

"Of course," she replied as she backed away.

As the door silently opened Jason forced himself not to move. When she closed it without leaving, he turned, placed the tablet next to him, flipped the thin blanket from his legs, and held his hand out to her.

"Why did you come in here?" Jason almost whispered. "To torture me?"

Once she was next to the bed, he took her cold hand in his; it trembled slightly.

She replied as her grip on his hand tightened. "No. To tell you that you were right. I should have taken someone with me."

"Why didn't you?"

She sat down then picked up the dark tablet. Her fingers traveled back and forth across the glass screen as she stared at it instead of Jason. He placed his hand over hers to stop the motion.

"Why didn't you take someone with you," he repeated as his hand pressed hers down on the cold screen of the tablet.

"I didn't think I needed an escort for a simple meeting," she lied.

"Based on the way you looked when you got here," he sighed, took the tablet out of her hands and dropped it next to him in bed, "I'd say nothing about your life is simple. But you did win, so . . ."

"Tell that to the nine stitches in my back," she smirked at him.

"Are you okay?" Jason asked as his hand landed on her knee. His hand was warm for some reason. Maybe he'd just fed.

"I just spoke with Leland," she replied. "They've got nothing."

"On the guys that attacked you?" he answered. "I'm

surprised."

"I'm not."

"Listen, I owe you an apology. I should have told you about Nikki and I before we . . ."

"I'm a big girl, Jason," she said. "I should have known she was more than just an occasional lover. But now that I know she is much more than that to you, I have to respect that, you know."

An awkward silence fell between them as his hand took hers. Poor timing might be to blame, but Alex knew better. He was never meant for her.

"And that's what I like most about you," he sighed. "Maybe in the next life."

"Says the immortal vampire," she stated.

He chuckled then brushed his nose over the vein in her wrist as it pulsed. It throbbed to the rhythm of her heartbeat. Frustration scratched at her insides when she felt his soft warm mouth pull at the thin layer of skin over the vein. He was ready to tap that vein, then her, if she let him. But she'd just made a vow to stay focused on the job and to respect his new relationship status with Nikki. Now she cursed her own pride as she ran her fingers through his hair and pulled free of his grip.

"There's always room for someone like you among our ranks," he sighed as his head rose, and they were eye to eye. Somehow he understood that nothing else was going to happen between them—not ever again. She was glad she didn't have to say it out loud. His hands came up, suddenly, and pulled her face close to his.

Alex let him kiss her slowly and deeply, then he pulled away.

"What an immortal vampire you'd make," he whispered on her lips. "Just say the word and I'll make you one of us, make you mine forever."

Alex stood, as her index finger moved across his bottom lip slowly, then she stepped away from the bed. At the door, she turned to him.

"Thanks," she grinned, "I'm good."

He'd seen that look before—the orgasmic stare of a killer who enjoyed the work. Tons of faces with that exact expression whizzed through his mind. Since a dream woke him from a deep sleep around two in the morning, he tried to count the number of times he'd seen that look on a stranger's face or on his own.

As he counted them like sheep, Tristan found the memories excited him rather than lulled him to sleep. But no memory brought him more pleasure than his very last one. His last real memory of the past before the darkness took over and he awoke, unable to move, inside the lab. Chained and chemically bound, the doctor in charge spoke gibberish into a device that hung over his head.

"I can't wait to give him a taste of his own medicine," Tristan whispered to the breaking dawn outside his bedroom windows.

His new body was young and strong, but it would take more time to return to the level of near invincibility of his old one. After almost two thousand years, it should have been invincible. Giselle stressed the importance of recognizing his limitations with this new vessel. He hated limitations.

"This body was once human," Giselle had said over dinner a few hours ago. "You may as well get used to having to be more careful with it."

Now, as he flipped through the images on the electronic tablet she'd given him, he wondered what it would be like to go head-to-head with today's Alex Stone. In their first encounter, she was much younger.

The older Alex Stone didn't look much different, but she had honed her skills. He could tell. Even still, he should be strong enough to take her, shouldn't he?

Maybe I should listen to Giselle, he mused as he clicked play on the video footage. *Let the pawns do the hard work for now*. There was time, after all. Once she was worn down, weak from the constant obstacles he planned to put in her path, it would be easier to convince her to join his cause. He needed her, and she would find, by the end of the conference, that she needed him too. Or she'd be stupid enough to think she could fight her way to her own freedom and then he'd have to kill her.

His laugh echoed through the room. The entertainment from last night stirred in the bed a few feet away, then they were still again.

"You're better than before," he said to the screen. "So much better than anyone I could send after you."

With a tap of the glass, the video stopped midaction. He tapped the play button again and she dispatched her attacker with very little effort. She would have been able to take them both, he was certain of that. But his interest grew when he was told who her companion for the night was.

Michael Gale had all the earmarks of a savage killer as well, but he held back. *Good breeding can do that, make one soft,* he sighed with a shake of his head. Tristan made a mental note to learn all he could about the Gale family in this century.

As he remembered, Conner Gale had been a very different man during the crusades. Some say he hid his fortune in Rosslyn Chapel then created a mythology that still stands today.

As a Templar Knight, Conner was brave and ruthless and legendary. He showed no weakness or fear in the face of his enemies, and his son had displayed those same traits the other night.

"I wonder," Tristan sighed. "Would you die for her? Would Conner allow such a sacrifice for a human? Doubtful."

He dropped the tablet on the table when his bed partners stirred again. They had done well by bringing this video back to him. Within the mass of tangled bed sheets, his new playmates were wrapped around each other, exhausted and low on blood. Last night's escapades still lingered. Of course he won that test of wills, but they did try their hardest to keep up.

Youth was no advantage when engaged in sex with a vampire as old as Tristan, even in a new body, they discovered. Stamina was king in that game. As members of his medical team back at the facility, they were in awe of him and everything that he was. For their help with his rescue, he'd promised to turn them, but they had to prove their worth before that would happen. So far they'd done well, but there was more to come for them, unfortunately.

Tristan would have been satisfied to take his time with them, but they insisted on showing him what they could do. Not surprisingly, they were spent somewhere around the third hour. The young man was the first to concede defeat. Tristan drank his fill before he granted him mercy though. The young woman fared a little better, but not by much.

"Humans," he whispered as they tried to sit up. Like clumsy animals, they groaned and struggled to untangle themselves from the sheets and each other. Then the door to the bedroom swung open.

Fiona and another servant walked in with fresh coffee, toast, and juice. They sat the trays down on a small table in the center of the massive room, then waited for further instruction.

"Get them cleaned up and paid when they're done," Tristan stated absently. "Burn those sheets too, if you don't mind. I hate the smell of humans in the morning."

Fiona bowed as her helper hustled the humans from the bed and toward the food. The helper stripped the bed quickly, gathering everything up in his long arms before leaving the room without a word.

"I will make sure they are taken care of, Sire. Your shower is hot and running. Hurry, or you'll be late, young man."

Tristan nodded to her. He left the room feeling strange. Maybe he was still hungry? Tired? No, he decided. He grappled with a memory suddenly. When his head began to spin, he sat down against the wall to wait for it to pass. As the dizziness faded, images began to play behind his closed eyes like a movie. His first look at her—Alex Stone.

"Careful," he had said as she stared coldly at him. He grinned at her. She didn't return it. "Little girls should play with dolls . . . not monsters."

He could almost see the grin she held back. Something in the way she blinked gave him the distinct impression she'd been told she would win.

"This girl doesn't play with dolls or monsters," she had replied as her sinister grin emerged.

He remembered clearly that look of determination on her bloody, but still innocent looking face. Even in the golden glow of the torch-lit vault, Tristan admired her natural brown skin, made darker by the desert sun. He wondered what strange twist of fate brought a child to this place to capture a creature such as him.

At a time like that, usually a human's thoughts were erratic, confused. Some spoke to a deity of some kind; they prayed for mercy or strength or both. But not her. This little girl said no prayer—didn't ask for mercy. To Tristan's surprise, a tune had played in her head. At the time, he had no idea what it was, but later, in the lab of death, he heard it play over and over and over again.

"What is that song?" he had asked her.

At first she was confused, angry at his intrusion. "Get out of my head!"

When the sharp stab of pain shot through his right temple, Tristan was surprised at first. The tune stopped because she had pushed him from her mind. He took a step forward. She took two back.

"How did you do that?"

"Magic."

Tristan tried to remember what came next, but it slipped away like smoke through his fingers. The harder he tried to hold on to the memory, the further away it retreated. As much as he wanted to, he couldn't remember why Alex Stone was still alive after their encounter.

He needed to find the pieces of his faded memory. How could some be so clear and others too hazy to grasp? Why, of all his memories of that day, had the ones of Alex remained the most hazy and formless of them all?

Returning to his dimly-lit bedroom, he noticed a tiny red light blinking on the smartphone he had left on his nightstand. Giselle had explained that this light meant he'd either missed a call or a text. As he dropped his robe, he pressed the button to see which one.

It was a text from Coop's little fly on the wall. Take-off was successful and, besides Alex's little skirmish in the parking lot, uneventful. *So disappointing,* Tristan thought. He had hoped Alex would have been hurt too seriously for them to leave the country, but no such luck. Apparently, she was much tougher than she looked. His attempt to keep her on the ground had failed. Tristan tossed the phone on the bed then headed for the hot shower.

In the foggy stall, under the hot cascade of water, he reviewed the video in his mind. Her eyes sparkled at the sight of her own blood. She moved with the confidence of a seasoned killer. But something had given her pause, if only for a few seconds—a physical reaction to something other than being skipped across the gravel like a stone over the surface of a placid lake.

Refreshed from his shower, at the mirror he dried and styled his dark hair and brushed his perfect new teeth. Once dressed, his phone pinged in the breast pocket of his jacket on his way downstairs. This time there was a video message from the fly.

Fiona, his dutiful maid, placed a hot cup of coffee to his left and a vial of fresh blood to his right as he sat down at the table. When she placed the electronic tablet next to the cup, he brought it to life, tapped the screen, and found the video.

The mole sat in front of the computer screen in a pale

pink tank and matching panties. When she propped her foot on the chair, her mocha colored leg glowed in the light of the machine. Her stringy wet hair was slicked back from her face. Beautiful, young, and evil as the day was long, Erin Sinclair, a.k.a. the fly, took a deep breath and grinned at the camera.

"Whoever you are," she purred, "I hope your pockets are as deep as Coop says because this is gonna cost you."

Tristan took a sip of coffee then frowned at the taste. He'd forgotten to flavor it. As he poured a bit of the blood into the hot liquid, Erin continued.

"I have some interesting news," she said, caressing her wet thigh as she sat back in the chair. "It's about Alex Stone."

A number crawled along the bottom of the screen. Tristan laughed as he committed the bank account number to memory along with the price tag that followed it.

"It seems that Ms. Stone is still on the supplement," she grinned, "according to her fanboy Sebastian anyway." Erin exaggerated a yawn then smiled at the camera. "Or she could still be nuts."

"Silly little girl," he chuckled as he took another sip of coffee.

"So," she purred then dropped her leg down again, "if you want more info, you know what to do. Once the funds have been secured, I'll send you the information. Tell Coop I said hi."

A second after her demand, the video dissolved. He was sure there was no way to retrieve it for later.

"Should I pay her?" he questioned Fiona as she refreshed his coffee.

"For what?" she groaned. "The secondhand information or the show?"

Tristan laughed again, shook his head at Fiona's obvious disapproval. She was old school. In her day, women may have been much more discreet when it came to business, but he had never known Fiona to go to such lengths to get what she wanted from anyone.

Then again, today's technology makes the whole negotiating business more impersonal, doesn't it? You can make demands from miles away with the tap of a screen. Morals seem much more fluid now too. For the right price, a young woman, or man for that matter, will sit in front of a computer and do just about anything. They call it being free, unencumbered by the restrictions of society. Tristan called it a new form of slavery—technological slavery, but slavery nonetheless.

"I think she believes you to be like all men," Fiona continued. "Guided by the carnal and obscene. I hope you will not be swayed by a barely dressed girl making demands at a computer screen. I would hope you would stay focused on your goal."

"Well, I hope she's not lying about the information," he replied. "That's a lot of money for a lie. I would hate having to kill such a talented girl over that."

"That's not talent," Fiona huffed. "It's her feeble attempt at trying to play in the big leagues with the only real weapon she has."

"Do you understand what it means if Alex Stone is still on those pills?" Tristan posed the question even though he knew Fiona couldn't care less. "It would mean the good doctor was a success after all. It would mean she is the key."

"The key to what, exactly?" Fiona asked. "You don't even remember what happened in that tomb, Tristan. For all we know, this is all just lies dressed up as truth to give you a false sense of security. Forget about Alex Stone for now. Focus on rebuilding your clan first."

"If what this girl says is true, the only way for me to build a clan strong enough to take over is with Alex Stone at my side."

He heard the low growl come from Fiona, followed by a hint of anger in the air.

"A child like that cannot be trusted," she hissed as she dropped down into the chair across from him. Her blue eyes turned a muddy black as her anger grew. Her worn hands lay one on top of the other on the table.

"You may be underestimating her, Fiona," Tristan grinned. "I know you find her methods distasteful, but she has managed to keep her true mission hidden all this time."

As her short nails grew to fine long points, Tristan could smell her blood in the air. Now he knew it was her blood in the vial that flavored his coffee.

"And you may be letting something else override your better judgment," she quipped. "You were always prone to weaknesses of the flesh, but this is not the time for childish machinations. I taught you better than that."

Tristan took one more sip of coffee then pushed the cup away. As he savored the taste of coffee and her blood, he stared at the dark screen of the tablet on the table. Fiona had told him early on that humans will do anything to get what they want, which included sexual favors of any kind. Although he enjoyed human women from time to time, he much preferred his own kind.

He glanced up to see Fiona waiting patiently for his reply. No doubt, from his silence, she thought she'd put him in his place as if he was still a child. She was usually very agreeable, but, for some reason, this time was different. It couldn't be that she didn't like Erin or any human, for that matter. It was something much deeper, he imagined.

"You also taught me never to let anyone disrespect me or my authority," he said slowly, "including you. I know you love me, but don't ever forget your place again."

The long, razor points of her nails disappeared as she retracted them. After she wiped her bloody fingertips on a paper napkin, she balled it up in her trembling hand.

"Of course, Sire," she whispered with a slight bow of her head.

"If she has information I can use against Alex Stone, then the money will be worth it," he continued.

She gave him a quick nod then rose from her chair. As she passed him, she took his cup of cold coffee with her to the sink. Once she rinsed and dried the cup, she placed it in the cabinet over her head.

Behind him, she waited in silence. Tristan stood, buttoned his jacket, then picked up the tablet. When he stopped in front of Fiona, she straightened his tie with steady hands.

"Thank you," he said with a small kiss to her pale cheek. "I have plans for dinner, so don't wait up."

Fiona gave him another nod and kept pace with him as he made his way to the front door. He could still smell her anger. Fiona had never been afraid of him. When he was a boy, she was the one who had taught him to hunt. She taught him why it was important to choose his donors carefully. Her stories of when vampires ruled where his favorite at bedtime. His dreams were always wild from her tales of blood and victory. He admired her, to be honest.

His driver held the back door of the SUV open, eyes locked on Fiona for some reason. Tristan handed him the briefcase and the tablet, which he put on the backseat.

"I love you, Auntie," Tristan said when he turned back to her, "with all my heart. But if you ever speak to me that way again, I will kill you."

"Of course, nephew," she glared up at him with fire in her blue eyes. She looked as if she wanted to take his head—like any good predator would have under the same circumstances. "I would expect nothing less of you."

"Who do you belong to?" Dr. Carlisle whispered to himself. Standing between the two corpses, he felt tired and frustrated. "Better yet, who gave you my drug?"

After the autopsies, he'd save some tissue samples then burn the rest, he supposed. As he dropped a sheet over the face of one, he closed his notebook and turned off the recorder. The other could wait until after dinner. He'd had enough.

He discarded the soiled gloves and surgical gown in

the proper containers, then washed his hands in the nearby sink. If he didn't hurry, he'd be late for his meeting with Ivy. She'd flown in as soon as Alex left Vegas last night.

Her genuine concern for Alex's safety was sweet, but ultimately misplaced. Ivy had grown too fond of Alex over this assignment. He thought he should replace her, but it was far too late now. For now, she was the closest person to Alex and Dr. Carlisle had to leave her there. Soon, Ivy's involvement with Mason Creed and her real reason for being in Alex's life would come out. Then Alex would probably bury them together for their betrayal.

Now wasn't the time for regret. Dr. Carlisle took a quick shower and dressed. On his way out the door, Ivy's text asked where he was. "On my way," he answered as he hustled to his car and waved at the guards on his way off the base.

Coop tried to understand all the science shit Tristan rattled off to whoever was on the phone, but he was never interested in that kind of stuff. He didn't have to be. But he sometimes wished he'd paid more attention in chemistry class back in the day.

Tristan kept saying things about genetic markers and DNA strands, and how he was unique and worth more alive than dead. Coop lost interest after a while. The conversation went on almost the entire trip to the airport. His brain drifted between the plan and what came after. The plan was to eliminate the entire team, all but Alex and Erin that is. What came after was money beyond anything he'd earned in a lifetime of service to his country. And life eternal. That was really the point of all the backdoor deals, wasn't it? In the new world, vampires would be on top again. Now that he was a vampire, that included him.

The Council wouldn't know what hit them when Tristan said the word. All those loyal subjects Conner Gale thought he had would turn on him and his family at

Tristan's command. He could always choose to side with Tristan, but Coop knew that wouldn't happen. Conner was way too arrogant and comfortable at the top rung of the vampire elite. No way he would just hand over the reins to Tristan. Coop couldn't wait for that title fight.

"Everything will be inside the men's room on the ground floor. Any questions?" Tristan's voice interrupted Coop's musing.

"Not really, no."

"Oh come on," Tristan smiled at him. "I know you want to ask."

Coop turned slightly in the seat to look him in the eyes. He chose his words carefully.

"It's Alex you want. Why does everyone else have to die? They're good kids; great agents. They could be very useful to us once you take charge of the Council."

Tristan's smile sank into a savage grimace. The look in his eyes—soulless.

"They won't understand. And they won't betray their country or her, not now. You should have thought about that before you made the deal. You asked for the girl. I let you have her, but the others are expendable."

"What's so special about Alex?" Coop hummed. "So what? She can tolerate the supplements better than any other female—big deal. How does that help us?"

Tristan seemed to be contemplating the question. "I'm not sure yet. But she isn't just tolerating those supplements, she's thriving on them. Better than any one of you ever did! Don't be so shortsighted, Mr. Cooper. There's a much bigger picture here and she fits into it. I just have to find out how."

Coop grinned at him. It was not going to be as easy as Tristan seemed to think it would be to get Alex on their side. In fact, she wouldn't be on their side at all. Not without a very good reason to flip like that.

"I know Alex," he said to Tristan. "She likes this team now. If we take them, she'll come for them—I'm sure of it."

"How sure?" Tristan purred as he leaned close to Coop.

His icy smirk gave Coop the chills. "Sure enough to stake your own life on it?"

He shook his head. Every day since the day he was turned, Coop was grateful to Tristan for the gift. He'd just had his first taste of human blood a few days ago. Nothing could have prepared him for how it felt. The smell of his donor's fear was fantastic. The way that chemical reaction gave her blood a spicy after-bite—that taste was embedded in every fiber of his being: sweet, warm, and fresh. He wasn't ready to give that up just yet, if at all.

"I didn't think so," Tristan chuckled as he faced forward again.

"Had to at least try, didn't I?" Coop replied as he did the same.

Chapter 15

Not even the sun could make thirty degrees feel like fifty today. But Alex and her team would be nice and toasty in their next-gen uniforms.

In stark contrast to Jason's usual security team in dark suits and even darker expressions, their first official sighting with him would be in winter white, leather jackets and pants made from the new fabric, complemented by deep wine-colored, form-fitted crew neck shirts underneath.

As they crossed the tarmac at La Rochelle Airport, Jason and Adam were dead center flanked by the Tracker team. Adam and Jason's usual personal security walked a few feet behind, scanning the perimeter. When they reached the line of black SUVs, Alex held Jason and Adam back as each car was checked again, underneath and inside. They didn't need any surprises here—not after everything that had happened over the last few weeks.

The last-minute change from Paris to La Rochelle made her uneasy. Adam seemed a little on edge too. But Adelaide had business here the night before and stayed, so here they were. Good news—they wouldn't have to stay overnight after all.

"*Combien de temps a la maison* (how far to the house)?" she said to the driver.

He looked surprised that she spoke French. "*Environ sept milles* (about seven miles)." He opened the door and she nodded to Adam and Jason to get inside.

"*Merci.*"

With Sebastian and Xavier with Jason, she took the rest

of the team with her in the lead car. As they rolled away, she checked to make sure the com devices were working.

"You guys stay sharp," she said. The two-way devices made it possible for them to speak to each other as if they were standing together. "The change couldn't be helped, so the route wasn't checked properly."

"Got it," Xavier replied.

She wanted to relax, but that was not a good way to keep anyone alive. As the countryside rolled past, Alex reminded herself they had done this before too.

The trip to Adelaide's winery was picturesque to say the least. The whole place looked like a postcard. Spindly trees lined both sides of the road they traveled. In the distance, small farmhouses dotted the landscape. She could only imagine what this would be like in summer and full bloom.

The big white estate rose ahead of them. Adelaide Margot's winery was suspended in time, almost. If not for the satellite dish in the far pasture, it would have been perfect. Adelaide and her staff waited in the arched entryway as they pulled up to the main house. Alex's car stopped in the curve of the circular drive to put Jason in front of Adelaide.

"Once they're in the dining room, we'll walk the gardens, make sure it's clear," she said to everyone. They took a position around Jason and Adam as they greeted Adelaide.

"*Bienvenue chez moi* (welcome to my home)," she said as she looked around the entire group, not just at Jason and Adam. Alex thought that was really decent of her. Her daughter, on the other hand, stared directly at Jason.

"*Merci,*" he said to Adelaide before he kissed her hand. Then he turned his eyes to Evangeline. "And this must be the lovely Evangeline. *Belle de vous rencontrer* (lovely to meet you)."

She smiled seductively as his lips grazed her pale hand. Her anemic complexion gave this damp day even more reason to be depressing. Before her mother could, Evangeline took Jason's arm in her grip and pulled him to her. Adelaide rolled her eyes as Adam offered his arm to her.

"Please forgive my daughter," Alex heard her say. "She's influenced by this modern world. No respect for tradition."

Alex wasn't really sure what that meant, but if that was her mother's way of calling her daughter a spoiled bitch, Alex had to agree.

They followed their hostess inside—Jason's old team spread out and covered the entrance and front door. Alex and her team would stay close to Jason and Adam. Two guards would remain in the dining room while the Trackers checked the gardens with Adam's security.

"Wow," Amy sighed as they entered the grand accommodations. "That's a Pollock," she gushed as she pointed to a canvas covered in dull blobs of paint to their right.

Original artwork hung on every wall. Glass and ceramic vases stuffed with fresh flowers sat on every ornately decorated table. Down a long hallway, at the very end, big wooden doors swung open, held by men in black jackets and white gloves. All at once, the smell of food and flowers mixed.

The team took it all in as they were led into the dining room by Evangeline and Jason. They observed every corner, every closed door. At first, Alex thought they were just overwhelmed by all the opulence, but they were on the job.

To her surprise, they were doing what they had been trained to do: checking doors to make sure they were locked; Kai marked the exits with his eyes; Sebastian checked dark hallways like a pro; and Xavier counted the number of windows they passed, she could tell. Amy had even managed to put herself between the couples to keep close to Jason. David had done the same with Adam. Erin and Alex brought up the rear.

With a reputation like theirs, she shouldn't have been surprised, but Alex had trust issues—especially when it came to this program. Her father had lied to her about so many things. He could have easily lied about this team as well. They could get into some scrap on the other side of the Atlantic and freeze up—then people would die. She wasn't too keen on getting killed anytime soon. As luck would have it, they were better than she gave them credit for.

"Don't look so surprised," she heard Erin whisper as she used a handheld scanner that could detect listening devices. "We do know what we're doing."

They entered something akin to a ballroom. A big round table was set in the center of the room, ready for the visitors.

"Please, everyone, sit," Adelaide said as Adam held her chair. "We don't want lunch to get cold."

Jason and Evangeline sat, as did Adam. There were seven more places set and Alex wondered who else was expected. Then Adelaide stood again and addressed her directly. "Ms. Stone, please," she smiled. "I'm sure your team is hungry."

"We're working, Madame," she answered. "We'll eat back on the plane."

"Nonsense," Adelaide frowned. "We are safe here. You have my word." She waved her hands at the empty places again. The look on her face and Jason's told Alex she was not going to take no for an answer. And Jason would not be embarrassed by her refusal either.

Alex nodded and they were all seated. The only place left for her to sit was the next to Adelaide. She got the feeling that was intentional.

"Now," Adelaide smiled again, "lunch is served."

The team couldn't drink on duty, even if the wine was Adelaide's pride and joy. She understood and had two cases of it loaded into one of the trucks; for the flight, she said.

Lunch went at a leisurely pace—too leisurely for Alex. Her senses were on edge, and she wanted to get outside and look over the grounds, since they had another couple of hours to spend here.

Alex wiped her mouth and placed the linen napkin on

the table. The others followed her lead.

She cleared her throat politely, "Madame, thank you for the wonderful hospitality, but we have to get back to work." She stood and so did the team. "I'm sure you have a lot to discuss with Mr. Stavros."

"I do, and thank you for being so polite," Adelaide answered.

Alex nodded and the team also thanked their hostess before following Alex toward the big French doors that led from the dining room to the gardens. When they were outside with the doors closed, Alex moved further away from the house without a word. At the giant fountain with a horse and rider in the center, she stopped and faced the team.

"I want every structure checked and cleared," she said. "She's planning on giving them a tour of the gardens after they're done. You have fifteen minutes."

They spread out in pairs to carry out her instructions. Alex took a seat on the fountain and tried to figure out what she was feeling. Her eyes traveled up the ivy-covered walls and went from drape covered window to drape covered window.

There were men posted on the three terraces that faced the garden. Each acknowledged her presence with a slight nod. The jumpy feeling wasn't because of them. When she stood, they all turned their attention to her. As she walked around the space, corner to corner, they watched her closely. Her hand was on the gun inside her jacket, and so were theirs.

"So much for trust," she mumbled.

"We won't ask you to report any personal holdings, Madame," Jason said as he sipped his tea; Evangeline was glued to her phone. "Just those that belong to your clan as a whole."

"Good," Adelaide sighed in relief. "This winery has

been in my family for six centuries; I was a small child when my father inherited it. I could not bear to have this taken from me."

"It won't be," Adam assured her with a pat to her hand. "We will be as honest with them as we can without compromising ourselves or you."

"Haven't you already compromised yourselves in a sense?" Adelaide replied.

"What do you mean?" Jason answered innocently.

"The human protection you have with you," she stated with a tilt of her head. "What's wrong with our own people?"

"Their government insisted," Adam hummed. "I'm sure you've heard of the problems we had back home recently. They're here to track that threat, that's all."

Adelaide nodded, but she seemed unconvinced to Jason. "Can they be trusted?"

"Absolutely," Jason smiled at Adelaide. "I trust them with my life."

"So, Jason," Evangeline finally joined in, "are you sleeping with her or not?"

Jason smiled at her. The look on her face was that of a bored child. Her pale, little fist propped up her small head as she stared at the smartphone in her hand.

"Sleeping with whom?" he replied. He already knew the answer though.

Word of their relationship had been placed, strategically, around both the main stream social media and the 'dark' web. Jasper now used that information to call attention to conspiracy theories and sinister plots that would compromise the integrity of the vampire community as a whole.

"That woman," she replied, still glued to her phone. "Jasper says it was all just bullshit to keep everyone busy while our leaders sell us out."

Jasper Jake had eyes everywhere. If he hadn't had the scoop on something in the last twenty years, Jason couldn't think of it right now.

“Jasper’s a busybody,” Adelaide sniffed then took a sip of wine. “I can’t believe young people still listen to him.”

Evangeline rolled her eyes then dropped her phone on the table. “Everyone listens to him Mother. He’s never wrong.”

“He’s wrong this time,” Jason hummed. “We’re not selling out. We are forging new alliances.”

When Evangeline smirked at him, he laughed. “Alliances? Is that what it’s called these days?” she asked.

Jason just laughed and shook his head at her. “We’re friends.”

“Is that what you tell Nikki?” she grinned.

“Evangeline,” Adelaide huffed. “*Ne soyez paz impoli!* (Don’t be rude!)”

“It’s quite alright,” Jason laughed as he wiped his mouth politely. “You shouldn’t believe everything you read on Jasper’s grapevine. And he has been wrong once or twice.”

“Maybe, but he says this meeting is more than just a friendly sit down between our kind,” she sighed as the picked up her phone again. Her long fingers zipped over the screen, then she read the post in a dramatic way: “*The big shots are gathering in the old country soon. What do you think they are doing? Selling out to the mortal world or about to take it over?*” She looked up at Jason and her mother. “Which is it, Jason?”

“The world is changing; we have to change with it,” he stated plainly. “Adapt or die.”

“I like our world the way it is,” Evangeline sniffed. “In case anyone cares.”

“I care, and I appreciate your honesty,” Jason replied. “So what do you think I should say then?”

“About what?”

“Whether or not we should make our existence known to the world at large?”

He saw her expression turn cold, then she shook her head at him. “Don’t.”

"Why?"

"Because we don't belong in their world and they don't belong in ours. What's wrong with the way things are?"

Jason thought that was a fair enough question. What was wrong with the current state of affairs, really? Adam cleared his throat and joined the conversation. He'd been so quiet that Jason had forgotten he was even in the room.

"They are becoming more aware of our presence. It's getting harder to keep our existence a secret."

"Then their government should figure out a way to explain us away," she frowned, "as they always have."

"Or," Adelaide interjected, "no more nightclubs and restaurants posing as places for humans to pretend to be like us—*ridicules!*"

"Oh Mother, please," Evangeline sighed. "They are legitimate businesses."

"They are lures," she sighed back. "The Council allows some to exist because they are a steady stream of income, but to be honest, the rest are just hunting grounds. If we do not get rid of them soon, the humans will use that against us in any negotiation."

Jason could see the amused look on Adam's face. He found her statements, though true, to be naïve. The human government received healthy returns on those establishments as well. He wasn't quite sure how they explained them to Congress, but income disguised as taxes and other subsidies were a welcomed boost in that economy.

"Evangeline has a point, Madame," Jason stated. "If the humans can't control their own then they're fair game. We've made quite a few concessions ourselves by keeping our numbers in check. We don't hunt indiscriminately," he grinned. "At least not always." He winked at Evangeline and she winked back. "We've held up our end. It's time they did the same."

"We'll offer up some of the enterprises that have fallen out of favor, Adelaide," Adam interrupted with a glance at Jason. "The Council provided us a list that should make everyone happy."

"I should hope so," she replied then emptied her wine glass. "*Nous ne sommes pas les monstres, qu'ils veulent que nose soyons—pas plus* (we are not the monsters they wish us to be—not anymore)."

Adam gave her hand a pat again. "*Absolument pas, Madame* (absolutely not, Madame)."

Jason stood, rounded the table, and helped Adelaide with her chair. "You promised me a tour of your gardens and winery," he smiled as he placed her arm through his. "I'm sure my team has had time enough to assure themselves that I am safe."

Adelaide smiled at him with a shake of her head. "I'm sure."

Adam and Evangeline followed as they strolled through the open doorway that led to the gardens. Jason wanted to ease her fears, and what better way than a leisurely walk down to the winery? He let her talk of random things that had nothing to do with the meeting tomorrow night.

As they made their way down the stone path, Alex and her team followed but not too closely. She seemed on edge, but Jason didn't have time to wonder why. It was her job to keep him safe and he had to trust that she would. For now, Adelaide's dulcet tones were a welcomed change from the "do it or else" tone he seemed to get from everyone else.

When they reached the main building, everyone felt more relaxed. Jason didn't feel the prickly vibrations of frustration in the air around him, not even from Alex. What he felt was relief. Alex was confident of their safety. Adam was confident in Jason's ability to put even the most hardcore detractors in their place. Adelaide was finally on his side. Evangeline wanted to be in his bed, but that was not on his agenda—at all. As seductive as she was, she was missing one component Jason found himself most attracted to in both Nikki and Alex.

Evangeline, heir to her mother's fortune and possibly her seat on the Council one day, would always have to answer for her actions. As a pure blood and an only child, she would always be Adelaide's daughter. And she would be expected to keep her bloodline clean. No humans and no turned vampires, period.

Alex was not bound to anyone for her actions. Sure, Nikki and Jason had a different set of rules to adhere to, but they decided what happened in their personal lives. Jason didn't demand that he be Nikki's only lover, nor did she demand that of him. But she was loyal to him when it counted and that meant a lot to Jason. The fact of the matter was he *did* love her, in his own way.

He pretended that was the reason he agreed to marry her. In the back of his mind, he knew a marriage to her was beneficial to his upward mobility. Nikki was held in great esteem by quite a number of higher-ranking Council members, which included Adam and Conner Gale.

Nikki tirelessly campaigned on his behalf for this seat. And he won. Soon, once he reached a certain level, he could bring about more meaningful changes for the turned and introduce initiatives that would push all of them forward in ways the Council probably never even imagined. No one would doubt his word again.

He mulled that over as Adelaide described her family history in detail. Boring stuff, but if it kept her happy for another few minutes, he could sit through the history class for a little longer.

Chapter 16

"We could take them now," the jittery blood junkie whispered behind him.

Coop turned toward him and grinned. "It's not time yet. Relax."

He peered at his old team and Alex through the binoculars because his vision was still slightly off. He was already stronger and faster than before. Those pills had messed him up though. Maybe that was the reason his power spiked then ebbed at the weirdest times. He needed to purge himself of their effects. With Tristan's blood, he would eventually. With every new day came a stronger sense of what he had become: not just a vampire, but a vampire made by a pure blood. That made him a member of a small minority.

"What are we waiting for, Coop?" the junkie whined as he scratched at his arm. "We can take them out and snatch up that bitch right now!"

"Really," Coop sighed. "The only person that's gonna get taken out is you, idiot!" When Alex moved closer to the perimeter, he pulled his companion out of her line of sight. They were far enough away and downwind, so she couldn't catch the scent.

"He said we were going to destroy them," the junkie continued. "I don't understand."

"Of course you don't," Coop said as he eased up and peered over the rise. They had moved back down the path toward the main house. Alex was bringing up the rear alone. "No one expects you to be smart, blood bag. So shut up and let me do all the thinking, okay?"

Back at the main house, Alex instructed the others to wait outside. Jason and Adelaide chatted quietly as she walked the edge of the room until they finished.

The blues and browns of an oil painting caught her attention right away. It was an original Romare Bearden, *Jazz Group*.

"It's lovely, isn't it?" she heard Adelaide chirp. "Romare was so talented. I miss him."

Alex turned and smiled at her. "You knew him?"

Adelaide laughed as she crossed the room toward her. "Oh yes! We were great friends, he and I."

"Was he a vampire?" Alex asked with the hope that she would say no; she did.

She'd met a few famous people, but no one she ever admired, like Bearden. His paintings and writings depicted life in Harlem during the early part of the twentieth century. Bold pictures of bold black people as they went about life in America. Alex wondered if he ever thought to write about someone like her—a bold black woman who fought monsters. If he had, he probably would have been the laughingstock of the Harlem Renaissance—a crazy artist that had sniffed too much paint.

If she had lived back then, she would have been invisible to them anyway. She'd have been just a girl in the background, unless the darkness came looking for them. Then they would believe in their own mortality and in her.

As they faced the painting again, Adelaide dabbed at the corner of her eyes with a crisp, white handkerchief. As she talked about her time with him, Alex could tell there was love there, platonic or maybe more.

"The others are on loan in the States," Adelaide concluded with a pat to Alex's shoulder.

Adelaide went back to Jason and Alex continued her patrol of the room. At the grand piano, she stopped again, but this time for a very different picture—a more recent photo of three people. Sandwiched between a happy Adelaide and a bored Evangeline was Michael Dean. She picked up the antique silver frame and interrupted the final goodbyes.

"Madame," Alex cleared her throat. "Who is this young man with you and your daughter?"

Adelaide took the photo and smiled. "Old boyfriend of Evangeline's. One of the better ones, in my opinion." She shook her head then placed the photo on the small table as they left the room.

As they walked down the hallway toward the exit, Adelaide continued to talk about Michael—how successful he was, how handsome and brilliant, and how it was such a shame her daughter couldn't stand not being the center of attention when they were together.

"But," Adelaide shrugged as the doors opened and a cold breeze sailed inside, "that's the price you pay when you date a Gale."

Alex stopped short and Jason almost ran into her.

"Gale," she hummed as she opened the door for Jason and practically pushed him inside the car. "As in Gale Enterprises?"

"Yes, he's Conner Gale's second son," she said absently. "Michael is lead counsel for his family, Gale Enterprises, and the Council when needed."

"Really?" Alex responded. She stepped up to Adelaide and into her open arms. A kiss to each cheek, then Adelaide looked her in the eyes.

"Yes," Adelaide continued. "There are six of them. Every available woman in our world is trying to wrangle an invite to the Ball this year. I had hoped Evangeline would have apologized for her behavior, but she is stubborn. I'm sure he's already asked someone else by now."

Alex just nodded and waved as she entered the car and the caravan drove off.

She wanted to be mad, but it was kind of late for that.

If he had been sent to spy on her, he was bad at it. She hadn't told him anything he could use, or maybe that was part of some game. But he had helped her in that parking lot that night.

Michael's lies would have to wait until she returned to the States. Right now, all her attention was on the wellbeing and protection of Jason Stavros. Nothing else mattered.

The plane was quiet at last. After dinner and the impromptu wine tasting, Alex took her team to the back conference room for a debriefing before they arrived in Romania. Adam stretched out in the common area with his laptop and jazz music. That left Jason alone in his quarters.

He tried to bring himself to read the gazillion emails in his inbox, but that just bored him. Everyone pretty much sent the same message: "we may be few, but we are stronger than the human race."

"Yeah, I know," Jason mumbled to no one. When the screen went dark, he laid the tablet on the nightstand with a sigh.

On his back in the soft bed, his eyes closed and his thoughts spiraled until he focused on just one idea—winning. He would win the delegates over to their side. He knew that for sure. But the Wolf Pack would not be in attendance, which disappointed him.

Jason had heard stories about Roland Wolfe over the years. Adam described him as a fair leader—strong and honorable. It surprised him that Adam would speak of a werewolf in such glowing terms, but, then again, he was no ordinary lycanthrope, was he?

He shook his head hard. Why was he even on the subject of the Pack? He had enough problems as it was.

In Romania was a woman he'd known for over seventy-five years. In the very near future, she would be his wife. That meant the other woman in his life would no longer be in his life. Somehow he couldn't see Alex Stone being anyone's mistress, not even his.

A low ping came from the tablet he'd laid aside. He tapped the screen to see a video call in queue. When he snatched up the bigger laptop with one hand, he smoothed down his hair with the other.

"Conner," Jason smiled nervously at his image on screen. "I wasn't expecting you to call. Is something wrong?"

"Not at all," Conner smiled back. He was relaxed and cordial. "I just got off the phone with Addie. She was very impressed with you."

Addie or Adelaide, as Jason would forever refer to her, had wasted no time in reporting back to Conner. He had hoped he'd made a positive impression on her and now he knew for sure.

"I'm glad," Jason replied. "I think I was able to put her fears to rest regarding the winery and vineyard. You were right, Sire. Her fear of losing her family holdings was keeping her from getting on board with our plans."

"Well, she will meet with her clan immediately," Conner continued to smile. "We have their vote."

With Adelaide on board, Conner now had the votes he needed in the High Chamber. One of the issues on the agenda for the next meeting of the Council of Pure Blood Vampires was a new chamber location. The Council had purchased land and an old resort in upstate New York. It was decided they would move the chamber out of the city. It had become too dangerous, too many human issues. The blood farms ran smoothly in New York City anyway. The supply of fresh human blood would last well into the next century. It was like that in almost every major city. The ones that needed more attention were on the Council's agenda for the next meeting as well.

The biggest issue on the ballot was one Conner and the three other heads of the Council had been deadlocked on for a whole year—what to do once Tristan was captured. The humans thought they would get him back, but that was not going to happen, not if Conner had anything to say about it. Jason was sure he had lots to say about the subject. Adam sure did.

Jason felt his confidence grow. "I'm glad to hear it."

"I had a chance to read over your opening statement as well," he said as he held up a tablet. "Are you sure you want to do this?"

"I like to grab an audience's attention right away," Jason boasted.

"I think you'll do just that," Conner agreed.

"If you feel announcing a possible traitor will hinder the investigation," Jason sighed, "I can change whatever you'd like."

He continued to smile. "I wouldn't change a word."

"Thank you, Sire."

Conner's happy demeanor turned somber all of a sudden. He straightened his posture and dropped his voice down an octave.

"She also mentioned Ms. Stone."

Jason stayed still. He concentrated all of his efforts on a straight face and cool demeanor. "She absolutely loved Ms. Stone."

Conner let a small grin spread across his lips. "Yes, she said that."

Jason reacted the way he should have at the insinuation that Alex may have done something to embarrass them. He didn't try to explain something that went unsaid. He didn't apologize before he knew what Conner was going to say. Conner was impressed.

"But Adelaide did seem a little uncomfortable for some reason," Jason added.

"Addie calls that intuition. She picked up on your interest in Alex," Conner continued. "I thought we discussed this before you left."

A nervous grin emerged on Jason's lips. "You told me to be careful with Alex, and I have been."

"Addie is a romantic, Jason," he sighed. He smirked as

he continued, "And don't play word games with me."

"Sire," Jason cleared his throat, "I didn't ignore your advice. I am being careful around her," he stressed *around* as Conner had said that night.

They laughed and Conner gave him a knowing nod. Jason found it easy to talk to him about Alex for some reason. More so than with Adam. Maybe it was because Adam didn't like Alex—hated her would be more accurate, actually.

Conner sighed, "Nicole is devoted to you and your plans to rise in this world. Don't jeopardize that for a human. Not even one as lovely as Alex Stone."

"Well," he sighed, "since the announcement, you won't have to worry about Alex and I being involved. We are just friends."

"Good," Conner smiled again. "Your life is about to change in every way. Whatever your understanding is with Nicole, you can't hold onto everything. We all have secrets, but Alex is not one that would stay that way for long."

Jason gave him a slight nod, but Conner could see the disappointment wash over his face. Conner dismissed him with a kind "goodnight."

Once he ended the call with Jason, Conner stood and stretched before he left his home office for the night.

As he turned the corner, Michael, Raph, and Sean came through the front door of the penthouse, all smiles.

"Welcome home," Conner said with a hug for each of his sons. "You look no worse for wear," he said to Michael as he went for the couch. He pulled his feet from his wingtips then plopped them on the oversized ottoman with a hard sigh.

"I'll live," he replied with a tired expression. "The Mother says hello, by the way."

"You should have seen him when we first picked him up," Raph chuckled. "I thought we were going to have to call ahead for an ambulance."

They all laughed when Michael shot the finger at Raph.

"Well, I'm glad that wasn't necessary," Conner stated, taking a seat next to Michael on the couch. He gave his leg a pat and Michael nodded that he was okay. "Thank you for making that little detour for me. I would have called to give our condolences for their loss, but I thought a more personal touch was needed." Raph and Sean nodded as they sat down in vacant chairs on each side of the couch. "So, tell me all the gory details."

"There's not that much to tell," Michael answered. "She was poisoned with some kind of rare toxin. The lab still hasn't been able to identify its origins. Fallon has made sure the case will be closed on her end with no further tie to Alex Stone."

"I meant about the attack," Conner grinned then tapped Michael on the chin playfully.

He sank down onto the soft cushions. "We exchanged a few pleasantries, then one of them took a swing at Alex."

"And a bat to you," Sean replied.

"Who do you think sent them?" Raph asked the group. "They didn't just decide they didn't like Michael's shirt. They were out there for a reason."

"Someone who knew you'd be there," Conner replied.

"I didn't even know where I wanted to go until I got to Vegas," Michael sighed with a shake of his head. "And I didn't tell anyone. I picked her up at Jason's casino and it just popped in my head."

"Then they followed you to her or followed you both to that place," Sean said.

Conner mused over that for a few seconds, then he sat forward. "Find out who they belong to and why they went after your brother and Alex Stone."

Raph and Sean stood and left the penthouse, each placed a mobile to their ear as the door closed with a small sound.

Conner scooted to the corner of the couch and turned

to Michael, whose closed eyes were surrounded by his still and pale face. "You need to feed."

"Later," Michael replied with a shake of his head, not even opening his eyes, but Conner was already at the bar with a black mug in front of him.

The thick, dark blood poured smoothly and silently. He placed it in the small microwave and 30 seconds later, it was on the table in front of his son.

"Drink."

Michael moved slower than usual which meant he hadn't fed enough. Externally, he looked fine, but internally, his body needed more time and blood. With the mug to his lips, Michael closed his eyes and emptied the contents in a few swallows.

"Thanks," he whispered. "I guess I needed that."

"So," Conner stated as he took the mug back to the bar and made another warm drink for Michael. "What's on your mind?"

"Why do you ask?" Michael replied.

"What happened out there?"

Michael sat back again with the mug cradled in his hands. Conner sat down in the chair and waited for him to begin.

"She's—" he paused and took a drink. "There's something different about her, Con. And not just that she fights like she's got nothing to lose."

"Meaning?"

Michael took another sip then put the mug down.

"She went all out on that guy. He didn't stand a chance against her."

Conner placed his elbows on his knees and stared at Michael. "That's not unusual, Michael. You read the report on the project and its participants. The soldiers on the supplement are practically invincible."

"That was not just being stronger or faster, Con," Michael harped. "I've only seen skills like that on people who have had hundreds of years to hone them—people like us."

Conner sat back again and shook his head. He'd hoped that Michael would have chalked up her abilities to her opponent not being as highly trained as she. But how could he deny what his son had seen with his own eyes? His fears were now confirmed.

"And you're sure it wasn't that her opponent wasn't that good?"

Michael laughed at him. "He was good enough. She was just way better."

"Well, maybe Dr. Carlisle was not as forthcoming as he should have been regarding what those pills actually do for the humans who take them," Conner offered.

Michael looked at his father then finished what was left of the blood before it got cold.

"I think we need to have another talk with the good doctor when they return from Romania," he said as he stood and stretched. "If those guys were dosed with the same formula then Alex should have had a harder time kicking that guy's ass. We should have tried harder to get that formula from him when we bought the company."

Conner stood as well and Michael followed him to the kitchen. As he washed the mug, then dried and put it away, Michael seemed deep in thought. Was it time to tell them about his suspicions or should he wait until they had a chance to meet with Dr. Carlisle?

"I've known Jon a long time," Conner said as he turned to Michael. "He's very shrewd and very protective of his work and his soldiers. He knew one day he would have to give up the company, but he never planned on giving up that formula. He had his government right where he wanted them. Soldiers, even his superpowered ones, can die in combat. His formula will always belong to him and he'll never let it go."

Conner put a long arm around Michael's shoulders as they exited the kitchen and took the stairs together. As they made their way down the hall, Michael sighed again.

"He could be leaving himself open to a threat not even his soldiers may be able to rescue him from," Michael yawned.

Conner nodded. "He could."

"Then why risk it? We could make him an insanely rich man if he were willing to sell."

They stopped at the door to Michael's old room. Conner pushed the door open and patted Michael's shoulder. Michael's room was just as he'd left it.

"I don't think money is a factor here," Conner lied. "I think it's more an ego thing. Right now, he has the most powerful human beings on the planet to protect him from just about any threat. That kind of makes him God. Who would give that up?"

Michael didn't reply. He just nodded and then said goodnight to his father. The door closed as Conner opened Drew's across the hall. He was asleep; his big red headphones were still on his head. Conner slipped inside and pulled them off gently. He turned off the music, then placed the device on the nightstand and turned off the lamp.

He watched Drew for a few minutes before he closed the door. Inside his own bedroom, he sat down on the bed and pulled his fingers through his hair. That always helped him think. Tonight, he had a lot to consider.

The future of his kind was at the top of that list. Then came the possible existence of a female hybrid—one that seemed more powerful than the last one he encountered 600 years ago, the one he had killed because she existed and could reproduce with the pure. Once Tristan remembered what she was, he would stop at nothing to make her his.

Chapter 17

"We use call signs from here on out," they heard Alex say. "So get used to them."

When she got a text that Jason was ready to leave for the meeting, she stood, and her team followed. As she adjusted her earpiece, it crackled, then the ambient noise settled in her head. It felt weird to have a gun strapped to her body again, but, somehow, she thought she missed that feeling.

Xavier and Kai headed outside to check the SUVs one last time. David and Erin double-checked the wireless access to all communication and tracking devices. One device was embedded in the jackets they wore. It not only fed GPS coordinates to the main tablet but vital signs too. Amy and Sebastian waited with Alex next to the bank of elevators. Jason would be down any minute.

"Casino on the way down," she said when a new text came through.

"Shooter and Linchpin ready at transport," Xavier stated. She could hear Kai's laugh cut through the announcement.

"I'm gonna kill you, Linchpin," she tried not to laugh but did anyway. "Get serious."

"Sorry, Nest," he snickered. "I'm good now."

Everyone laughed, then the elevator doors slid open with a weak gust of trapped wind. With Adam in the lead, Jason came into view dressed in an Italian wool suit, brown leather boots, and a gorgeous smile. He didn't look nervous at all.

Amy quickly moved to his right and Alex to his left while Sebastian brought up the rear of the group.

"Casino on the way out," Alex said.

"We're ready," Xavier answered.

"Casino," Jason chuckled. "That's original."

"I ran out of ideas," Alex smiled at her phone. "Sorry."

A sharp blast of cold air hit them as the main doors opened wide. Today, even with the sun playing hide-and-go-seek in the clouds, winter in Romania was full steam ahead. Later, the forecast called for light snow. Three black SUVs waited as exhaust puffed from their tailpipes. The driver of the middle vehicle held the back door open.

"Amy, Erin, Kai, and Sebastian are with you," she told Jason as he tossed his briefcase inside. "We'll be right behind you."

Jason stepped close, his right shoulder butted up to hers. "I was hoping we could talk."

"Maybe later, Mr. Stavros," she answered. "Right now, we have a schedule to keep. Get in."

She didn't wait for him to say another word. A gentle nudge toward the truck and she heard him sigh as he climbed inside, Amy on one side, Erin the other. Sebastian took the wheel and Kai was shotgun.

When she turned, Adam had already situated himself in the last truck. David pecked away on his tablet in the front passenger seat and Xavier tapped on the steering wheel as they waited for her. Alex shook her head and climbed in back behind Xavier.

A huge silence settled over the entire group inside the SUV. Normally, it wouldn't have bothered her. The less said the better, but for some reason Adam's hum touched her skin like sandpaper.

It was the hum of his life-force and it was awfully strong this morning. Maybe because they were mere inches from each other. Or maybe he'd just fed before they came down. Whatever the reason, they couldn't get to their destination fast enough for Alex.

"So are you excited?" Adam said out of nowhere. It startled all of them.

"It's just a job," Alex replied. "I've done lots of these."

Adam chuckled as his meaty finger tapped the screen of his tablet. "I meant the party tonight."

"Oh, sure," Alex answered as she checked her phone again.

"As I understand it, Esmeralda and Morgan are your oldest friends. I would think you'd be happy to at least see them, wouldn't you?"

Alex cut him a sideways glance. His eyes stayed glued to the tablet.

"I am, but that's not the priority right now," she replied.

"Good," Adam actually smiled, put the tablet away, and turned slightly in the seat to look at her. "I was hoping you'd say that. To be honest, I didn't have much confidence in your ability to focus on the job. I've always found humans to be easily distracted." He turned forward again.

Xavier's eyes, reflected in the rearview, clouded with anger. David's posture was rigid. Alex remained calm and relaxed. Adam wanted to rile them, all of them, but Alex had expected that.

"Me too," she grinned at him. "But, lucky for you, we're here. So relax, Adam. You're in good hands—mine."

A full, deep rumble of laughter almost rattled the windows. Adam's broad shoulders shook for the few minutes it took the caravan to reach their destination. At the fountain that separated the entrance from the exit, they went right, circled around the grassy knoll, and stopped at the white stones steps that would take them inside the Palace of the Parliament.

Chapter 18

The approach to the seat of Romanian government was uneventful, and Jason was glad. At the second largest administrative building in the world, the white stone steps and columns welcomed the caravan. Plush, red carpet led to the very top step and the front door.

Jason felt his pulse quicken at the sight. All this pomp and circumstance was for him. From the red carpet to the military guards who stood at attention when he exited the vehicle, everyone was here for him. Even if it was at Conner's request, he was center of the vampire world right now, and he loved it.

Alex sent his official bodyguards ahead. She wanted her team to walk him in, past the press corps that was allowed to film and photograph the first-day festivities. Although none of this would air on the mainstream news, it would appear in every newspaper, newsfeed, and entertainment show owned, operated, and broadcast by the supernatural world. This was easily the most exciting thing that had ever happened in the supernatural community. Jason was about to make supernatural history.

"*Binevenit* (welcome)," an older gentleman greeted Jason. He shook his hand, then kissed his signet ring out of respect. "Please to follow me."

He made a big flourish with his hand toward the stone stairs. With Alex and her team behind them, they climbed the carpet-covered steps, and the man spoke about the architecture and history of their kind in Romania.

"We are sorry the castle was not available," he said, his

voice just above a whisper. "It was the oddest thing, the fire. But Mr. Gale's generosity will help to restore it in no time. Please give him our sincere appreciation."

"*Voi Sire* (I will, Sire)," Jason answered in perfect Romanian. He'd practiced that simple response on the drive over. Although vampires could learn quickly, he was never good with languages other than Greek and English.

They entered the main hall to the sound of violin music as it settled down from above them. The new leather of his shoe soles barely squeaked as they moved over the slick marble floors, which had been polished to a high shine. True to all the pictures he'd seen of the grand staircase, it rose in front of them covered in a thick, deep red carpet.

With Alex and Xavier at his Jason's side, the others climbed the first flight of stairs, turned, and waited for them to ascend. In their black combat uniforms, the second skin they wore under their jackets matched the carpet perfectly. Wild flashes from the paparazzi would have blinded them in the dim light of the foyer, but they also wore dark glasses.

"Can you believe this?" Kai mumbled out of the side of his mouth. As the photographers and reporters snapped pictures and yelled questions at them, they stayed focused—as Alex expected. They were working after all.

"Yeah, this place is pretty awesome," Amy chirped next to him. "It must be pretty ancient."

"It was actually opened in 1997," David announced as he gave the press corps a small wave. "It has twelve floors above ground and eight below. One of the them is big enough to house a partial government in case of nuclear attack. Oh, and it is the heaviest building in the world."

They all looked at him, then laughed.

"Thanks for the Wiki, Sheldon," Kai cracked then laughed again.

"Shut up," David chuckled as he elbowed his twin.

Who could have imagined this scene as it unfolded in front of her? Alex let her eyes scan the filled conference room from corner to corner as she walked slowly around its perimeter. Representatives from supernatural communities all over the world were seated in a conference room, much like a United Nations assembly. Alex's brain processed the sight with fear—not fear for anyone's safety at the moment but for her own in the not too distant future.

These beings were debating whether or not to bring credence to all of humanity's fears one day soon. How long would it be before her secret came out if theirs did? Where would she fit in then?

"You may think your request is simple—benign," a little round woman with stringy red hair mused at Jason, "but it isn't."

From her seat in the second row in front of Jason's seat, her very Irish accent struck Alex as odd. Ms. Clayton's diction felt overly pronounced, like she didn't want to make a grammatical mistake and appear uneducated to the rest of the representatives.

"We are a small clan, Mr. Stavros. Your reach and influence is global; ours is not. And we like it that way. Our arrangements," she took a sip of water, "are hundreds of years old. We don't wish to rock the boat, so to speak."

Jason stood and casually slipped out of his jacket. As he laid it over the back of his leather chair, he smiled at Ms. Clayton.

"We do understand that, Ms. Clayton," he replied. "No one is asking you to 'rock' anything—just to consider the possibility that we may be asked to renegotiate our deals."

The name card indicated Ms. Rowena Clayton was from County Cork, Ireland, Eastern Region, whatever that meant. She also represented the Clayton Clan. Her neat, dull-gray suit was in stark contrast to the shock of red hair that framed her round head.

"Our goal," Jason continued, "is to make that as painless as possible—for everyone. We are willing to bring your community under our umbrella of protection, if you wish."

Ms. Clayton shared a table with one Mortimer Gentry, London, Bromhall Clan. She sat when he stood, as if on a counterweight. His bushy eyebrows and weathered expression gave Alex the impression that he was less than pleased with everything going on right now.

"What would we need protection from?" he barked in a large full voice. "Like the House of Clayton, our agreements have served us well. No one has asked for a new agreement."

Jason turned his full attention to him. Alex figured that was his intention—to get the entire proceeding focused on him.

"The humans, at this very moment, are discussing this matter just as we are discussing it now," Jason replied. "Someone means to expose all of us, Mortimer. If we can't help stop this threat, we will need to be ready for whatever comes next."

Now it started to make sense. The signal for the video conference with Dr. Carlisle came from a Pentagon line. Most of the rooms in the Pentagon had been remodeled after 911, but not the one he was in this morning. She no longer wondered why the Trackers were here and not on some bullshit assignment right now. All the human bigwigs were in the most fortified building in the world. Who needs fancy bodyguards when you have that?

Everyone was figuratively running scared. The Council of Pure Blood Vampires wanted what information Tristan possessed. They weren't going to let the Trackers just give him back to Dr. Carlisle to keep experimenting on—not without a fight. Alex knew a fight like that would spill out into the real world eventually. Her stomach flipped at the thought.

Dr. Carlisle wanted answers that weren't in Tristan's head. Whatever he was looking for had to be inside his body. Why else would he keep him for so long? She could only imagine what her father had been up to all this time.

Tristan was valuable to both sides, and he knew it.

He was just arrogant enough to auction himself off to the highest bidder.

Alex searched her brain for someone she might still know on the inside, someone who was part of the Pentagon meeting or close enough to it that she could get something to help her. Whatever the Council thought was being discussed, they were way off. That could work to her advantage. Being here could actually give her time to build a case against Tristan Ambrose.

She turned her attention back to the meeting when Mortimer cleared his throat. Mortimer pulled absently at his waistcoat of rich emerald silk. It fit his bulky frame nicely, Alex noted. His style, reflective of the late nineteenth century, reminded Alex of a stuffy banker or railroad man from an old movie. Everything about him, from his dark suit and tie to his white starched shirt and perfect leather shoes, reminded her that he was from another time. One end of a gold chain, attached to the center button of the vest, disappeared inside a watch-sized pocket on the right side. She was sure the timepiece would be as old as he was.

"And how can we trust these humans?" Mortimer murmured in a polished British accent. "How do we know this isn't their doing? A way to squeeze even more from our ailing coffers?"

"It's not," Jason answered with a bit of irritation in his voice. "The covenant is still in effect. This threat is not coming from the humans."

Mortimer took his handkerchief out and dabbed at his brow. "How can you be sure?"

As Jason loosened his tie, he kept a calm expression. Alex felt her temper burn at Mortimer's insinuation.

"Our investigation has led us in a different direction, Mortimer," he answered. "Right now, we know one thing for sure."

"And what is that?" Mortimer asked with a surprised expression.

"This threat is inside our community," he answered.

A hum of whispers filled the chamber among the representatives as well as the onlookers. Jason turned, picked up the white mug, and took a sip as he locked eyes with Adam.

Alex's heart fluttered in her chest and her palm began to itch. Jason had just baited the hook. It was up to the Tracker team to reel in the catch.

As Jason tried to bring everyone back to order, Erin slipped quietly through the door. She nodded in Alex's direction and was allowed inside. Alex met her halfway.

The slip of paper Erin handed her was folded neatly. She opened it then looked up at Erin who nodded as Alex folded the paper once more.

"We'll be right out," Alex said.

As Erin exited, Alex noticed her glance in the direction of the Warren delegates—more specifically, the young warlock they'd all met at this morning's meet and greet. Their exchange had seemed familiar. That struck Alex as strange; Esmeralda introduced him as her new protégé. When she disappeared through the door, the warlock's eyes followed her until it closed. Then he grinned at his feet.

Chapter 19

Jason felt her hand on his right shoulder as the slip of paper came over his left. The note had three words on it: "Coop is alive."

"Are you sure about this?" he said in a low tone.

"Not yet," Alex replied. "They have the vid ready outside."

He looked up to see Nikki and Adam at the side exit staring at their exchange. Nikki left the room as Adam made his way over to them again.

Jason stood and let Alex help him with his jacket. He tapped the water glass with his pen.

"I think we should take lunch early," he announced politely. "How about we meet back here in two hours?"

The wave of relief that sailed around the room washed over Jason. Everyone was tense. They'd been meeting for five hours with no breaks. Even Jason felt tired and in need of some fresh air.

As he and Alex exited the room, he let her lead him through the crowd headed to the commissary. They reached her team huddled in the far corner of the courtyard, lined up like good little children. Erin held the tablet out to her.

"This just showed up in a secured vid box," she stated as Alex tapped the screen to start the playback.

Over Alex's shoulder, Jason watched the scene unfold. The cold winter wind pushed the smell of Alex's excitement, intertwined with her natural scent, into his face.

From the slight movement of the video, he could tell it was shot by a handheld device. Jason watched as two men walked at an easy pace away from the camera. Overhead, electronic boards displayed flight information and people stared up as they rushed in all directions through LAX.

A few short minutes later, the two men stopped at an international gate that displayed a flight to France. The date was two days before Jason and the team had boarded their own flight. From the profile, both Jason and Alex knew it was Coop. His curly locks looked even curlier now that he was turned. As Coop's full lips moved, his companion grinned with his hands in his pockets. Tailored and gray, the suit his companion wore fit like a glove. His height gave him a more sophisticated appearance.

"Who's the suit?" Alex asked no one in particular.

"Erin ran facial rec when he faced the camera," Sebastian replied. "His name is Brice Campbell."

"We pick him up yet?" she said as she continued to watch.

Jason picked up on her anger and backed up just a bit. For some reason, it stung him all over.

"For what?" Erin smirked.

"That's the second time his name has come up, or have you forgotten?" Alex answered with a smirk of her own. "He's connected to this. Have him picked up."

The men hugged, then Coop walked away. Brice faced the camera and smiled. Then the screen went black.

"On what charge?" Xavier joined the conversation. "Giving a dead guy a ride to the airport?"

Alex spun around and stepped into his personal space. "Did he look dead to you?"

Erin cleared her throat. "Only Coop boarded the flight—under an old alias. Brice Campbell is still on US soil."

"Brice Campbell just moved to the top of our shit list," Alex announced. "Bring him in."

Jason followed as she crossed the courtyard toward the commissary tent. He pulled her to a stop at the entrance.

"What's wrong?"

Alex gently pulled her elbow from his grip. "Coop's here and God only knows what he was able to do before we got here. He has to be found."

"Then we will find him," Jason whispered.

They entered the noisy tent and Jason waited for her to get a cup of tea before he led her to a table in a quiet corner. He could see Adam across the tent. He looked to be in a very intense conversation with Mortimer.

"Brice is working for someone," Alex began in a low tone. "Maybe whoever turned Coop. We pick him up, sweat him—he'll tell us what he knows."

"And if he doesn't?"

She looked up from her hot tea with a frown on her face. "He'll tell me."

"You can't go cracking skulls like the old days, Alex," Jason grinned. "If he's the middleman, wouldn't it be better to let him lead us to his boss?"

Her hands wrapped around the ceramic mug as she blew over the hot liquid. When she nodded her agreement, Jason let out a sigh.

"Good," he smiled as he stood and buttoned his jacket again. "We need to talk."

She pushed the mug away, looked up at him. "Talk."

Jason stepped in front of the small table she sat at and leaned over. "Not here. Tonight? Dinner?"

"I can't," she shook her head then sipped the tea. "The solstice thing is tonight, remember?"

"I forgot," he replied as he forced a smile. He didn't want her to see his disappointment. "Have fun. See you back in the chamber."

She just nodded, seemingly lost in her thoughts. Jason joined Adam on the other side of the room. His back was to Alex for a reason. Adam just grinned as he continued to read the documents in his hand.

"Where's Nikki?" Jason asked half-heartedly. He didn't really care.

"She said she left something at the hotel," he answered.

"She'll be back shortly."

"Did she go alone?" he asked, suddenly interested in the answer.

"No," Adam answered. "I sent Peter with her. Relax."

With her back against the far wall of her private suite, Peter swallowed a mouthful of Nikki's spicy blood then finished satisfying his boss's soon to be wife. Nikki licked at his bloody earlobe and sighed as she came down again.

After they were done, he zipped up and excused himself with a bow and a breathless "Sire," to her. The bathroom door closed as her phone buzzed.

"Yes," she said to her reflection in the mirror.

"Are you alright?" Jason's voice spiked anger in Nikki—ruining her afternoon quickie just like that.

"Of course," she giggled as she fixed her lipstick and smoothed down her hair. "Worried about me, lover?"

Jason chuckled. "I was more worried about Peter. Make sure he's presentable before you return him to me."

Nikki glared at her own reflection. "Don't worry, darling," she purred sweetly. "He'll be just perfect when we return—so will I, by the way."

"Good. You have twenty minutes, sweetheart," he replied. "Tick, tock."

He was gone before she could curse him. Peter appeared refreshed and grinning from ear-to-ear. She stepped up to him and pecked him sweetly on the cheek.

"Bring the car around," she stated. "I'll be right down."

Peter backed away with a smile. "Sire."

Nikki took her time making herself presentable. She picked up her briefcase, checked her makeup one last time, then left the room.

The elevator didn't stop on its way to the lobby. As she stepped off, she felt a quick wave of something that felt like desire hit her skin. She didn't stop to see where it came from. Instead, she picked up the pace and practically jumped through the sliding glass doors to the outside. There, Peter waited with the backdoor open wide.

"Something wrong, Sire?" he asked as he took her briefcase and helped her inside.

"No," she answered. "Thank you."

As the truck pulled away from the entrance, Nikki forced herself not to look back. It was probably nothing anyway—just some horny little newbie who hadn't been told not to troll the lobby for a fresh meal. Or maybe it was just some residual vibe from Peter. He could be insatiable that way. He probably liked the fact that he could brag about doing the boss's fiancé most of all. Why did it matter? Jason couldn't care less who or what she did, if she was discreet. The way he thought he had been with Alex. Nikki tapped her sharp nail on the handle of her briefcase.

As much as she wanted to drop Alex in the "just another human" category, Nikki knew she didn't belong there. Jason's initial attraction to her unnerved Nikki, if she was being honest with herself. He'd never had such a hunger for a human woman before. But that fire seemed to have dimmed just a bit. Maybe the time apart and the wedding plans had knocked some sense into him. Nikki straightened her posture then pulled a small black velvet box from her bag.

He'd gotten it in her luggage somehow. She had found it as she unpacked at the hotel. It was the exact ring she had asked for—right down to the pink diamond center stone. His note simply read "*For You.*" The hinged lid opened with a soft creak. Nikki felt her heart jump at the sight of her engagement ring.

The center stone—a 5.15 carat pink diamond—bounced the natural light back in her face. Its 18 karat rose gold and platinum band consisted of 103 small round diamonds that lined both sides and around the center stone.

Beautiful is too small a word, she thought as she eased it over her ring finger. Jason wouldn't do the honors in front of everyone at the conference, of that she was sure.

"Oh, what the hell," she smiled at the ring as it sat on her finger.

Jason knew what looked good on her, as always. No need to have it sized. It fit perfectly. With this ring on her finger, it felt real. For the last few months her free time had been filled with caterers and bakers, reception halls and dress hunts. All the while, she wondered how long it would take for Jason to actually make it official, and now that day was here. Then she paused.

"If I embarrassed him like this, he'd kill me," she sighed then slid the ring from her finger and placed it carefully back in the black velvet box. It pained her to put the ring back in her bag, but she did.

"Were you talking to me, Sire?" Peter asked as they approached the Palace of Parliament once again.

"No, sorry," she replied. "Just going over some notes."

He gave a slight nod as traffic at the entrance slowed in front of them. Everyone returned from lunch at the same time it seemed. Once they passed the fountain, it took no time at all until they reached the front entrance. Peter helped her from the back of the SUV. Another guard arrived to escort her back to the meeting hall as Peter parked the truck in the designated space.

"Don't let the pretty face fool ya," Coop said when he noticed his blood junkie backup drool over the sight of Nikki as she sauntered through the lobby.

She moved on six-inch heels like she walked a wire with no fear of falling.

She covers pretty good, Coop thought. Even he could feel the creepy lust oozing from his partner as she made her way to the exit.

"What do you think our sire will do with her once she's served her purpose?" he moaned and licked his lips. He couldn't take his eyes off her. "Do you think I could have her for a while? I'll bet her blood . . ." he stopped to lick his lips again. Coop felt like his stomach just turned inside out.

"Really? Get a grip, you little freak," he growled.

His companion's nervous energy disturbed Coop's calm. That tightly wound vibe sprang from him and spread over Coop like ants. Tristan told him he'd be much more sensitive to human vibrations, but this junkie vampire's were almost unbearable.

When he focused hard, it eased, but only slightly. If he wasn't careful, this guy would be dead by sundown. For half a second, Coop thought that might not be a bad idea. He could just drain him dry—blame it on someone else. Tristan would never know. Then he decided against that plan. He knew who he wanted his next meal to be, and it wasn't some trashy blood whore jonesing for his next bite.

"Should we follow?" he whispered as he bounced slightly in his chair, risking drawing attention in the hotel lobby. With Alex and the team still occupied at the conference, nobody would recognize him, but there was no need to tempt fate.

"No," Coop answered with a shake of his head. "She felt your . . . whatever that was. If we follow, she'll get spooked and give my," he growled low, "*her* team the heads up. We need them to not see us coming, okay?"

He nodded absently as he continued to bounce. To Coop, the long plastic tube the junkie pulled from his pack looked like one of those yogurt things for kids. After it was empty, he balled up the tube and stuffed it back in his pack. The smell of fresh blood used to creep Coop out, but now it smelled like a Porterhouse, medium-well, with a baked potato.

It seemed long enough now. Coop stood, blood junkie at his side, and made his way outside. Behind the wheel of his rented BMW, Coop took a right off hotel property at a leisurely pace. Nikki's car had been tagged. A red dot blinked on the handheld as they drove in the direction of the super-secret meetings.

At least the scenery is nice, he thought as he took it all in.

Unfortunately, he wasn't here to sightsee, even if everyone here looked at him like a tourist. He couldn't pass as a local. Neither he nor Alex looked like anyone around them. Her advantage was she was part of Jason's entourage. So *tourist* Coop it was. Except he wasn't here for postcards and snow globes. His mission was to take a hostage and kill anyone who got in his way.

He stayed a few cars behind them all the way to the Palace of Parliament. The traffic ahead slowed. Coop figured everyone had rushed back at the same time. As they passed the fountain, he saw Nikki's SUV ease up to the front entrance in line with the other dignitaries. When her driver jumped from behind the wheel and opened her door, her long legs came out as her pale hand took his.

Coop could see her shiny red nails scratch at his wrist and the small grin on his lips at her gesture. Their little secret was not lost on him.

"So Nikki had a quickie for lunch," Coop chuckled as he steered the car to the right where visitors had to park and presented paperwork to be cleared to enter the building.

"What?" the junkie sniffed.

"Nothing," he replied. "Stay with the car. I'll be right out."

In the parking space, the engine died as his companion exited the passenger side and slid in behind the wheel. Coop took a black leather briefcase from the back seat, put on dark sunglasses and made his way to the visitor checkpoint.

If everything went as planned, and it had so far, the burly guard would allow him inside with a glance at his credentials and nod of his head. Tristan's reach extended inside this facility and practically into Jason's face.

Coop fell in line with the other visitors as they made their way to the viewing gallery. These people were allowed inside because they represented smaller factions that had some interest in the outcome but no voting privileges. His credentials were the best forgery Tristan's money could buy. He hummed a tune as he entered the building and followed the small group up a flight of stairs that led to the balcony in the back of the meeting hall.

From here, he could see the entire room. Every voting delegate, the one assistant they were allowed, and their security teams were in clear view. As he made himself comfortable in the front row, he spotted Jason and Adam as they chatted at the table in the front of the room.

"Big boy table, huh?" he whispered as he made a mental note of everything he saw for later, when he would return with help and take what he came here for.

The tiny camera on his lapel recorded everything—an instant record of the proceedings as they played out in front of him. On the tiny screen built into his sunglasses he could zoom in on anyone in the room with a quick tap to the right side—zoom out with a tap to the left.

Technology is grand, isn't it? he thought.

He had to laugh at how easy it was to get inside even though she had taken over his team. Just the thought of that made his blood boil. Then she walked in.

Alex had an air of confidence he'd never seen on anyone, especially a woman. She could be larger than life or more shadow than substance depending on her mood. Despite everything, he had to admire the way she reinvented herself. Though she was still tethered to Strategic, she called her own shots—until now, that is. Now, she was bound by her stupid pride to protect a vampire. Coop smiled, reached up, and tapped the right side of his sunglasses and her face filled the small screen.

She looked as she always did: cool but ready to strike. Coop found he admired that about her too. What would she think after this was all over? After she gave up that Dagger guy and Tristan either killed her, tortured her, or both at the same time? Would she beg for her life or would she just let it happen? Either way, she wasn't strong enough to handle what Tristan had planned for her, not for long anyway. She'd give up the name. Then he'd take his time with her. Coop just hoped he'd get to taste her before she died. Tristan had promised him that.

His new fangs ached to descend and his mouth watered at the thought. Little Miss Tough Girl reduced to a blood bag just for him. Her holier-than-thou attitude would disappear when he fed from her veins as she screamed and begged for mercy. He zoomed out again as the camera on his lapel continued to record the action. He wanted to watch her with his new eyes. Suddenly, she stopped dead in her tracks and faced the balcony.

"Shooter," she said as a new scent drew her attention up. "We've got a problem."

"What kind of problem?" Xavier answered.

"Meet me at the balcony entrance now," Alex replied.

Everyone made their way back inside to take their seats once more. Jason and Adam stood next to the center table; Jason's personal security was close by. Even Nikki was safe with two handsome accessories at her side.

Alex's eyes traveled from one end of the balcony to the other. The few invited onlookers were spread out around the upper seating. The head count should always be the same: ten. Six men and four women. Alex had memorized the face, fashion sense, and mannerisms of each person about five minutes into the first speech yesterday. Suddenly, there was now eleven.

Just as she scanned from one end of the balcony and reached the opposite side, eleven had made his way up the stairs headed to the exit. The black man with a curly brown afro and a cocky stride disappeared down the exit ramp, as she signaled one of Jason's guards.

"I need to leave this room," she told him. "Stay close to Mr. Stavros until I return."

"Is there a problem?" he asked. "Should we evacuate?"

"No, just stay close."

She locked eyes with Jason briefly. Then she tapped the device in her ear.

"Shooter, you read?"

"Yeah. We're headed for the balcony exit," he said, his voice jumpy as if he were running.

Alex trotted toward the exit doors. Outside, she ran toward her team; her boots squeaked on the polished marble floor. Just ahead, she saw Sebastian, Kai, and Amy. Then David, Xavier, and Erin came around the far corner. Xavier shook his head at them.

"Nothing," he huffed as he adjusted his weapon under his jacket.

"We didn't see anyone," David added doing the same.

"He's here," Alex said. Her heart thumped in her chest at the thought.

Alex took a deep breath. His scent had changed, but there was still some hint of humanity for now. He was moving effortlessly fast through the building. He couldn't do that by himself.

"Parking lot," she barked as she ran toward the guarded exit. The others were close behind her. "Did you see a man," she asked the guards in her best Romanian, "like me, black man, leave through here?"

One of the younger men nodded and pointed. As they ran through the exit door, she could hear him on the outdated walkie-talkie tell security in the parking area to stop any cars attempting to leave.

On their way down the stone stairs, Alex barked for them to spread out. Each one of them drew a weapon and walked quickly through the cars—cautious, but ready. Nothing. Every car had official plates and drivers waiting to be called for pick up.

Alex reached the guard shack before anyone else. The guards told her no one had attempted to leave in the last thirty minutes or more. She cursed in English, but they understood and grinned.

"He's gone," she said as the team regrouped at the

guard station. “He had help getting in and out. Shit! Let’s get back inside.”

Back inside the building, Alex handed her black leather jacket to Amy then went to the ladies’ room. It was quiet and clean. The smell of cleanser and perfume filled the air. Harsh overhead lights gave her brown skin a strange tint. She splashed water on her face, dried it and her hands, and went back to the team.

“Get me every video of this parking lot starting a week ago,” she said to Erin and David. “I want names and pictures of everyone on parking lot duty since last night. We’ll match them up after the party tonight. Understand?”

“Yeah,” David replied. “We’re on it.”

He tugged at Erin’s arm and they headed toward the main security room on the bottom floor of the building. They would get anything they asked for—anything.

“Everyone else, keep making laps on this hall until I tell you to stop,” she hissed over her shoulder at them as she went back inside.

Down in the bowels of one of Tristan’s many safe houses, he walked the dimly lit corridor alone. All the sounds and smells mixed together, making a hollow echo around him. The steel door creaked open and he stepped inside.

She was perched on a neatly made bed brushing through her wet hair. Freshly showered, but woefully undernourished, Sasha looked up with a relieved grin on her bruised face. Had she fed properly, those bruises would have been long gone.

“They starved you,” Tristan whispered as she stepped into his open arms and he stroked her hair. “It must have been horrible.”

“It was agony, Sire,” she whimpered. “Rats! That’s all I had for two weeks. Sometimes, nothing at all.”

He could smell the salt tears as they rolled down her

face. When he pushed her back and placed his hand on her cheek, she leaned into his touch. Her once full frame was thinner than before. There was some color in her cheeks, but Tristan had left instructions to have her properly fed by the time he arrived. He couldn't put his finger on it, but something was still not right about her.

"Well," he said as he stepped back to get a better look at her. "I'm just glad you were able to escape. I'm glad you're home safe."

Sasha smiled as she sat back down on the bed. Her hands trembled as they rested in her lap. The silk robe she was given was loosely tied at the waist and her breast practically spilled out. She was not shy about that at all. Her hair was slicked down on her round head, curling slightly at the ends as it dried.

Malnutrition had taken away almost all that he loved about her. It didn't take much to damage the turned. Whoever took her knew that, and they were good at their job.

"I'm sorry that I don't have much to report, but it was all I could to do the stay alive and come back to you," she sighed and untied the sash. The robe opened, but didn't reveal her nakedness completely. In a weak voice she said, "My captors were cruel, Sire, so very cruel. They kept me like an animal in cage!"

"There was nothing left in that building you were held in," he said as he looked down on her upturned face. "Do you remember anything at all?" Sasha shook her head, keeping her eyes focused on him. He could practically taste her lust in the air.

Tristan stepped up to the bed then sat down next to her. Her cold hand squeezed his as she composed herself. Then he noticed it—her strong and steady pulse. Her heart had the usual weak beat of a vampire who wasn't afraid or tormented at all. There was just her desire as it built up slowly.

He placed a soft kiss on her forehead as he stood again.

At the door, her turned back to her. "I'll send someone healthy and beautiful for you to feed on when you wake. You need more rest."

Sasha rose slowly and approached Tristan with a fire in her eyes. As she approached, the robe slipped from her shoulders then to the floor. Her only clothing—lacy panties. Her breasts, bared to him, were full and round with pert and pink nipples.

"Someone healthy and beautiful is already here," she purred as she picked up his hand and placed it over one firm breast. "I missed you, Sire."

Her slightly cracked lips pecked at his clean cheek. Supple and warm to the touch, Tristan gently squeezed the breast in his hand. A warm sensation tickled his ear as she nibbled at his neck. Then her hands pushed his jacket away. She dropped it on top of the robe at their feet.

Once her arms wrapped around his neck, he wrapped her in his embrace. She began to unbutton his shirt then unzip his slacks. Before her abduction, Sasha was curvy and exciting—strong. And, if he closed his eyes, she wasn't the fragile little victim wrapped around him now.

Shockingly cold, her hand slipped inside his slacks and gently coaxed him, just as he'd taught her to do. She pulled him forward. On the bed, she ended up on top. As she rubbed against him she moaned, "Touch me, please, Sire."

Tristan wrapped her wet hair in his hand and she squealed as he pulled her head away. He stared into her eyes and saw a smoldering lust. Longing, desperation, a need for his approval appeared there. But something else bothered him. As the low buzz reached his ears, he tried to ignore it. He licked at her mouth, squeezed her butt to stoke the fire deep inside him—anything to shut out that sound.

"Did you really miss me, Sasha?" he asked as she moved against his growing erection. When he flipped them over, Sasha wrapped her legs around his waist as he ripped away the frilly fabric of her panties. Then the air filled with her excitement as Tristan entered her in a smooth motion.

"Yes," she moaned and purred as he began to push her into the soft mattress. "I missed you so much I wanted to die!"

A gasp escaped her mouth as he plunged deep again. The vein in her neck appeared as if he'd asked for it; his incisors dropped to a fine point. He hissed when she drew a long nail down his neck and licked away the blood. Before the wound closed, she did it again. With a wicked grin, her fangs sank deep into his skin. Her pull was strong and she fed greedily from him as her body began to shake and prepare for her climax.

Stained with his blood, Sasha kissed him roughly, then he pulled her mouth from his, raised his head and sank his teeth in her soft neck. She screamed and laughed as he drank. The sex satisfied his perpetual hunger for it. Her blood, when it mixed with his, helped him enter her mind.

Tristan blew past the unimportant things he found there. What he was after should have existed in her present mind, but he found very little there. The buzzing grew more annoying.

He barely heard her moans of pleasure and pleading for more. He was concentrated on her thoughts. Fragments of the fight with Alex Stone came and went. Images of how Sasha was beaten to a pulp by the woman. Then blackness, total and complete. As he fed on her rage, his emerged—rage at being kept like a comatose pet, and his fear of never seeing the world again. He felt her sharp nails sink into his thighs as he pumped harder and harder.

The buzzing amplified in his brain. It felt close. *Close enough to touch,* he thought.

"Now," she pleaded and writhed underneath him. "Please, Sire!"

His rhythm quickened as he let go of her mind and came in one last deep, hard thrust. Sasha screamed his name through her release. He pressed his ear close to her neck and the buzzing sound almost shattered his eardrum. She tried to keep him in her embrace, but he was up and straightening his clothes before her eyes completely opened.

He stepped up to the door and banged hard. It opened and a young woman handed him a long knife. It had some weight to it as he adjusted his grip on the jewel encrusted handle. The young woman stepped back and he could hear Sasha rise from the bed.

"You're lying," he whispered at the young woman in front of him, but his words were for Sasha. "They turned you against me."

When he felt her close behind him, he turned. The knife slid easily into her body, and he could smell her flesh as it began to burn from the inside. Made from pure silver—except the handle, of course—it tapped her heart. Because he had taken more than enough of her blood, she would not be able to withstand the poison of the silver. Had she been in better shape when they released her, it would have taken longer—much longer.

"Sire," Sasha moaned as she looked down at the blade in her chest.

Tristan stepped back as her skin sizzled and cracked. Blue veins turned black by the poison. She began turning to ash from the center of her chest first. The knife hung there for a few more seconds. Her tears turned to tiny puffs of smoke as they dried on her hot skin. "They will pay for this; I promise you." Then the knife dropped on top of the ashes as she crumbled at his feet. A little device sat in the pile of her remains; its red light blinked wildly. He crushed it under his heel then turned to the young woman.

"Is he ready?" Tristan whispered. She nodded. "We have about ten minutes before they get here. I'll be right out."

"Yes, Sire," she replied then followed him out of the room.

Chapter 20

"Are you just going to sit here all night brooding?" Esmeralda frowned at Alex.

"I'm not brooding," she replied, taking another shot of really good vodka. "I'm plotting. My brooding face looks like this." Alex pushed her lower lip way out then slumped back in the fluffy oversized chair she and Esmeralda occupied together.

"Please don't ever do that again," Esmeralda laughed before she kissed Alex's cheek.

Alex grinned as the party of all parties raged on around them. Esmeralda's Solstice parties were always loud, sexy, and all night long. Only Alex didn't have all night. She and her team had an early call with Jason.

"Alex," Esmeralda pulled her face around, "you can't do anything about it now. Enjoy the fun, please." She gave Alex her best smile as she stood. Her slender mocha hand hovered at eye level. "Come on. I wanna dance!"

She let Esmeralda pull her to her feet and out into the center of the shiny, happy people of the "invite only" celebration. They mixed in with the bodies on the dance floor and danced to a thumping beat. Under purple lights and fake smoke, Alex tried to put the day's shit out of her head. She felt Esmeralda's back against hers then a strong set of muscular arms wrapped around her.

Morgan Warren was a creature of habit. He always wore the same colored tie to every meeting. His cologne was always some exotic mix of essential oils that he refused to tell anyone—not even Esmeralda, and she was his wife.

It intoxicated and soothed her and as the music slowed, Alex swayed in time with him.

"As irresistible as ever, I see," he whispered in her ear.

"Don't tease me," she replied. "Your wife's right over there. She might turn me into a toad or something. I bet you'd be able to resist me then." He chuckled and the vibration tickled her spine.

"Never."

The song surrounded them as Morgan guided her side to side. Then he spun her around and dipped her over one strong arm. When she was upright again, he kissed her hand softly then winked at a smiling Esmeralda to their right who squeezed against Sebastian, who blushed bright red.

Morgan's big, brown bedroom eyes closed when a lone saxophone began to wail. He rotated his hips which caused Alex to do the same. The arm around her waist pulled her even closer and his hand held hers in a warm grip. On her toes, Alex let Morgan lead her away from the crowd and into a darkened corner of the dance floor. As they continued to dance, he looked into her eyes.

"You haven't given me a proper greeting," he hummed. "Is that because of him?" He gave a quick nod then angled them so she could see who he was talking about.

Jason, with Nikki on his arm, walked in as if they were just announced husband and wife. Alex leaned closer to Morgan. His full lips displayed a slight grin as she brushed hers over his smooth brown cheek. He chuckled again.

"Sorry," she sighed.

"That's more like it," he smiled at her. "Did you know?"

At first she frowned then shook her head at him. "No. I just thought it was a casual arrangement. I was wrong. So I'm done."

"Is he?"

She cut her eyes to see him strolling toward them. Morgan kissed her cheek then extended his long arm out to shake Jason's hand. A guy hug was exchanged as Nikki stepped up to Alex and held her slim left hand up to her.

"It's beautiful," Alex stated. "Congratulations."

"Thank you," Nikki beamed at the rock on her finger. All the lights bounced off it like it was the sun. The stone was perfect; Alex could see that much. What else would a woman as beautiful as Nikki be given except perfection? "He just surprised me at dinner. It was very romantic."

Alex just nodded with a glance over Nikki's shoulder at Esmeralda, whose pink tongue shot out as she pretended to stick her finger down her own throat. The group around her laughed. Alex shook her head and looked away.

"I need a drink," she stated absently. "Can I get you anything?" A shocked look passed over Nikki's face.

"I'm fine, thank you," she replied.

She stepped between Jason and Morgan, took Jason's hand and placed a small kiss on his cheek. "Congratulations." He squeezed her hand and tried to keep her next to him.

Alex excused herself and joined Esmeralda and the rest of her team at the bar.

Nikki swallowed her evilness as Alex walked away. She had expected anger or smugness. Instead, she was . . . nice! Why wasn't she mad or even jealous? Nikki embraced a smiling Morgan as he congratulated her as well. *He smells wonderful*, she thought as his scent took her mind away from Alex's lack of emotion.

"So when's the big day?" Morgan asked as he held her close. She didn't mind and neither did Jason from the looks of it. He was stealing glances at Alex and her friends at the bar. Their laughter cut through all the other noise in the nightclub for some reason. At least that's how it felt to Nikki.

"We haven't set a date yet," he replied as he turned back to Morgan, whose arm Nikki still clung to. "These meetings are priority, I'm afraid."

Morgan gave a nod to him then looked down at Nikki.

"I'm sure you've already picked out your gown."

"Of course I have," she giggled. "And his tux."

"Well, all he has to do is show up then," Morgan hummed. "That's easy."

"Let's hope so," she said and took a drink from a pretty waitress who then nodded toward the bar. Alex and all the others raised a glass to them. Jason looked ready to run, but Nikki knew he would find a way to get close to Alex tonight and try to explain.

What did it matter? She was now officially about to be his wife. Once that happened, she would have no need to hang onto the "place holders," as she called them, because Jason would be hers alone.

The power was in the union. With the right mate, anything was possible. Jason had just proven that with the decision to move forward with their wedding plans. Nikki knew that once it was official, she would be that much closer to her own seat at the table. The Lower Chamber was just the beginning for both she and Jason. They were poised to be the first couple to shatter the glass ceiling in the "pure" parade.

No one ever expected her to have aspirations of her own—not even Jason. Although she loved him, she would not allow anyone to relegate her to the station of silent trophy wife. As Jason and Morgan went on and on about some sporting event, Nikki contemplated her own bright future. She straightened her posture and put on a bright smile. If nothing else, she knew not to show anyone the chinks in her armor.

Jason would come back around soon. Now that Alex was out of the picture, he would desire her again. She had admitted defeat just then, hadn't she? Alex upset the delicate balance Nikki had set for their lives. In that moment, Nikki decided to do whatever she had to in order to get that balance back. If that meant Alex Stone's destruction, so be it.

Alex had to escape the noise for just a few minutes. In

the dim corner of the hotel lobby, she found a little bit of peace. Inside the bar, every thought and desire pounded on her skull. To shut them out, she'd have to get as drunk as everyone else was or retreat and regroup. She chose the latter.

Outside the big lobby window, snow had begun to fall. It tumbled down in a weird pattern as she let the movement soothe her and disconnect her from the force of the party a few feet away. One deep breath and the voices disappeared. Another breath and so did the music and smells. One more and the only voice inside her head was her own.

Her team would be no good to her tonight; that was for sure. It didn't matter. She could go over the videos by herself. Let them enjoy the party.

She lowered her body down into the fluffy chair behind her and closed her eyes. At first, all she could see was the snow, then it faded to black. The lobby was filled with the smell of pine and fresh snow. Someone had just walked in from outside.

Without even looking, she could hear the heavy footfalls as they approached the front desk. In her hiding place, their whispers barely reached her. They may not have been whispering, but as long as she controlled her power, it sounded that way to her.

The desk clerk pecked the keys at the computer roughly. The new guest, male, asked for two rooms with king-size beds and a fireplace. The clerk stated they were the last rooms in the entire hotel and how lucky he was to get them. With the convention, as he called it, and the snow, he may have had to drive to the next town had he not stopped at that very moment. They shared a laugh, then silence.

Before she noticed that nothing had been said in at least a minute, she opened her eyes, and there he was in front of her. He stared down at her with a strange expression on his bearded face. The twinkle in his blue eyes was familiar. His heavy jacket was still dusted with snow. The boots, brown and worn, were slightly damp. Their water-proofing held strong.

"You look tired," he said as he removed his gloves, stuffed them in his pocket, then scratched at his beard.

"You look like a stranger," Alex replied as she straight-ened her posture. "My mama always told me not to talk to strangers."

He grinned and the hairs on his face twitched.

"And here I thought I was unforgettable."

When he laughed, Alex's brain clicked to a picture of the man she knew without the beard and the years that had creased around those blue eyes. She stood. He stepped back into the light.

"Becker?"

"In the flesh!"

K.C. Becker had put on a few pounds of muscle and added a beard to the mix. As she stepped into his arms, the scratchy face-warmer rubbed against her cheek. As he laughed, he rocked them back and forth.

"What the hell?" she laughed in his ear.

He released her and held her at arm's length as he looked her over. With a shake of his head and a big smile this time, he studied her closely.

"What the hell right back at you," he said. "You grew up."

Alex invited him to join her with a nod toward the empty chairs. Once he shrugged off his jacket, they sat down and stared at each other for a few seconds. He kept the black watch cap on his head.

"What are you doing here?" Alex finally broke the silence. "I thought you were dead."

Becker laughed and scratched at the beard again. "Well, don't sound so disappointed, Dagger."

"Sorry," she sighed. "You look good."

He nodded as if he didn't want the compliment. Becker never really was much for compliments as she remembered it. "I'm on assignment—new team."

"Really? The doctor never said anything about a second team," Alex stated, suddenly uncomfortable. He smelled different.

"I'm not with Strategic anymore," he replied. "I got kicked out when I couldn't tolerate the supplement."

That's why he smelled different. He wasn't on the pills. But from everything she'd been told, without them, their bodies would break down and eventually kill them. Becker looked fine—perfect, in fact.

"Don't look at me that way," he said. "Don't believe everything the old man tells you. I've been off the supplement for about three years now. I'm good. I mean, not bench pressing small cars or healing overnight good, but I'm human again."

She watched him look at his rough hands with a sense of satisfaction and peace. Underneath the sweater she could see muscle definition. Not like before, lean and cut, but regular muscle tone for a man his age. He was human again.

Without thinking, Alex took his wrists in her hands. He let her squeeze his forearms, biceps, triceps, then his shoulders. His heartbeat was normal, his breathing steady. But his scent was very different and that bugged her. When she placed her hands on either side of his hairy cheeks, his eyes closed.

He opened his mind to her for some reason: the time he spent in the hospital with the others after Sandbox, being poked and prodded like meat on a hook, her father taking blood samples from him with a grim expression. Then the image shifted. Becker was as he is now—out of the program, off the pills, and normal. Before she released him, she wiped the name "Dagger" from his brain. He'd feel the effects in just a second.

"How did you do it?" Alex said as she disconnected and his eyes opened again. He squinted and rubbed his temples. "Sorry. I'm still working on doing that without hurting people."

"That's okay," he chuckled as he popped his neck. "You

were never that good at it anyway."

"How did you stop the side effects?" she asked again, but he just sat there with a grin as he stared at her.

"That's not why I'm here," he replied then stopped. He looked as if he'd forgotten her name. It worked. "Alex," he chuckled. "Maybe I didn't stop all the side effects," he said with a shake of his head. "Memory screwed up for a second."

"Then why are you here?" she said.

"Working," he stated, "just like you. Lucas tracked me down." His expression went cold and hard. "Any word on who did this?"

"I'm close," Alex replied and his eyes clouded with pain. "Tristan's out, with the book. Coop's—"

"Coop's what?" Becker growled low. "A backstabbing traitor? Yeah, I know."

"So you're working for the Pack?"

"Yeah," he nodded. "Have to earn a living somehow. I'm not filthy rich." He winked at her. "Wait, I thought Coop was dead."

"Nope. He's turned and here in Romania."

"Did he kill Matt?"

She shook her head. "But whoever did, I'll find them and hand them over to the Pack. I promised Roland. So why send you?"

Becker shrugged. "Just to be safe?"

"They don't trust me?"

"They don't trust the bloodsuckers."

Alex sat forward and so did Becker. "Did you hear what I said about Tristan? He's out."

"I know, but he's not my problem. We're just here to get Matt's killer. The rest is on you."

"We?"

Becker nodded toward the entrance as the door swung open once more. Longish brown hair, worn away from his face and dusted with fresh snow, this man was familiar as soon as he smiled at them. Like Becker, he had an impressive beard. It was speckled with gray, trimmed, and shiny. His easy stride indicated he felt safe. As he moved toward them, he reminded Alex more of a college professor than a priest.

The only jacket he'd ever worn was brown tweed with a patch at each elbow. A heavy, gray wool scarf twisted loosely around his neck. He dropped his bulky bag next to Becker's at the desk as he approached them. He still had that same grace of movement he had in Mexico.

That day, he seemed timid as he asked if they had to kill his mentor and friend. What Ben tried to explain to Father Tomas was his mentor was already dead. The more he fed on human blood, the further from human he became. Father Tomas didn't seem to understand at the time, but somehow, now, Alex got the feeling it had finally hit him.

"Alexa," his voice registered surprise when he spoke her name. He cut a glance at Becker as she shook his hand firmly. A proper pronunciation of her name sounded so much better with an accent. "My, you haven't changed one bit."

This was the first time she'd noticed he was Italian. He'd spoken Spanish so flawlessly back then that she'd assumed he was a native.

His slim hand held hers in a tight grip, so unlike the first time they'd met. Now, he was confident and self-assured. She could feel the coldness of his hands creep up her arm as he put her warm hand to his lips. They were cold too.

"Father," she began but stopped when both men laughed.

"I left the priesthood years ago," he replied with an elbow to Becker. "It's just Tomas now."

Alex felt a strong need to apologize for her mistake. "Sorry."

He smiled. "Don't be. After everything I saw in Mexico, with . . ." he paused to shake his head. "Well, I can better serve the cause without the strictures of the church. At least that's what I tell myself."

"What cause?" she asked.

Before either could answer, the desk clerk stepped up and announced their rooms were ready. Becker excused himself to gather the bags.

"We can talk more tomorrow if you have time," Tomas stated. "I will be speaking at the conference in the afternoon session. Perhaps you could join us for lunch?"

Alex took his outstretched hand in a tight grip. "I'd love to."

"Signorina," he said in a low tone.

Inside the small elevator, they both nodded at her as the doors closed.

Chapter 21

"Did you see where Alex went?" Jason said to Morgan.

"Lobby," he replied. As Jason began to stand, Morgan pulled him back down on the couch they were sharing while his wife and Nikki shared a partner on the dance floor. "Leave her alone, Jason. You've made your choice."

Jason stared into Morgan's deep brown eyes. He may have been a little drunk, which explained his boldness, but he wasn't so drunk as to think he could tell Jason what to do. He released Jason's arm with a tilt of his head.

"Are you worried about me, Morgan?" Jason grinned.

Morgan sat forward then emptied the drink in his hand. Once the glass was on the low table in front of them, he turned to Jason. "I'm not going to let you hurt her."

"I'm not trying to hurt her."

"Good. Then back off before someone does get hurt."

Jason emptied his glass too and parked it next to Morgan's.

"If she tells me to back off, I will," Jason replied as they both stood up. "Until then, mind your own business. This is between me and her."

Morgan stepped into Jason's personal space much to his surprise. He'd never thought of Morgan as an aggressive person. He always seemed more of the romantic type—able to talk his way through an unfavorable encounter rather than fight. He was wrong.

"In case no one told you," Morgan grinned as he pretended to brush off Jason's shoulders. "You can't have her."

Jason smiled and returned the gesture. "Someone already said that and you're both wrong."

"You're used to getting whatever you want," Morgan sighed with a step back. "I get that. But why do you want Alex so badly?"

"Why do you?" Jason replied. "Don't deny it. I see it in your eyes, even now."

Morgan turned toward the dance floor, waved at his wife as she smiled at them. Nikki did the same. "I love my wife more than life itself. No one will ever come between us. Alex is ours to protect until there is someone who can do that better. That someone is not you."

He turned back to Jason with a frown on his face. Jason was confused by the statement and Morgan's painful expression. Why would Alex need protection?

"She's not your child, is she?" Jason joked but Morgan's attention was on the empty doorway. Jason stepped up to him again to get his attention, but he felt a strange sensation move between them.

Morgan was a powerful warlock; Jason never doubted that. What he felt now, in the space between them, was more than just Morgan's display of power. This was something much more raw and unchecked. He turned to the doorway too. A hot wave of emotion hit him in his chest.

"What the hell?" Jason whispered as he took a step forward.

"You felt that, didn't you?" Morgan whispered back as he gripped Jason's forearm.

He pulled him around again to face him. Instead of the hate he expected to see in Morgan's eyes, Jason saw fear—real fear.

"What's wrong, Morgan? Tell me."

"Have you tasted her blood? Tell the truth, please Jason."

For some reason Jason's first thought wasn't to lie to Morgan. He wanted to tell him.

"Yes. A while back."

"What do you remember?" Morgan continued to whisper.

"I don't understand," Jason replied.

"About the taste."

"Nothing really," he answered. "I mean I can't describe it. And I can tell you every flavor of blood I've ever tasted. But not hers."

"She let you bite her?" Morgan asked with a look of terror.

"No. She cut her finger and fed me from it. Not very much though."

Morgan looked relieved. He looked almost happy at the answer.

"And now?"

"I don't really remember what it tasted like. I've had others since her, and I remember them all. Can you explain it?"

Morgan led him to the bar and ordered two shots of vodka. When they arrived, he picked up one, handed the other to Jason.

"No, I can't," he answered then raised his glass.

Their glasses tapped together with a heavy sound. Jason tossed his back and it burned all the way down his throat. For some reason his brain did a back flip, then he felt like his knees would give out. When he opened his eyes, Morgan had helped him to a stool at the bar.

"Are you alright?" Morgan's smile filled his line of sight. "I didn't think you were a lightweight, Jas."

Jason shook his head a couple of times. "What happened?"

"We were talking about the heavyweight bout coming up at your casino, took a shot, and boom, you almost did a face-plant on the bar."

Morgan waved at the bartender and there was a glass of blood on the bar like magic. Jason could smell it as the scent crawled up his nose and wrapped around his brain.

He drained the glass before he knew it was empty.

"Thanks."

"No problem," Morgan replied with slap to his shoulder. "Maybe it's time for you to call it a night. I'll get one of my guys to bring your car around and have someone get Alex."

"Yeah," Jason nodded. "Thanks again."

As her team climbed into one SUV, Jason and Nikki, drunk and giddy, were loaded into the other. Esmeralda stood in her husband's arms as he shielded her from the cold wind and watched.

The least inebriated of her team, Erin took the wheel of the SUV. Kai stretched out in the cargo space in the very back. They were only a couple miles from their own hotel anyway.

"I'm right behind you," Alex said to her. She watched the truck pull away behind Jason's. Snow crunched under the weight of the tires as they rolled away. A small Jeep 4x4 pulled up as Morgan met her on the walkway.

"What happened?" she said to him, but she knew the answer. He'd done something to Jason—a spell of some sort.

"You gave him blood," he replied. "I had to do something."

"He couldn't have remembered the taste," she answered. "I made sure."

Morgan looked down at her, folded his arms over his chest. "Did you?"

"I know what I'm doing, Morgan!"

He turned to Esmeralda, nodded at her and the others. Esmerelda led the others back inside the hotel. When Morgan turned back to Alex, he was angry.

"Obviously not, Alex! What were you thinking? Why would you risk it?"

"You had no right!"

"Neither did you," Morgan barked. She watched him pull his temper back then sigh. "How much did you give him?"

"Not much," she replied. "He's had others since then. He can't possibly remember what it tasted like after all this time."

Morgan's cheeks were a rosy red color from the cold around them. Alex barely felt it.

Morgan stepped into her personal space, took her chin in his fingers. "But, he did remember you giving it to him. That's the problem! If I hadn't erased that memory, who knows what might've happened?"

"I didn't ask you to," she exhaled and pulled his hand away. "I don't need your help."

Morgan pulled her into his arms. His embrace was caring and warm. "You will always need us, Alexa. You are special. You keep forgetting that."

She tried to pull free, but he wouldn't let her go. After a few seconds, she slipped out of his arms and stepped back.

"I should've known better," she said. "I *do* know better. I just wanted . . . to be close to . . . never mind."

He brushed snow from her hair as they walked toward the Jeep. A young man opened the passenger side door and waited silently. Alex was wrapped up in Morgan's arms again before she could say goodnight.

"I know you want to be like everyone else," he said as she shut her eyes tight. "But accept who you are, Alex. It's so much better."

Alex nodded, kissed him on the cheek, and slid into the warm car. She looked back and he was still standing there in the snow as they drove away.

Their floor was silent except for the hum of the poor lighting that lined each side of the hall. Alex could hear breathing, deep but steady, at each door. Even Sebastian was out cold. She tapped on Erin and Amy's door. Amy answered with a bottle of water in one hand and a bottle of aspirin in the other.

"Hey, you okay? We thought we lost you," Amy grinned as she popped the aspirin then chased it with a gulp of water.

"Yeah, just checking on you guys," she answered. "Everyone else tucked away, I guess?" A lump on one of the beds indicated Erin was already asleep. Alex turned her attention back to Amy.

"I just did a drive-by before you knocked. We're good, Boss," she replied and tossed the little blue and white aspirin bottle into a small bag that sat on the floor by the empty bed.

Alex said goodnight. A few doors down, she slid her key card through the electronic lock and pushed her room door open. A lone lamp blazed on the desk by the foggy window. Jason sat on the edge of the bed, eyes locked on a silent television.

"Welcome back," he mumbled as he watched a soccer match.

"What are you doing in here?" Alex asked. The door closed with a muffled sound. She kicked off her shoes and tossed the key card on the nightstand as she did. When she shrugged out of her jacket, it landed on top of the shoes.

There were two queen-sized beds in the room. One she slept in, the other she placed her overnight bag on. All of her clothes hung neatly in the small closet, and all her toiletries were in the bathroom. Jason sat on the bed she wanted so badly to climb into and sleep.

"Waiting for you," he answered then turned off the television to give her his full attention. "What took so long?"

As she pulled her sweater over her head, she tossed it over the chair at the desk, then she crossed over to the other bed, straightened her undershirt, and sat down.

Jason was dressed in a t-shirt and Adidas soccer shorts. His white tube socks were pushed down just above his ankles. The smell of soap filled the room.

"Shouldn't you be with your fiancée right now?"

"She's passed out in her own room."

"Okay. That still doesn't explain you being here instead of there."

Jason leaned back on one elbow and propped his knee up to lay his arm on top of it. Alex leaned back against the bag behind her.

"I think we should talk."

What could he possibly say that would make any difference to her now? He was sorry? So what? She was too, but that wouldn't change the fact that he was engaged and she had made a mistake. She never should have let him in. Never should have given him a taste. All her mistakes . . .

"Talk about what?"

Jason smirked at her as he picked absently at the thin blanket underneath him.

"Us."

"There is no 'us,' so good talk, and see you in the morning," she grinned and stood. Before she could turn to open the door, he was in her path. The movement was swift, impressive considering the amount of alcohol he'd had tonight and the spell Morgan had used to wipe his mind.

"I'm sorry I didn't tell you about my arrangement with Nikki before we . . ." he paused with a nervousness she didn't understand. "Before we got involved."

"I think you mean engagement," Alex smirked. "It comes before the actual marriage. And, yeah, you should have told me. But what's done is done."

Alex tried to step around him, but he moved as quickly as she did.

"Move, now."

"No. Not until I've said what I came here to say. So shut up and sit down," he frowned.

Alex plopped down on the bed again, and he sat next to her. When he took her hand in his, she didn't try to pull away. "Fine."

"The word I meant was arrangement," he continued,

"because that's what it is, an arrangement. Nikki and I have been friends for almost eighty years, Alex. I couldn't imagine myself without her or Adam in my life."

She just nodded because there was nothing really to say, was there? He'd made his choice and it wasn't her. He certainly didn't have to drive that point home now.

He sighed. "Adam and Nikki worked tirelessly to help me get that seat in the Lower Chamber."

Alex looked him in the eyes. "Wow," she couldn't stop the surprise in her voice. "Congratulations! That's a big deal for a second-gen, Jason."

Jason smiled, gave her small laugh. "Yeah, it is. Thank you."

There were very few second-generation vampires in the Lower Chamber of the Council of Pure Blood Vampires. For Jason to be among their ranks was a huge coup for him and Adam. For a turned human to get a coveted seat was a feather in Adam's cap as well.

"I'm sure Adam and Nikki are very proud of you," she said as he kissed her hand with warm, soft lips. "I'm sure no one will be expecting that announcement." When she pulled her hand free, he sighed.

"Conner's making the formal announcement at the Dark Ball in December," his voice trailed off.

Alex stood and pulled him to his feet. At the door, he wrapped his arms around her and held on tight. She could feel his heartbeat through her back. The heat of her body mixed with his until she kissed the arm closest to her mouth and he released her.

"I wasn't expecting to feel this way about you," he whispered as he stopped at the door and faced her. "I wish things were different."

"Things are different," she replied.

The anger reached him before the door flew open. If he'd been stronger, he might have been able to defend himself, but his strength wouldn't have been a match for Tristan anyway.

"Who is it?" Tristan snarled as he plucked Ben from the cot then flung him into the concrete wall across the cell.

His lungs spit out air on impact. Ben had just enough time to take in a little more before Tristan's hand clamped around his neck. He felt his feet leave the dusty floor as Tristan forced him against the wall and held him there.

"Something wrong?" Ben croaked and forced a smile. He squeezed his eyes shut when Tristan's fangs dropped to razor sharp points. Ben prayed his death would be quick.

Instead of the pain of teeth ripping through his neck, he felt hot breath against his ear.

"They made me kill one of my children, Benjamin," his voice slithered down and tapped on his eardrum. "She betrayed me without even knowing. You will tell me who the Dagger is!"

Ben's feet hit the floor, but Tristan's hand pressed against his chest. The pressure made it hard to breathe. He didn't struggle; what would be the point? He was as close to an ordinary man as he'd been before he joined the program. Even if he wanted, he couldn't come up with enough power to break free.

"I told you, the Dagger doesn't exist anymore," he exhaled.

The pressure weakened slightly, then Tristan removed his hand, stepped back, and straightened his posture and his demeanor.

Ben moved cautiously toward the bed. Once he was seated, Tristan pulled the stray chair close and sat down as well.

"I only want to speak with him," Tristan stated sweetly. "We have much in common."

Ben chose his next words carefully. One wrong turn of phrase and it would all be over.

"Well, the Dagger is gone, so I guess you're gonna have to figure something else out."

"You're lying."

"Prove it."

An eerie feeling moved over Ben's skin. Tristan's power was limited, but he did have some tricks up his sleeve. He reached into his inside jacket pocket. The smartphone he tossed over landed next to Ben's hand on the bed.

The screen popped to life and a video started playing. Alex, dressed in black gear, entered a large meeting hall. She looked like that kid he remembered from the past—in charge of the situation and ready to defend Jason with her life.

"I couldn't figure it out at first," he heard Tristan say. "Why everyone is so determined to protect her when she seems very capable of protecting herself."

Ben pushed up from the bed. "She is."

The device slid across the rumpled blanket back into Ben's line of sight. This time a still photo appeared. A group picture of the team outside a very official looking building. The sign read "Palace of Parliament" in Romanian and English. One after another, single shots of the young Tracker team appeared on screen. Then Jason, Adam, and Nikki.

"Then I realized that one of them is the Dagger," Tristan announced as he stood. When his shadow covered Ben, he wanted to stake him, but didn't have the strength or a weapon. "Something no one believed could exist, not in 600 years."

He barely felt the sharp blade slide between his two ribs. The point stopped at the wall of his pounding heart as Tristan's steady hand held it there. Pain crawled out in all directions from the point of origin. In the next few seconds, he would bleed out or Tristan would push the blade into his heart and end him quick.

"She told them a hybrid exists," Erin's giggly face announced from the device as Tristan held it up to him. "She's either crazy or I should have asked for more money."

Tristan slipped the phone back in his pocket, still

holding onto the blade.

"She should have asked for more money," Tristan hummed as he released the blade. It hung in Ben's chest as he stared at Tristan.

"Me too," Ben moaned. "Maybe I woulda died a millionaire," he tried to laugh, but it hurt like hell.

When his time came, Ben always thought it would be in a hail of gunfire. Not that this wasn't poetic, being staked by a vampire. But he had hoped for something more dramatic. His knees buckled slowly, or maybe it just felt that way to him. Slumped against the wall, he grabbed the hilt of the knife as he smiled up at Tristan.

Tristan knelt and stared at Ben as he died. He didn't seem happy, or sad for that matter.

"You'll die with honor," Tristan whispered. "You were loyal to the very end. I'll make sure she knows that."

Ben coughed up blood as he laughed. "That's not really a consolation, Tristan, but thanks for trying, I guess."

Tristan twisted the blade away from his heart. Ben stifled a scream. He wasn't going out like that. He'd bleed out, slowly, but he wouldn't beg for his life. Whether he would end up in heaven or hell was anyone's guess. He would leave this earth with one clear thought in his head. Once it was all said and done, Alex would make sure Tristan Ambrose died screaming.

Chapter 22

"Hey," a voice seemed to bark from miles away. "Alex! Hey!"

Darkness, black and complete, was everywhere she looked. And that voice still miles from where she felt her body suspended in the dark. It was so black she couldn't even see her own hand in front of her face. *Wait. Is my hand in front of my face?* she thought.

A stinging sensation spread over her senses. All at once she felt like she was being propelled forward at an unimaginable speed. So fast, in fact, that she felt like whatever she was headed for would kill her on impact. Then she felt the sting again.

Her eyes popped open and she reached out just as Sebastian's hand headed toward her cheek again. The grip she had on his wrist would have snapped it if he'd been human.

"Wow," he said as he sat next to her on the bed she was laid out on. "We were about to call the morgue, man. You were gone."

Alex blinked to bring him and the entire room filled with people into focus. Jason sat on the other side of her with her hand in his. He looked pale and worried, as did everyone else.

"What happened?" she moaned as Jason helped her sit up. The room spun like a top.

"You passed out," Jason replied. Erin tossed him a wet cloth. He pressed it to her forehead and the motion of the room stopped. "What's the last thing you remember?"

Alex reached out for that last memory; she was talking with Jason. Then a searing pain stabbed at her temple. After the heat came an icy feeling—as if she had just touched death.

"You were leaving," she groaned. "Then everything went black."

As she looked around the room, everyone glanced at each other. Their fear felt like a solid wall around her. It pushed at her. It swallowed up the oxygen around her. To everyone's surprise, Alex sprang from the bed and pushed open the French doors then landed on her knees on the snow covered balcony.

"Alex," she heard Jason behind her. "Breathe."

That's when she noticed she wasn't breathing; not at all. She took in a lung full of icy northern air and held it in her body until it forced its way out through her mouth in a trail of white smoke. Then she did it two more times before she climbed to her feet again.

Her hands were wet and cold, but she could feel her blood as it rushed through her body and that was a good thing. Amy handed her a bottle of water and Xavier held the chair for her as she sat down. The smartphone on the nightstand pinged and vibrated like a slot that just hit the jackpot. Then, one after another, everyone's phones did the same.

"It's 51," Sebastian announced. He looked grim and pale as everyone waited for his next sentence. "They found Ben."

Each one of her team members fished out their devices, and each one looked like Sebastian as they read the message. Amy was the first to cry. Big tears spilled from her eyes as Sebastian took her in his arms. Xavier made the call to confirm. The twins, Erin between them, wore silent but deadly stares on their faces. But Erin's deadly stare looked more like boredom than sadness.

"Alex," Jason's tone was smooth and even. "Everyone. I'm so sorry."

“They just found him in an abandoned warehouse,” Xavier said in a heavy tone. “Along with the crushed receiver Adam planted in that girl. She was dust.” He shoved his phone in his back pocket.

Alex licked her dry lips, swallowed what was left of the water, then threw the empty bottle at the trash bin by the door. She missed. Her device vibrated and pinged again. Kai tossed it to her.

“The doctor would like a word,” she hummed. “Go get your tablets and meet me downstairs in the conference room. I’ll get the manager to open it.”

They filed out in silence. Doors opened and closed down the narrow hallway. Jason was already on the old desk phone with the manager. At her door, he told the team that the room would be opened and ready as they filed out into the hallway. She could hear the elevator bell as the doors opened.

As she reached into her pack to pull out her own tablet, Jason waited for her. One of his personal bodyguards stood outside her room with a grim expression.

“Don’t let anyone on this floor until we return,” Alex ordered. “And no one comes down. Am I making myself clear?”

“Understood,” he answered as he escorted her to the elevator where her team waited inside. “Shall I send someone down with you?”

“No,” she shook her head and stepped inside. When she turned, Jason was at his own door with Nikki in his arms.

“We should get started on the guest list,” he heard Nikki say as she poured herself a cup of coffee. He declined when she asked if he would like one as well. “Maybe we could work on it on the way home.”

Alex and the Tracker team had been downstairs for over an hour. The sun was about to rise over the mountains and the morning session would begin in three hours. Nikki continued as he sat at his desk, towel tied securely around his waist, wondering what was going on downstairs.

"I wonder if Conner will let us use the Chamber Ballroom," she gushed as her polished nails tapped the screen of her personal laptop. "It's a beautiful venue."

"Shut up," Jason groaned.

"What?" Nikki barely noticed the growl in his tone. She was so wrapped up in her own world, Jason could have been on fire and she wouldn't have noticed.

"I said shut up, Nikki! Someone is dead," he grunted at her as he crossed the room to take down a suit for the morning's meeting. Dark gray wool, the suit was tailored to his physique by the best designer in Vegas. He'd had it made specifically for this meeting. Just the feel of it on his skin gave his ego a boost. "That stupid guest list can wait!"

"Whatever," she sniffed and rolled her eyes. "Why are you so bent out of shape? It's not like you knew him."

"Because I happen to care when someone I know loses a friend," he sniffed back. "Have some sympathy!"

Nikki unfolded her Lenovo Yoga so that it resembled a standard laptop again. After she placed it on the table, she stepped up to Jason and began to caress his damp chest with her cold hands.

"Jason," she said calmly, "God made them weak, mortal. They lost a friend, and that is sad, but it's really not our problem, is it?"

Jason pushed her hands away with the sudden urge to toss her from the balcony. An outraged expression covered her freshly scrubbed face.

"You can skip this session. I'm just finalizing the agreement with the Warren Coven—nothing I can't handle by myself."

"Why? Because I'm not weeping buckets over someone I didn't even know? That's so childish, Jason," she snapped.

"Just do as I say, Nikki," he grunted.

The feel of her hand in his made his stomach turn. The sweetness of her voice was like nails on a chalkboard for some reason. She kissed his palm then slid his index finger in her warm wet mouth.

"Don't think this is going to win you any points with her," she said as she made him draw his wet finger down the exposed skin between her full breasts. Jason pulled free and put some space between them so he wouldn't choke her with his bare hands. "Now that we're official, I won't tolerate the things I did before. I'm going to be your wife, so you may as well get used to that."

"I still have time to change my mind," he purred as he crossed over to the room service table. He poured a hot cup of coffee then poured a vial of blood in it.

"You won't," she said from the bed.

She was naked under her silk robe. It lay open to her flat stomach. When she shook her blonde hair loose, it sat on top of her pale shoulders like spun gold.

Jason didn't move, so she did. With a seductive grin on her face, Nikki stepped up to him and pressed her nakedness against his bare chest. Her coldness pushed through the towel still wrapped around his waist.

Nikki snaked her slender hand under the towel and began to stroke the solid flesh she found there. Jason grew even angrier at the involuntary response to her external stimulus.

"We're better together," she purred again. "You can't deny that, Jason."

Her cold lips touched his and he shivered. Warm, with a hint of blood, her breath tickled. Then her tongue slid over his mouth until he parted his lips and touched his tongue to hers.

"I'm not denying it," he whispered, "but don't pretend we're the couple of the year, Nikki. That bullshit is for the public." At his groin, a powerful desire pushed blood through him. He kissed her deeply as she jerked the towel free.

"Why are you always trying to pick a fight with me?" she panted on his lips, tossing the damp towel to the floor behind her, then dropping the robe on top of it. "You know how much that makes me want to fuck you senseless."

Jason swept her up in his arms effortlessly. Once they were on the bed, he was inside her in the blink of an eye. A euphoric cry pierced his brain as Nikki pleaded for him to go deeper. She clawed at the tangled sheets beneath her and he obeyed.

At the last forceful plunge, Nikki screamed, and he felt her body buck underneath him as she released. Her satisfied purr vibrated off his lips as he kissed her forehead and pushed away.

"I need another shower," he announced as he headed for the bathroom. "Go get dressed, please."

It didn't take long before he heard the door open and slam shut. As he stepped under the hot water, the anger returned.

Forensics only had a blurred picture of what had happened. The team stared at their screens as the doctor's dull, uninterested tone narrated the crime scene as it unfolded shot by shot. Dirty, damaged walls and dank dim corridors set a stage Alex didn't care to see.

"They had been feeding on him over some time," Dr. Carlisle droned. "If he hadn't died, he would have transformed pretty soon anyway."

"Transformed? You mean turned, right?" Amy sniffed, wiping at her red nose.

"No, transformed is the correct term," Dr. Carlisle answered. "He wouldn't have turned into a vampire, Amy. There was no infected blood in his system. They meant to make him something less than vampire—more like an animated corpse."

"Like a zombie," she whined. More tears sat in her already puffy, red eyes.

"A true zombie, as we know, doesn't exist," he answered. "His memories would have remained, but he wouldn't have connected them to a life he lived. He wouldn't have been Benjamin Palmer anymore. A shell, if you will, of his former self."

"A bite junkie," Sebastian groaned at his screen then cut a glance at Alex. "As long as he got his fix, he'd do whatever for the next one."

"Who did this?" Xavier grunted.

Dr. Carlisle's face appeared on screen. He looked somber and tired.

"We're not sure yet," he said. "The only DNA found was the dead girl's and Ben's."

"Bullshit," Alex said under her breath.

They all looked at her and Dr. Carlisle frowned from the screen.

"We combed the entire scene, Alex. There was nothing."

Alex sat straight and planted her hands on either side of the tablet. "Tristan is behind this and you know it! Pick up Brice Campbell and sweat him. Jesus!"

"We can't do that, Alex," Dr. Carlisle sniffed.

"Why not?" she exclaimed. The drinking glasses and empty pitcher rattled against each other when she slammed her hand down on the table.

"Need to know," he replied. An obvious smirk spread over his lips.

"Need to know? Doc, are you freaking kidding?" Kai squealed. "He was one of us. He was her friend. We deserve to know why Brice Campbell is untouchable."

Dr. Carlisle stood and someone else took his place in front of his computer. At first she didn't recognize him. He'd gotten older, as everyone does, over the years. She remembered him with a full head of dark, curly hair and a confident smile. Even though his expression was somber, his eyes still seemed bright. His head, however, was now as bare as a baby's bottom.

Major General Walter Diaz, late fifties and about to retire, looked fit and alert. Chances were they had just finished lunch because it was late afternoon in DC. In his fatigues, General Diaz made a striking figure of a modern soldier. As she remembered they used to call him "Dragon" Diaz. The guys under his command used to say he'd breathe fire down on you if you screwed up.

Alex and her team hadn't even had breakfast yet. In t-shirts and various styles of sweatpants, they looked like college kids home for the holidays. Beyond the plaster walls of the meeting room, day had broken and the sun had begun to melt last night's snow.

"Good morning," he said with a nod. "My condolences, Commander Stone. The President sends his regards to the entire Tracker team. We will wait for your return to make arrangements. He will, of course, have full military honors and burial at Arlington."

A lump formed in her throat as she nodded at the general. She hadn't fully wrapped her brain around the fact that Ben was gone. No one had.

"Thank you, sir," Xavier replied for the group. "We will wrap things up here by tomorrow night. Our plane is scheduled to depart at zero hundred hours, sir."

"Understood," General Diaz answered. "An escort will be waiting at Nellis when you touch down. Sorry, but you'll have to catch some shuteye on the way to Andrews."

"Yes, sir," they all answered except Alex.

"General," she cleared her throat. "I'd like us to be read in on Campbell. He's the key to all of this. I think we deserve to know why he still hasn't been brought in for questioning."

Diaz cut his eyes away then back. He raised his chin and the brightness of his eyes dulled just a bit. Everyone saw the same image on their screens. As the team Commander, Diaz addressed her directly.

"We need to keep him in play," he said.

"In play," Alex repeated. "He's an operative?"

"Civilian contractor," he replied. "He's been passing us intel for about five years."

"On what?"

There was that glance again. As if Dr. Carlisle approved or rejected his answers before he gave them.

"He was hired by a woman named Giselle Marafioti," he answered. "Her family migrated to the States from Romania when she was fifteen. She is said to have the second sight and was billed as such in her family's travelling circus."

"So she's a fortuneteller," Kai sniffed. "Big deal."

"She's more than that, son," Diaz frowned. "Tristan knows talent when he sees it."

"Meaning what?" Alex interrupted.

"Meaning she can translate most any language or write code that will translate the ones she can't. She has some magical skills as well. Mostly spellcasting."

"So what did she hire Campbell for?" Xavier asked with a hint of frustration.

"He has set up various off-shore accounts that we monitor. He has also purchased several parcels of real estate," he replied. "That warehouse was one of the holdings."

"I thought he was a cheesy entertainment lawyer," Alex asked the obvious question. "How'd he get into off-shore accounts and real estate?"

"Let's just say, he hasn't always worked in show business. He used to put trash back on the streets instead of on the big screen," Diaz said.

"Defense lawyer," Alex shook her head.

He didn't respond or change his expression at all.

"Wait," David spoke up. "This has been going on for five years? Why did we only learn about Tristan a few months ago?"

"That's not something I'm prepared to read you in on right now."

Alex trusted her instincts, and right now they screamed *set up*. David was right. The Trackers should have been brought in the moment Tristan escaped. As Strategic's top team, the assignment was theirs, automatically Alex should have been notified the moment after that. That still didn't explain why he wasn't in custody though.

"He's way off the reservation," Alex stated. "You can't bring him in, can you?"

"No. Not without jeopardizing several other operations," Diaz stated. He took a deep breath, then let it out slowly. "Right now, we need you to finish this assignment. We will keep tabs on Campbell."

After a few seconds, he stood and Dr. Carlisle sat down again.

"Any other questions?"

"Just one," Alex said. "Who's Campbell's handler?"

"Ramsey. Why?"

"Just curious," she grinned at him. "We have work to do. Keep me posted?"

"Of course," he grinned back. "Stay safe."

She disconnected before anyone else. On her feet, she gathered up her tablet and phone and left the meeting room without a word. The others caught up to her at the elevator.

Once they were inside and moving up, she stayed quiet even as the others stared at her in hopes of some sort of explanation. She didn't have one. She couldn't tell them why they'd been left out of all the details, why they should have known Campbell was in play as a contractor. But they weren't and that should have bothered them. Somehow, she could tell it didn't.

They filed out of the elevator one by one. In pairs, they entered their respective rooms with the understanding that they should be showered, dressed, and back downstairs in thirty minutes. No exceptions.

Alex entered her room, stripped as she walked through, and stepped under the shower spray as it heated up. For a few seconds, the water was ice cold. It helped wake her fully. It also helped to clear her clouded mind, which was why she stepped in before it was hot and ready.

Ben was dead. Coop was here, and she wasn't any closer

to finding out what was really going on. To top it all off, one of the six people under her command was a traitor. She was sure of that now. Tristan did not escape the DPG alone. Coop was turned for a reason. Becker now belonged to some other outfit. And no one had even bothered to ask the one question that haunted her from the moment she agreed to this assignment. *What the hell was wrong with this picture?*

Chapter 23

They weren't just pictures on his wall anymore. Each one was an obstacle in his way. If he wanted back in, he'd have to prove these "kids" were flawed.

Freelance work paid the bills, but now that the program had real money behind it, everyone associated with Strategic was riding high. Everyone but him. K.C. Becker regretted the ultimatum he had given Dr. Carlisle all those years ago.

With Alex on the bench, it only seemed logical, right? Matt had gone back home and Ben had been reassigned to DC. Why couldn't he be lead on the next assignment? Coop, that stooge, didn't know a vampire from a kick in the head. He had barely made it through boot camp. The new team should have been Becker's. He'd put in more time than Coop at that point.

Becker felt the irritation, even now, as he remembered those days. No love was lost between him and Coop during that time either. What qualified a chump like him to lead the rookies?

"He's doing much better on the supplements than you are, Becker," Dr. Carlisle had said. "I'm still working through your results. It just seems strange that you are breaking down without any warning like this."

Truth be told, Becker had noticed it right off: night sweats, muscle fatigue, nausea. He didn't tell Ben because he knew his report would go straight to the doctor and he'd be off SandBox.

Dr. Carlisle shook his head as he looked over the file.

"Every time we increase the dosage, your vitals go off the charts. I need to be able to keep you stable at those levels, Becker. I won't clear you for field duty until I can."

That sounded final and it was. Coop took over the new team and Becker was stuck at 51 like a rat in a cage.

"Doc," Becker remembered the plea clearly, "please. I'll be fine. I'm all you got left of the originals anyway."

Dr. Carlisle was quiet for a few minutes as he flipped the pages back and forth. Becker thought he'd convinced the doctor to give him a chance. Then Dr. Carlisle sighed.

"We'll keep you under observation for one more week," Dr. Carlisle stated. "If you hold steady at this level, we'll revisit letting you lead the next mission."

Becker tried to hide his disappointment as Dr. Carlisle gave him a quick pat to his sore shoulder.

"Doc! Come on," Becker harped.

"Trust me," he said with another pat then he left him on the exam table.

For the first three days, Becker felt like his old self again. Power, stamina, all of it was in check. On day four, he found out Alex wouldn't be back. In fact, she went MIA after she was released from the loony bin. He couldn't, for the life of him, understand why. And no one offered any kind of explanation—not even Ben.

"Becker," he heard Ben say over the small conference room speaker. "She's just taking some time, you know. That assignment was pretty rough, on all of us."

"Yeah, but she's disappeared," Becker replied. "The doc's freaking out, man. What's up?"

He remembered a strange feeling touched his skin at Ben's silence. Ben was never silent and had never lied to them until that day.

"Nothing," he chuckled. "She's a girl, right? Teenage rebellion and whatnot. Just let it go, Becker."

Later that night, Becker increased his dosage without permission. He told Ben he'd let it go, but he wanted to find Alex on his own—bring her back and prove his worth to the organization. He felt great for most of the evening. During the exam around midnight, the doctor bumped his meds too. He looked pleased at the progress he thought Becker had made. Becker didn't say a word because he wanted off the base, soon. By the time his test results came back, he'd be so fantastically fit that they'd have to release him to active duty again.

Early on day five, the sweating started. At first, he thought the AC had quit. It was set to sixty degrees when he checked around four in the morning. On his way to breakfast, everyone else wore sweats and jackets because it was so cold. Becker was in shorts and a t-shirt and he was still hot.

By noon, the smell of sweat overtook the oxygen in his room. All the way up the elevator to the main level, Becker coughed and sticky sweat poured from his body. Once he was outside, he threw up his breakfast burrito then passed out on the concrete outside the hanger.

When he opened his eyes, Dr. Carlisle, a nurse, and Ben stood over him. Every word seemed to be on the lowest setting. The only sound that hurt his ears was the sound of his own heart as it raced in his aching chest.

He had missed his window of opportunity to take over the new team. Afterward, he split from Area 51 and roamed around for a while. A chance meeting brought him to his current outfit. It was not as well funded as Strategic or as well equipped. But the pretty doctor that headed the facility fixed the damage the supplements had done to him, albeit temporarily. She was able to keep him stable while the genius Dr. Carlisle could not.

Money wasn't a problem for Becker. Strategic had paid well for his silence. The jobs were shit and the pay was worse with this outfit though. The good part was he got to lead his own team finally. Mostly washouts from other high profile programs, his team learned fast, took direction without question, and cleaned a scene with near precision.

Strays and rogue elements had been the targets until

now. Now they were on the trail of a traitor and an escapee from DPG. He didn't know who paid for the hunt and, to be honest, he didn't really care. He just knew the take was bigger than any other job and everybody needed the fix—especially him.

As he stared at the photos again, he wondered which was the traitor. They all seemed like regular kids—if you considered a vampire, a witch, a computer genius, a couple of bombmaking twins, and a former rookie SWAT member regular. *Maybe that was the point,* he told himself. *Who would suspect evil in those innocent faces?*

He laughed out loud. "Anybody who's ever seen a horror movie."

Tomas knocked then came in through the connecting door. He was dressed for this morning's meeting at the Palace. Becker still couldn't get over how different he looked without the collar.

"I'll try to get this meeting done as quickly as I can," he said as he poured a cup of fresh coffee. "I'd like to have more time to speak with Alex."

Becker grinned at him. "You're not going to convince her to join us; you know that, right?"

"Why not? I think if we present our case, she's intelligent enough to understand how dangerous it is for a creature that is half vampire and half human to walk among us," Tomas replied.

Becker couldn't help his boisterous laughter. Even he had a hard time with the information they'd stolen from the lab at 51. How could such a creature exist? And how come no one had told them it was even possible for vampires and humans to mate and conceive?

"Yeah! Tell her a vampire and a human had a kid and see if she believes you."

"We have proof," he replied with a scowl.

"We have a bunch of scattered notes," Becker corrected him. "Carlisle is kind of an evil genius. So if he was able to create a hybrid and hide it in the world, she's gonna want to help us find it. But we have to have more than the diary of a mad supergenius before she'll come over to our cause."

Tomas laughed. "She will listen. She's a reasonable person."

"She'll listen because she knows monsters exist," Becker said. "This hybrid thing . . . She may have to see it to believe it."

They finished their coffee as they discussed things besides the cause.

Chapter 24

"As you can see," Jason said as Morgan and Esmeralda looked over the ten-page agreement, "this truce will stay in effect until the threat has been neutralized. Your personal holdings, the plantation in New Orleans, and the island in the West Indies are off limits."

Esmeralda nodded as Morgan continued to review the small print. Alex could see his brow furrow at each new line. He tapped the page and Esmeralda looked down.

"What about line 15, section D?" he asked as he looked up at Jason. "You're asking us to allow agents of your choosing access to our new training house. Why?"

Jason sat back in his chair. "Our agents will need a base of operations soon. The training house is fortified and protected by the most powerful witch in world," he smiled at Esmeralda. "If there's trouble, they'll need as much help as possible."

"What kind of trouble?" Morgan asked.

"We have reason to believe Hellclaw has reestablished a house somewhere in Washington DC."

"So?" Morgan frowned.

"Your recent purchase of an entire brownstone in Georgetown will be perfect. The renovations have just been completed and it is ready for its new occupants," Jason grinned.

Morgan didn't mask his surprise very well. Alex had the distinct impression they wanted to keep that a secret. Somehow, Jason found out and Morgan was not happy about it.

"What's your point?" he replied as Esmeralda laid her hand over his fist.

"We'd like to put our team in that brownstone," he answered.

"For how long?" Esmeralda asked.

"Until we can secure a place of our own," Jason replied. "We know we're behind the curve on this and we were hoping you'd assist us—just for a few weeks, a month tops."

Morgan's jaw immediately set tight. His eyes narrowed on Jason as he sat comfortable and smug a few feet away. If not for Esmeralda, he would have already jumped the table to get at Jason.

"No," Morgan huffed. "We'll not let you use our training house for this hunt." He pushed the paper away, unsigned.

"I understand your hesitation," Jason continued to grin. "But you agreed to join this alliance. In doing so, you also agreed to certain terms—one of which is the use of any property not deemed personal, for use by designated agents of the Council of Pure Blood Vampires. We're only asking for a few weeks. If we start moving people in now, they could get suspicious. You were there first. Another round of moving trucks could send up a red flag."

"Your mistakes are your own. I didn't agree to be used by you or the Council," he growled. "Hellclaw exists because your kind didn't have the stones to have them eradicated completely."

When he stood, so did Jason. His personal bodyguards moved in from the perimeter of the room and so did Alex. Jason raised his hand and they stopped.

"You were foolish to think, with Tristan gone, they would just abandon all that he had taught them to survive," Esmeralda joined in. "He wanted them to infiltrate the other houses, learn their weaknesses, and, when Tristan returned, use all of that information to bring down your Council."

"We'll find him and the rest of his followers," Jason replied. "But make no mistake. He sees every group that signed the covenant as an enemy. Do you think you're strong enough to take him on alone?"

"Maybe not," Morgan sneered. "But allowing our property to be destroyed, on the off chance your team can find his, seems like an awful lot to ask."

"Morgan, I can assure you that your property will be taken care of," Jason stated. "Any damages will be fully covered by the Council. We'll do our best to be out before anything bad happens to the facility. And we'll do our best not to break anything while we're there."

Morgan chuckled as he stared at Alex over Jason's shoulder.

"How nice of you, Jason. You have a deal under one condition. We get to add a stipulation before we sign," he smiled broadly at Jason.

"Which is?"

"The team must be led by Alex Stone," he announced.

"I can't speak for Alex," Jason began, only to have his mouth waved shut by Morgan.

"She leads the team or no deal."

"She's a contractor, Morgan," Jason sniffed. "We can't make her do this. We can extend the contract for the others, easily. But she doesn't belong to Strategic—not really."

"Then maybe you should make her an offer," he replied with a laugh. "Because we will not let you put vampires under your rule in our training house without her."

Jason turned toward Alex, a mask of agitation covering his face. He thought this would be easy. Unfortunately for him, Morgan didn't want to make this easy. His dislike of Jason was evident, but it went deeper than that.

"I'll have to take this to the Head of the Council," Jason sighed as he turned back to Morgan and Esmeralda.

"Go ahead," he answered then sat down again. "We'll wait."

At least she had the morning off. Nikki took in the

sights as she thought about all the plans that needed her attention. Jason's childish dismissal of her for the session with the Warrens turned into a blessing. She could window-shop instead of watch Jason pretend not to be watching Alex every chance he got.

The little café was perfectly quiet and quaint, she thought as she took the empty table by the window. Once her coffee and pastry arrived, Nikki thanked the little lady and took her time with her breakfast. The last thing she was worried about was Jason, for once.

She'd decided on a beautiful black box invitation. Each satin box would contain the official invitation, RSVP card, and a black return envelope neatly bound together by a deep red silk ribbon. The three hundred guests that Jason had limited her to would be selected by Jason and Nikki. This was going to be the event of the year. And when Conner made the announcement of Jason's appointment to the Lower Chamber, everyone that was anyone would want to attend.

Her pride and ego swelled as she thought about all the excitement that would buzz around her wedding. She suddenly felt a little panic flutter in her chest. Did she have the right dress? She sighed and giggled to herself. Of course she did. The wine red strapless gown was beyond dramatic. The mermaid design wrapped her body in silk all the way to her knees, then opened up around her legs in gorgeous folds of tulle. A diamond tiara was being made specifically for that dress. She would be the talk of the social circuit for years to come.

"May I warm your coffee miss?" the lady's voice intruded on Nikki's musing.

"Yes," she sniffed as she pushed the small, white cup toward the edge of the table.

Fresh coffee scent surrounded her. She put the tablet down and stirred in real cream as she admired the picture of her dress again. A quick sip to test the temperature, Nikki tapped the screen again to move to a back view of the dress.

The taste of that first sip bounced around her mouth. She put down the tablet and took another sip. She couldn't remember the last time she'd tasted coffee this good. Aromatic and rich, it didn't need a thing, not even a bit of blood to kill a bad taste. It didn't have a bad taste.

"May I ask," Nikki said over her shoulder to the woman as she wiped down the small counter. "Do you grind this here?"

"Yes, miss," she smiled. "Would you like to buy some?"

"Yes," Nikki smiled back. "One pound please."

The woman disappeared behind a dull colored curtain. When she returned, she had a small bundle wrapped in plain, brown paper in her wrinkled hands. Nikki immediately put the package to her nose and took a big whiff of the coffee. It was heavenly.

On her walk back to the hotel, she let that smell invade her senses. The short walk was pleasant. Inside the elevator, her vision blurred. When she reached the room, she had to lean against the door because the room began to spin. Before she could catch it, the package dropped from her fingers and broke open on the carpet at her feet.

She thought she heard her phone ring deep inside her purse.

"Paul? Come to my room, please," she slurred and the phone dropped from her hand.

Not long after, he ran through the door and caught her as she fell.

"I got you," she heard a deep voice say next to her ear.

Paul laid her gently on the bed then went to the bathroom. He returned with a cool cloth. As he laid it over her forehead, he put his phone to his ear and answered the door.

Nikki heard the scuffle, but she was too weak to move. When the smell of sulfur and ash reached her nose, she felt her stomach flip. Then her body began to rise from the bed. She must have blacked out because a sudden blast of cold air popped her eyes open.

A warmth spread over her cold skin as a man slid her

inside the back seat of a pristine sedan. He got in next to her and her head dropped to his shoulder. She could no longer fight the darkness as it came crashing down on her. Then she heard him laugh.

"We haven't been properly introduced, Ms. Hanson," he chuckled as he held her face in his cold hands. "Jesse Cooper, at your service," he smiled. "Everyone calls me Coop, though."

She tried to form that word, but her mouth would not cooperate. She even tried to push him away and reach for the door handle, but the drug was strong and growing stronger as she fought her heavy eyelids.

"Don't try to fight it, Nick," Coop's watery voice told her. "It was in the coffee you had too much of." He and the driver she was suddenly aware of laughed together.

He took her purse, dug out her phone and tossed it from the car window. The last thing she heard was a cackle of a laugh come from the driver and something about a small taste before they killed her.

"You don't have to do this," Morgan said to Alex.

"Neither do you," she replied.

"I'm just trying to get you a way out of this."

"I don't see a way out of this."

Morgan tapped the table with his thumb as he stared at Alex. Jason was still on the line, supposedly with Conner. It had been almost thirty minutes. Esmeralda sat silently behind them. *That's very unusual for Esmeralda—to be quiet, that is,* Alex thought as she turned in her seat to look at her.

"What? Nothing to say?" she hummed.

"Don't be ridiculous," Esmeralda purred. "I have plenty to say. I'm just waiting on you two to stop the staring game for two seconds."

Alex sat up straight, crossed her legs, and blinked.

"Whatever you're planning on doing with that weapon, don't," Esmeralda announced.

"How'd you find out about it, anyway?" Alex frowned. No one could keep a damn secret these days.

"Please," Esmeralda waved her off. "Bianca called me the second you came to Ashblood asking for that favor she owed you. Do you understand what the spell will do?"

"Not really. I was kinda hoping I wouldn't have to find out," Alex grinned. "Now I'm intrigued."

"It will interrupt our spell," Morgan joined in. "It will allow you to bring her to the surface again."

With a few magic words, all the pain they went through to help her put a lid on her rage could all be wasted. How fair was that? When she needed them, they were there with Roland to save her from herself. Once she had been physically freed of Creed, his mental hold on her had to be broken for her to truly start over. Blood bonds could only be broken one way—death. She had died and been reborn, in a way.

Esmeralda, Morgan, and Roland had brought her back from death. Now, Alex was considering breaking the spell just to have an edge on Tristan. But how strong was she now? She talked a good game, but was she really any stronger now than she was then?

Alex was afraid to answer that question. They hadn't had time to study the bracelet and text that the Cantu had brought her properly, but she trusted Esmeralda. If she said the bracelet's own magic would block the current spell, it would. She'd be soulless once again.

"If it helps me get Tristan, I can handle it," Alex said.

"You couldn't handle it before," Esmeralda replied.

"That was only because of the blood bond," Alex stated. "It was broken when I died, remember?"

Alex grinned at them because she thought she'd won the argument. Esmeralda sat forward and glared at her. Maybe the argument had just begun.

"Your bond with Creed was broken, but that thirst for blood and pain existed in you before that happened," Esmeralda said. "Remember?"

"Yeah, I remember. I remember what I used to be, Esmeralda. Thanks for reminding me I was a psycho bitch! I can control that now. I was different then."

"Were you? Or did you just get tired of fighting what they'd turned you into?" Morgan hummed as he still tapped the table. "You came to us begging to be freed! Begging for a chance to make things right. Now you want to go back to that? Just to arrest Tristan again?"

Alex moved closer to Morgan. "I'm not going to arrest him. I'm going to kill him this time, just like the Mistress told me to. Just like I should have been able to do all those years ago, but couldn't! I wasn't strong enough back then, but I am now."

"Then don't use that thing," Esmeralda was next to her now. "You don't need it. Like you said, you're stronger now."

Her slim hand smoothed Alex's hair as she tried to not to be afraid. But she was, and Alex could feel it.

"I need it," Alex whispered. "If I try to do this like I am now, I'll fail."

"Why?" Morgan whispered back as he took her hand in his.

"Because," Alex swallowed the lump in her throat—that sign of weakness she tried hard to conquer. "Because I care about this team. I don't want them to get hurt or worse. Because they deserve to live a little while longer. And if I don't bring that part of me back—that part that doesn't give a damn about anything or anybody—I can't beat Tristan."

"He'll use that against you," Esmeralda sighed.

"Yes. He'll make me choose."

"Your life or theirs?"

"No," Alex stood up and stared down at them. "Their lives or the lives of everyone else."

A loud bang caused Morgan and Esmeralda to jump to their feet as Alex ran for the door. "Stay put," she yelled at them over her shoulder.

She pushed the door open as smoke and screams filled the hallway. Her earpiece buzzed and crackled. It was out.

As she turned the far corner, two of the Warren guards practically ran her down.

"Go! They're both in the meeting hall," Alex yelled over the chaos.

In the next hallway, Sebastian and Xavier pushed their way toward her. Xavier's head bled above his right eye. Sebastian was covered in dust.

"Where are the others?" she demanded as they pushed back through the crowd and desperately ran for the exit.

"David is with Jason," Xavier yelled. "They're getting him to the truck."

"Kai's trying to shut down the exits with the palace guards. Everyone is being evacuated to the commissary tent on the far lawn. Erin and Amy are there now. No one leaves the grounds until we say," Sebastian replied.

"Xavier, you head to the tent," Alex ordered, then yelled at his back. "See if Erin can get comms back online!" He threw his hand in the air to let them know he heard her.

As they cleared the crowd, Alex and Sebastian headed toward the guard house at the entrance to the grounds. The bomb had taken out an empty wing of the palace. That was a warning. If they didn't move fast, the next one would kill people.

"No one's left," he said as the palace guards stood, assault rifles in hand, at the exits.

"Should we head over to the blast site? Kai should get as much evidence as he can before the locals mess shit up," Sebastian stated.

"Be careful," she warned. The rock in the pit of her stomach told her this wasn't over yet. "Five minutes, then meet us at the tent."

They ran in one direction; she ran toward the main stairs. Jason was being rushed to his vehicle when he saw her.

"Jesus," he huffed as he took her in his arms. "What the hell happened?"

"Not sure yet, but we'll see you at the hotel," she

answered then pushed out of his arms. "Don't stop for anything," she said to the driver and the two bodyguards. "When you get to the hotel, lock down the floor and the stairwell. Two guards on the elevator in the main lobby and the floor. Where's Adam?"

"He's already at the hotel," Jason announced. "He's checking on Nikki."

She just nodded as Erin's voice came through the earpiece.

"Boss, we're up again," she said sweetly.

"Thanks."

"We need to get to the tent," David stated as he waved his phone at her. "Kai's got something."

She followed David away from the truck with one more glance at Jason.

At the commissary tent, the atmosphere had begun to calm a bit. Palace guards stood outside and patted down everyone who approached the entrance, including Alex and David.

Once inside, Alex scanned the crowd. As people sat in tight groups close to the entrance, Erin stood in the far corner on her phone. Her back was to the crowd for some reason. A tight grip closed around her elbow before she could start toward her.

"Need some help?" Becker's grim expression surprised her.

"What are you doing here?" she responded.

He looked over his shoulder at Tomas and another man she didn't recognize. They seemed to be in deep conversation. The man had a cut on his arm that Tomas attended to.

"He had a meeting right next door to the blast," Becker answered.

"Is he hurt?"

"No, but we'd like to help you, if you need it."

Alex glanced back; Erin was gone, and so was Amy.

"I think they're trying to get everyone out in an orderly fashion. We've got guards checking out the cars and the drivers before we let anyone out of here."

"I'll give them a hand," he smiled at her. "Tomas is pretty good at keeping people calm in a crisis. Maybe it's the former priest in him."

Becker stepped outside and she could see him take control of the situation with the wave of a badge of some sort. She didn't have time to worry about that though. She tapped the device in her ear and called for Xavier.

"Where are you?"

"In the guard tower, like you said."

"The guard tower?"

"Yeah, Erin said you wanted us to meet you in the guard tower above the tent. Right?"

Alex rolled her eyes up as she yelled for Becker. He was at her side in a flash, along with Tomas.

"We have to clear this tent now."

Becker didn't ask any questions. He and Tomas began to calmly direct people toward the exit as Alex backed toward it herself. In the crisp early afternoon air, she felt her body began to warm up as adrenaline pumped through every vein. Her leather jacket, light as a second skin normally, seemed heavy now as she shook it from her body.

"Tent's clear," she heard Becker yell as he took one last look inside.

She gave him a wave as she began to run toward the elevated guard station directly behind it. Erin ran toward her with a young man by her side. They parted ways when she spotted Alex.

"What's wrong?" she asked innocently.

"You tell me," Alex answered just as innocently. "Why aren't you up there with the team? You know, since I sent you to get them together and all."

Alex glanced up. Sebastian and Xavier appeared to try pulling the door open. From her vantage point, she could see the stairs were wired and so was the door. If they opened it, it would blow both of them, as well as Kai and Amy, to pieces.

"Don't open that door" she yelled. They stopped and the four of team members appeared in front of the observation glass. "The door's wired. You gotta jump."

Erin began to laugh uncontrollably. Alex grabbed her arm, twisted it behind her back, and forced her to the cold ground.

"Are you crazy? That's gotta be like twenty feet," she heard Kai squeal.

David came up next to her as she held Erin down. "What the fuck?"

"That whole building is wired," Alex nodded toward the rest of the team.

David ran toward the guard house at full speed. Alex released Erin and followed.

"Well," Xavier hummed as he pulled his weapon from the holster. "I always did like that scene in *Butch and Sundance.*"

Kai nodded as he, Sebastian, and Amy copied Xavier. They aimed at the glass and fired. The sound of breaking glass reminded Sebastian of wind chimes. A blast of cold air rushed inside the room.

Xavier and Kai began to toss furniture out of the way then ripped the desk from the wall. They turned to Sebastian and Amy.

"If we get a running start, we might hit the tent," Xavier surmised. "It might break the fall, a little."

"Or not," Kai shrugged with a grin.

Sebastian turned to Amy. "I might be able to keep us both airborne for a bit. Or at least slow us down. I'll pull in when we clear the building. Just hold on tight."

"What?" Amy looked at her teammates with stunned surprise.

"Oh yeah," Kai smiled. "He can levitate."

"Kinda," Xavier added.

"Kinda," Amy sighed and tightened her grip on Sebastian's hand.

They heard Alex's jumpy voice blast through the earpieces.

"Aim for the tent!"

They all laughed, backed up and ran.

Alex and David were blown back by the blast. With all the smoke and fire, it was hard to see where any of them might have landed as she tumbled head over heels down the slope. As wood and glass and metal rained down on them, Alex finally stopped. She didn't see David right away. When he struggled to his feet, he waved at her.

The tent had collapsed in on itself. It was covered in debris as the smoke began to clear. She and David tossed mangled chairs and steel rods out of the way as they searched. To her right she saw movement. As she reached the spot, Xavier's head came up as he pushed trash off of his body.

"Talk to me," she said as he moaned.

"I'm good," he groaned and snapped a finger back in place with a grunt. "Nothing that won't heal." He tried to laugh, but it came out as a grunt instead. She helped him to his feet.

"Hey! Over here!" They ran toward David's voice.

They had to climb over the twisted remains of a wall to reach him. As more smoke cleared, he sat in the middle of the chaos with his brother's head in his lap. It was hard to tell if Kai was conscious. With all the noise around her, Alex couldn't focus on anything.

"He's hurt bad," David sniffed. "We gotta get him to a hospital."

Xavier ran toward the sirens she had just noticed blaring in the distance. David slipped out of his jacket and placed it around his brother. As she knelt down, she heard another moan and cry for help—Sebastian.

"The uniform should help to keep him warm," Alex

gave David a pat on the shoulder.

"Go help Sebastian. I got this, boss."

He wasn't far away. A small hill of metal and wood separated him from David and Kai. As she climbed over it, she saw his back. The material of his shirt was slashed like someone had taken razors to his back. Pieces of metal and wood were embedded in his skin. His head was bowed and his body was shaking.

Alex stepped up to him. Amy, pale and still, was attached to him by a long metal rod. It had gone straight through her heart and into his side. All Alex could hear was one heartbeat—his.

"Come on, Amy," he whimpered and sniffed. "Open your eyes. Please."

Upon closer inspection, the rod was silver and so were the random pieces of metal embedded in his skin. The longer he let the rod stay in his body, the more the poison would leech into his bloodstream.

"Sebastian," Alex whispered as she took hold of the rod. "I have to take this out or you'll die from the poison. It's silver."

He just shook his head as the tears rolled down his pale face. She could smell the silver now. As it hit his blood, it would soon kill all the blood that kept him alive.

"Don't," his voice cracked. "You'll kill her."

Alex moved in closer, wrapped her arm around his shoulders and put her lips to his ear.

"She's already dead."

She jerked the rod free of Sebastian, then Amy. He fell back then dropped to his side as Alex laid Amy down in a patch of snow. She covered Amy's face with Sebastian's jacket.

Chapter 25

The best medical bay in this country was on Jason's plane. Alex had Sebastian and Kai sent there while the rest of the team headed to the hotel. Adam said there was an emergency there.

On the way, it had been decided the conference was over. Everyone would leave immediately. She promised Esmeralda and Morgan she would call them before takeoff. She wasn't sure how to tell them about Amy.

David stayed with his brother and Sebastian. Xavier and Alex were the only members of the team left to fight. Erin was the next target.

"We'll find her," Xavier hummed as he pushed the SUV faster and faster toward the hotel. "And when we do, she's done."

"We have to make sure Jason and his group are secured on the plane first. If she hasn't found the tracker I planted on her, then she'll be easy to find."

They pulled up to the hotel and were escorted to Jason's floor. As they exited the elevator, the smell of ash wafted toward them.

"Someone's dead," Xavier whispered.

Alex entered the room to see it in shambles. Jason sat next to the window, a pile of ash at his feet. Adam was on the phone next to the rumpled king-size bed. He spoke in low tones.

"What happened?" she asked the room.

"Nikki's missing," Jason's weary voice announced.

"Mobile?"

"No answer," he sighed. "We're trying to track it, but so far nothing."

Alex walked around the mess hoping to spot a clue. She didn't think Nikki was in on this, but she had to be sure.

"Who's dust?" she asked.

"Paul, probably," Adam answered before Jason could. "He was assigned to her, and that's his ring there in the middle."

A small signet sat on the dust, charred and warped from the heat of his body as it burned. Jason just stared at it without blinking. Then she spotted something odd—the pile of coffee grounds next to the ash.

"Coffee grounds. Where'd they come from?"

Xavier picked up the busted wrapper with a knife he took from the room service tray.

"Looks like they're from a café around the corner from here."

Jason stood, crossed in front of Alex then punched the flatscreen TV dead center. The glass spiderwebbed but stayed bolted to the wall. He stepped up to a silent bodyguard.

"Go down to the café and find out if she was there," he ordered.

"Yes, Sire," he said, taking the paper from Xavier and leaving the room.

"Why wasn't she at this morning's meeting?" Alex asked Jason's back.

"I told her she could have the morning off," he said. It didn't sound like the complete truth to her.

She turned to everyone else. "Give us five minutes please. Then take Mr. Stavros and Mr. Craig to the plane."

When the room was empty, except for Adam, Jason, and Alex, he turned to her. He looked angry and tired and ready to kill someone. He didn't want do this in front of Adam, but right now his pride wasn't the most important thing, was it?

"Why wasn't she with you this morning?" Alex

repeated.

"We argued, so I told her to stay here."

Adam took a seat on the bed.

"What did you argue about?"

"Us," he answered. "You and me."

Jason glanced at Adam, who was still as a statue. Unlike Alex, he knew Adam could mask his rage into a nonchalant gaze of indifference.

"So you got mad and made her stay here," Alex said. He nodded. "Did you notice anything unusual when you left?"

"Nothing."

He watched her approach the pile of ash and pick up the ring. She stood as she studied it closely. Then she slipped it in her pocket. That's when he noticed the rips and tears in her uniform. That's when he noticed she had blood on her hands too.

"When was the last time you fed from her?" she asked in the most unemotional tone he had ever heard.

His anger burned through him. Was she trying to embarrass him? Scold him in front of his sire?

"A couple of days ago," he replied when he realized why she asked the question. "I don't think I can track her now. I've never been very good at it and she's fed from someone else recently."

"Who?" Adam joined the conversation.

Jason dropped his gaze to the ashes then back up at Alex. She shook her head as she rubbed at her temples. They all turned to the door when it opened again.

"We got a fix on Erin," Xavier announced.

"The tracker worked?" Alex asked, a little excited.

"No. She's on the phone," he replied as he held his out to her. "She wants to speak to you."

"He wants her back, you know," Alex heard Erin giggle. There was some commotion in the background. Nikki's voice screamed and Coop's familiar chuckle cut through it.

"Yes, I know."

"You seem awfully calm for someone who just got

dumped," she giggled. "But, you're probably used to it by now, huh?"

"Let's get to the part where you tell me where you are," Alex sneered. "You know it's me you want and you know you're gonna tell me to come and get Nikki."

"You're so smart, aren't you?"

The line went dead then a text came through—the address to Dracula's Castle.

"Who was that?" Jason said. "Do they have Nikki? Is she alive?"

"Yes and we'll get her back. I just need to get you to the plane safely."

Adam stepped in her path to the door. "Who was that?"

"Erin."

"Erin," Jason stated. "Your Erin?"

"Yes. She and Coop, and probably Creed, have Nikki. We're going to get her back, alive, and then we're leaving this place."

"I'm going with you," Jason announced as he dropped one last bag on the cart and watched the bellhop roll it away.

"No, you're not."

"Why is it just you and Xavier here? Where are the others?"

They followed the cart to the elevator. Jason let Adam get on first, then he told him they would take the next one. The doors closed with Adam glaring at them.

"Where are the others?" he repeated.

The car came up and they stepped inside. Alex pressed the button and kept her back to Jason. He spun her around.

"Where is the rest of the team?"

"Sebastian was hurt in the explosion," she said as she faced forward again. "Kai is in critical condition. David is with him."

"And Amy?"

Alex faced Jason and she fought back tears with everything she had.

"She's dead."

The stunned look on Jason's face almost made her cry. The doors opened and she waved him out first. As they walked behind his bags, two bodyguards fell in line behind them. Everything was already loaded in the trucks when they stepped outside. It had become overcast and began to snow again.

Erin didn't like to wait. Not for permission. Not for action. Not for anything. All that time spent training with Alex and learning from her had paid off though. *I know Alex pretty well,* she thought to herself. *Alex will come for Jason's whore just to look like the bigger person. She won't let Jason come with her though—not smart. And, if nothing else, Alex is smart.*

"Idiots," Nikki hissed at them, "all of you!"

With a grin, Erin turned from the dirty window she had watched the sun set through. Nikki, held to a metal chair by pure silver chains, grew weaker by the minute. If they didn't hurry, it would be too late and Jason would hate Alex forever.

She took a step toward Nikki with the intention of causing her more pain, but Coop stopped her. His hazel eyes sparkled as he spoke.

"Don't let her in your head. It's not worth it."

"Is that the best advice you can give?" Nikki moaned as her head lolled from side to side. She coughed up blood as she laughed. "How about, 'run before it's too late'—before I get free?"

The yell brought dust from above. The old theater had seen better days. Its stage was scuffed and dirty, littered with old costumes and sheet music. The once red velvet curtains were moth eaten and filthy from years of neglect. The audience seats were in disarray. Some were tossed carelessly in the orchestra pit. Others had been pulled loose during an abandoned renovation attempt.

Above them, rusted chains held backdrops high. They looked as if they'd fall any minute.

"You should stop struggling, Nick," Coop said with a smile. "That only helps the silver move faster through your body."

Coop peered out from center stage. The spots of lights from the damaged roof made it possible to see some of the darker points of the room. But as the sun died, so would the light, so Erin had left a trail for Alex to follow.

All at once, Coop could smell Erin's blood. Alex had slammed her to the ground pretty hard back at the palace. Her lip was busted. The pain of his fangs as they cut through his still-adjusting gums was bearable, but not by much.

When he stepped up to Nikki, the smell of silver made him queasy. Her once ocean-blue eyes were milky and pale now.

"Bet this isn't the first time you've been tied up, though," he chuckled as she snapped her teeth at him.

A little giggle came from Erin, but a deeper laugh came at them from the back of the theater. When he stepped from the shadows of the house lights, he looked ten feet tall. As he reached the orchestra pit, dressed in dark slacks and a gray sweater, Mason Creed appeared to float up the stairs.

Creed had a new sense of confidence about him. Coop noticed it right away. A warm glow to his skin, even in the cold, dank place, signaled a recent meal. He'd been dosed and Coop was suddenly jealous.

"Don't be rude, Cooper," he smiled as he entered the pool of light Nikki sat in. "She's our guest, after all."

Creed frowned as Erin took the handkerchief he held out to her. The scent of her blood and sweat mixed with silver tickled at the back of his throat.

"Wipe her face, please," he said. "Can't have her looking like a wet dog when they come."

Erin did as she was told. Nikki jerked at the chains, but

she was too weak to break free. After Erin smoothed her hair back, she took a stance next to Creed.

"Honestly," she sighed with a shake of her head, "what's so great about Alex? I mean, I was with her for two weeks and I was ready to kill her in her sleep."

Creed and Coop laughed. Creed, better than any of them, understood that side of Alex that made you want to kill her. Her judgements were harsh. She found fault in almost everything he had done except when they were in bed. And, come to think of it, she may have held back on her criticism there too. He shook that thought. She never held back, especially when it came to other people's faults.

"She can be a bitch," Coop said. "Especially when she's training someone. Be glad you only had to train for two weeks. I spent six with her before SandBox," he shook his head slowly. "If I could have spiked her Gatorade, I would have, trust me."

Creed stood back as Erin and Coop traded war stories about Alex. He could have joined them in the bash, but he couldn't bring himself to do it. Even with the harsh way she forced him to end their relationship, he still felt some fondness for her. In a way, he probably always would. But now was not the time to have sympathy for Alex Stone. She was marked by his new sire for something even he was not privy to just yet. And, whatever it was, he wanted to be witness to it, even if he had to watch Tristan destroy her.

"You loved her," he heard Nikki whisper.

Creed moved close and knelt so he was at eye level with her. The space between them was heavy with the mixture Tristan had created: silver and some other compound formed a cocktail of pain for vampires. He secretly hoped he would get a chance to use it on Coop soon. There was no love lost between them. From the moment Coop had turned and swore his allegiance to Tristan and this plan, he had strutted around like a rooster in a henhouse.

"Yes, I did," he grinned. "Just like Jason does now."

Her fangs dropped to sharp points as she managed

a weak growl at him. When her eyes opened slightly, her irises were solid white with dilated pupils. The handcuffs were heavily coated in the mixture. At this rate, she'd be dead by the time help came for her. Creed almost felt sorry for her.

"He doesn't love her," she hissed and moaned. "He loves me!"

"I know when a man can't get Alex out of his system," he sighed. "One word from her and he'll leave you at the altar. Sorry."

Blood tears rolled down the sides of her face as her head dropped back. Her long blonde hair fell from the loose bun as she whimpered softly. Then she struggled to raise her head again and growled at Creed.

"He's coming for me. And I'll make sure he kills you first!" At that, she lost consciousness. Erin and Coop turned toward them.

"Something I said," Creed shrugged and stood up again.

He dropped a long arm around Erin's shoulders and kissed her forehead lightly. Her swollen lip had a small bit of blood on it still. He tipped her chin up and kissed her fully after he cut the tip of his own tongue with a sharp fang. She moaned as he licked her lip with his bloody tongue. Erin pressed her body to his. When he pulled away, the mixture of his blood and hers had healed the cut on her lip almost completely.

"Thank you," she purred sweetly.

"Sebastian's not doing so well," Xavier said as they prepared to leave the plane and rescue Nikki. "Jason's doctor says there's something in his blood that he doesn't recognize. He needs a professional lab to identify it."

"This won't take long," she replied. Her phone buzzed with a text. Help was on the way to the castle now. "What about Kai?"

He just shook his head. "Same thing." David took in a

deep breath and stepped closer. "Can't Jason help? I mean, at least heal some of the damage?"

Alex had thought of that, but whatever was in Sebastian's bloodstream could also hurt Jason. That was not an option. As far as Kai was concerned, there was too much physical damage for even the pills to repair. Shrapnel from the explosion had ripped through him like bullets. For him to have sustained this much damage, he was most likely in the first stages of degeneration anyway. If that were true, how long would it be before Xavier and David started to display symptoms too? Then she thought about Amy.

From what the doctor was able to tell, she died the instant that metal hit her body. No vampire on earth was strong enough to bring back the dead. The impact had sent the pole through Sebastian and straight through her heart. And it was coated with the same compound as was found in Kit—a new poison with some sort of cryogenic base, her father said. Laced with pure silver nitrate, this new poison would be a problem for all vampires, especially the youngest ones. Unless they could find an antidote, any vampire under a couple hundred years old was susceptible to it. Even the oldest of the pure could be slowed down by it.

"He can't risk it," Alex answered. David's face morphed into a deep sadness. "Sebastian was exposed to that toxin. Amy died instantly," she took David in her arms, placed her lips close to his ear. He trembled as he let her hold him. "Stay with them," she whispered. "I need you focused."

When they heard voices in the distance, David moved out of her arms with a quick nod as he wiped away his tears.

Jason came from the back of the plane with a look of determination. He also had a bodyguard and a gun with him.

"You're not going," she said with a shake of her head.

"Try and stop me," he replied.

She glanced at the guard then Xavier, who shrugged.

"You stay close and do as I say," she ordered Jason. "When we find Nikki, you get her out and don't look back."

"You and Xavier are not going to win this alone," Jason hissed.

Alex adjusted the earpiece and the weapon under her jacket. "We're not going to be alone."

Xavier led the way to the exit ramp. Adam appeared from the cockpit. His stare stopped them all in their tracks.

"Where do you think you're going?" he growled at Jason.

"I can do this, Sire," he said. "I'm going to do this. I don't need your permission."

Adam turned his clouded eyes to Alex. "He dies, you die."

Alex just nodded and waved Xavier forward.

"Jason and the big guy will be back here shortly," she said as Adam followed them to the doorway. At the top of the ramp, she turned to Adam. "If we're not back one hour after they arrive, take off. If your doctor can keep Sebastian and Kai stable, 51 will be waiting for them. No one touches Amy. Your doctor knows what to do when Nikki gets here."

Adam's expression softened. "Understood."

Tomas looked nervous, but Becker was more so. He didn't want to let Alex down and he sure as hell didn't want to lose whoever was responsible for Matt's death. Every waking moment over the last few weeks was spent monitoring Strategic and the Tracker team for any information on Matt's killers.

As he checked his weapon for the fifth time in as many minutes, he kept the image of Matt's dead body in his mind. It would help him do what needed to be done to bring the bastards responsible to justice. Not the justice anyone would be familiar with though. He wanted justice to be in the Circle, with Lucas Wolfe. The toughest bastard in any pack in the world. If the guilty were lucky, he'd take them out quick. But, from the looks of Matt's remains, they didn't go easy on him, so turnabout is fair play. Money talks in the merch business, and, as of five minutes ago, someone had talked their organization into a capture instead of a termination.

"K.C.," Tomas interrupted his thoughts. "Are you okay?"

"Yeah, just peachy," he grinned.

"I don't understand," he frowned over the passenger seat.

"I'm good," Becker replied.

His driver and right-hand-man, Marcus, glanced at Becker in the rearview. He was a former Navy Seal. But it's hard to give up the rush of hunting and war sometimes. When he lost his right foot in combat, he was sidelined.

"Becks," Marcus said over the heater. "We sure this Stone chick ain't gonna screw us on this deal? I mean, our client paid us a good chunk of change to bring whoever in. You sure you can handle her?"

Becker understood the hesitation. In this line of business, it was hard to know who to trust, even if that someone saved your life once or twice. "She's good."

"Okay," Marcus sighed. The truck picked up speed. Becker glanced back to make sure the others were still close behind them. He wanted to get there in one piece though.

Dracula's Castle rose slowly ahead of them in the darkness. Spotlights, yellow and dim, lit up the concrete path all the way to the front entrance. They wouldn't use the front door this time. Marcus killed the headlights when Becker ordered. He slowed down and eased the four-wheel drive vehicle off the main road.

"There's a caretaker's path to your left," Becker announced. "You should see it soon. Park there."

True to the map in his head, it was there. Muddy snow piled on either side, but it was there. The two trucks parked. Four big guys exited the truck behind them. As they stood between them, Becker repeated the drill and made sure the comms were in working order.

Two men headed toward the back entrance. Deliveries were made there and a flimsy lock held the bay doors in place. The other pair, led by Tomas, headed back to the main road. Just to the right of the main entrance was a set of French doors. They would gain access from there. Becker and Marcus would take the scenic route.

With their climbing gear secure, Becker, Marcus, and their team stepped up to the lowest wall and scaled it quickly. It would have been much easier if he were still on the drugs, but it felt good to do this as a regular guy. At the top of the building, they dropped the gear, checked weapons and comms, and made their way to a roof entrance. In the near dark, the rusty stairs looked about ready to collapse. At the bottom, a red fire alarm light focused a beam on the hardwood floor. Reaching the bottom without much noise, they waited in the darkness to see if anyone heard. Thirty seconds went by—then all hell broke loose.

Chapter 26

Alex saw flashes of light as they approached from the wooded area to the north of the trucks they found on the muddy path. Xavier and the bodyguard went toward the lights. She and Jason took the loading dock because it was still open.

"Let me lead," he whispered. "My night vision's probably better."

She pulled him back and rolled her eyes. "Just stay close. These guys are not very stealthy."

He chuckled low and followed her through the small storage area and up the door that led inside the main building. Gunfire cracked in the distance. Voices echoed down the corridor as they moved quickly toward Xavier and his partner.

"Two down," he said in the earpiece. "I see three just ahead of your current location." They heard another crack of gunfire. "Make that two," he returned.

She raised her bio-watch and tapped the screen. At the bottom of the small screen her heat and Jason's cold signatures were side by side. With a swipe of her finger, Xavier and the bodyguard popped up. A tiny compartment on the side of each watch held miniscule amounts of their blood. Developed by Strategic just that year, the bio-watch could separate and register the owners of the samples as long as they were within twenty-five feet of the device. She swiped back to the screen displaying her and Jason.

Two white dots moved in fast. If they were human, they would have registered red, like hers or Xavier's. If she had a sample, the watch would have chosen a random color, and initials of the donor, if known, would show on screen like Jason and the bodyguard. They were vampires.

She dropped to her knees, fished a silver dagger from her boot, and signaled for Jason to move to the blind corner across from where they stood. It was dark enough to hide him, she hoped. For some reason, a suit of armor sat in the center of the hallway. Alex moved into the darker shadow and hoped it would give her enough time.

As the figure of one man came slowly around the corner, she flipped the dagger so that she held it by the sharp edge. He stopped and turned toward a noise behind him. When he turned back, she threw the dagger as hard as she could. Just like that, it struck dead center and he began to burn from the inside out. Jason smiled at her.

She ran toward the man as he crumbled and caught the dagger before it hit the ground. Jason yelled and she ducked. He put two silver bullets into the chest of the next vampire but missed his heart. The vampire opened fire in the narrow hallway as he backed up and Jason wrapped Alex in his arms and spun around the blind corner again.

"You hit?" he whispered. She shook him off and pulled him with her as she ran.

"You got a fix on Nikki yet?" she said to Xavier.

"I got a couple of Becker's guys with me now," he answered in a jumpy voice as if he were running. More gunfire and grunts filled their heads through the communication devices.

Alex realized they were on their own. She turned to Jason and he closed his eyes. The muscles in his arms and chest bulked suddenly. Under the dim red light of the fire alarm, he turned toward the giant staircase and nodded. A tattered sign hung loosely on the wall. Its arrow pointed up to the ceiling; it read: Theater and Ballroom, Floor 2.

She looked at the bio-watch. Xavier and the bodyguard were surrounded by white dots. But there were also green ones—Becker's guys hopefully. She had to keep moving forward.

It didn't take long to climb the winding staircase. Almost at the top, they stopped. Jason raised his head first and peered over the last step to make sure it was clear. He pulled Alex with him and they made their way down the wide corridor. When Jason grabbed her arm, he faced a door halfway down the hall. His hand hovered over the entrance.

"Here," he whispered.

Alex pulled out her modified Sig p226 and checked the magazine. With the safety off, she chambered a round as she took one side of the door and Jason took the other. She pushed it open with her foot. It groaned and creaked as a weird smell tumbled out at them. Jason peeked through the narrow opening where hinges met wall. When his eyes widened, she knew.

She covered his back as he swept through the door. Nikki, in the fetal position, groaned and shivered on a dirty cot against the wall. Jason moved to gather her in his arms but Alex stopped him.

"Don't touch her," she sniffed. "Smell that? That's pure silver and it's pouring out of her in buckets—just like Sebastian."

"She's dying," he sniffed back. "I have to get her out of here."

One more glance at the bio-watch and she saw a green dot move in their direction. She put her finger to her lips and waved Jason down. As she moved toward the side, a thin shadow inched toward the door. When it stopped, she raised her weapon chest high, bent her right elbow slightly to account for the kick, then aimed.

Hands in fingerless gloves came into view, then Becker's bearded face. He cocked his head to the one side and arched a furry brow at her. She lowered the weapon.

"Jeez," he said as he moved inside after checking the hallway again. "Where's the love?"

"How'd you know it was us?" Alex said.

"With this," he answered as he held up an identical bio-watch.

Alex's heart jumped in her throat. "Is Xavier dead?"

Becker shook his head. "He's fine, sorry. I borrowed it because he's watching the exit for us."

"I need you to take her for Jason," she said.

"Why?"

"She's pumped full of some kind of silver compound and it's killing her," Jason replied.

Alex nodded at Becker and he gathered Nikki up in his arms after wrapping her in the dirty sheet she was laid out on. His nose twitched at the scent, she was sure.

"Make sure they get to the Jeep. He knows where to find it," she said to Becker as they made their way back to the stairs. Xavier had a slight limp but looked fine as the bodyguard moved toward them. When the smell hit his nose, he looked ready to vomit.

"Payne will get them back," Becker said as a wiry-looking, tattooed white guy stepped out of the shadow. "He's a pretty good field medic too. He knows what to do."

Jason looked afraid as Becker handed Nikki over to Payne. He followed them to the main entrance, looked back once, then left, gun raised.

"Drive faster," Payne ordered as he wiped at Nikki's face and tried to get her to take in some of his blood. Jason saw a gentleness to this man—a man who was killing his kind without a second thought just a few minutes ago. "Come on, darlin'," he heard Payne drawl. "Just a little." A weak moan escaped her pale lips.

He had to crack the window to thin out the thick odor as it poured from Nikki's body. Jason took practically every corner on two wheels. When the airfield came into view, he heaved a big sigh of relief. The gate swung open when he flashed the headlights at the guards. At the plane, a stretcher waited.

"I'll get her loaded and settled in your med bay," Payne announced as the truck rolled to a stop next to the stretcher. David waited with the doctor and nurse.

Once Nikki was out and strapped in, Payne help David carry her up the ramp and into the plane. Jason stripped off his holster, jacket, and earpiece. One of his assistants took the gear as he hustled to the medical bay. Inside, his doctor, gloved and masked, attended to Nikki. As an unconscious Sebastian lay shaking next to her, David wiped her body down with wet cloths as the nurse prepared the intravenous blood bags they would use to put as much clean blood in her as possible. She screamed when the needle slid into her arm.

"Jason," Adam whispered from behind him. "Let them work."

He let Adam pull him from the room. At the end of the narrow hall, he stopped and turned back around. Adam leaned on the wall across from him.

"She'll be fine," he whispered again.

"Any word from Alex?" he whispered as he stared straight ahead.

"No."

Jason turned, sat on the arm of a leather seat, and sighed. Half of him worried for Nikki as she fought for her very life right down the hall. The other half worried for Alex, who had risked hers to get Nikki out. And how easy was that? A few stray vampires sent in to sacrifice themselves for The Cause—barely turned dupes put in their path to slow them down. And that other team, where did they come from?

"What did she say to you before we left?" Jason demanded as he rubbed his chin.

"We are to leave here in one hour," Adam replied. "With or without her."

Jason stood quickly; he moved closer to Adam. "You're not serious! We are not leaving her here to die."

"That's not your decision to make, Jason. It's hers, and

she's made it. The flight plan has been filed. Area 51 is on full alert. The clock is ticking."

He stepped back and sat down again. Adam wouldn't let him leave this plane, not without a real fight this time. That would be a fight Jason would not win. When Nikki screamed again, he jumped to his feet. A few seconds later, David appeared in the hallway, haggard as he removed his bloodstained gloves. Payne appeared behind him as he rubbed at the inside of his right arm.

"The doctor says whatever they used, its new and very aggressive," David stated to Jason. "They're trying to slow it down with fresh blood, but with both Sebastian and Nikki affected . . ." he shook his head. "It may not be enough. Adam, he wants to get some blood from you to see if pure vampire blood might have a better effect."

Jason rolled his head from side to side until it popped. Adam made his way to the medical bay without a word. Payne stepped next to David.

"I'll be on my way then. I hope what I gave helps your friends."

"Wait," Jason put his hand out for a handshake. Payne's grip was strong and warm. "Thank you."

"My pleasure," Payne grinned. After he shook David's hand and said he'd keep them all in his prayers, he hustled from the plane. A few seconds later, they could hear the Jeep burn rubber on the tarmac.

"Who was he?" Jason asked. David led them to the galley. Fruit and bottled water was lined up on the narrow counter. He took an apple and sat opposite Jason at the square table.

"He said he worked for some outfit K.C. Becker heads up," David answered. "He was a doctor at one time."

"Becker? He was a member of the original team, right? Night Command? Why didn't she tell me she had backup?"

"According to Payne, they just ran into each other yesterday. Kinda lucky, if you ask me."

"I think Becker helped us get Nikki out," Jason said,

mostly to himself. "I saw him and another guy at the Palace today too. What's the outfit called?"

David shrugged. "He just kept referring to 'The Cause' when I asked," he said with air quotes. "I'll see what intel I can get on them when we're in the air." He stood, stretched and grabbed a bottle of water. "I'm gonna go check on Kai."

"Of course," Jason nodded.

When David was gone, he folded his arms on the table then dropped his head on them. Images of what had transpired over the last hour bounced around in his head: the smell of the castle and the sound of gunfire, how he had found Nikki so easily seemed strange to him.

His head popped up suddenly. The plane was still and quiet. Back in the direction of the med bay, Jason followed the smell of alcohol and blood. He reached the door to find Adam with a laptop propped on his knees as he sat between an unconscious Sebastian and Nikki.

"You should get some rest," he said when he noticed Jason at the door. "They've been sedated, heavily." He watched as Adam glanced at his smartphone. Thirty minutes had already gone by in a flash.

"I'm going back for Alex," Jason announced. He stepped up to Nikki and let his hand hover above hers, afraid to touch her. The doctor had warned that the toxic mixture could be passed through such innocent actions.

"No, you're not," Adam shook his head and folded the laptop up again. "She left specific instructions. We won't deviate from her plan. She's in charge, even if she's not aboard."

"You'd see her dead," Jason hissed, "rather than letting me go help her, wouldn't you?!"

"If the choice is you and Nikki or her, then the answer is yes."

Jason felt like punching something. But Adam was right—not about her life or theirs, but she was in charge of the assignment. Her job was to keep him alive and returned in one piece. It wasn't supposed to be fair, was it?

"It's a setup," Jason snapped. "You knew it, didn't you?"

"We suspected as much," he answered to Jason's surprise. "We had hoped we were wrong, but . . ." he stared at Nikki. "I hope she's as good as everyone seems to think she is."

"You wanted to draw Tristan here," Jason continued as he paced the small room corner to corner. "Maybe end it before it reached home. But he's not here, is he?"

"It doesn't appear that he is," Adam stated. He sat back down and watched Jason continue to pace. "But Creed and Jesse are."

"Creed," Jason hissed. "I knew that lying piece of shit was wrapped up in this somehow."

"Well, he's made his choice as well," Adam replied. "I know you thought you could save him, but if she doesn't kill him, Tristan will—if he fails. Nothing you can do about that now."

"How does she know Creed?" Jason asked. "Was he a target or something?"

Adam stretched his leg out in front of him. "Lovers."

Jason sat on the metal stool he pulled from the corner. As he scratched at his chin, he wanted to scrub the image of them as lovers from his brain.

"I thought he was lying about that," Jason replied.

Adam continued, "She's the reason Cyrus is dead. Creed killed him defending her. They both testified that it was self-defense—Cyrus lost his mind and shot her twice for some reason. I tried to prove it was an elaborate scheme to get his money and holdings, but I could never gather enough evidence."

"I don't see her doing something like that," Jason waved his hand at the accusations. "She's a good person."

"She was a different person back then, Jason," Adam rolled his eyes. "People can change. She may be good now, but even you had your vices when you were younger."

Wine, women, and song, he thought with a grin. Adam had indulged that side of him for quite a while. Anything he desired, he got, as long as he remained loyal to Adam and the Council—and he did. Everyone has to grow up sometime though. Jason had learned to reign in some of his childish tendencies, but beautiful women were still his weakness.

"I was a teenager, human, and being given everything my heart desired," Jason replied. "And immortality!"

"Yes. And, like her, you grew up," Adam grinned.

"Well, they didn't part ways on good terms," Jason stated. "In fact, he betrayed her in some way. I can tell. She will kill him and good riddance."

Chapter 27

Michael received word about Romania while he was at a late lunch with the new clients. The small pharmaceutical company had agreed to their terms and their money. A few blocks from K Street, they met to finalize the deal. When the message came, Michael's appetite evaporated.

"Something wrong, Mr. Gale?" the CEO said as she laid her warm hand on his arm. He could feel the heat of her blood as it rushed through her veins. "You look pale."

Michael slipped his phone back into his inside jacket pocket with a grin. He'd planned on a more private encounter with her before the end of the day, but that wasn't going to happen now. He could feel the tip of her high heel glide up his leg. At no time did her expression change though. Her lustful scent circled his nose. Everyone else just stared at their menus and nursed fresh coffee.

"I've got an emergency, I'm afraid," he said as he waved to their waiter. "It's on me."

Michael explained the tab should be charged to his personal account, as always. He stood, made another apology, and left the restaurant with a promise to call the CEO when he returned to New York.

On the ride up to his room on the fifteenth floor, he called his father.

"Michael," Conner answered in rather a happy tone. That was odd.

"Con, what's going on? What happened in Romania?"

He heard a door close in the background and the noise

that surrounded Conner was gone.

"First, I don't have any updates on Alex or Xavier Ramos," he started. "Nikki and Sebastian Rayne have both been poisoned with a compound we have yet to identify."

Michael rushed down the hall and practically kicked in his door. As he threw clothes into his bag, he cradled the phone between his ear and his shoulder.

"Where are the others?" he asked. "You said Sebastian was hurt. What about Alex and Xavier? And the twins and the young women, Erin and Amy?"

There was silence, then Conner heaved a hard sigh.

As Michael waited for his father to reply, he checked out of the room with the television menu, grabbed his bag and briefcase, and left the room. He tapped the elevator button with his foot.

"Con? You still there?"

"Yes," he replied then cleared his throat. "One of the twins has been badly injured. His brother is on board the plane with his teammates, Jason, and Adam."

"And?"

Conner cleared his throat again. Michael didn't like the feeling of doom that settled over him as he stepped from the elevator into the noisy lobby. The doorman flagged him a cab.

"Erin Sinclair is the traitor we were worried about," Conner stated. "Alex and Xavier are in the process of trying to capture her. Apparently, there's another team in play—freelance most likely. I don't have any details on that yet."

"And Amy?"

He knew the answer before Conner said it. She was dead—killed by someone they trusted. Conner explained how it happened in detail, but it didn't really matter. Michael knew what if felt like to lose someone under his command. Even if they knew what they signed on for, no one expects to die.

"I'll be at the airport in about an hour," Michael groaned as he craned his neck to see the afternoon traffic as it stacked up.

Music, like a full orchestra, floated down the hallway at them. Becker sent Marcus and the others to get the trucks and meet Payne out front. Tomas and Xavier backed him and Alex up. They moved down either side of the wide hallway in pairs. They closed and locked doors that were not already secured, if they could.

Xavier marked the rooms they'd checked with an X in chalk. Tomas followed close behind him, watching their backs. He seemed nervous, in an excited sort of way. She remembered a timid and kind man who had been replaced by a priest turned vampire. He prayed over them before they set fire to his mentor. He'd said a prayer over the building as it burned with him inside.

Now, as he held a gun at their backs, she wondered if he still knew a prayer or two.

The music grew in volume and intensity as they reached the double doors of the ballroom. Strings and brass instruments fought for the lead in the piece. Alex didn't recognize it. She was not a classical music fan. Suddenly, it stopped.

"Tomas," Becker whispered. "Stay here. Shoot anybody who comes at you."

He nodded as he held up his weapon.

Inside, they found more broken furniture scattered around the enormous room, tables turned on their sides. A crystal chandelier hung overhead. Harsh, white light splashed a wide circle in the center of the dance floor. The three of them kept to the shadows on one side. Movement in the darkness on the other side of the dance floor prompted them to raise their weapons all together at once.

"You made it," they heard Erin giggle as she stepped from the dark into the harsh circle of light. "And you brought friends."

Alex stepped into the light, Erin's weapon still drawn on her. "And so did you, I see."

Creed and Coop slid into the light as well. Coop smiled and winked at Alex. His vampireness was beautiful. Everything about him was intensified.

When Xavier stepped up next to Alex, his finger hovered over the trigger. He was wound so tight that the slightest sound would set him off. He clearly had his sights set on Erin. Singular and cold, his stare seemed to bore right through her.

"Damn," Coop harped. "I thought you were dead."

Becker stepped up to his group and smiled. "Look who's talkin'."

Becker and Coop laughed while the others stood there. Alex shifted her focus from Erin to Creed. He looked and smelled different, like in Vegas. She could feel the mental blocks in place so she didn't even try to push past them.

"Good girl," Creed purred in her direction.

"Is this the devil you mentioned, Coop?" Alex grinned. "You know, right after he put a bullet through your chest?"

"Better the one you know, right?" Coop replied. "Besides, look at me now! Good as new."

Alex nodded. She glanced back and Tomas was still at the door. But now he looked scared and ready to run.

"So now what?" Coop smiled. "You try to take us in?"

"Nope," Alex answered. "Which one of you killed Matt?"

Creed and Coop glanced at each and laughed. Becker took a small step forward.

"We could just take you both to the Pack, I guess," Becker replied with a scratch of his beard. "I mean, neither one of you will beat Lucas."

"If you want me," Coop growled. His new fangs extended fully and his well-proportioned arms bulked even more. "You know what you can try to do."

Alex felt a familiar twinge deep inside. Her scalp tingled and her muscles tightened. She wasn't sure how much of her power she could unleash and not give away her secret. To her surprise, it wasn't Creed's anger she felt crawl up her spine from across the scuffed dance floor. It wasn't Coop's jealousy, which she could feel all around his still-changing body, that caused her hair to stand on end either.

All of the anger and pure hatred she felt driving into her body from across the space between them was Erin's. It spiked every time Alex moved or spoke or blinked.

"That sounds like a dare," Becker grinned, shaking off his heavy jacket and his shoulder holster. "I've been hoping to kick your ass since that training session in Utah."

"Yeah," Coop laughed as he popped his knuckles. "I did kinda sucker punch you, but you could take it then." He shrugged. "Now you're just an average joe. I can smell your body aging from here," he frowned and spat on the dirty floor.

Before anyone could blink, Coop reached back, pulled a long shiny blade from underneath his leather jacket and let it go. It planted itself in Becker's left shoulder. The power from the throw knocked Becker off his feet.

A shot rang out before Alex or Xavier had time to react. Tomas sent two rounds straight up. Both shots clipped the tenuous wires that held the old chandelier in place above them. It crashed down—right on top of Coop. That gave Tomas time to reach Becker.

"Get him out of here," Alex ordered. One quick jerk and Tomas pulled the blade from Becker's shoulder. He howled in pain. "Get to the plane!"

Becker protested, but Tomas pulled him toward the exit anyway. As she turned back, Erin charged full force. They sailed through the air. Alex felt her back bounce off the floor, then she slid over the dirty hardwood with Erin's hands around her neck. They took out a group of chairs like a double sized bowling ball as it made a strike.

Erin grunted and growled as Alex easily removed her hands and catapulted her back toward Xavier and Creed, whose battle had begun as well. Alex jumped to her feet as Erin crawled from a pile of crumpled tables. Her eyes were wild with hate. Blood leaked from a cut just above her left brow. The feeling of blood tracing down her face angered her even more.

The windows along the far wall were busted. Some black-out drapes hung haphazardly over a few of them, but the snow still jumped into the room on the wind as it howled outside. A storm.

Great time for a freaking storm, Alex thought.

Erin had ditched her uniform. That was a big mistake.

Alex and Xavier wouldn't have to battle the temperature as it fell like Erin would. On the supplements, she must have felt invincible. That was a big mistake too.

Alex dropped her jacket. She wouldn't actually need it. This uniform worked with or without it.

As Erin's anger spiked, Alex could smell her body as it rejected the chemicals. The first clue was her shiny brow. The sweat on her upper lip glistened. The reaction seemed to escalate as her temper did. Alex had to use this to her advantage.

Erin was not going to make it without another dose or two. Alex, however, felt stronger than ever. She took a deep breath and straightened her posture.

"They told me I was better than you," Erin groaned. "Younger, stronger! Everything you are not!"

She took a swing and missed. But her roundhouse sent Alex back a couple of steps. There was some power behind it and Alex was impressed. She tried two more kicks, which Alex easily blocked. Alex clocked her with two quick jabs and Erin was on her ass again.

"You should probably stay down," Alex suggested as she pushed up her sleeve. She knew Erin wouldn't stay down. She knew Erin's sole purpose in life, at this moment, was to kill her. It wouldn't hurt to convince her . . .

Erin jumped to her feet with blinding speed. The punches they traded, the kicks and other Taekwondo moves they performed, lit a fire in Alex that she hadn't felt in a very long time. Every time she landed a solid punch or executed a perfect backflip to avoid one from Erin, she felt her blood pick up speed. Then her ego got the better of her. She miscalculated and missed a right hook. Erin's booted right foot slammed into her left side and she felt two ribs crack.

"You should probably stay down," Erin mocked her as her knees hit the floor.

The next thing she felt was Erin's hand grab her by the hair and pull her to her feet again. The pain from her side shot through her in vicious strikes. When Erin's fist bounced off the spot again, she screamed. It mixed with Xavier's howl of pain as she saw Creed practically drop kick him through an exit door.

"Xavier!"

Alex bent forward and flipped Erin over her back with her full strength. Her body hit the floor so hard she could have sworn the floor boards cracked. When Alex dropped her fist on her abs, Erin released a hard breath. It smoked from between her puckered lips. Before she could regroup, Alex picked her up by her neck, and, as she pressed her left elbow into her own side, she slammed Erin back down with enough force to make an impression on the hardwood.

Her next move was to put her fist through her face, but Erin rolled away. Alex's fist bounced off the wood and her index finger snapped. She snapped it back in place even as pain rumbled up her arm. Her body, as it healed, sent spikes of pain through her.

Another scream, either Xavier or Creed, took her attention for a few seconds. That was long enough for Erin's quick left jab to snap her head back hard enough to blur her vision. When Erin tried to sweep her feet, Alex was surprised that she was able to jump out of the way with her head still spinning. She landed on a pile of sturdy debris directly behind her. It was balanced enough to keep her upright.

Erin gave her a nod of approval. Alex jumped down so that her body was at an angle to Erin. From that vantage point, she was able to catch Erin by the ankle while she swung her leg out. With all of her strength, Alex pulled Erin toward her and planted her right knee in her gut as hard as she could. With Erin's lungs emptied, she took hold of her belt with her left hand and her neck with her right and lifted Erin from the floor. She only had a few seconds before the pain in her side would buckle her knees again. As if Erin was a bag of trash, Alex threw her halfway across the room. She landed on top of a pile of tables with a loud crash.

In less time than she had hoped, Erin was back on her feet. She threw a chair then charged her again. Erin came headfirst at Alex. She drove deep into her stomach and Alex's feet left the floor. Again, they were airborne. This time, they only stopped because of the wall. Its already warped and weak plaster caved when Alex crashed into it. Almost the entire wall crumbled around them when they came to an abrupt halt.

Erin took her by the front of her shirt and bounced her off the frame inside until it broke. More plaster fell around her and she breathed in the sheetrock dust. Alex forced her foot between them and pushed. Erin lost her grip and stumbled backward. Alex coughed and untangled herself from the rubble. When she could breathe again, Erin was already on her feet.

This time, the flurry of Erin's kicks sent her backward until she had no other choice but to let some of them land just to bring Erin close enough to grab hold of. The pain was excruciating, but Alex had her right where she needed her to be.

"Don't make me do this," Alex huffed and coughed.

"Do what?" Erin coughed as well, but she coughed up blood, not sheetrock dust. She wiped at her mouth then looked at her hand. It was covered in the blackest blood Alex had ever seen. She laughed as she wiped her hand on her jeans. "Kill me? I'm winning, in case you hadn't noticed."

From too far away for Alex to help, she heard glass break and a howl of pain. At this distance, she couldn't even recognize who was in pain and who was the cause of it. It was time to end this.

She didn't know what Erin had expected, but Alex jumped straight up and planted both feet in Erin's chest. The surprise on her face as she soared through empty space was worth the pain as Alex landed on her left side. The noise Erin made as she demolished the already trashed furniture in her path echoed for a few minutes. Bats that had taken refuge in the rafters scattered above them.

She noticed the struggle it took for Erin to get to her feet again. She also noticed the presence of a sweet candy smell, just like with Coop. But it wasn't just Erin's sweat she smelled. The odor was doubled because Alex's body had begun to change too. She'd felt it, but she just thought it was her healing abilities kicking in. But maybe it wasn't.

The pain to her right thigh was sudden and sharp. She looked down to see a piece of metal lodged there. The wound immediately began to itch and burn, so she yanked it free.

"Won't do you any good," Erin sighed and coughed up more blood. "The poison's already in your system now."

A rush of anger flooded Alex's body. Without a second thought, she and Erin traded hard punches again, but this time Alex didn't hold back. She let all of her power go. If she was going to die from some poison, she wouldn't be the only one. Erin grunted and howled as Alex unleashed a blinding series of kicks and jabs to her face and body. Her brain kept saying stop, but her muscles wouldn't listen.

The taste of her own blood when Erin's backhand cracked her cheekbone forced more adrenaline through her system. That, coupled with the poison, made for a weird kind of reaction in Alex—a reaction that felt familiar for some reason. Every gift she had woke up with one big bang. She could hear everything around her for miles. Every scent was amplified and covered her like her own skin. Her sight was clear and sharp. She could see every pore on Erin's bloody, sweaty face.

Erin came at her again, but this time she was ready. She blocked every punch and kick like she was reading Erin's mind. Then she realized that she was. She could hear every word as it popped up.

Erin slashed at Alex wildly—using the piece of metal Alex had pulled from her leg. The sharp edge caught her under her left breast with a stinging cut. When Erin raised the makeshift blade high, Alex caught her by the wrist, twisted her hand down, and plunged it into Erin's heart. Alex felt the tip bounce off her ribs and then enter the organ.

Honest surprise covered Erin's face as she stumbled backward. Someone had told her she'd win. As Alex pushed the knife deeper, she almost wished they'd been right. As Erin slid to the floor, Alex looked over at the chandelier. During the fight, Coop had managed to free himself and escape.

She pulled the knife free, wiped the blood on her sleeve, and left Erin's dead body crumpled in a pool of her own blood.

"That was for Amy," she said as she walked away.

Before she even reached the exit, she heard heavy footfalls coming toward her. With a good grip on the knife she stepped into the hallway. There she saw Becker, Tomas, Payne, and Marcus as they walked her way. Xavier was being helped by some guy she hadn't noticed before.

"Where's Creed?" she said as she turned to enter the ballroom again.

"Body bag in the truck," Becker replied as he followed her.

On her way to her jacket and gun, she barely glanced at Erin's body. She leaned over to pick up her things and the room began to spin.

"Whoa," Becker harped as he grabbed her around the waist. "You're hurt pretty bad. Take it easy."

He grabbed her jacket and weapon for her. She turned to see Xavier balanced on one foot and staring down at Erin. His handsome face was covered in bruises and scratches. His left ankle was broken. His right wrist too. But the supplements meant he'd be healed by the time they were home.

"Where's Coop?" he mumbled without even a glance at Alex.

"Got away, sorry," she answered. "Let's go. We'll miss our ride."

That was the last thing she remembered saying before the room flipped and Becker barked at someone to either grab her or Erin's body; she couldn't really tell.

"Stop!"

David's voice startled them both. Adam almost dropped his laptop and Jason's neck popped when he jerked his head up as it rested on Nikki's bed. The hollow thump of David's boots as he ran down the aisle toward the cockpit brought Jason off the stool and through the door.

He heard David yell at the flight crew as the ramp was almost pushed away and the door sealed. The engine's whine died as one of them called the cockpit. David disappeared through the doorway and Jason followed.

"They made it," he yelled at Jason with a big smile on his face. He descended the ramp and ran toward the caravan of Jeeps headed in their direction.

"Thank God," Jason huffed as he did the same.

"Looks like we took it to the wire," Becker grinned down on her. "You okay to walk on your own?"

Alex nodded as he tightened the bandage around her thigh then checked her ribs again. Not broken any longer, they were still tender. She'd lost count of how many times they'd been broken over the last month.

When the truck came to a complete stop, Alex let Becker help her out. Xavier still needed more help. His ankle wasn't healing as quickly as her ribs. He'd have to dose when they were inside and settled.

David's yell over the noise and wind was a relief. Jason in a full-out run behind him made her grin. She saw Becker grin at her out of the corner of her eye.

"What?"

"Nothin'," he shrugged and released her. "I just don't remember ever seeing you smile."

"Yeah, well, don't get used to it," she grinned at him. "Coop got away. I'll smile again when we get him and Tristan."

Jason and David reached them at the same time. Jason brushed past Becker with a muffled "thanks" as he scooped Alex up in his arms. He hadn't showered and he smelled of alcohol and salt. He'd been crying.

She watched Payne and David carry Xavier up the ramp and inside the plane. Two others carried the black body bag up behind them. Then Payne and the others came out and down the ramp again.

"Ugh," she grunted when he squeezed her to him. He dropped her to her feet when he realized she was in pain. "Broken ribs again."

"Really? Again," he grinned.

Becker cleared his throat. "We'll get going then."

Alex stepped up to him and took his hand. "Thanks, Becker. Really. Anything I can do for you, just call. Anytime."

"I'm gonna hold you to that, kid," he smiled and kissed her hand. "I'll let Roland know you're okay."

He whistled and his men climbed into the trucks again. Tomas came up behind him and smiled at Alex.

"Take care of yourself, Alexa," he said with a sad expression. "I think this is just the beginning. We have a common enemy. Together, we can defeat him."

"He's mine," Alex frowned and grabbed her side because the painkillers Becker gave her were wearing off too soon. "He killed Ben. He wants me to come for him.

I'm going to grant his wish."

"We're not going to tonight," Jason interrupted. "We have a plane waiting. Do you need a ride? We have room."

"No, thank you," Tomas replied with a shake of his head. "We have a way back to Rome. It was a pleasure to meet you, Mr. Stavros. We will be seeing each other again soon." Before Jason could react, he turned back to Alex. "It was certainly good to see you again, to see how you have grown. We will speak soon, no?"

"Soon," she let Jason lead her toward the plane as the engine roared again.

At the top of the ramp, she turned to see the trucks roll down the tarmac in a straight line. Something about the way Tomas said goodbye didn't feel final. The last time she had seen him, Tomas was frightened and clung to his faith to explain away what he'd seen. This new Tomas had lost that fear and replaced it with something else—knowledge. Bold and brave, Tomas seemed committed to his new path, more so than when he was a young parish priest in Mexico. His newfound knowledge of the world underneath this one was probably the reason.

The doctor checked her side and leg and gave her a nod of approval. Alex felt more like herself again. The sweat was gone and so was the sweet smell. Her senses were back to normal, too. She wanted an explanation for what had happened, though.

His fingertips were rough and cold as he touched her side cautiously. She held her breath to keep from punching him in the nose. Sharp pain still shot through her when he touched the bruised spot.

"Healing quite well. Fascinating how those supplements work," he hummed. He looked up as though he'd realized he had just said that out loud. "I was under the impression there were severe side effects with women. Isn't that why Dr. Carlisle stopped giving them to his female recruits?"

Alex didn't answer him and he didn't seem to notice

it because Jason had walked into the room. He stood up, removed his gloves, and faced him.

"Sire," he bowed. "She is healing rather nicely. The young man will need more rest."

Jason took the gloves from his hands and asked him to leave them alone. Once the door closed, Alex relaxed back in the bed and pushed out a hard breath. He sat down and handed her the gloves.

"I know how protective you are," he whispered.

"Have to protect the program, right?" she replied, gloves balled up in her fist. "How're Nikki and Sebastian?"

"No change," he shook his head. "The doctor's not sure if they'll make the trip back."

Alex popped the painkillers the doctor had given her and swallowed them without water. She nudged Jason up and stood. "I need a shower."

He stared at her and she could feel how exhausted he was now. His eyes were bloodshot and puffy. Pale and in need of fresh blood, she pushed him toward the door gently.

"I'll come see you and Adam when I'm done," she said.

The door closed before he could say anything else.

Chapter 28

After his shower, Jason collapsed on the bed and closed his eyes. He told himself his worry was for everyone, but that was a lie. He wasn't prepared to lose Nikki. She had been by his side for almost one hundred years. She was going to be his wife. She was his best friend in the world next to Adam.

To watch her just lie there, motionless and pale, he didn't think he could do it right now. He couldn't sit there, helpless and afraid. His soul ached. Maybe he did love her more than he wanted to believe. But how could he love Nikki and want to have Alex next to him right now? She would bring him the comfort that Nikki never seemed able to. It didn't make sense.

Suddenly, he noticed the sound of his laptop alarm. He was supposed to call Conner with an update. As he pulled the machine onto the pillow he placed over his legs, he ran his fingers through his clean hair and rubbed at his tired eyes. Conner appeared, dress shirt opened to his undershirt, but still with a jacket on.

"Jason," he seemed concerned. "Are you alright?"

"Yes, Sire, thank you for asking."

"And the team, how are they?"

Jason rubbed his cheek absently. "Considering the losses, I think they're doing fine."

"Losses?"

"Yes, Erin Sinclair is dead, Sire. She died in the fight. Cooper disappeared during the confusion. And you know about Amy."

Conner nodded. "And Creed?"

"I believe he is on his way to Roland's compound. Sorry, Sire. I couldn't get him back."

"Maybe it's for the best," Conner sighed. "He let Matthew die, so he must face the consequences of his actions."

Jason wanted to see those consequences. He wanted to watch Creed die at Lucas's hands. He didn't want to get him back. Creed had made his choice.

"And Alex? How is she?"

"I believe she's talking with 51 about Kai and Sebastian. I could get her for you, if you wish."

Conner shook his head and waved off the idea. "We can talk when she returns. I believe they'll be in DC for a few hours. I can catch up to her there."

Jason straightened his posture and took a deep breath to settle his nerves.

"Why wasn't I told about the real reason you wanted her on this detail?"

Conner didn't seem surprised. He smiled at Jason and nodded.

"I was wondering when you'd get around to asking. I didn't want to give her any reason not to trust you. If she doubted you, she might not care to keep you safe."

"And if Tristan had been here? What then? Would you have just let him kill her?"

"He doesn't want her dead," Conner answered with a frown. "He left his prison with information he needs to confirm with her. He'll keep her alive until he gets what he wants."

"And then?"

Conner didn't answer and Jason swallowed the bitter response he wanted to let out.

"You look exhausted," Conner said. "Get some rest and we'll speak again when you get back to Vegas. Goodnight."

He wanted to crush the laptop in his hands. Instead, he set it to the side and closed his eyes again as he laid back. A door opened in the distant quiet of the plane. He sat up and peered out of his door to see Alex follow David into the cabin he shared with his brother.

"Hey," Kai had to whisper. "Did we win?"

"What do you think?" Alex grinned at him. She put her hand on his arm and it stuck to his skin. The sticky sweat covered his body like honey. David handed her a wet cloth.

"It's the supplements," he said as she wiped gently at his arm then her hand. "Everything's working overtime."

She looked up at David as she handed the cloth back for him to wet again. Tears sat in his bloodshot eyes. When he gave the cloth back, it was warm and clean. "Could you bring me that pack in my room please?" Alex asked.

He hesitated, but left when Kai nodded.

"Can you save me?" Kai groaned. He was in pain, lots of pain. She raised the blanket that covered his legs, saw cuts and bruising that weren't healing. His pinky on his right hand sat out of place, twisted. She lay the blanket back down as softly as she could, but he moaned anyway once it was over his body again. "It keeps poppin' outta place," he coughed. "Stupid finger."

"I can't stop this," Alex whispered "I wish I could. Only Dr. Carlisle can fix this."

Kai closed his eyes and the tears that filled them rolled down the sides of his head.

"I don't think I wanna die," he said, "but I don't think I can hold on much longer."

"Yes, you can," she sniffed through gritted teeth. "You can."

David returned, dropped the pack at the door. "What's wrong?"

He replaced Alex at his brother's side, tried to take his hand, but Kai screamed from the pain at the slight contact. David jumped to his feet apologizing.

"That hurt," Kai tried to smile, but it looked more like

he wanted to punch his brother.

"Sorry," David held back tears as his voice broke. "I'll get you something for the pain."

He left the room quickly. Alex sat down again. Kai's good hand trembled as he took her index finger like a baby.

"Did you get her?" he asked, and she could feel the pressure on her finger. She could feel how painful it was for him to even speak about her.

"Got her," Alex answered with a grin. "I'll take care of the other thing in a minute."

He barely nodded, but he grinned. "Let David do it, okay?"

"I don't think that's a good idea."

He opened his eyes and they were all pupil. She could barely see the deep dark iris anymore. It broke her to know that he was down to his last minutes on this planet. Erin should die a hundred deaths for this. But you can only kill someone once—sometimes.

"I'd want to if she—" he winced at the next wave of pain that shot through him. He squeezed her finger hard against the pain. "Took my brother from me," he finished once the pain passed.

Alex couldn't be sure what Erin had done as a mole inside Strategic. And she couldn't be sure that she hadn't been drinking blood as well as being fed upon. Taking her head would ensure that she wouldn't come back as something not quite vampire, but just as deadly.

"I know, but she was your friend," Alex whispered. He frowned. "She was. You can't deny that."

"She betrayed us," he hissed. "If you hadn't killed her, any one of us would have gladly done it."

David returned with a syringe filled with a clear substance. He injected it in the bag attached to his brother. After a few seconds, Kai's body relaxed and he was asleep again.

"I'm gonna check on Sebastian and Nikki," Alex said as she hauled the pack from the floor and swung it over her shoulder. She turned to David and watched him wipe his brother's chest and arms again. "I have to take care of Erin in a minute. If you want, you can . . . but you don't have to if . . ."

"I'll do it," he responded as he stood and squared his shoulders. "For my brother and Amy and Ben." Alex didn't argue. She left quietly.

The med bay was empty except for its vampire patients. She removed two syringes from the pack then dropped it at the door. Nikki shivered and mumbled. Her skin was stained with her own blood. Alex put the entire contents of the syringe in the blood supply attached to her, then she used the other one on Sebastian. If it was going to work, it would take just a few minutes.

As she waited, she thought about all the things she would have to put in order once she returned: the company, her affairs, sell the apartment in the city, open the emergency accounts no one knew about, because this was a major emergency. If she was going to fight, she'd fight with the knowledge that she had nothing to lose.

Nikki stirred first. A weak moan escaped her lips as Alex took her hand. It was ice cold, but her grip was strong. Her eyes fluttered open then turned to Alex.

"Please tell me we didn't have a chick moment," she groaned and coughed.

"No chick moments," Alex replied. "How do you feel?"

"Like I got hit by a really big truck," she answered. "And I'm having a bad hair day."

"Well," Alex giggled. "No big truck."

"God," Nikki groaned again as she brushed at her messy hair weakly. "I'd rather have had the big truck."

"Sorry," Alex said.

"I'm assuming I have you to thank for saving me?"

"Saving you?" Alex's heart thumped in her chest.

"From the idiots that took me," Nikki hummed.

"Oh, not really," Alex sighed. "I mean, not by myself anyway. Jason helped."

Nikki gave her hand a squeeze, although she probably didn't realize it. Her lips formed a small grin at the news of Jason coming to her rescue. She raised her head slightly when Sebastian coughed.

Alex moved to him and pushed him back down as he tried to sit up.

"Take it easy," she said. "You're still pretty weak. Both of you," she said as Nikki tried to do the same. "Just relax. I'll get the doctor and Jason."

Michael was glad to hear Alex was safe and on the way home. He settled down in his bed and tried to rest. His phone buzzed just as he was about to drop off. He glanced at the name and FaceTime image as it blazed on his screen.

"Fallon," he yawned. "You have to worst timing ever."

"Sorry, Michael," she giggled from the screen. "I have a report from the medical examiner."

He sat up. "Well?"

Fallon rolled her eyes as she began. "The compound is a combination of silver and something cryogenic in nature. He can't identify that yet. He says it's some next level scifi stuff," she laughed. "His exact words. The other chemicals haven't been seen in modern medicine in centuries."

"It took him almost a week to come up with 'centuries old chemicals' as an explanation? I could have done that. Besides, all chemicals are centuries old." Michael picked up the glass of blood on the night stand and emptied it. "And why would silver have any effect on a shifter? They're not allergic to it."

"I said that," she replied. "He says it's not the silver by itself that's lethal. It's the combination of the cryogenic stuff that's the kicker. Until he can identify all the chemicals, he can't come up with an antidote."

"Great," Michael hissed. "Thank you for the update. I need you in New York by tonight."

"Sure. Why?"

"Alex and the team will arrive in a few hours. She's lost two team members so far. Maybe we can help with the hunt for Tristan Ambrose."

Fallon frowned then replaced it with a wicked smile. Her green eyes danced and she looked like she wanted to do a jig. "Ambrose? Seriously? I thought they had him locked away for good. I mean, I've heard the story and all, but I didn't think he would ever get out."

"Well, he did and she's going after him," Michael replied. "I think we can convince her to let you join the team, temporarily."

"Cool," Fallon smiled.

"Our jet will pick you up in three hours," Michael continued. "I'll send you the location of the private airfield. Don't be late."

"Aye aye, Captain," she barked and gave him a sloppy salute with the wrong hand.

He shook his head and disconnected. After he made arrangements for a jet and sent her the address, he tried to sleep again. It was no good. Too many questions rambled around in his head. He sat up and listened to see if anyone else was up yet. Conner had insisted he stay at the penthouse last night. They were all going to DC in a few hours to meet with the Secretary and watch Alex and the team debrief.

There was movement in the kitchen. He climbed from the rumpled bed, slipped on a t-shirt and socks, then made his way downstairs. Drew sat at the high bar with the New York Post in one hand and a spoon of Cap'n Crunch in the other. His mouth covered the spoon as Michael walked in.

"You're up early," Drew mumbled as he stared at the newspaper.

"So are you," Michael replied. "How come?"

"Just got back from a run," Drew answered and dropped the paper. "What's your excuse?"

Michael noticed a slight hint of fresh cold air and sweat around the kitchen and his school hoodie draped over the other stool at the bar. Shoes were stacked one on the other at the small table behind him. A bright orange watch cap and his phone had been tossed absently on top of that same table.

He stood on the other side and stared at his little brother. His brown hair was kind of spikey from sweat and snow, his cheeks still bright red from the cold air of New York.

"Going to DC in a few hours," Michael answered. "Fallon woke me with a report."

Drew was well aware of what his brothers did aside from working at their father's company. He'd begged Michael to take him on a recon mission once, but Conner nixed that.

"He's too young," Conner said as Michael and Drew stood in his office that day. Drew was fifteen. "What if something goes wrong—as it so often does when you go on recon?"

"I can take care of myself," Drew's voice broke and both Michael and Conner smiled.

"Con, I'll look out for the little bastard. It'll be fine."

"Not this time," Conner shook his head.

Drew didn't speak to anyone for weeks after that.

"She's sooo hot," Drew's voice stopped the memory. "You sleeping with her yet?"

"Jeez, Drew," Michael frowned at him. "A gentleman never kisses and tells."

"That's a no then," he grinned and took another spoonful of cereal into his mouth.

"I'm not her type, little brother," Michael smirked.

Drew looked confused then the lightbulb popped on. "Damn," he sighed. "That's too bad. Guess I'll have to settle for the fantasy then."

Michael laughed. "Please keep that to yourself."

"Whatever. So what's the assignment this time? Unicorn uprising?"

"Shut up," Michael chuckled.

When the coffee pot clicked on, they both laughed. Its digital clock read 7:00 a.m. In a few minutes, the kitchen would be filled with the aroma of fresh coffee. Conner would be down shortly.

True to his routine, he entered the kitchen in a robe and messy hair.

"Good morning, Con," they sang in unison.

"Good morning, my sons," he laughed as he poured hot coffee into a black mug then poured a vial of blood in it for taste. "Why is everyone up so early?"

"He went for a run in a blizzard," Michael offered as Conner handed him the first mug then took down another.

"He couldn't sleep 'cause the hottie woke him," Drew replied.

"Hottie," Conner mused.

"Fallon," Michael sighed, then shot Drew the finger when Conner turned his back.

"Oh. What did she want?"

Conner sat down next to Drew at the bar. Before he took his first sip, he leaned over and kissed his forehead.

"The medical examiner in Texas found a compound he can't identify in the shifter. The base is something cryogenic in nature and silver, but the others are too rare for him to recognize right now. I should have the full list by the time we reach DC."

"We know what to look for," Conner replied. "Send the list to lab once you get it."

"Have you heard anything else about Alex?"

Michael noticed that Drew had tuned them out until he mentioned Alex.

"She's fine, Michael," Conner said. "But Cooper did get away."

"If he went back to Tristan, we'll find him."

"What about Alex?" Drew said. "Alex Stone, right?"

"Yes," Conner said with a wink at Michael. "His current crush, I believe."

"She's a vampire," Drew gushed.

"No," they both answered.

"Then she really is screwing that Jason dude? Ugh!"

"She's not," Michael frowned, but Conner stopped him before he gave away any other information. "Eat your cereal."

"Will she be in DC?"

"Drew, don't you have plans with your friends today? I thought you were going to a concert tonight," Conner interrupted.

"Yeah, but that's tonight. And if I get to meet Alex Stone then I'm not going. I'm going to DC with you guys," he smiled at them.

"You're not going to DC," Michael grinned. "It's Council stuff, little brother."

"So?" Drew frowned at his brother. "I've been to Council stuff before."

"Not this kind," Michael frowned back. "This is not a fundraiser or a social function."

"Dad," Drew said as he rolled his eyes at Michael. "Can I?"

Conner was quiet for a few minutes. They watched him go back to the coffee pot and refresh his mug. When he was seated again, they looked like they were on pins and needles. Michael thought his hesitation was Conner trying to figure out a way to let his youngest son down easy. It wasn't.

"Yes," he finally said. "I think you should go with us."

"Really?" they both squealed.

"Yes, really. It can't hurt. Go get ready," Conner said to Drew.

He jumped from the stool and ran out of the kitchen and upstairs. When they heard the door slam, Michael looked at Conner with surprise.

"Con, are you rethinking your position? I mean, about not turning him when he turns eighteen?"

"Not at all, but he needs to be sure being turned is what he wants, more than anything else. If he wants in, he needs to see what that means."

"I guess, but starting him with this assignment," Michael shook his head. "This really is high profile stuff."

"Yes, it is," Conner agreed, "but right now there's nothing going on that he can't be privy to. He just wants to see what we do outside of the company. What could it hurt to show him the boring stuff?"

Michael just shrugged and left Conner to his morning routine. Upstairs, as he passed Drew's room, music blared and the shower was running. If he focused, he could hear Drew singing in shower.

He rushed to answer his mobile as it chimed on the nightstand. He glanced at the call screen; it was Alex.

"Hey, long time no hear from," he tried to say nonchalantly. He wasn't supposed to know where or what she was doing. She sounded cheery.

"Yeah, just getting back into US airspace," she replied. "Did I wake you?"

"No," he sighed. "Early bird, you know?"

She laughed and it made him feel good. The way Conner spoke last night, he expected her to sound weak and worn out from the ordeal. Instead, she had a light tone to her voice.

"Yeah, well, I would expect nothing less from an heir apparent," she giggled. "Don't wanna miss any important goings-on in the world, now would you?"

Michael dropped his head, and the pit of his stomach dropped too.

"I can explain," he said.

"What's to explain?" Alex replied, still with that lightness to her voice. "You played me at the manor. Let me make a complete fool of myself, as a matter of fact. Did you and 'Daddy' have a nice laugh at my expense?"

"That's not what happened," Michael replied. "I didn't even know you would be there that night. And I didn't have a laugh at your expense with anyone."

She was silent, and he couldn't really tell if she was still there until she exhaled.

"You could have been straight with me," she finally said. "That's all I'm saying."

"You're right and I'm sorry," he answered.

It was silent again, an awkward silence he didn't want to have between them. They were going to have to get past this fast. It would make it harder to work with her if she didn't trust him.

"Alex?"

"Yes."

"I didn't intend to deceive you, I swear," he said softly. "I just wanted you to relax. I wanted you to trust me."

"But you did deceive me and I don't trust you. Why didn't you just tell me the truth that night at the batting cages? Why didn't you tell me the truth when I called you afterward? I don't like being used, Michael."

Michael couldn't answer without sounding like a complete tool. Orders were orders, right? This was an assignment now despite the way he felt about keeping her in the dark. He figured she would just go with it and this would be over. "I'm not using you. We're trying to help you."

"When did I ask for your help? I took this job because I wanted to find out who killed my friends and I did!"

"You still need us," he snapped at her. "You're not going to get to Tristan without us. And even if you do, you can't kill him! He belongs to us, and we decide how he dies, not you!"

He swallowed hard and stifled the urge to punch something.

Alex began to laugh again. "It's you who's not going to get Tristan without me! I bet you don't have the first clue as to where he is, do you?" He was silent. "I thought so. Neither of us will find him until he wants to be found. And when he surfaces, you can bet your ass I'll be the one to take him out! Don't get in my way."

"Or what?" Michael hissed. "Big bad Alex Stone is going to take on one of the oldest vampires in existence by herself and win? Don't be a fool, Alex!"

"I did it before," she replied.

"And we know how that turned out," Michael chuckled. "He broke you so bad that you spent three months in a mental ward! He's had five years to decide what he's going to do when he faces you again. You've been selling underwear and sleeping with athletes in your spare time! You're not ready for him, Alex—trust me. You need our help, our resources."

It was her time to be silent. Michael reeled in his temper during the lull.

"I have my own," she said, "of both. And you're right—I failed back then, but that was then. Things change. I've changed, and I was trying to convince myself I hadn't. I know what I'm doing. I know who I'm dealing with. I'll be ready for him, and you, if it comes to that."

Michael took a deep cleansing breath. He steadied the pounding in his chest and closed his eyes. "We are not your enemies, Alex. You're not the only one with a reason to see Tristan captured and brought to justice for his crimes. Be smart about this!"

"Matt and Ben are dead," she hissed. "I'm bringing three bodies home with me! Three people who are gone! One of them by my hand!"

"Three," he sighed.

"Kai died an hour ago."

"I'm sorry . . ."

"Don't tell me you're sorry," she snipped. "Don't tell me to be patient and trust you and to be smart. Tell me you will do everything you can to help me find him. Tell me when we do, he dies!"

Michael frowned. "I can't do that. I can only tell you we will help you find him and he will answer for his crimes. That's all I know for sure."

"Fine."

"Alex," Michael took another deep breath. "Tristan is a threat to all of us. You're not in this alone. Please believe me when I say we are with you. But, make no mistake, my father wants him brought in alive. Get good with that. I know what my father does to his enemies. I've helped him do it."

The line went dead and Michael tossed the phone back on the nightstand instead of crushing it in his fist.

Chapter 29

As they stood on the tarmac—Alex, Xavier, Sebastian, and David—the northern air of Washington DC cut through Alex like a knife. Even with everything the uniforms and fabric did to keep them comfortable under almost any weather condition, the coldness inside was not quelled by the technology.

Three coffins, carried by military personnel, were placed on a tram for transport to the next aircraft they would board. The Boeing C-17A Globemaster would escort them from Nellis to Joint Base Andrews in Maryland in five hours. It would be late afternoon by the time they landed in DC for debriefing. It would be well past dinner before they finished at this rate.

As they walked behind the procession to the transport, Alex led what remained of her team. People watched at attention as the coffins rolled toward the open cargo bay wrapped in white parachute-like material—even Erin's. No one would ever know she was a traitor. No one would ever know she didn't deserve this attention.

Erin's parents refused to let 51 keep the body. They had that right. They did agree to blood and tissues samples being examined—not that the real results would be released to them, but they didn't know that. David brought Alex a blood sample after he took Erin's head anyway. Alex would have someone she could trust examine it when they got back to Texas.

They watched from the top of the ramp as the coffins were secured. Each taking a jump seat, they strapped in as the engines whined to life. David closed his eyes immediately. Xavier put on headphones and Sebastian sipped on a bottle of blood as he stared at Alex. He gave her a weak grin and she returned it. The ramp rose slowly then locked into place for take-off.

Once they were in the air, Alex took out her tablet and checked her email. Tons of updates on the summer launch filled the virtual box. Some junk mail too. As she separated the trash from work, she came upon a message from Jason. The timestamp showed he'd sent it early that morning. Her finger hovered over the touchpad. The cursor sat on the message. All she had to do was click it and read. Part of her wanted to. Part of her had already put him behind her. She clicked anyway.

Thank you for all of your hard work. As per our agreement, you and your team have received final payment for your services. Kai's share was transferred to his brother. Amy's to the Warrens to be distributed to Amy's last known relatives, if they can find them. Erin's was donated to the charity you indicated. Nikki sends her thanks again and Adam as well.

Yours,
Jason

P.S. Be careful.

She slid the device back in her pack.

"How are you?" Jason asked as he closed his laptop. Nikki walked over clad in a robe with a towel wrapped around her head. She had just finished a long, hot bath. He could smell expensive bath soap.

"Better," she sighed as she eased down on the bed next to him. "Much, much better."

"Good," he said with a pat to her leg. "You look better, but the doctor said you should rest more."

She unwrapped her head and let her hair fall loose. It was still wet but shiny again. As she dried the long strands with the towel, Jason looked on in relief. She did look much better. Everything about her seemed renewed. Maybe it was the blood.

"What do you remember about being held?" Jason asked.

She shrugged and shook her head. "Just those idiots, Jesse Cooper and Creed, and the girl. I mean, they didn't really ask anything. It was strange."

"How so?"

She folded her legs underneath her and sighed as she dropped the wet towel over the side of the bed. "They just wanted Alex to come. That's all I remember picking up from the girl—a huge amount of hate for Alex."

"What else? Did they mention any names?"

"Nope."

After she stretched her arms over her head, she lay down and curled into a fetal position behind Jason. His bed welcomed her weight. She sank into the folds of expensive silk and Egyptian cotton with a sigh.

"What else do you remember?"

"The next thing I remember is Alex standing next to my bed," she frowned. "You saved me," she yawned then grinned. "I knew you loved me more."

Jason leaned down and kissed her forehead. She was asleep. After he pulled the cover over her body, he left her in the room alone. Downstairs was quiet. Inside his private office was too. In the dim afternoon light, he sat at his desk and tried to read emails, but it didn't help. It didn't help him not think about Alex, not think about what Nikki said.

"They didn't ask me anything," he mumbled to no one. "Huge amount of hate for Alex."

He turned the flat screen on mute. Evening news had just started, some bullshit stories about drug busts and robberies in surrounding neighborhoods. Then, a story on his return. The false item indicated he had returned from some tech conference in Geneva concerning new slot technology. He couldn't believe the lies people bought from the media sometimes.

Conner was holding back; Jason knew that. Alex was too and he wanted—no, needed— to know why. His first official day as a member of the Lower Chamber was Monday. According to his briefing, the topic of discussion would be the upcoming Dark Ball. He sighed.

"What are we, party planners?" he murmured to himself.

Away from the desk, he poured himself a drink and stood beside the window to watch the light fade once again. A week went by so fast. He had accomplished what he was asked to accomplish. There was some action, some bloodshed, and death. He couldn't remember the last time he'd had such an adventurous week. But people he knew were dead now—people Alex was close to.

His phone buzzed with a text from Alex. Her short message had a big impact on him. She could have called, but that's who she was, wasn't it?

It was my pleasure to protect you. I hope that Nikki is well, and let Adam know he's full of shit. Good luck on your upcoming nuptials and I wish you both the best.

He laughed as he sat back down again. Then his phone buzzed again.

"Stavros."

"How's your lady?" Coop's familiar chuckle scratched at Jason's eardrum.

"Perfect, no thanks to you," Jason snarled.

"She's tougher than I thought," Coop replied.

"What do you want?"

"I just wanted to give you and Nikki my congrats on the wedding thing and kudos on getting into Alex's pants," he laughed—howled, really.

"Sounds like you tried and failed," Jason laughed. "She does have standards, turns out."

"Please," Coop crowed. "This will be so much better. I'm like you now. Apparently, she's into that."

"You're nothing like me," Jason replied. "She's going to find you and Tristan, and you're going to die. I just hope the Council lets me help her."

Coop laughed for what seemed like forever to Jason. "The Council will fall, just like he planned. You're going to have to choose sides, Jas—soon. No one will be safe once the truth comes out."

"I have chosen," Jason answered.

"Choose again."

Coop was gone before Jason opened his mouth again. He dropped the phone on the desk and finished his drink.

"We're almost done here," General Diaz stated as the stenographer's long fingers flew over the keys. "Are you sure Cooper is alive? I mean, a vampire now?"

"Yes," Alex answered.

"Are you sure he was responsible for Matthew Wolf's death?" he continued.

"Yes," she said.

"And Tristan Ambrose has resumed his place as the leader of HellClaw?"

"No."

"No?"

"He's back in the world, yes," she replied. "But Hell-Claw was destroyed. The new clan doesn't have a name yet. At least not one he's revealed to us."

"Do you know where he is?"

"Not yet."

"Can you find him?"

Alex didn't reply. She glanced at Sebastian, Xavier, and David as they sat at the door with a guard on either side of them.

"What happened to him at Dugway?" Alex asked.

Diaz immediately straightened his back. He placed his

hands on the table and stared into Alex's eyes. He was in a battle with himself. In his mind, she could hear him tell himself she needed to know. But his duty got in the way.

"I'm not at liberty to discuss that with you at this time," was his reply.

"Then I'm not at liberty to tell you whether or not I can find him."

"It's not us you should tell, Ms. Stone. The Council has offered the Tracker team unlimited resources and help with bringing him in. Do you understand what that means?"

"Yes. That means you're rolling over and playing dead. Just like I knew you would. You're handing the team over to the Council. Problem with that is, they don't have to go, if they don't want to."

"You're right, they don't have to go," Diaz sniffed. "The Justice Department doesn't own the contracts anymore for Strategic. Gale Enterprises does. So they do what they're told or they lose their jobs."

Alex turned her head to the young men. "Anybody care about that?"

"No," was the unanimous reply from the group.

Alex grinned at General Diaz because she knew she'd won. "We're done."

She stood and so did the young men. Diaz got to his feet and had asked the stenographer to leave the room. Once she was gone, the guards were dismissed as well. He went over to the viewing window, turned off the surveillance, and flipped a switch on the wall, opening a secret observation room to reveal several Gales.

They had been watching the whole time. She locked eyes with Michael first, then went from face to face until she reached Conner. He smiled as a guard opened the door and he led the way out of the room.

They filed in one after the other. She hadn't bothered to do any research on the family for some reason. Now she wished she had. Conner, Aiden, and Michael stood on one side of the table while the four young men of various age and skin color blocked the exit.

His own little United Nations, she mused. The youngest couldn't have been more than a teenager and he was still human, she noted. He was actually the first to speak.

"Big fan," he nodded and grinned at her. One of the others, a young vampire with beautiful, dark skin and silky twists of hair tapped him on the shoulder with a shake of his head.

"My youngest has been eager to meet you," Conner replied as he extended his hand. She shook it, even though she didn't want to. "You've met everyone else."

"Yes, I have," she looked at Michael again. "In Vegas, yes. Nice to see you all again."

"I'm Andrew," the young man stepped forward again with nervousness about him. "Drew. Really nice to meet you."

"Same here," she stated and turned back to Conner.

"I think Ms. Stone and I should speak privately," Conner stated to the room. Sean held the door while his brothers and the General filed out. Her team remained.

"Gentlemen," Conner said as he walked over to them. "I can assure you, she is safe."

They didn't respond or move; they just turned their eyes to Alex. She excused them with a nod. The door closed with barely a sound. On the other side was the vampire elite and the team that had nothing to lose by pissing them off.

"My mother is meeting me at the airport," David sighed as he stared at his phone. "Arrangements are being made."

Xavier put an arm around his shoulder. "We're here for you. We'll get 'em—all of 'em." Sebastian leaned against the wall and nodded.

Being inside the Pentagon was intimidating enough. Add to that Marine guards ordered to shoot to kill if anybody got twitchy, and Sebastian started to worry. He watched the other vampires with curiosity and a slight bit of anger. They had put their lives on the line for Jason and what did they get for it? *Thanks* and *see ya later*.

"Holy shit," he heard Xavier whisper as he leaned over David so he could see the screen of his smartphone. "Am I seeing that right?"

David scrambled inside his pocket and pulled out his phone too. "Holy shit."

Sebastian moved over to them. "What?"

"Pull up your account," Xavier whispered then glanced over his shoulder at the Gale brothers. They were huddled on the opposite end of the hallway.

"Umm," Sebastian hummed. "Is this for real?"

The sum was not their usual pay for any job they'd ever done. And they all had an equal sum. Except David. Both Sebastian and Xavier figured he'd gotten his brother's share as well.

"How come this is so much?" David hummed.

Xavier moved closer to his friends. "Alex."

Conner Gale was a classically handsome man—didn't matter that he was almost two thousand years old. He looked like a fit and healthy middle-aged guy. How anyone could believe he was the father of six was beyond her. But the younger four were adopted, so maybe it was easier for people to accept.

"How are you?" he said.

"Glad to be home," she replied. "Well, almost home."

"And the others?"

"They'll survive."

"Mr. Yun has lost his brother," Conner stated with a sad tone.

"They've all lost their brother," Alex replied with a lift of her chin, "and their sisters. They will learn to live with what's missing."

"Spoken like someone who's been there," he grinned.

She figured it was an attempt to appear supportive, empathic.

"Where's my father?"

"On his way to my facility in New York," Conner answered. "Our lab is state-of-the-art. He'll be able to identify the compound a lot faster at Gale Enterprises."

"And Leland?"

"That I don't know."

Alex inhaled and pushed the air out slowly. She focused her power on the sound of Conner's very slow heartbeat. Since she couldn't read his thoughts, she'd listen for any lies through that.

"You should probably try to find him. He was Brice Campbell's handler. He may be able to shed some light on him for us."

"Maybe, but the most important thing right now is to find out what this compound is and how to combat it," Conner sighed. "Now, I have a question for you."

"Shoot."

"Why did you let Cooper go?"

"I didn't. I was kinda busy saving Nikki and my team."

"You let some off-the-books team take Creed—why?"

"It wasn't my job to bring him back to you. So . . ." she shrugged.

"You know what will happen to him in the Circle."

"So?"

Conner appeared frustrated. His green eyes darkened as he tried not to yell at her like she was one of his children. She could tell because her father used to get that same look on his face.

"So he may have been able to lead us to Tristan," he replied. "Now that's not possible."

"Creed is very resourceful," Alex grinned. "He may just surprise all of us and talk his way out of getting his ass handed to him in the Circle."

"That is a fight to the death," Conner grinned back.

"It's Lucas's call," Alex replied.

"He is going to let Creed live after what he's done? I wouldn't."

"That's you. Sometimes, it's not about revenge. Sometimes it's about justice."

She could see that he didn't get it. Few people did unless it happened to them. To let one's enemy live was sometimes the worst punishment of all. The rest of the supernatural world had always seen the Pack as wild animals. Alex knew a different side to them.

"What does he want?" Alex asked.

"Who?"

She frowned at Conner and his tell was the absent way he straightened his tie. He was going to lie, if he could.

"Tristan. What does he want?"

"What he's always wanted," Conner scowled. "He wants to rule the vampire world, alone, and enslave humans, and not necessarily in that order."

"He could have done that already," she said with a shake of her head. "He wants something he doesn't have the power to get. What is it?"

"You tell me. He seems to be fixated on you right now. What do you think he wants that he doesn't have the power to get?"

Conner could tell the wheels in her head were working overtime. She didn't know any more than they did about what Tristan wanted. Her tough demeanor and barrage of questions proved that. Of course she was afraid, but she would never show it. Conner was afraid too. When she showed her fear, he would too.

"Unfortunately, he's gone underground," she said. Conner felt the pain it took for her to admit it. It amused him. "And whoever's funding him has deep pockets."

"He hid a lot from us," Conner admitted. "He had loyal followers and a plan. We underestimated him. Do not make that same mistake."

"I won't," she stated with the same pride he had seen in her the night they met.

After she saved Jason's life, Conner decided her skill had been underestimated as well. Like Tristan, she had secrets and a plan. If she revealed those to anyone, it most certainly wouldn't be him. He'd hoped it would be Michael, but that was probably a long shot as well now.

"I need to see my father," Alex said.

"I'm sure you can reach him anytime you like," Conner replied.

"I need to see him," she repeated.

"Oh, of course. We can be in New York in an hour if you need a ride."

She just stared at her own hands. They were clean, but he could still smell a faint hint of blood. Hand soap and sanitizer couldn't completely kill that smell.

"I'd like to see David off and meet his mother as well. Sebastian and Xavier are coming home with me."

"Absolutely," he replied, crossing the room to open the door. "Raph?" His dark-haired son of Spanish descent walked over to them. "Let the pilot know we will have three more passengers on the ride home."

He smiled and pulled a sleek smart device from his jacket pocket. As he spoke, he walked away from the noise of conversation around him. With Conner and Alex behind him, the rest of the young men followed.

Back down a long marble hallway, the group was flanked by Marines. The General waited at the exit with more guards. He offered his condolences once more, thanked Conner for some reason, and watched them exit the building.

People were used to the sight of official-looking SUVs on the streets of Washington DC. As they rolled toward the interstate and Dulles, no one seemed to care. They were too busy shopping or meeting others for dinner. The snow fell in big, silent flakes around them. Alex was suddenly tired of the snow. Its beauty was lost on her and the others as they prepared to see that special casket one last time.

David and Kai's mother was striking to see in person.

The bad lighting and angles on CSPAN didn't do anyone justice. Her long, dark hair was full and healthy. Like her sons, she was tall and slim. Kai had her smile.

She thanked them for their service and for bringing her sons back to her, even if one of them was in a box. Alex didn't expect her to be so calm. But she was a politician and they didn't do anything without an audience—not even grieve. Conner had somehow managed to have the press banned from the terminal.

Her hands were cold when she shook Alex's. She didn't say anything, just nodded at her with tears in her eyes. Then she pulled Alex into her arms and whispered in her ear, "Kill them."

"Yes, ma'am," she answered as she stepped back.

"I'll see you guys in San Francisco," David said to his friends, his brothers, his family.

"Yes," Xavier said then hugged him tight.

"And Amy?" David asked as he stepped up to Sebastian next.

"The Warrens will wait for us then plan her service," he answered as he wiped the tears from his eyes.

David turned to Alex and held her eyes with his. Once he took her in his arms, she could feel his body shake and she squeezed him hard. He pulled away and wiped his face.

"He liked working for you," David's voice was raspy and worn.

Alex nodded as a tear slid down her face. "We're not done yet. Not by a long shot."

"I'm ready," he said.

They waited until David and his mother were down the boarding ramp before they turned away, heading to the boarding gate for their own flight.

"You lit into Michael pretty good," Sebastian said as they found a vacant spot of seats across from the VIP lounge. "You're still willing to work with them after that?"

Conner and his sons were inside that lounge in a super secret conversation. He'd text her when they were done or the plane was ready, whichever came first. She was fine with that.

"I just wanted to see how much they knew," she replied, "which is next to nothing. I would have done the same thing, I guess."

"You hungry?" Xavier asked as he stood. "I'm hungry."

"Sure," Alex replied.

Sebastian stood too. "What's your poison?"

"Anything that's not leafy, green, and good for me," she grinned. "And don't say poison."

She could see a hot dog stand a few feet away. Sebastian and Xavier immediately engaged in small talk with the pretty clerk. What she thought was fatigue—manifested as a sharp pain in the temple—was really something else.

At an easy stroll, Brice Campbell appeared out of nowhere. With four very large vampires at his side, Brice looked relaxed and confident, an easy feat considering he had switched bodies with Tristan, whose age had taught him how to master his emotions.

Brice-Tristan sat in the row in front of her—a comfortable conversational distance away. His entourage was dispersed two on either side of her at the end of the row, and two were on either side of him.

Out of instinct, she reached for a weapon that was not there. They had been checked and loaded on a plane bound for New York City. For the first time since this all started, she felt completely alone.

Chapter 30

"Where's a shiny, silver dagger when you need it, huh?" Tristan hummed as a grin spread over his rosy lips.

He wanted her off her game—isolated. Manipulating the two young men was easy. Her feeling his mental sting took some effort—another thing he remembered about her. How hard it was to hurt her.

Once he was comfortable, he pulled the Zippo from his pocket. With it balanced on his knee, held steady by his index finger, he smiled at her.

"Do you recognize this?" he said to her.

"No," she answered dryly.

"Of course you do," Tristan laughed and flipped the lid up with his thumb. "If you want it back, you're going to have to ask me nicely."

"Keep it," she hissed.

Tristan sat forward on the seat, placed his elbows on his knees, and cradled the lighter in both hands. "Are you sure?" he growled low. "You were very fond of this trinket once." He frowned at her. "You killed a priest with it, remember?"

Tristan opened his hands then flicked the lighter to life. He raised the flame and his gaze to Alex as he did.

"You can't smoke inside airports anymore," she grinned.

He grinned too. "You can't do a lot of things inside airports anymore."

Her expression seemed odd to Tristan. She didn't seem afraid or worried that he'd kill her where she sat if he wanted. She probably knew that anyway. Then he saw a flicker of recognition in her brown eyes. Bloodshot as they were, they still danced the way he remembered.

"Brice is dead, isn't he?" she said, having realized to whom she was actually speaking.

"In a manner of speaking," Tristan smiled as he let the flame die.

His eyes traveled around the space. Outside the windows, artificial light illuminated a passenger jet as it taxied to a stop. When the ramp was connected, her phone buzzed.

"You have changed. There was a time when you couldn't care less about the life of a vampire. Must be the company you're keeping."

She eased down in her seat and crossed her legs. As her top leg swung its foot up and down, Alex continued to grin.

"Money's money, right?" she grinned. "I go where the stacks take me."

The sharp pain at his temple surprised him. It blurred his vision for half a second before he shut her out. Maybe Giselle was right. This body would need more time to adjust.

"Nice! Very nice," he chuckled. "Your power has grown so much. And so have you, by the way."

Being this close to her now, the memories of that night were coming back. He shuffled through the mental deck of memories and reached a startling conclusion. She was more than just a successful female test subject. Alexa Stone was the Dagger and now Tristan could move forward with his plan.

Alex sat forward, arm slung across the top of her thigh. Never to be outdone, Tristan did the same.

"That's why you took the Seventh Grimoire," she sighed and shook her head at him. "You needed a spell powerful enough to switch bodies. My father was an idiot to leave that thing anywhere near you."

"Yes on both counts! He's perfect, right? I mean, now that I'm in charge."

"It's too late to save him."

"Ever the hero," Tristan laughed freely. "Yes. It is too late."

Alex raised her eyes to meet Tristan's gaze. His delicate features couldn't hide the monster inside—the one she knew so well. This creature had changed her life. In that cave, in the dimly lit dungeon he called home, he had pushed her over to the other side for a while. And now that she was back, he wanted to do it again.

"What do you want?" she asked. "Why all this drama? You could have a new life anywhere on the planet and no one would even know."

Tristan's grin faded; his eyes clouded with anger. "I liked my old life. But since I have this new body, I may as well make the best of it. You can't imagine what I'm going to do now that I can walk in the light! Darkness can no longer hold me."

She wouldn't let him shake her; not this time. Control of the situation would go to the one who controlled themself the best. Alex was determined to be that person. And as the fear slowly lost its bite, she knew she would be. Now it was just a low rumble like hunger. Nothing she couldn't ignore.

With the lighter bouncing in his palm, the sparkle of his dark eyes wasn't so scary. That slight tilt of his head? Amusing.

"Oh, was I supposed to react to that?" she grinned. "My bad."

He placed the lighter on the arm of the chair next to him. He waited to make sure it didn't fall before he turned his eyes to her again. A look of satisfaction spread over his face.

"How's your father?" he asked.

"Fine," she answered with a shrug of her shoulders.

"You seem unsure."

"That's because I am."

"He's never been much of a father to you, has he?" he

sighed.

"I guess that's a matter of opinion," she replied.

His pale lips pressed into a thin line as Alex watched.

"Is that all you have to say on the subject?" he quizzed.

When she didn't answer, he shrugged. To her relief, Sebastian and Xavier appeared. The guards seated on either side of her row jumped to their feet. Tristan remained seated as the ones on his side jumped up as well.

"Welcome, gentlemen!"

Xavier pushed one big guy back as the guard attempted to frisk him, she guessed. Sebastian had to do the same to another.

"Who the fuck is this guy?" Sebastian said as he stared at Tristan.

"Language, young man," Tristan smiled at him then waved to the empty seats next to her. They remained standing as she and Tristan stayed seated.

"This is Tristan," Alex replied, "wearing Brice Campbell."

They looked at her, then Tristan, then back at her with confusion.

Tristan shook his head. "More like a hostile takeover."

"What?" Xavier frowned at him.

"Long story," she answered.

"Doesn't matter," Sebastian hissed. "He's responsible for the loss of our friends. Can we kill him now?"

Tristan was up with his hand wrapped around Sebastian's neck before anyone, even Alex, knew what had happened. Alex jumped to her feet and kicked the vampire that tried to grab her. He slammed into the wall, just under a giant flat-screen.

Xavier was on his stomach with a gun to his head.

"I could snap your neck, little boy," Tristan growled as he held Sebastian high.

"Not before I put two in your fucking head," Michael growled as he flipped the safety off his Beretta with a wicked grin on his face. "Let him go—now."

Michael and his brothers reined in the situation quickly as Conner and his teenage son looked on. Raph pulled Xavier to his feet.

Tristan let Sebastian go then ordered his men to stand down. With Sebastian and Xavier next to her, Alex nodded to Michael. He kept his gun trained on Tristan as his brothers watched the others.

"You care too much for these people," Tristan said as he stared at Sebastian.

"Thanks for the update," Sebastian's voice rasped.

"I wasn't talking to you," Tristan replied as he stepped up to Alex. "You can't trust them and they don't trust you."

"Maybe not," she said as she stepped forward too, "but we have a common enemy."

Tristan smiled at her. She wasn't sure why, but she let him place his cold hand to her cheek. Then she felt him inside her mind.

Don't make me do this, little soldier, his mind said to hers.

Do what? hers replied.

Tristan's eyes clouded again, but this time he looked sad.

"They'll create more like you," he said out loud. She didn't even feel his mind disconnect from hers, "Or they'll try."

"Let them try," she said.

With his hands in his pockets, he smiled at all of them. A quick jerk of his head sent his men to the almost empty concourse again. They waited, patient and quiet. He took a deep breath.

"It's already begun," he sighed. "Erin was just the first. She was expendable. They wanted to see where your weaknesses were. Now they know."

"Put a face to 'them,'" Alex said, "and you just might walk away from this."

Tristan shook his head slowly as he turned to wink at Conner. "I've done too much to answer for I'm afraid. The Council won't turn a blind eye this time."

"This time," Sebastian joined the conversation.

"Do you really believe they cared about those people back then?" Tristan grinned at Alex again. "At least I was merciful."

"What?" Xavier growled. "You bled innocents dry for your own amusement!"

Alex was struck by the honest look of confusion on Tristan's face. He had no idea what Xavier meant.

"Those people were a failed experiment," Tristan stated plainly. "An experiment your government was conducting."

Michael stepped around him, lowered his weapon and took the empty spot between Alex and Xavier.

"What kind of experiment?"

"What were they trying to do?" Sebastian added before Alex could ask.

His dark eyes swept from face to face with more confusion. Then Tristan smiled as they stopped on Alex again.

"The women and children in that village in Africa," Alex's dry throat morphed the sound of her voice. It sounded sinister, mean—even to her. "We found you there first. We were told you started with them—trying to expand your clan. But that's not what you were doing, was it? Those women were surrogates with their offspring?" Tristan didn't react at all. "You didn't send those children after their parents, did you?"

"They were programmed to do that," Tristan answered. "The ones that couldn't be controlled had to be eliminated. That was my job. And I enjoyed it."

"No one survived," Alex barked at him and everyone jumped. "You killed all of them!"

"I had to," he barked back. "I knew humans couldn't be trusted."

"Why capture you?" Michael added. "Why not just kill you too before you blew the whistle on the whole thing?"

"She missed," Tristan smiled. "That was her mistake."

"I didn't miss," Alex replied. "I would never have left a loathsome creature like you in play if I hadn't been ordered to."

Tristan turned his deep brown eyes to Alex. He turned up the wattage on his smile as he slipped his long hands into his pockets. "Loathsome? Well, someone's been to college."

One thing about working for a government, any government, is when you're given orders, you follow them. Good soldiers don't ask questions. Good soldiers follow orders or people die. She'd heard that in a movie. So they followed orders. Tristan was to be captured and contained, not killed. No one was happy about it, but they were just doing their jobs, right?

"The doctor needed a pure blood to perfect a new supplement anyway," Tristan continued. "The Council offered me. I guess they figured I wouldn't survive, so . . ." he shrugged again then turned back to Alex. "By the way, you're welcome."

"He needed something else too, didn't he?" Alex hummed as he stepped into her personal space. "He needed to see if a hybrid was possible. A creature with traits from both species."

"She," Tristan replied, "and, yes, she did."

"She? Who are you talking about?" Alex asked.

"The doctor doing the reproductive experiments," Tristan replied. "You thought I meant Dr. Carlisle? He had a partner in his crimes."

Alex felt the room tilt just a bit. She took a deep breath and stepped back.

"Did it work?" Alex ignored her dizziness. She felt her heart pound inside her chest.

"I don't know," he said as he moved back, "but she's still out there somewhere. Find her and you can beat it out of her yourself."

She stepped back again and bumped into Michael, not because she was afraid of Tristan being so close, but because she couldn't be sure what she would do if he said yes to her next question.

"What's her name?" she asked him as he stared at Michael.

He didn't answer. He just nodded to Michael and walked away. He and Conner passed each other without a glance. Once he was safely surrounded by his guards, he turned to the group again. The Zippo sailed through the air in her direction. She caught it with one hand, closing it in her fist.

At that, a plane disembarked and emptied tired passengers into the seating area all around them. The noise and scents upset her. Then she heard his voice inside her head.

Watch your back, he thought to her. *Eventually, all of our secrets will come out. Imagine how the world will change, for you especially.*

Chapter 31

Although the luxury of Jason's 747 was gone, it was still nice not to have to fly commercial. Gale Enterprises owned two G650ERs. The Gulfstream accommodated the group, no problem. She could even grab a nap if she wanted. Alex stretched out on the small two-person couch in the back and read email instead. The others sat at the front.

Sebastian and Xavier, seated on an identical couch, were preoccupied with Drew. His mouth moved a mile a minute as he sat in the narrow aisle in front of them. They nodded and smiled as he seemed to explain something in an animated sort of a way.

Conner and Aiden, across the narrow space from them, sat side by side engaged in casual conversation. Every now and then Alex would glance up and around the plane. Everyone appeared relaxed under the circumstances.

Michael and three of his brothers sat in four leather seats, a table between them. Two worked on tablets. One slept peacefully. Michael's eyes turned to her suddenly. When his brother pushed a tablet his way, Alex went back to her own work again.

Her inbox was packed with updates and meeting notes from Ivy. At the end of each one, she wrote "Don't worry. Everything's fine." But she was worried. And nothing would be fine again. Soon, she'd have to decide what was more important: the company or the world.

In New York, she'd speak to her father and try not to throw him from a window. He was responsible for Tristan's release; she knew that now. Even if no one else did, it would come out soon enough.

As she stared at yet another note from Ivy, she emptied the water bottle in her hand. She dropped it in the bin next to the couch and decided she needed another. Before she could move, Michael stood over her holding a fresh, cold bottle out to her.

"Thanks," she said without even a glance at his face.

"May I join you?" he asked.

"Your plane," she shrugged as her booted feet landed on the floor with a low thud. It was all but drowned by noise of the plane and conversations.

She tried to rise, but Michael pushed her back down as he sat beside her. His cologne had almost completely faded. His navy dress shirt was still tucked in his brown tweed slacks. The jacket had been discarded as soon as they boarded the plane. When his long legs crossed toward her, she lost sight of everything else around them.

"You're being childish," he said as his hands rested in his lap, one on top of the other.

"Bite me," she replied, tablet still in her hand as she pretended to be working.

He pulled the device from her fingers and she tried to get it back. With one flick of his wrist, it sailed through the air and landed in the empty seat across from them.

She could have brought it back and scared the shit of everybody, but her head still hurt and that would only cause more pain. *Besides, I don't want to bring the plane down with me in it,* she thought with a grin.

"What's so funny?" Michael inquired, slightly annoyed.

"What do you want?" she returned the tone. "I was working."

He stretched a long arm over the back of the small couch. His hand hung over the edge at her shoulder. He barely felt her body heat, even being this close to her. It was the materials they used to make the uniforms. They had all been very impressed with the results.

"What did you mean by a hybrid?" he asked. "Is that what your father's been up to all this time? Trying to create the impossible?"

"Nothing is impossible," she replied. "The supernatural is proof of that, isn't it?"

"I guess, but he never mentioned a hybrid program."

Alex shook her head, but he didn't think it was in response to his statement. Her body temperature spiked, slightly, then the heat was gone.

"Didn't you buy Strategic and everything it owned? Maybe you missed that part," she grinned at her hands as she turned them palms up and wiggled her fingers.

"Apparently we didn't get everything, as it turns out."

She didn't seem to mind his closeness. The way his leg crossed over hers as they sat together. Her closeness, however, had an effect on him—a familiar effect, one he thought he'd felt before.

"Not my problem," she kept that grin as she turned her head toward his, "turns out."

"What did he mean by Erin being expendable?"

Her head turned only slightly as she answered. "Designed to be used once then discarded."

Michael grinned despite his desire to curse at her right then.

"I know what the definition of expendable is," he sighed. "She was a wealth of information, and she was on the inside. Why allow her to be killed?"

"I think my previous answer fits here too," she replied. "They got what they needed and discarded her."

"She seemed to be tolerating the drug so far," Michael stated.

"Obviously not," Alex said plainly. "The side effects magnified the more she used—I could tell. That's what happens when women take those things. Didn't you read the files on the experiments?"

"Yes, but someone still gave her those pills," Michael said. "Why would they do that knowing what would happen to her?"

"You're asking the wrong person," she answered.

He felt a twinge of pain as he tried to enter her mind. The mental block forced his power back at him. The wave watered his right eye.

"You're on those pills and you seem to be just fine," he moaned and wiped his eyes with the back of his hand.

"What's your point?"

"What went wrong in every other female recruit that's not going wrong in you?"

She shrugged her shoulders and he suddenly wanted to punch her in the face.

"Mind if we take some blood? Have a look?" he asked, but he knew what her reply would be.

"Yes, I do mind."

"And you killed the only other female specimen that could tell us what was going on."

"She tried to kill me," Alex frowned at him. "Let's not forget that little detail."

"You're not curious?"

"Why should I be?"

"There are others," Michael replied. "Tristan said that."

One confession couldn't hurt, could it?

"There are no others," Alex replied. "It was my job to find them and bring them back to 51. The last one was killed almost a week ago."

"Are you sure?"

"Yes."

"Then why did Tristan say there were others?" Michael mused.

"To see my reaction."

Michael stood and turned to her. As he looked down on her, she just stared at her hands again. Maybe he was wrong about her. She wasn't one of the good guys after all. Too hardened by her past, she'd turned cold and heartless.

"We don't have time for these games! Xavier and David need answers, Alex, not riddles. Don't you care about them, at all?"

She raised her head and her eyes were hard and clear. As her back straightened, her chin rose too.

"Did anyone care about me, about what was done to me? Of course not. You cared about the supplement and how much money it would make once it was perfected. Isn't that why you bought Strategic in the first place? The tech. The results. The program. All of it was to make money! You can stand there and judge me all you want, but you know it's true."

Michael noticed all eyes on them suddenly. He backed up as she stood, picked up the tablet, and sat back down.

"We bought Strategic because your father practically begged us. He said he wanted to save them and you!"

Michael didn't move when she jumped to her feet again.

"I didn't ask to be saved! I don't need your help either!"

"Yeah? Well, the three bodies you brought back with you say otherwise!"

Conner was behind Michael before he could say another word.

"Alright, you two, break it up."

"Sorry," Michael growled with a bow of his head. "I think it's been a long day, for everyone. My apologies, Ms. Stone."

She took his hand and gave it a strong squeeze before he let go first. Without a word, she sat back down and went back to her tablet. He retreated to the other end of the plane with his father and Aiden. Sebastian and Xavier joined her in the back corner for the remainder of the flight.

Sebastian stared at his hands as Xavier urged him to just suck it up and ask. The large conference room at Gale Enterprises reminded him just how much power Conner Gale had in this world. State of the art technology was everywhere: holographic projector in the ceiling, WiFi voice conference capability. There were even individual monitors that popped up from the round table for more personal meetings.

"Go ahead," Xavier whispered to Sebastian as Alex sat quietly at the far curve of the conference table. She was texting and looked intense.

"I am," Sebastian whispered back and nudged him away. He stood and walked slowly to where she sat. "Busy?"

Alex didn't look up from her phone.

"What's on your mind?"

He sat down only because she pushed a chair out for him. As she waited, he tried to find his voice. "What happened on the plane?"

"What do you mean?"

"The doctor said we were practically gone," he replied in a hushed tone. "What happened?"

Alex placed her phone, screen down, on the table. She leaned closer and dropped her voice even lower than before. "I helped you along."

"What does that mean?" he asked.

"I gave you something to help your body heal itself," she replied.

Sebastian moved closer. "What?"

Alex looked up into his eyes and her brown orbs sparkled from somewhere deep inside. That fire that always seemed to simmer inside her was now stoked by whatever secrets she kept hidden.

"Me. I gave you my blood, and it worked."

"You sound like you weren't sure it would," he grinned.

"I wasn't," she grinned back. "You're connected to me now, Sebastian. I'm not sure for how long, but we're connected."

"And the others? David and Xavier?"

Alex shook her head and her right hand balled into a fist. "It doesn't work on humans. I can't help them the way I can vampires. If I could, Kai and Amy would still be here."

Sebastian felt her sadness and it surprised him. She

never seemed to have that kind of emotion for them—for anyone, come to think of it. But she was sad and angry, just like them. He wanted to understand how she came to be, but he'd keep her secret instead. He'd protect it with his life—they all would.

Xavier moved closer to them. He dropped his voice as he sat down.

"What else can you do?"

Somewhere deep inside her brain, she was afraid to answer that question. It meant admitting she was not human or vampire, but both. One day, if Tristan had his way, she would have to choose a side. Alex wasn't sure which she would choose.

"I'm getting better at moving things with my mind. I've noticed that I can read thoughts more clearly now too," she answered.

"Any increase in strength?" Sebastian asked. "Speed?"

"Some."

"Healing," Xavier added. "You're healing faster than before, aren't you?"

She nodded. Then she felt a vibration come at them from the hallway. Someone was trying to eavesdrop on their conversation. She shook her head and cut a glance over Xavier's shoulder. Sebastian changed the subject. "Alex," he said as he stood. "Thanks."

Michael walked through the glass doors of the conference room.

"If you guys are ready, I'll show you where you can shower and change," he announced.

Xavier picked up a bag and tossed it to Sebastian before he grabbed his own. They followed Michael from the room.

She was ready to get this over with. A shower and food was what she wanted most right now.

"My brother thinks he's smarter than everyone else," Drew's voice came through her thoughts. "He's kind of a pain sometimes."

As Sebastian and Xavier showered and changed in the

Gale Enterprises gym, Alex was kept in a big comfortable conference room to wait on her father and Conner. Drew was left to keep her company, she guessed. His brothers were no longer in sight.

"Yeah," she replied as she sat in one big, black leather chair with her feet in another. "I agree; he is a pain." She tried not to take another pill, but she was going to need it to take the edge off.

When Drew chuckled and turned his back, she moved a short bottle of water from the center of the long table with a her mind. Inside the backpack, she pulled the pills out and shook one into her hand. Drew turned to her when he heard the sound.

"You okay?"

"Headache."

He watched her closely. If he reported this to his father, which he would, Conner would most likely assume the pill was the supplement. In reality, it was just a very powerful pain reliever—prescription strength. Dr. Gilcrest had been kind enough to give her the maximum dosage allowed by law.

"Those pills help with a simple headache?" he asked as he watched her empty the small bottled water in three gulps.

"We don't get simple headaches," she answered. "And they help with just about everything."

"What don't they help with?" he asked as he pulled a chair out and sat down across the table.

"Annoying questions," she said as she closed her eyes. Then she felt ashamed of that response. It wasn't his fault. "Sorry," she apologized and sat up straight again.

He looked unaffected by her response. Probably because he was used to being around very powerful people. "No problem. My brothers do the same thing."

He began to rise from the chair, but she stopped him.

"That's no excuse for me to be rude. Please stay."

He sat back down again after he took a bottle of water

from the center of the table.

"How'd you move that water?" he asked with an honest expression. "The pills?"

"You saw that?" she smiled.

"No, I heard it slide across the table," he answered. "Plus, you didn't stand up to get it. I know that for sure."

Alex realized she might be in a bit of trouble. She had taken it for granted that this boy was no threat. That was her first mistake. Her second? Agreeing to come back to Strategic in the first place.

"Yes, the pills," she lied. "They enhance abilities. I could be picking up some latent telekinetic abilities from the donor. It doesn't last long though."

"Can you move anything? I mean, like people, for instance?"

"No. The pills are a combination of a lot of things, including vampire blood. The other chemicals water down the telekinetic ability," she answered. "In me anyway."

He looked disappointed. He had probably hoped she'd fly him around the room or something while they waited. "That's too bad. Who wouldn't want to throw people around with their mind, right?"

"Right."

His smile was warm and sincere. She could tell he had more questions, more serious questions, that he was afraid to ask: Did she hate vampires? How did she get into this business? Was she going to try to kill his family? All of that whirled around in his mind until she shut him out.

"Where are you going after you leave here?"

Alex looked up at him. "Home."

Drew sat forward and sighed. "Maybe you guys could stay here. Have dinner with us tomorrow. It's Thanksgiving."

She hadn't realized that until he said it. Then she thought it was strange that they celebrated such things anyway.

"They do it for me," he said as if he'd read her mind.

"Do what?" she said as she matched his posture.

"Thanksgiving," he rolled his eyes. "I don't really care about that stuff, but it makes them feel better, so . . ." he shrugged.

"I didn't say anything."

He grinned as he absently rubbed his right temple. "Yeah, but I figured you'd be wondering why vampires would care about that stuff. I'm not a vampire, yet," he added with a raise of his index finger. "So they try to give me as much of a human life as they can."

Before she could ask another question, the doors opened wide. In stepped Conner, Aiden, and her father. Sebastian and Xavier brought up the rear, along with Detective Andrade. Alex and Drew stood.

"Drew," Conner said as he motioned for him to come over to him. "Michael is waiting in his office. He's going to get you home. I'll see you later." Conner kissed his son on the forehead.

Quickly, she reached into his mind and took the conversation about the pills from his head. He squinted and rubbed his temple again. "Thanks for the talk."

"Thanks for keeping me company. Happy Thanksgiving," Alex smiled at him.

Chapter 32

"What's wrong with you?" Michael huffed as he finished with his email reply.

Drew sat in the chair on the other side of the desk with his leg bouncing rapidly. That annoyed Michael. It distracted him.

"Nothing," Drew said. "I thought you were ready to go?"

"Give me one more minute," he replied. "I need to get this email out."

"It's Thanksgiving," his brother groaned and sighed. "You guys never stop working, do you?"

"It's the day before Thanksgiving," Michael corrected him. "And I'm almost done, so chill." He looked up and Drew's leg still shook, but now he chewed on his nail as he stared into space. "What?"

"What?" Drew spit out a nail and frowned at Michael.

"Why are you so nervous?"

He watched Drew mull over the question. "I'm not nervous," he answered then chewed at another nail. "I'm just ready to go home. I'm hungry, I guess."

"Well, quit bouncing around. You're freaking me out."

They would have to pass by the conference room to leave the building. Michael gathered his briefcase and phone and shooed Drew out the door. Through the glass he could see Alex, his father, and her father in deep conversation. The others sat quietly. Fallon winked at them as they passed. He wanted very much to know what was being said, but he had to get Drew home.

Drew reached the elevator first and pressed the button.

Its doors opened with a burst of tepid canned air. Inside, a holiday tune played and Drew hummed along.

"You like her, huh?" he heard Drew ask.

"I told you, I'm not her type," Michael said as the numbers ticked off. "Besides, she works for me. I never mix business and pleasure."

"I wasn't talking about Fallon," Drew replied.

Through the lobby, they walked side by side to the exit. The town car waited at the curb; white smoke spilled from the tailpipe as they climbed inside.

"How was your trip?" their driver and long-time butler, Jeffrey, inquired as he pulled from the curb.

"Okay, I guess," Drew answered. "I did get to meet Alex Stone though."

"Good for you," Jeffrey answered. "I know how much you like her work. And how did you like the Pentagon?"

"It was kinda cool," he smiled as the black car made the first right.

All along Central Park West, Christmas lights filled the barren trees and fake potted plants in front of buildings along the way. In the distance, their building was trimmed in green lights.

"She's stubborn," Michael finally stated as he looked out his window. "Arrogant as hell too. That's gonna get her in a lot of trouble one day."

Drew laughed. "Dude. It took you, like, a year to answer that question. And that's how I know you like her a lot!"

"Whom are we discussing?" Jeffrey asked through the rearview mirror.

"Alex Stone," Drew chuckled. "Michael picked a fight with her on the plane. She almost tossed him out of it." He laughed again.

Michael rolled his eyes at his brother as he continued to laugh. "Shut up."

"Can I drop you somewhere, Michael?" Jeffrey asked as the car came to a stop at their destination. The doorman opened the backdoor and Drew stepped out.

Michael shook his head as he grabbed the briefcase and handed it to Drew through the door. "I'll stay."

"That's probably best," Jeffrey frowned. It had begun to snow again. "It looks like it will snow all night."

Fallon felt claustrophobic in a giant room over New York's financial district. As the snow continued to fall past the windows, she looked on the exchange with a slight bit of anxiety. Alex and her father traded insults like a married couple. The young men just sat there like stones. After all they'd been through, who had the energy to fight more? Apparently, Alex and her father.

"Are you fucking kidding?" she exclaimed. "You knew what Coop was doing and you allowed it to happen."

"I didn't know for sure," he replied. "I suspected they had a sexual relationship. I had no idea he was giving her those supplements."

"Did you know he was your traitor?"

Fallon stepped closer to the window. A vibration hit her square in the chest. It came from Alex and she was sure every vampire in the room felt it too.

Dr. Carlisle dropped his gaze and then slid his eyes toward Xavier and Sebastian. That's when Alex felt Sebastian's tension with Xavier's anger followed closely behind it. Fallon's fear bounced off the windows she stood next to.

It was hard to believe no one on this team knew about Erin and Coop—especially Sebastian. How was that even possible? But they knew Coop was a suspect.

"We had been alerted to some things he was tied up in," Dr. Carlisle answered slowly. "I had the team investigating him."

"Even Erin?"

"Yes, she was the one to bring us most of what we had on him. We were going to bring formal charges after this conference."

"Who alerted you?" Alex asked with every bit of control

she had left.

"That's classified," he replied with a hint of arrogance in his voice. *He always had that arrogance,* she reminded herself.

"Fuck classified! Who alerted you?" she yelled and slammed her hand down on the table. The water glasses tumbled over.

"I did," Conner announced from the end of the table. He turned his full attention to Alex. His hands, fingers entwined, were on the table in front of him. "In some circles, a man like him with huge gambling debt and an even bigger drug habit . . . it attracts attention."

"Attention," she repeated. "What kind of attention?"

"People, desperate people, will try to sell just about anything," Conner answered. "The information was relatively inexpensive."

Alex didn't like Coop much, but it was hard to believe he could have sold them out like this. "Gambling and drugs; that's all you had? There are worse things going on in the government these days. That barely scratches the surface for bringing charges."

"That wasn't all we uncovered, no," Dr. Carlisle answered. "He was stealing classified information to cover his debts."

"Then why even consider letting him lead the assignment? Why not just arrest him?" she asked.

"We needed to follow the money," he answered. "And it led us to Mr. Campbell."

"Three people are dead because you followed the money," Alex accused.

"They knew the risks," Dr. Carlisle hissed back. "It's what they do, isn't it?"

"Is that what you told her parents?" Alex snapped at her father. "'Sorry, folks, but I allowed your daughter to take potentially dangerous drugs and she went ballistic and tried to kill her entire team,'" she exaggerated the shrug of her shoulders. "'But she knew the risks.'"

"She was a traitor," he sighed with a wave of his hand. "We still don't know what damage she actually did to us. We have no idea what she passed along to Tristan at this point. Possibly information on the advancements I've made with my research."

"She and Coop were working together," Alex said. "So who did they give the intel to?"

"Mr. Campbell," Conner said. "He was put in play to help us keep track of the money. He came highly recommended. So don't think we just trusted him with millions sight unseen. He lies very well for a human."

Alex, who was still fixed on her father, wondered what else he had lied about. Most certainly he'd lied about her, that was clear.

"That's what assets do," Alex explained. "He was playing both sides. What did you think he was going to tell you anyway?"

"What Tristan's next step would be," Conner hummed back. "What he took with him when he escaped Dugway."

"He took the Seventh Grimoire," she announced. Fallon, Sebastian, and Xavier looked confused. "It was supposed to have contained passages from a larger text that is being kept by The Vatican. That book contains some of the most powerful spells and incantations in the world. The problem is no one alive can decipher the languages. That's why the Church wanted him so badly, isn't it? They wanted that book."

"Yes," Dr. Carlisle answered. "After his capture, I copied some pages and had it sent to The Vatican, but the complete text never made it there. I have no idea how Tristan got it back."

"What were you using Tristan for?" Alex finally asked.

Dr. Carlisle looked uncomfortable. Fallon turned toward the group again when she asked that question.

"His DNA carries a very specific marker," the doctor replied. "I was able to isolate it."

Fallon looked in Conner's direction. His controlled

anger punched her in the gut.

"What does it do?" Alex asked.

"Slows down the negative effects of the supplements," Dr. Carlisle answered. "The formula that Ramos and Yun are on anyway."

"But you can't reverse them," Conner added.

"No," he sighed and shook his head as he reached for the small bottle of water in front of him. "But, I was getting close. When he escaped, so did my research—so to speak."

Alex sat back. Fallon glanced down to see her stretch her fingers out. Dr. Carlisle pushed a box of tissue her way and she balled the clean, pale material into her fist. Then Fallon smelled a slight hint of blood.

"Why can't you take what you have so far and duplicate what you found in his blood?" she asked. "Try to cure them and get them off those stupid drugs?"

"As you know," Dr. Carlisle cleared his throat and took a sip of water, "vampires regenerate at an accelerated rate. Their lifespan far exceeds that of humans. But once the sample is extracted, the tissue is only good for about a day, then . . ." he blew across palm, "It disappears."

"Disappears?"

Dr. Carlisle grinned at her. She had always hated his grin. "It disintegrates."

Both Fallon and Alex looked at Conner. On the surface, he appeared in control and calm. But Fallon could feel his rage barrel through his two-thousand-year-old body like a battering ram. If he unleashed it, Dr. Carlisle would die and Alex would too, if she tried to save him.

Conner stood slowly and placed his hands behind his back as he paced the space behind the doctor. "How long do the young men have before they start to show the signs?"

"If they continue with the current regime, they will run out in about ninety days," he answered as he tapped his smartphone. Then he smiled. "Losing Kai, as unfortunate as that was, does buy them another thirty days or so."

Alex straightened her posture in the chair. Before she

could open her mouth, Conner shook his head at her. The stern look in those green eyes frightened Fallon too.

"Can they skip a couple of doses? Try to extend the time," Conner continued.

"No."

"Do you have anything in reserve?" Alex spoke up. "You couldn't count on us bringing Tristan back alive."

She was agitated and she had every right to be.

Alex swallowed hard as he father mulled over her question. Somehow she knew the answer was no. He shook his head and placed the phone on the table.

"But I'm sure, under the circumstances, you want him captured as badly as I do."

Her muscles tensed. The only thing keeping her seated was her own doubt. Could Conner catch her before she reached her father's throat? There was really only one way to found out.

"I want him dead!"

With a blink, Conner was on her side of the table, hand placed firmly on her shoulder. She was trapped in that chair.

Anger sparked in Dr. Carlisle's eyes. As he moved to the edge of his seat, he pushed the phone further away from him.

"You can't kill him," he barked. "Not yet! I told you I'm close to fixing this. If you kill him, Xavier and David will die too. Is that what you want? Just to get back at me?"

"Get back at you for what?" Conner interrupted Alex as he pressed harder on her shoulder.

Dr. Carlisle's gaze shot up to Conner, then over to Fallon, and finally back to Alex. She pulled in a deep breath to slow her heart as it raced in her chest. A tightness squeezed her chest and her vision blurred.

"We're done here," Dr. Carlisle pushed out a hard breath as he stood. "I trust you will do what's right, Mr. Gale. We have an agreement." He let his gaze slide down to Alex again. "I never meant for this to happen, I swear. I was just trying to save this program. Tristan doesn't know anything about magic anyway. That text is useless to him."

"Right," Alex sniffed. "Well, he figured out at least one of the spells. Now he has a new identity—Brice Campbell. That body is vulnerable, for now, and that will work to our advantage. I want those pages you copied translated, please. You should get started on finding out what that compound is and get an antidote before Tristan surfaces again."

"When did you start giving me orders?" Dr. Carlisle frowned at her as she stood.

"When Tristan escaped on your watch," she replied. Conner helped her with her jacket. "Don't like it, take it up with him." She pointed at Conner.

Dr. Carlisle stared at them for a few more seconds then left the room without another word. A guard escorted him down the hall and out of their sight.

"You gonna just let him walk out of here like that?" Alex asked Conner as she stood next to Fallon. "He thinks he still has a chance at getting Tristan back. You're not going to hold up your end of that agreement, are you?"

He let her into his personal space for some reason. Fallon stayed close though.

"You're right," he answered honestly, "we're not." He slipped his hands into his pockets as he stared down on her. "Tristan will face the Council when he is captured."

"Then what?" Alex sighed. He could feel all of her energy begin to drain from her body. The effort it took for her to try getting out of that chair wore her down a bit. For a minute or two, he hadn't been sure if he could keep her still much longer though.

"A tribunal will decide his punishment," he answered.

"Tribunal," she snickered. "You pretend to care about the lives he took, then pass judgement? Big deal. He gets a few hundred years underground and then he's out again."

"We are taking this very seriously," Conner hummed. He tried very hard not to lose his temper, but Alex's defiant smirk tested his resolve. "His actions make us all look guilty. The terms of our agreement—"

"Agreement," Alex interrupted him. "People are dead, Conner! People who played by the rules of that agreement and they died anyway. If he broke your rules, why keep him alive?"

"He does get to tell his side of the story," Conner answered.

Alex stepped back and took a deep breath. After she let it out, she folded her arms over her chest and waited for Conner to continue.

"We don't know what was done to him while under your father's care," he continued. "He was to be treated humanely. We didn't agree to torture."

Conner recognized the look of someone wanting to yell, but she stood silent for a few seconds.

"Then you should have kept a closer eye on my father. He's a scientist. If he would experiment on his own daughter, what made you think he'd care about humane treatment?"

"Maybe you're right," Conner conceded, "but the fact still remains. Tristan Ambrose will get to tell his side of the story. As long as he lives, your teammates have a chance at survival. If he dies, so do they."

Conner expected a snide remark or a thinly veiled threat to expose them. But she stared at the floor and nodded.

"He can't be the only one," she said when she looked up again. "The marker has to exist in another."

Conner considered that for a few minutes. "That would make sense, but there are two questions that come to mind."

"How do we find another vampire with the marker?" Alex verbalized before he could.

"And," Conner jumped in, "do we have time to do the research before Xavier and David start to break down?"

They turned to the windows together. The snow fell in heavy clumps past the glass.

"Looks like you're stuck here for the night, I'm afraid," Conner said. "Detective Andrade will escort you to the hotel. The pilot expects the storm to clear by midafternoon. We should have you back in Texas by tomorrow night."

"Great," she answered. "I'm ready."

Fallon couldn't imagine that kind of animosity toward her own father. They had a great relationship right up to the time both her parents were killed in that accident. She had a great relationship with her mother as well. They were supportive and loving, and she missed them terribly.

No one spoke on the ride to hotel. Even with light traffic, it took a while to get there with the snow. Fallon had spent most of her assignments in warm places. She spent the longest in Texas. Texas didn't get much snow. She didn't like it here.

Once she checked them in, Fallon escorted them to the floor Conner had secured for them for the night. They didn't need twenty-seven rooms, but they had them anyway. Fallon and two other vampires had the rooms next to the elevator. Alex had a suite at the end of the hall. Sebastian was on one side and Xavier the other. The rest of the floor was empty.

"If you're hungry," Fallon said as Alex looked around, "you can call room service or they've got a great bar downstairs."

"Thanks," she answered in a quiet voice. Fallon could see the exhaustion wrapped around her as she sat down and sighed. "I'll see if Xavier and Sebastian are up for dinner."

"Sebastian has a fresh supply in his mini-bar," Fallon replied. Alex nodded again. "I'm very sorry for your loss, Ms. Stone. I'd like to offer my help, if you'll have me."

Alex looked up at her with a strange gleam in her tired eyes. She looked like she wanted to say something, but she didn't. Then she nodded as she kicked off her boots and curled her toes until they popped. While she shrugged from her jacket and pulled a thin sweater over her head, Fallon stayed where she was.

"Is that what Mr. Gale wants? Does he think we can't handle this?" she sighed.

"He thinks you need help," Fallon replied. "Tristan won't take any chances and neither should you."

Her body was toned and her skin taut. After a week in the cold and sunless climate that was Romania, her skin still held a brownness that Fallon found appealed to her. Being part Brazilian, she longed for that tone to her own skin sometimes. Vampires only held color when they fed and that was only for a short time.

Alex stretched her arms over her head and Fallon thought she heard her muscles sigh. Her undershirt clung to those muscles quite well too.

"What's good here?" Alex finally asked as she picked up the room service menu.

"Not sure," Fallon answered. "It's my first time in New York."

"Well, in about an hour it will be Thanksgiving Day. Think we can see the Parade from here?" Alex nodded toward her balcony. She stood and dropped the menu on the table again. "I say we get turkey sandwiches and champagne. Do you mind?" She nodded at the phone.

Fallon smiled at her and picked up the receiver. She watched Alex walk into the bedroom and then the door closed. A few seconds later, she could hear the shower. On her way to her own room to do the same, Fallon told the guys the plan. They would meet in Alex's room in one hour.

Chapter 33

Drew couldn't sleep. As he tossed and turned, his brain tried to grab onto one thought that would take his mind to that something he had a sinking feeling he'd forgotten.

Finally, he gave up and jumped from the bed. It was three in the morning, and everyone else seemed to be asleep or doing whatever vampires did in the early hours of morning. He always thought that was strange. That the old myth turned out to be untrue disappointed him somehow.

Conner told him stories of when sunlight was a danger to them, but that problem had been solved ages ago. As long as they used the synthetic, sunlight didn't hurt them. But silver, in a large enough doses, could. Now that this new mix was on the street, they were all worried.

He stopped at Michael's door. For some reason, he was still awake. Drew heard him through the thick wooden door. He tapped twice then let himself in.

Michael sat in bed, laptop to his side and a glass of blood in his hand—working, of course. Drew took a seat in the overstuffed chair across from the bed. It had belonged to Michael's mother, Conner had told him. He kept it here for safekeeping.

"Why are you up?" Michael hummed as he stared at the screen.

"Couldn't sleep," Drew replied. "Why are you up? Surfing porn?"

Michael glanced up at him then rolled his eyes. "Working, little brother."

"Imagine my surprise," Drew sighed. He swung his legs over the arm of the chair and sighed again. "Whatcha working on, big brother?"

"It's sort of complicated," he said back to the screen. "Dr. Carlisle's research is fascinating."

Drew rose from the chair and crossed the room. Once he was on the bed, Michael turned the computer toward him. All he saw were jumbled sections of numbers and equations, and they gave him a headache.

"What's he trying to do?" he asked.

"I think he's trying to create a hybrid," Michael hummed with a look of delight and fear in his eyes.

"A what?"

"A cross between us and them."

Drew felt his heart rate pick up speed. Michael must have heard it too because he looked up and grinned. "Is that even possible?"

"Not that I know, but I'm not a geneticist," he shrugged. "Looks like he's been at it for years, though."

Michael took a long draw from the glass then set it on the nightstand. Drew wasn't much for the smell of fresh blood, but he was used to it. Raph said, once he was turned, it would smell like a gourmet meal. He highly doubted it.

"Maybe that's what that Tristan guy was talking about?" Drew smiled as the thought occurred to him. "Erin Sinclair was becoming a hybrid, but she couldn't take the transformation."

Michael rubbed his chin as he continued to stare at the screen. He nodded absently then closed the laptop. "Maybe. Raph and Sean are working on the formulas. We may have to ask the good doctor for some help. He's gonna be pissed we didn't tell him this already."

"He probably failed and just abandoned the research," Drew added. "I mean, he knew he could enhance abilities with the pills, so why mess that up by trying to create the impossible?"

He pushed from Michael's bed, stretched, and yawned

big. Michael did the same. As he turned to leave, all the thoughts in his head shut off. It was quiet and he felt calm and suddenly very sleepy.

"Turning in?" Michael asked as Drew headed for the door.

"Yeah, all that boring science stuff did the trick," he yawned again. "I'm done."

He closed the door and headed to his own room again. Inside, he turned off the light and crawled under his warm comforter. As he drifted off to sleep he thought he could hear the snow hit the roof high above his head. That's stupid, he told himself as he pulled the cover over his head. He was in a deep sleep before the next snowflake fell.

Alex always felt the most alive in the early hours before sunrise. She had learned the smallest creatures made the loudest sounds. Worms pushed through earth and snow in search of food. Winter birds stretched wings that had covered them through the night to prepare for flight when the sun rose again. She stood at the window, glad that the snow had stopped, and waited for those first rays to appear.

Sebastian and Xavier had committed themselves to the fight, with her as their leader. David too. After San Francisco and New Orleans, they would return to Texas and begin to train for what came next—Tristan's death.

She closed her eyes and focused. The traffic outside was still light. It was a holiday. Inside the hotel, on this floor, everyone was asleep except for Fallon. She walked from one end of the hall to the other in a sort of a quick step. Like a dancer, she balanced on her toes then dropped to her feet when she stopped. Alex could hear her groan and stretch.

On one side of Alex's room was Sebastian's. He slept off and on, like she did through the night. Xavier, on the other side, slept through the night like a baby. He got up once to use the bathroom. When she pulled back her thoughts, her phone vibrated on the table.

A message from Becker. He wanted to meet when they returned to Texas. Any place she wanted, his message said. Just let him know when she was home. At the end, *"The Cause needs you."*

"What cause?" she hummed out loud to the empty room. "What are you into now Becker?"

She stopped her solo conversation when a noise got her attention. It came from the bedroom. The window opened, then she heard heavy boots on thick carpet. Alex slipped her bare feet into the boots she'd abandoned hours ago. In a tank and track pants, she crouched behind the loveseat and peered around it at the bedroom door.

Two muffled shots from a silencer reached her sensitive ears, then the whispered curse when the person realized that she wasn't in the bed. The bedroom door eased open and she saw the muzzle of the gun first. With a blink of her eyes, the lamps went out before a figure came into view. In the muted darkness, that figure moved with caution toward the center of the room.

Gun held at chest level and close to the body, the masked figure swept the room twice before the mask was removed. His face was flushed from the heat inside and being covered by a wool mask. Alex thought he looked familiar now, more so than when she barely paid attention to him last night when Fallon introduced him and the other.

Alex crept back behind the small loveseat and to the other end to get behind him. When he turned to go back through the bedroom, she took him in a full nelson before he knew what was going on. He squeezed off more rounds into the ceiling then dropped the gun. They were about the same height, roughly. He bent at the waist to try shaking her loose, but she was stronger. Her feet were in the air long enough for him to spin them around and knock over everything on the desk and one of the lamps with a loud crash.

Alex hoped someone heard the noise. Suddenly, he slipped from her hold and slammed an elbow in her chest.

She slammed into the wall. As she dropped to the floor, Sebastian and Xavier forced the door open, followed closely by Fallon and the other guard.

The young man took two giant leaps and was up and over the couch and through the French doors to the balcony before anyone caught up. Alex ran out on the balcony and followed him over the edge. A second building sat four feet below. He made the jump with very little effort. Alex almost missed the edge as she landed and rolled through the snow to a stop.

Like a shot, she was on her feet and close behind her would-be assassin. Sebastian and Fallon made the jump. Xavier and the other guard took the old-fashioned way down to try cutting him off.

A narrow set of stairs took Alex into a donut shop. She could hear the young man crash into everything in his path as she gave chase. At the front of the store, he jumped through the plate glass window. She followed as shards of glass pelted her bare arms.

He slipped and stumbled down the snow-covered sidewalks of New York. Central Park West had probably never seen anything like this before. Alex ran at full speed; her boots seemed to have more traction than his. When she caught him by the hood of his jacket, she jerked him back with all her strength. His feet came straight up and his head slammed the pavement first. If not for the snow, it would have most likely cracked like an egg.

Behind her, Sebastian and Fallon rushed in their direction. In the distance, Xavier and the other guard did too. Alex grabbed the young man by the front of his jacket and slammed him on someone's Mercedes. The alarm blared.

"You missed," she hissed at him, her breath wispy in the morning air.

He didn't speak, but he head-butted her and that sent stars through her head. When her vision cleared, he was up and over the car like he had wings. She jumped to its roof and onto his back as he slipped again in the street. A yellow cab came to a screeching halt as they tumbled away from its tires.

With a flurry of kicks, which she blocked, he sent Alex back a few feet and onto the hood of the cab as the driver cursed them both.

"Crazy fucking kids," he yelled and waved his fist out of the window. "What the hell!"

She heard Sebastian apologize, and then Fallon, Xavier, and the other guard surrounded them. Alex slid off the hood as the young man unzipped his jacket and shook it off. He grinned at them as the sun broke through a cloud over head.

"For The Cause," he smiled at her.

As the rays stabbed through the clouds, light splashed over them. The young man's skin began to darken then turn to ash as the light grew stronger. He caught fire and screamed until he disappeared into ash that turned the snow underneath him black and inky.

"Holy Christ," they heard the driver howl. "Holy . . . did you see that?"

Fallon stepped up to the stunned driver and flashed her badge. As she dealt with him, Sebastian and Xavier stood by Alex's side.

Chapter 34

"What the fuck?" Sebastian whistled.

"No synthetic," Xavier answered. "Does it every time." He shook his head then took Alex's arm in his hand. "You're hurt, again."

Alex stepped up to the pile of soggy ash when something shiny caught her eye. She pushed the soot away with the toe of her boot. A scorched vial lay in the center of the mess.

"What do you think that was for?" Xavier hummed to her right.

"Blood," Sebastian offered.

They both looked at Alex, and Sebastian fought the urge to run. This whole thing was about her. People were dead because she existed. Even though they were the only ones who knew what she was right now.

The sound of the yellow cab as it turned around the next corner caught their attention. The car went on at a leisurely pace as if nothing had happened. Fallon was on the phone as she approached them.

"Get back to the hotel, we're leaving," she said, then went back to her phone conversation.

As they made their way inside the hotel, guests were up to start their morning routine. Most were here for the Thanksgiving Day parade. They'd just missed the fireworks.

Inside her room, Xavier patched her arm. She popped two painkillers, then Fallon escorted them out into the elevator, through the lobby, and into a black SUV idled at the curb.

"Nice, Andrade," their driver said. "Michael's not gonna be too happy to know one of your guys was crooked."

"He was cleared months ago," she growled at the man. "He can't blame me for this."

"If you say so," he smirked then chuckled.

"Just drive, Spider," she growled. "Silently."

Sebastian heard him chuckle again as the truck picked up speed on the expressway. He could smell Alex's blood. That reminded him he hadn't fed properly. And it reminded him he had her blood inside him too.

"You okay?" he said to her and she just nodded. "What now?"

"San Francisco," she answered as she rubbed her arm. "Xavier," she said over the back of the seat they shared. "Call David. Let him know we're on the way and to have security beefed up around his mother and the services." He nodded as he tapped on his smartphone screen.

"What about the Warrens?" Sebastian asked.

"They're always protected," she said.

Sebastian nodded then turned back to the window. The sun was on full blast as the snow began to melt around the city. He could even see more blue than clouds now.

"Andrade," Sebastian said. "How'd you get that cab driver to back off so fast?"

She turned her green eyes to him and grinned sweetly. Her dark hair was pulled into a messy ponytail and her skin was clean of any makeup.

"I told him you guys were magicians," she laughed. "You were working on an illusion for a television special."

"He bought that?" Xavier yelled from the back row of seats.

"That and a grand," Fallon smirked then laughed too.

Gale Enterprise's lab sent the results as soon as they were in the air again. Turns out the bullets he put into the pillow weren't bullets but high tech tracers laced in tranquilizers. So not only would she not know she was being tracked, but the plan had been to knock her out and take a blood sample too.

"Who would choose not to be on the synthetic?" Fallon said as she sat down across from Alex. "That's kinda crazy, right?"

"Not necessarily," she replied. She closed the laptop and slid it back in her pack. "Tristan was always old-fashioned. He opposed the creation of the synthetic from its inception. He was always against the clans 'joining' the human race."

"We're much stronger at night, but still," Fallon shrugged. "I'd rather see the sunrise, even if it does knock off a few hundred years, you know?"

"Not everyone sees it that way," Alex stated. "To you, what's a few hundred years? To Tristan or even Conner, two thousand years isn't really a long time considering."

Fallon nodded. "The synthetic speeds up our aging process only slightly."

"Yes, and it's still way slower than ours. Without it, you could have centuries and a near invincible body. The synthetic is like chinks in the armor."

"I guess someone could always back off the synthetic," she sighed.

"Sure, but when the effects wear off, you're stuck in whatever climate you were in at the time. Who'd want to be in Jamaica and not be able to enjoy the beach?" she grinned.

"Yeah," Fallon smiled. "Plus, I look awesome in a bikini."

"I'm sure," Alex replied. She stretched and yawned and Fallon did too. "I'm gonna catch a nap. Wake me when we're close."

"No problem," she yawned again. "You may have to wake me though."

Fallon kicked her feet up on the rolling bag next to her seat and was asleep in a few seconds. Xavier had been asleep since they took off, and Sebastian had stretched out only a few minutes after he did.

She'd be glad when they landed. The idea of David alone in San Francisco didn't sit well with her right now. Something felt off and she wanted the feeling to go away. Once she successfully shook the uneasiness, she sank down on the sofa, fluffed the pillow behind her head and closed her eyes.

Sleep came quickly. The exhaustion wrapped around her like a warm blanket and she gave into the feeling of flight as her brain dropped into REM sleep.

The thick, black plastic began to move on the table. At first, one weak punch got his attention. It stopped for a full five minutes while Becker watched from a stool in the corner of the exam room. Then, a low moan followed by a harder punch from inside the bag. Payne was crouched against the exit door. Marcus had fallen asleep on the other exam table.

"You gonna just let him punch his way out?" Marcus yawned without opening his eyes.

Becker sighed then hopped off the stool. He unzipped the bag and folded the top part away from Creed's face. Pale and almost blue, Creed's cold body warmed as the sedative wore off and his body began to thaw from the refrigerated ride back to the States.

"Thanks," Creed moaned as he propped himself up on his elbows. "How long was I out?"

"Twelve hours," Becker replied. He handed him a bag of blood from underneath the table. "Give or take."

"Give or take," Creed repeated. "Where are we?"

"New York," Marcus yawned again, still stretched out on the table.

Creed opened the top of the bag and began to feed in hungry gulps. Becker was impressed with how he didn't spill a drop. When the bag was empty, he asked for another. Becker obliged.

As he opened the second bag, Creed swung his legs

over the side of the table. The body bag crunched as he did. Bag number two was empty in no time. When Creed sighed and stretched, he grinned at Becker. His color changed before Becker's eyes. He went from pale blue to just regular pale in seconds. Must be whatever was added to the blood.

"Better?" Becker grinned back.

"Much," Creed nodded. "Is everything ready?"

"Yep," Marcus harped as he jumped from the other table with a grunt. "Car's waiting downstairs."

"Good. I need a shower and a real meal before we get started," he smiled as he stood slowly. Becker moved back and watched Creed take two shaky steps. Then he straightened his posture and gave them a big smile. "Have you contacted Roland yet?"

Becker nodded. "He was pretty disappointed to hear you'd been killed in the rescue of Jason's girlfriend. I think he was looking forward to watching you die in the Circle."

"And Alex?"

"On the way to the airport," Payne answered as he stood up. "Your guy failed, by the way."

"He died for a good cause," Creed replied. "It was a long shot anyway."

As the others waited, Creed slipped his feet into a pair of boots Becker had bought for him. He pulled a navy hoodie over his head and left the hood up.

When they exited the room, parts of the hallway were dark and others dimly lit. They stopped at a door marked "Research," which Creed knocked on three times. When a voice bid them to enter, Creed pushed it open.

"Mason," a woman said with a sweet smile and glasses perched at the end of her nose. "You look like you're feeling better."

"I am, thanks to you," Creed crooned as he stepped inside and took a seat. Becker and the others stayed in the hallway. "How will I ever repay you? Brunch, perhaps?"

"I can't," she pouted and removed the glasses. Her dark

hair hung loosely around her shoulders. In a white lab coat, she got lost in the fabric. It was much too big for her slender frame. "Raincheck?"

Creed shrugged and dropped a booted foot on the edge of her desk. Becker's body took up the entire space of the doorway. "Only for you, Kat."

Becker saw the woman bat her long lashes at Creed and shake her head as if scolding him. He would never have called her that. She was far too sophisticated and worldly to be called Kat. Katherine Grayson, Doctor Grayson, was the head of this little research facility and his savior. He had a giant crush on her, as everyone did, from the moment he laid eyes on her.

"Becker, you're so quiet," she purred at him. "Are you feeling alright?"

"Yes, ma'am," he replied as he stood up straight. "Long flight. Ready to get to the hotel and grab some shuteye. Got a lot on my mind."

"Yes. I can imagine. By now, Tristan has probably already told her about the reproductive experiments, so she's going to have a lot of questions," she said as she pushed her round glasses back up her nose with her index finger.

"She's smart," Becker said. "Once we've had a chance to talk to her, she'll join us. I'm sure of it."

"For your sake, I hope so," Creed chuckled.

"What's that supposed to mean, bloodsucker?" Becker sniffed.

"If she finds out I'm alive, she'll figure out you're not the Becker she knew back in the day," Creed answered. "She does not take betrayal lightly."

"You let me worry about that, and you stay out of sight," Becker winked at Creed. "We covered our tracks. Everything is going according to plan."

"Yes, you did, Becker," Katherine said as she stood and slipped out of the lab coat. "Excellent job, by the way."

"Thank you, ma'am," Becker answered.

"Please," she waved at him. "Stop calling me that. You're

off the clock as of right now."

The others gave a hushed cheer behind him. She giggled and smiled at Creed again.

"Well, don't let us keep you from anything. We can talk in a couple of days," she stated. "Happy Thanksgiving, gentlemen."

She remained behind the desk which indicated to Becker she wanted to speak with Creed in private. He nodded and backed out. After he pushed the door closed, he and the team walked a few more feet down the hall and took the stairs down to the garage.

"What do you think they're talking about?" Payne said as they climbed into a Ford F150 crew cab; Becker was behind the wheel. Marcus climbed in back and stretched out with a long groan.

"Who says they're talking?" Marcus chuckled.

Becker ignored the obvious stomach-churning innuendo. He couldn't imagine a woman like her with a dude like Mason Creed. He was way too slimy and low-class, right? Granted, he was probably someone's idea of handsome. And he did have a body women swooned over, but he cheated; he was a vampire. Who could compete with almost eternal youth?

As they waited at a stoplight, the sun melted the ice that had formed overnight. He turned up the heat when Marcus complained. Payne stared at his smartphone, earplugs in, and laughed at the screen. The light changed and Becker weaved around the scattered taxis and buses in his way. Parked in a small lot somewhere in Brooklyn, he led the way to a 24-hour diner. The scrawny Christmas tree in the window was what drew him in.

It was warm inside—cozy, even. They took an empty booth in back and grabbed the plastic menus one by one. Their waitress looked to be about twenty years past retirement. She moved quickly though and greeted them warmly. Her name was Jackie and she owned the place. Her brother, Marv, was on the grill and was one hell of a cook, she remarked.

"What can I get you?" her smile stopped on each of them. In that moment, Becker knew he was going to leave a her a great tip. Smiles go a long way.

Once she'd taken their orders, Marv hustled out with a fresh, steaming pot of coffee while she went to the kitchen. Jackie came back with coffee mugs as Marv gave them a crooked grin with his chef's hat squarely on top of his round head. Tufts of gray, wiry hair sat away from the sides.

"How come you fellas aren't home with your families?" Marv asked. "It's Thanksgiving."

"This is family," Marcus smiled and dumped too much sugar in his coffee.

"Yeah," Marv sighed with a sad shrug of his hunched shoulders. "Me and Jackie," he nodded, "that's it for us too."

"Well, then you guys should pull up a couple of chairs and join us," Payne replied as he poured cream in his coffee, no sugar.

Becker just watched and sipped his black coffee. He didn't really care much for holidays, and this one was no different. If the doctor hadn't said anything, he would have been happy with thinking it was just another Thursday in a long line of them in his life.

"We don't want to interfere," Marv shook his head as he backed up.

"You're not," Marcus replied. "It doesn't look like you got much traffic coming in this morning, so why not? You do eat your own food, right?"

Marv laughed with them and agreed. Jackie came from the kitchen with a big smile on her face and a tray perched on her arm. The smell of pancakes, eggs, bacon, and sausage filled the air.

Becker stood and welcomed her into his side of the booth as she blushed. He called her darlin' and that made her smile. He noticed she'd fixed her hair a bit and put on some lipstick.

As Thanksgivings went, Becker figured this was the

most festive one he'd ever had—friends, old and new, around him, hearty breakfast, and good coffee. As Jackie and Marv told stories about their childhood, Becker sat quietly. Marcus and Payne laughed loud and hard.

It's weird being with regular people, Becker thought. It was weird they didn't ask what they did or why they were in New York. Maybe they didn't really care. They were lonely and welcomed Becker and his friends with open arms. Maybe that's what holidays are really supposed to be about—not just family, but being welcomed when you're not family.

"Becker," Marcus mumbled with a mouth full of toast. "Eat up, man! Jackie's got pie!"

Becker took a forkful of pancake and eggs and joined the conversation. He put the last few days behind him with each bite. He also put that little voice inside his head to bed for the night. That voice had started to annoy him with all the "you betrayed your friend" jazz.

Even if it was right, he didn't want to worry about it right now. Jackie had pie, and it was Thanksgiving, after all.

Acknowledgments

The best thing about doing a series is that you get to say thanks to more people. Jonathan, thanks for being there and never letting me forget I really am a writer. Chandra, no one on this earth is more proud to be your blood than me! Hold on. Kai, my third sister, my mother loved you like her own. Stay strong. Aunt Maryann and Uncle Mac, you are the light in the fog which I have come to depend on. Shine on. Robbie, Traci, Peggy, Helen, and Wynata, without you I would never hear my sister's voice again; blessings on high. And Barbara B. and Deanna M., my unofficial and unpaid Street Team, thank you from the bottom of my heart!

About the Author

Being an introvert doesn't mean you have no voice. It just means you have the ability to communicate in different ways. For author and champion introvert, Janice Jones, that way is writing. She began by reading anything she could get her hands on, but after college, she found herself in roles that required business-focused writing rather than fiction. This didn't stop her; she continued to create her own stories to feed her passion for the written word.

Honing her skills as a paralegal for several years, Janice continued to feed the beast by spending every spare minute she could creating the world of her first fictional character, Alexa Stone. The idea for *The Dagger Chronicles* came during a rough time in Janice's life, but she continued to write and focus on improving every way she could. Earning a Master's in Creative Writing from Southern New Hampshire University, Janice was encouraged to continue *The Dagger Chronicles*.

Since *In Her Blood* was released, Janice has enjoyed meeting and hearing from new readers and writers. Although she can't use all the feedback and suggestions, she does try to incorporate what she gets into all her writing. Janice is currently working a few new projects, including writing a screenplay for *The Dagger Chronicles* with her brother, Jordan. She appreciates all the feedback and encouragement she has received and is looking forward to the future. Janice would like to thank her family, friends and the team at Amberjack Publishing for this exciting opportunity.